DRONE THREAT

DRONE THREAT

MIKE MADEN

G. P. PUTNAM'S SONS | NEW YORK

PUTNAM

G. P. PUTNAM'S SONS
Publishers Since 1838
An imprint of Penguin Random House LLC
375 Hudson Street
New York, New York 10014

Library of Congress Cataloging-in-Publication Data

Names: Maden, Mike, author.
Title: Drone threat / Mike Maden.
Description: New York : G.P. Putnam's Sons, [2016] | Series:
  A Troy Pearce novel ; 4
Identifiers: LCCN 2016029298 | ISBN 9780399173998 (hardcover)
Subjects: LCSH: Special operations (Military science)—United
  States—Fiction. | Special forces (Military science)—United
  States—Fiction. | Terrorism—Prevention—Fiction. | Drone
  aircraft—Fiction. | BISAC: FICTION / Action & Adventure. |
  FICTION / Suspense. | FICTION / War & Military. | GSAFD:
  Suspense fiction.
Classification: LCC PS3613.A284327 D78 2016 | DDC
  813/.6—dc23
LC record available at https://lccn.loc.gov/2016029298
p.   cm.

Printed in the United States of America
1   3   5   7   9   10   8   6   4   2

BOOK DESIGN BY NICOLE LAROCHE

Bernie, Celestin,
Mark, Martin, Roger,
Scott, Tad and Wes.
Faithful. Friends.

MAJOR CHARACTERS

THE UNITED STATES OF AMERICA

Alyssa Abbott	White House Press Secretary
Clay Chandler	Vice President of the United States
Melinda Eaton	Director, Department of Homeland Security (DHS)
Jim Garza	National Security Advisor
Jackie Gibson	Lane's Chief of Staff
Stella Kang	Pearce Systems (security, drone operations)
David Lane	President of the United States (POTUS)
Carl Luckett	U.S. Army Ranger
Ian McTavish	Pearce Systems (IT)
Margaret Myers	Former President of the United States
General Gordon Onstot	Chairman, Joint Chiefs of Staff (JCS)
Ilene Parcelle	Partner, Seven Rivers Consortium
Troy Pearce	CEO, Pearce Systems
Julissa Peguero	Attorney General of the United States
Mike Pia	Director of National Intelligence (DNI)
Norman Pike	CEO, Chinook Charter
Steve Rowley	U.S. Army Ranger
Sarah Swift	Pearce Systems (combat medic)

THE STATE OF ISRAEL

Daniel Brody	Mossad agent
Tamar Stern	Mossad agent, former Pearce Systems associate
Moshe Werntz	Mossad chief of station, Washington, D.C., head of North American operations

OTHER NOTABLES

Abu Waleed al-Mahdi	Caliph of the ISIS Caliphate; Iraqi national
Kamal al-Medina	ISIS unit commander, Iraq; Saudi national
August Mann	Pearce Systems (Director of Nuclear Facilities Deconstruction); German national
Aleksandr Tarkovsky	Russian Federation Ambassador to the United States

ABBREVIATIONS AND ACRONYMS

AUMF	Authorization to Use Military Force
COTS	Consumer Off-the-Shelf
CTE	Chronic Traumatic Encephalopathy
IAI	Israeli Aerospace Industries
LaWS	Laser Weapons System
MALE	Medium-Altitude Long-Endurance
MWDSC	Metropolitan Water District of Southern California
PTSD	Post-Traumatic Stress Disorder
ROEs	Rules of Engagement
SOG	Special Operations Group (CIA)
SVR	Foreign Intelligence Service of the Russian Federation
TBI	Traumatic Brain Injury
TXDOT	Texas Department of Transportation
VTOL	Vertical Take-Off and Landing

AUTHOR'S NOTE

As with the previous novels in the series, the drone and related systems described in this story are currently deployed or are based on patent filings, prototypes, or research concepts. In some cases, I've modified or simplified their performance characteristics for the sake of the story.

He who fights with monsters should be careful lest he thereby become a monster. And if thou gaze long into an abyss, the abyss will also gaze into thee.

FRIEDRICH WILHELM NIETZSCHE,
Beyond Good and Evil, Aphorism 146 (1886)

DRONE THREAT

1

ZAKHO DISTRICT
KURDISTAN REGION
NORTHERN IRAQ

The sun's bloodred halo framed the Christ hanging from his towering crucifix.

Or so it seemed to Ahmed. He cupped his hands around his eyes to get a better look, his spent RPG launcher heavy on one shoulder and his battered AK-47 on the other.

Not a Christ. A Christian, and a Kurd.

It was a *kafir* they had crucified, he reminded himself. His limp body hung from a utility pole on top of the hill, his arms tied at the elbows to the crossbar with baling wire and duct tape. The *kafir* wouldn't submit, wouldn't renounce his infidel faith.

He crucified himself, Ahmed thought. He spat in the dust at his aching feet. The boots he wore were too small, taken from a dead Iraqi weeks ago.

He glanced back up. The blowflies swarmed around the moist tissues of the pastor's mouth and nose, laying their eggs. The orifices were caked with black blood. The eyes would be next, Ahmed knew. He'd seen it before, in the last village. And in the one before. The hatched larvae would begin their grim feast and in a week the pastor's skull would be picked clean. Disgusting. Ahmed spat again.

Brave, this one. Not like the Iraqi soldiers who fled like women when his convoy of pickups arrived in a cloud of dust yesterday, black ISIS flags flapping in the wind, each vehicle crowded with fighters like him. The Iraqis just dropped their gear and ran.

Well, not all of them.

Was it the flags that scared the cowards? Or the head of an Iraqi colonel hanging like a lantern on a pole on the lead truck? The Iraqis were probably Shia. Worse than infidels. Cleansing the Caliphate of all such nonbelievers was their sacred duty. Only through such cleansing and blood sacrifice would the Mahdi come with the prophet Isa and defeat the Antichrist. Has the Caliph not rightly taught that all of the signs are pointing toward the Day of Judgment? And was it not their duty to bring this about, one infidel corpse at a time?

Ahmed turned around. A line of utility poles marched down the long sloping hill. He counted ten more bodies hanging on them, including three children.

The pastor's children. Children of iniquity.

Dirty work, that, Ahmed thought. Glad he wasn't asked to do it. He would have, of course. Allah commands it. And if not, Kamal al-Medina ordered it, and he was more afraid of his commander here on earth than he was of the Exceedingly Merciful on His heavenly throne. He'd never seen Allah behead a screaming *kafir* with a serrated combat knife nor listened to him sing while he did it.

Such zeal. *It is to be admired*, he thought.

A Dodge Ram pickup honked behind him. He turned around as the truck skidded to a halt in the dust. A sharp-faced brother called out from the cab. He was a twenty-five-year-old Tunisian from Marseille. A French national like Ahmed, though Ahmed was a lily-white redhead of Norman stock and only nineteen.

"The commander has called for you," the Tunisian said in French. He threw a thumb at the truck bed. "Hop in."

Ahmed felt his stomach drop and the back of his neck tingle.

"But I'm on guard duty."

"I'll take your place after I drop you off."

"Why does he want me?"

The Tunisian lowered his voice. "Does the Black Prince consult with lowly commoners like us?" He flashed a crooked smile.

The pejorative reference to Kamal al-Medina's royal bloodline would have earned the Tunisian ten lashes with a whip if Ahmed reported the slur. He wouldn't, of course. Ahmed used it, too. They all did. And they all admired Kamal al-Medina as much as they feared him. The Saudi had given up everything—palaces, gold, power—to fight for the Caliphate and the *ummah*.

"No, he doesn't." Ahmed unslung his RPG launcher and rifle and clambered into the back of the Dodge. He slapped the cab roof and the truck whipped around, speeding toward the center of the small village of squat cinder-block houses, well kept and brightly painted in hues of red, blue, and yellow. Most doors were defaced with a spray-painted red Arabic *N* for *Nasrane*. A slur for Jesus the Nazarene and his followers.

It was also a mark for death.

Their truck sped past still more utility poles with a Christian corpse hanging from each, their sightless, downcast eyes keeping silent vigil over their lost village. The long shadows they cast were quickly fading in the dimming light. It would soon be time for the brothers to wash for evening prayers.

If only these Christians had submitted, Ahmed thought. Submitted to the will of Allah and signed the *dhimma* contract and paid the *jizya*—perhaps that would have kept them from death. Easier still, they could have just lied to save their lives and fight another day. Was *taqiyya* not permitted in their book as well?

He liked this village. It was neat and well organized and surrounded by fertile fields. A village not much different from the one he came from in Normandy. He wondered how soon before those utility poles back home would be filled with Crusader corpses, too. He hoped he would live long enough to see it and to see even the whole world under the great Caliphate of God.

Inshallah.

THE PICKUP SKIDDED to a stop in front of the church guarded by two jihadis, an almond-eyed Kazakh and a graying Uzbek. Both good fighters, Ahmed knew. And zealous.

Ahmed leaped out of the truck bed and the Dodge sped off. Ahmed stood a moment, unsure of his situation. Had he sinned? The commander's zeal for God knew no bounds. Just last week he punished a brother who kept smoking cigarettes in secret. Sharia forbade it. Smoking was *haram*. "There are no secrets here. God knows all and he will not honor us if we don't keep his law," al-Medina proclaimed before personally delivering the forty lashes to the brother's back with a thick leather whip.

Ahmed weighed his chances against the two guards. There were no bullets in his battered rifle and his RPG had no grenade—not that he could've used either in close-quarters combat. He had his grandfather's old folding knife in his pocket, but that wasn't much of a weapon, either. Both guards were well armed and could kill with their hands. He'd seen it himself. Perhaps he could run, but then they would shoot him in the back like a dog.

The Uzbek nodded a dour greeting and pushed open one of the two front doors and signaled him to follow.

Ahmed hesitated before the open door. He hadn't stood in a Christian church since he was a child—his first communion. The small stone church in his village had long since been abandoned by the last Catholic faithful and converted into a bike shop. Still, he wondered what judgment might be waiting for him inside this holy place after a day of slaughter. The sun had fallen beneath the hills and the long shadows had given way to a general gloom.

"He's waiting for you," the Uzbek said. "Follow me."

Inshallah, Ahmed said to himself again with a shrug. He followed the Uzbek in. The old fighter limped heavily on his left foot into the broad expanse of the sanctuary and down the rows of mostly empty pews. The aisles were littered with chunks of broken plaster, half-melted candles, torn hymnals, and spent cartridges. A few of the brothers were passed out on the long benches, snoring from exhaustion. Three unit subcommanders stood on the raised platform and used a communion table to study a map they had laid upon it. A few dim bulbs in a chandelier overhead threw a sickly yellow light around them. A black ISIS flag hung from the rafters.

Ahmed's eyes drifted to the smashed ceramic Christ crunching beneath their feet, broken into a dozen pieces and tossed like garbage around the floor. This pleased him. A false Christ these *kafir* worship, and an idol at that.

The Uzbek led Ahmed to another door to the side of the sanctuary. He knocked on it. "Enter!" boomed from the other side. Ahmed recognized al-Medina's commanding voice.

The Uzbek nodded curtly to Ahmed, then hobbled away.

Ahmed took a deep breath, then pushed open the door.

Kamal al-Medina sat behind a small wooden desk, and his two senior commanders sat on a worn leather couch against one wall near him. The room was spacious and lined with crowded bookshelves. A small side table was dedicated to framed photographs of the pastor, his wife, and three children. The wife was stunning. This must have been the pastor's office, Ahmed concluded.

"Brother Ahmed!" Al-Medina stood. A wide grin spread beneath his dark, wooly beard. His lieutenants rose as well, also smiling.

Al-Medina came around from behind the desk and wrapped Ahmed in a bear hug. The other two commanders did likewise.

"Emir?" was all Ahmed could muster in his confusion.

Al-Medina laughed and spoke to him in French. "No need for the formalities. We're all brothers here, yes?"

Ahmed nodded, tried to answer him in faltering Arabic. Al-Medina held up a hand.

"I attended a private school in Switzerland, so French is no problem for me. But we can speak English or German if you prefer."

"I like, eh, want the language of the Prophet, peace be upon him," Ahmed insisted in broken Arabic.

"But I prefer to practice my French, if you don't mind," al-Medina insisted.

"*Ça va*," Ahmed said.

"Excellent! Can I get you something to drink? Water, coffee?"

"No, sir. I'm fine. How can I be of service?"

Al-Medina clapped him hard on the shoulder. "You already have, my young lion. I heard what you did yesterday." Al-Medina pantomimed holding an RPG on his shoulder and firing it. "You killed those three Iraqis barricaded in the house, firing their machine gun. They had the front echelon pinned down with their murderous weapon. But you jumped into the street and put a HEAT round right into their window. BOOM!"

Al-Medina clapped his hands when he said the word and laughed. The others laughed, too.

Al-Medina switched back to Arabic. "You saved many brothers that day. I just wanted to take the time now to properly thank you, and to reward you. Do you understand?"

"Yes, a little," Ahmed said, embarrassed by his poor Arabic skills.

Al-Medina signaled with his hand. "Follow me."

Al-Medina led Ahmed and the other commanders to an adjoining room. Stacks of American rifles, grenade launchers, ammo boxes, and even fresh Iraqi uniforms still in their plastic bags lined the walls.

"Take your pick. All courtesy of the United States government," al-Medina said with another laugh.

"For me? Anything? Truly?" In his excitement, Ahmed fell back into his French. He snatched up a brand-new M-4 carbine still glistening with lubricant.

"Anything you need or want." Al-Medina opened up a box. "Here, brand-new boots if you need them."

"Boots!" Ahmed set his new weapon down and raced over to the box of boots and began sifting through them, looking for his size.

"But there's something more for our young hero," one of the commanders said, chuckling.

"Ah, yes. I almost forgot," al-Medina said through a wide grin.

Ahmed looked up.

"Come, boy. Something better indeed."

The other men laughed.

Al-Medina led the nineteen-year-old to yet another door that opened to a great room. A dozen women sat cowering on the floor, their faces covered by hijabs. But their downcast eyes told all, dazed and red with tears. Some were even blackened.

"Take one."

"Sir?"

Al-Medina shouted an order. The women all jumped to their feet as one, startled by the harshness of his voice. They immediately pulled off their hijabs. Some were younger than Ahmed. Two were blond. Al-Medina saw Ahmed's gaze fall on one particular girl a few years older than he. Her dark blue eyes were wide with terror. She covered her bruised mouth with one trembling hand.

"That one is an American. An aid worker. The trucks are coming first thing in the morning to pick them all up and take them to market. But you can have her until then." He nudged Ahmed. "She's good, I can tell you."

"And it is not *haram*?" Ahmed had been taught that sex outside of marriage was forbidden by the Koran.

"It is *mut'ah*. A temporary marriage for your pleasure," al-Medina assured him. "The imam will bless it."

Ahmed's face flushed crimson, matching his thin beard. He couldn't believe his good fortune. He'd never been with a woman before.

The three older jihadis laughed at the boy's innocence.

"That one, then" Ahmed said, pointing at a dark-eyed beauty in the back, trying to hide her face.

Al-Medina pounded Ahmed's shoulder. "The pastor's wife! Excellent choice."

HE PRAYED TO GOD before he raped her. They all did.

So did she.

Not the same prayer.

Not the same God.

The red-haired boy lay next to her, sleeping. He looked more child than man in the light of the single bulb when he first took her. But he was no child. More like a rutting pig. He stank of his own urine and sweat after days in the field. Too eager to care to bathe before the filthy act.

She had wiped herself clean of him with the sheets after he had finished but otherwise didn't move. He passed out soon afterward. She lay in the dark with her eyes fixed on the invisible ceiling, praying for the strength she'd need in the coming hours. She counted his breaths again, deep and long. Satisfied he was fast asleep, she reached for the razor blade she'd hidden in her garment folded neatly on the floor next to the mattress. Everything in her wanted to slit his throat and let him bleed out in his "marriage" bed. But there was too much at stake, and too many other lives hung in the balance. Her husband, she knew, was watching, too. He wouldn't have approved of her killing him even though the boy had raped her in his own bed. Her husband was a true Christian.

Certain the pig was out for the night, she carefully extricated herself from the tangled sheets. She stood slowly, then bent over to fetch her garment.

Suddenly he stirred.

No! She caught her breath. But he just rolled over and fell back into the deep rhythms of exhausted sleep.

She uttered silent thanks and dressed quickly. It was pitch black, but this was her bedroom and she knew every square inch of it, so there was no need to turn the lamp back on. She stepped blindly but carefully toward the small nightstand and reached behind it. Her groping fingers found the hidden cell phone. She listened again for the jihadi's breathing. He was still asleep. She opened the phone. 1:35 a.m. She panicked. Was there still enough time? The signal showed only one bar and less than 10 percent of charge left on the battery. She prayed it would be enough.

She prayed she wasn't too late.

She texted her message, hit Send, and prayed again. She touched the blade in her garment, a small comfort. She would use it on herself if tonight failed.

God forgive me.

2

Troy Pearce stood in the dark on the gravel mountain road marking the border between southern Turkey and northern Iraq. He reminded himself that not too long ago he was in the East China Sea.

Literally.

President Lane called him a hero for stopping a war with China. But, standing here on the edge of another killing ground, it didn't seem to matter much. He didn't feel like a hero. He was just doing his job. And the cost he paid was high. Too high. He pushed the thought away.

Pearce wore black tactical gear with an olive-drab *shemagh* wrapped around his neck. His dark hair was flecked with silver and his pale blue eyes were tired. He rubbed his beardless face to push away the fatigue.

The tablet in his hand read 03:48:21 in the top right-hand corner but his eyes were fixated on the strand of ghostly white shapes on the black screen meandering steadily in his direction. The lead figure was a burly Kurdish guide and the thirteen others were the women he was helping escape on foot through the moonless night up the steep, grassy hills that lay between them and freedom. The image on his tablet was broadcast from a Heron TP medium-altitude long-endurance (MALE) UAV. It was being piloted remotely via satellite by his number two man in the company, Ian McTavish.

"Got a visual?" Pearce asked Ian in his comms.

"Not yet. They're still on the other side of that ridge." Tariq Barzani had a pair of night-vision goggles pressed against his worried face. A woolen cap covered his bald head. Pearce noticed that his bushy mustache had grayed considerably since he had last seen him years before, but he looked tough as ever.

"Just five kilometers. They've still got time," Pearce said. "But they need to hurry." He handed Tariq the tablet. The Kurd studied it closely.

Pearce worried about the Turkish border guards. The Gendarmerie was heavily gunned and as brutally efficient as the rest of Turkey's armed forces. They patrolled this area regularly with armed vehicles and overhead drone surveillance, but a ten-figure baksheesh placed in the hands of the regional commander bought Pearce a nonnegotiable four-hour window. That window would slam shut in just seventy-two minutes. The women were making good time, but if the Turk border patrol suddenly decided to show up early, the whole operation would be blown.

Or worse.

"They know the danger, trust me," Tariq said. His sister's text earlier confirmed their departure from the village, but nothing more. His cousin leading the way confirmed their arrival at the rendezvous point, but for security reasons they all agreed beforehand to maintain communication silence until the group arrived at the border.

Five pickups were parked on the gravel road, a Kurdish driver and gunner in each. Plenty of room for the women and two friendlies who tagged along, Carl Luckett and Steve Rowley. They were ex-Rangers who had served under Mike Early, Pearce's closest friend during the War on Terror, now dead. Early had brought the two of them along on a mission he and Pearce had run a long time ago in Iraq—the same mission where he had first met Tariq, their translator. When Pearce picked up the phone twenty-four hours ago, the only thing he had to say was "Tariq needs us." The Kurdish peshmerga fighter had saved all of their asses and never asked for so much as a thank-you at the time. So when Tariq came hat in hand to Pearce's place and begged for help, Pearce dropped everything and pulled together a plan. They had a very narrow window, and this was the best Pearce could do on short notice. But, all things considered, it was a better play than others he'd made in the past, and he was still vertical and breathing after those. Besides, he hated ISIS, and anything he could do to frustrate them was a good day's work as far as he was concerned.

Pearce checked the screen again. With any luck, they'd be loaded up and rolling out of here with the women in the next forty minutes and landing in Beirut within three hours at the latest.

God, how he missed Mikey. There was no safer place on the planet than standing next to the big, hulking Ranger when the bullets started to fly. He hoped it wouldn't come to that tonight.

Pearce's private Bombardier Global 5000 corporate jet was waiting on the tarmac at an airfield nearby in Cizre. A few more well-placed bribes and a couple of hard-pulled strings generated all the necessary paperwork and travel permits they needed to fly unmolested in and out of Turkish airspace on a supposed business trip. Pearce Systems was an international security company, but much of Pearce's drone-based business was connected to commercial enterprises, so his cover wasn't too much of a stretch, especially with former president Margaret Myers working the phones on his behalf. Fortunately, the military-contracting side of his business was running the Canadian army's Heron TP operations in Afghanistan. With the Heron's range and endurance, it wasn't any trouble to reroute one for tonight's mission, and Ian had become a crack UAV pilot. Pearce couldn't imagine running any kind of mission anymore without eyes in the sky.

Tariq handed him back the tablet. Pearce resized the image.

"Shit!" Pearce tapped his earpiece. "Ian, we've got Deltas coming in hot."

A speeding convoy of trucks was racing toward the women.

"I see them," Ian said. "But—"

"No time to talk!" Pearce shouted at the others. "Saddle up!"

Luckett and Rowley leaped into their pickup as Tariq barked orders in Kurdish. He hardly needed to. Truck engines fired up and machine guns were racked.

"You've got company!" Ian shouted.

Pearce was already in the bed of his truck and pounding the roof to take off when the roaring *whomp-whomp-whomp* of helicopter blades came thundering over the hill behind them. The sound was deafening as two T-70 Black Hawks swept overhead. One hovered directly above them and poured a blinding searchlight on the convoy. Grit and dust from the rotor wash stung Pearce's face. The other chopper dropped thirty yards on the Iraqi side of the border, blocking the way forward with its heavily armed fuselage and another blinding searchlight.

"Stay or go?" Luckett shouted in Pearce's earpiece. Tariq's anxious eyes asked the same thing.

Pearce checked his tablet. The ISIS convoy was less than a mile from the women, who hadn't changed course or speed. They clearly didn't know that they were being hunted. It was now or never but—

The other chopper landed just a few yards behind them, the blades dangerously close. A squad of Turkish special forces leaped to the ground and charged toward them, weapons forward, shouting. Pearce's instinct was to turn the machine gun around and open up but his mind checked his gut—they'd be cut to pieces in a flash.

The Turks surrounded the trucks just as a middle-aged American woman in civilian clothes and a Kevlar vest jogged up. Her name was Hyssop, the embassy trade attaché. The slowing rotor wash fanned her short, thinning hair.

"What the hell is going on, Pearce?" Hyssop demanded. "I didn't authorize any of this!"

"I don't have time to explain. Call your dogs off and let us through—"

"Not going to happen! You're supposed to be on a trade mission, not an armed incursion!"

"We've got lives on the line out there!" Pearce said. "You've got to let us go. Now!"

The Turkish army commander, a captain, shouted orders to his men. They raised their weapons to fire.

"Troy! The women!" Ian's Scottish brogue shouted in Pearce's ear.

Hyssop grabbed Pearce's sleeve. "These guys aren't screwing around. Stand down now and I can still get you out of this—"

A truck engine gunned. Tariq's pickup leaped forward, scattering the two Turkish soldiers standing in front of it. Before the others could open fire, the captain shouted another order and the squad lowered its weapons.

"Tariq!" Pearce screamed.

Pearce watched as Tariq's pickup made a suicidal charge straight at the other helicopter. The chopper lifted off before the truck reached it but as soon as it passed underneath, the Black Hawk's door gunner opened up with a salvo from its Vulcan machine gun, shredding the Toyota's thin steel and erupting the gas tank in a fiery explosion.

The Turks gathered around Pearce's vehicle howled with laughter.

Pearce shouted as he swung his size-fourteen combat boot. It cracked into the braying face of the soldier standing closest to him with a sickening thud. Pearce leaped down and crashed into the next Turk, driving the surprised trooper into the ground. Pearce lifted a fist to smash the second soldier's face when a pistol exploded just behind his head. Pearce's ears rang with the shot as red-hot ice picks stabbed his eardrums.

Pearce's fist froze in midair. He turned around. The captain's pistol was six inches from his face.

"Pearce, you asshole!" Hyssop sped over to him, throwing herself between him and the captain as she hauled Pearce up to his feet.

The Turkish soldiers manhandled the Kurds, seizing their weapons and cuffing them with PlastiCuffs. Two more soldiers dragged Luckett and Rowley out of their truck and hauled them roughly over to Pearce.

"You are in violation of Turkish law and Turkish national sovereignty. I have every legal right to execute the three of you right here as foreign invaders," the captain said. He glanced with disgust at his two fallen men, one still clutching his broken jaw and moaning through bloody fingers. "And for assaulting my men."

"Give me ten more minutes and I'll finish the job," Pearce said.

The captain held out a gloved hand. "Your comms."

"I'm sorry, I can't hear a word you're saying—"

The captain's face hardened as he raised his pistol again.

"Idiot!" Hyssop snatched the earpiece out of Pearce's ear and tossed it to the captain. He pocketed it, then pulled out a pair of PlastiCuffs.

"Just try," Pearce said.

"Pearce, it's not just your ass on the line. You're about to make this into an international incident. There's a lot more in the wind than you're aware of here."

"Those shit bags just killed my friend—"

She got in his face. "And a lot more people will die if you don't shut this down right now."

Pearce glanced at Luckett and Rowley. The Turks were cuffing them behind their backs. But the ex-Rangers were still dangerous men, even tied up.

Luckett read Pearce's mind. He grinned.

"You call it, boss. We're with you all the way."

It would be a stupid move, Pearce decided. Gotta get back to the plane. He held out his wrists. The captain zipped the cuffs tight, then yanked the tablet out of Pearce's pants pocket and the pistol out of its holster.

"Let's get out of here. Now," Hyssop said, pulling him toward the first chopper.

"What about them?" Pearce nodded in the direction of the Kurds already being marched toward the other chopper.

"That's none of your affair," the captain said. He barked an order to the sergeant standing nearby, who signaled two others. The three armed Turks prodded the four Americans back toward the first helicopter.

A minute later, Pearce, Hyssop, Luckett, and Rowley were airborne. Pearce watched the Kurds get thrown into the other Black Hawk, their hands bound behind their backs. Pearce knew the bloody history between the genocidal Turks and the hapless Kurds. He assumed the Turks would toss them out of the chopper like sacks of garbage as soon as they reached altitude.

Maybe the four of them, too.

As they pulled away, Pearce's eyes fixed on Tariq's truck down below, still burning in the dark. He swore.

Jesus, what a goat fuck.

As soon as they were airborne, the Turk captain opened up Pearce's tablet. He pressed buttons until an image pulled up. He stared at it. A feral grin spread across his face in the red cabin light. He turned the tablet around and held it close to Pearce's face.

Pearce's heart sank. The ISIS trucks and men were on the women like a pack of wolves. But instead of rounding them up, they were killing them. A half dozen bodies already lay scattered on the ground as the rest fell in a dead run, one by one.

The captain's grin grew wider.

Pearce grunted with rage and launched at the captain, aiming his skull at the Turk's jaw. But the captain saw it coming and clocked Pearce across his ear with the butt of his pistol and Pearce crumbled to the steel floor, knocked out cold.

3

Pearce awoke when Luckett dropped him into the plush leather seat. His head throbbed with a splitting headache, and his eyes blinked in the harsh cabin lights of the Bombardier 5000.

"He's back with us," Luckett said over his shoulder, a worried look on his unshaven face. The turbines whined as the engine power increased.

Rowley dashed over. He lifted each of Pearce's eyelids, checking for dilation. "You better get that noggin checked when we land, but I think you're okay for now."

Pearce stood up on wobbly legs. The plane was already rocketing down the tarmac.

"Whoa, boss. We're taking off. Better sit down and buckle up," Luckett said as he plopped into his own seat and strapped in. Rowley did the same.

Pearce pushed past both of them, steadying himself with the leather headrests as the plane angled steeply into its climb. He made it to the front of the cabin and fell into a chair facing an open console attached to the bulkhead. It was a remote-control station. He pulled on the headphones and dialed up Ian.

"Ian, you still there?" Pearce powered up the computer monitor and pulled out the sliding keyboard and joystick.

"Troy! Thank heavens. It's good to hear your voice. I was getting worried. Your men filled me in. I'm sorry for what happened. I didn't know what to do."

"There wasn't anything you could've done. Please tell me you tracked those dickheads back to their rat hole."

"Are you at the console yet?"

"Just opened it." The computer monitor flicked on. Another ghosted image appeared, but this time it was a small village. A crosshair was fixed on a large building. Several trucks were parked outside, still glowing from the engine heat.

"What am I looking at?"

"That's where they all ran to ground. The whole stinking lot of them."

"Any civilians inside?"

"None that I'm aware of."

Pearce flipped a few more switches. Seized the joystick.

"Ian, I need you to log off."

"Troy, I don't think that's a good idea—"

"Not asking your permission. Sign the fuck off now."

"Troy—"

"I'm trying to protect you. Now do as I say or I'll fire your ass."

There was a brief silence as Pearce armed one of the two Hellfire missiles slung under the Heron's wings.

"Logging off, under protest," Ian said. His line went dead.

"Duly noted," Pearce said.

He pressed the trigger. A moment later, the screen flared with a blinding white light. When it faded, it revealed a heap of hot, smoldering ruins where the building and trucks had stood.

Pearce stared at the screen. Armed the other missile. Fired. It struck the flaming wreckage and the screen flared again.

Pearce wished he had another one.

He fought the urge to scream.

He dialed up Ian and turned the control of the Heron back over to him, then powered off his console. He leaned back in his chair, the horrific images of the night flashing in his brain like a strobe light. He covered his face with both heavy hands.

And wept.

———

THE SUN ROSE pink in the early dawn.

The Turkish special forces captain stood in the midst of the ruins of the church, a pile of smashed rubble and smoldering wood. His men were fanned out, turning over splintered pews and shattered brick, searching for human remains.

The captain glanced up at the pink-gray sky. The blast shattered one of the nearby utility poles. Its grim human cargo had been tossed through the air and now lay twisted in the dirt, still attached to the crossbar. But the rising light revealed the gruesome line of bodies high in the air that still remained, leading away from the church and down the long, winding road away from the village.

Butchery, the captain thought. But useful. The Kurds were a problem and ISIS a convenient solution for Ankara. His own country had slaughtered the Armenians in the same way years before. He shrugged. His moderate Islamic government knew what it was doing and he wasn't in charge of the Kurdish operation. He shouldn't even be on this side of the border. His duty was to obey orders, but the army didn't pay enough money.

"Captain!" a short, stocky corporal called out.

The captain picked his way through the ruins and made his way over to the corporal, who pointed in earnest at the corpse beneath the burnt timbers.

The captain nodded at the wood. "Move that."

The corporal lifted a big chunk of wood with a grunt and tossed it aside, wiping his hands onto his camo pants, staining them with ash.

The captain knelt and examined the corpse. It was only half of a human torso, relatively intact from the gory waist up. The face was partially charred and badly disfigured, but there wasn't any doubt.

The captain pulled out his cell phone and framed the shot to make the gruesome figure less so. The important feature was the face. He snapped a few shots until he got one he was comfortable with and even took a few minutes to crop and edit it.

"Good work, Corporal. There's a thermos with black coffee in my kit. Go get yourself some."

"Thank you, sir!" The corporal threw a hasty salute and scrambled uneasily toward the chopper as the captain speed-dialed a number.

"It's me, sir. Captain Orga. We've found Kamal al-Medina. I have a photo." The captain attached the photo to an encrypted text message and sent it. He waited for a few moments for the man on the other end to receive the picture and process it.

The man asked a question.

Orga answered. "An American drone strike, certainly."

Another question.

"Hyssop said he's ex-CIA. Goes by the name of Troy Pearce."

4

WASHINGTON, D.C.

Breaking glass.

Pearce awoke, startled out of a fitful sleep. Head pounding. He glanced at his pistol in its holster on the nightstand, but something stopped him from snatching it up.

Bacon.

He smelled bacon.

His stomach was sour, but the bacon smelled like maple and sweet pork fat. His mouth watered. But that meant someone was cooking downstairs.

More glass broke.

He rubbed the sleep out of his eyes and pulled on a pair of jeans that lay crumpled on the floor. He sniffed the wrinkled T-shirt. Not good. He tossed it aside.

The white marble tiles felt cool under his bare feet as he made his way unsteadily toward the staircase. The air in the stairwell was heavy with the smell of fried potatoes now, too. Maybe he really had died and gone to heaven.

But, judging from the way his head throbbed, it could've been the other place.

He carefully picked his way down the floating white oak stair treads until he reached the kitchen. The whole downstairs was a huge open-concept floor plan of glass and marble. Ultramodern and elegant, just like the woman in the kitchen.

"Morning," Pearce said.

Margaret Myers looked up from the frying pan full of potatoes. Another was larded with scrambled eggs. She wore form-fitting athletic wear that complemented her healthy physique. The former president only pushed herself harder in the gym these days out of spite for her adult-onset type 1 diabetes. Her brand-new wireless iLet Bionic Pancreas receiver was strapped to her waist and hidden beneath her shirt.

"Good morning. I'm sorry if I woke you."

Pearce glanced over at the stainless-steel garbage can brimming with beer bottles, its electronic lid jammed open.

"Sorry about the mess. I thought you weren't coming back until tonight."

"Caught an early flight. Thought we could spend the day together instead of me hanging around in a stuffy old hotel. How are you feeling, by the way?"

"Better than when you left." He stepped closer to her.

She pushed the pan of eggs off the burner and wrapped her arms around his neck. "I was so worried."

He pulled her in closer but his mind was somewhere else. "I know."

She leaned back. Cupped his face in her hands. "You need to shave." She sniffed, grinning. "Maybe a shower, too. Breakfast will be ready in ten."

"Tea?"

"Green as grass and steeping in the pot." She gently touched the nasty bruise on the side of his head. "You sure you're all right?"

"Shower and some caffeine and I'll be right as rain."

"Did you get to the doctor?"

Pearce shrugged his wide shoulders. "I'm fine."

Myers caught herself admiring his bare, broad chest and powerful arms. He'd spent more than half of his life throwing punches—or worse. A myriad of minor scars bore witness on his skin to his years in combat.

"Call him today, please."

His face darkened. He let her go. "Will do, Madam President."

Meyers turned around and picked up an already cooked plate of bacon, his favorite. "The bacon is a strictly volunteer mission, should you decide to accept it."

He stared at the bacon and then her fake-scowly face. *She deserves better*, he thought. A slight smile stole across his face. She knew how to make him laugh at himself. He picked up a piece of bacon in his fingers and crammed the whole thing into his mouth, caveman style.

"Verdict?"

"Perfecto," he said, still chewing.

He snatched another piece and plopped it into mouth. "Back in a flash." He dashed back upstairs, his mood lightened.

She watched him jog up the stair treads, then pulled the eggs back onto the burner to finish them up, still worried.

A QUICK GLANCE in the bathroom mirror told the story. He examined his stubbled face closely. His exhausted blue eyes were shadowed by dark circles. The place above his ear where the pistol had struck him was swollen and still hurt like hell. His head hadn't stopped pounding since the Turk hit him, but two days of heavy drinking didn't help, either. Maybe she was right. Maybe it was time to see a doctor.

He didn't have any of his things at her place, but she had been thoughtful enough to buy a couple of disposables and some shave gel and leave them in the all-glass shower enclosure. She was old-fashioned in a funny way. They were in love, for sure, but he hadn't asked her to marry him and she wasn't going to shack up. "Not my style," she'd said with a smile. Not his, either, actually. They were serious but taking it slowly. They'd been friends for a few years now but only recently had become lovers.

Pearce's blood pressure suddenly dropped.

When, exactly, was their anniversary? Sometime soon, he knew. Not the kind of thing he should be forgetting, but it had been more than a decade since he had to worry about such things, and if he missed it, well, Margaret wasn't the kind of woman to lord it over him. But then again, she was a woman, and something told him it might be a good idea to figure that out before she called him on it.

The plan had been to land back in D.C. after the mission and lay over for a day in order to give her a status report and reconnect, then fly on to California to check up on Tariq and his family while Margaret attended to business in Denver.

But Tariq was dead. No reason to head out.

He decided to stay in town at his hotel, but Myers saw his heavy fatigue and insisted he crash at her place for a few days and recover. What she really wanted to do, he knew, was take care of him, at least that first night.

He took her up on the offer. His company suite was sterile and he wasn't big on room service.

It was the call to Tariq's wife the next day when Myers was out of town that finally set Pearce off on a bender. He hadn't boozed like that in years. At least he had the sense to do it here and not get hammered in some crosstown bar like he used to do in the old days.

He flipped on the shower and let it run good and cold. Nothing like a blast of freezing water to sober a guy up and get the blood flowing. A small mirror suction-cupped to the slate tiles helped him slather on the gei and shave pretty close with the triple blade without cutting any parts off, and a quick splash of shampoo and liquid soap rinsed off the mess of the last few days. He wished he could rinse out the image of Tariq's truck lighting up the night or the ghost-white images of the women getting gunned down on that mountain slope so far away now.

He pushed open the glass door and toweled off briskly, pushing all of the negative thoughts out of his mind and crowding it with images of the breakfast he was about to consume. He learned on the long, hard marches in the mountains of Afghanistan that the only way he could make a steep climb was to focus on just the next step. The cold shower even managed to push away the queasy feeling in his gut. He dragged a brush through his longish hair, then pulled open the one dresser drawer that held a few of the things he'd left here before and pulled them on: boxers, Levis, and a Denver Broncos T-shirt Margaret bought him to remind him where his new football loyalties belonged. The thought made him smile a little.

He was a lucky bastard, for sure.

5

By the time he made it back downstairs she'd already set the breakfast bar in the all-glass nook overlooking the busy street below. As he sat down, she placed a thick Navy mug of steaming hot green tea in front of him and he took a big slurp.

"Bless you," he said. His plate was heaped with fried home-style potatoes, bacon, and scrambled eggs. His absolute all-time favorite breakfast.

"Dig in," she said with a hopeful smile. She didn't cook this kind of fare often.

He glanced at her plate as he splashed spicy Tapatío sauce on his eggs. She had just one piece of bacon, a small mound of egg whites, and a few cut strawberries—low-glycemic fruit. She knew her bionic pancreas would compensate for whatever she ate with automated dosing of glucogen and insulin. But she wanted to maintain as much control as she could over her own body and preferred to eat sensibly rather than allow the machine to correct her bad choices.

They ate in silence for a few moments.

"Is it okay?" she asked.

He grinned, his mouth stuffed with food. He swallowed. "Yeah, that's why I'm not saying anything. It's great. Thanks so much."

"By the way you're wolfing that down, I'm guessing the liquid diet you were on wasn't quite doing the trick."

Ouch. He deserved that. "Yeah, well, a bad habit from the bad old days. It won't happen again."

She laid her hand on top of his. "I'm not judging you. I'm just worried, that's all. You said you'd been fighting this battle for a while now. I hate to see you give in to it."

She was right, of course, he reminded himself. He half blamed the booze for a friend's death in Mozambique, and the bender he went on afterward nearly got another friend killed in the Elephant Bar down by the docks. He went clean and sober after that and hadn't touched a drop until yesterday. Even after what happened at Fukushima.

"I'm no teetotaler, you know that," she said. "But the drinking is a symptom."

Troy felt the heat on the back of his neck. He dropped the fork. "What's that supposed to mean?" The words came out harsher than he intended.

Myers set her fork down and wiped her mouth neatly with her napkin, gathering her carefully selected words.

"I know things went sideways on this mission and I'm deeply sorry. I know you did everything you could, but—"

"But shit happens. That's all. Shit happens. Not my first fucking rodeo." He picked up his cup and took another sip of tea, trying to tamp down his rising anger.

"You told me this had been a pattern in your life and that you were determined to change it. I just want to help you, that's all."

"I appreciate it, but I've got it under control. It won't happen again. I just needed to blow off some steam." He set his empty cup down. She filled it back up.

"I get that, I really do. But you said your dad was an alcoholic, right?"

Pearce nodded, then lifted the cup to his mouth.

"And he was a combat vet, just like you. And he brought the war home with him, and he took it out on you and your mom and your sister."

"That's all water under the bridge."

"I know you've put all of that behind you. But he drank to self-medicate."

"Is that what you think I was doing?"

"I'm just asking."

"He had PTSD."

"I know," she said, nodding.

Pearce saw something in her eyes. "Are you saying I have PTSD?"

"Did your dad ever admit he had it?"

"That was different. He was old-school."

"Maybe."

"What's your point, Margaret?"

"I think you should see a counselor. Maybe try and sort a few things out."

"To stop drinking?"

"No. Like I said, the drinking might just be a symptom."

"It was just a one-off. You know I swore off the booze."

"I know."

"I just slipped up."

"It's a slippery slope."

Pearce set his cup down, sat up straighter. "And if I don't stop drinking?"

She shrugged and smiled. "Then you don't."

"And if I get worse?"

She glanced over at the mountain of bottles in the garbage. "I guess I'll have to buy a bigger garbage can."

Pearce felt a sudden rush in his eyes, blurring them. *I don't deserve this woman.*

He stood up. Paced the floor. "I tried, I swear. I really tried. We could've saved them if that bitch from the embassy hadn't shown up—"

"Then you might be dead."

"But Tariq *is* dead. And so are those women. And it's my goddamn fault."

"You didn't kill him or those women. Those bastards did. You tried to help."

"And how'd that turn out?" He ran his hand through his damp hair, thinking. "Hyssop didn't do us any favors either."

"It's her job. She was trying to protect the interests of the American government as she saw it."

"So you're on her side?"

"No, I'm on yours. Always. But I'm trying to help you see hers. She had a job to do and she did it, and as far as I'm concerned, I'm grateful. If she hadn't been there, the Turks might have decided to kill all of you."

"You know I had to go."

She nodded. "Of course I do. You explained it. And you're a loyal guy. It's one of the many things I adore about you. But the truth is, you were conducting an illegal operation on foreign soil. It was a risk you were willing to take because you loved Tariq, but a risk is just that— you take a big chance that something might work or it might not. This time, it didn't. But not because you didn't try."

"What else was I supposed to do?" Pearce headed for the living room. She followed him.

"I don't think there was anything else you could do. We talked about Tariq's situation. President Lane wouldn't have helped—his 'no new boots on the ground' policy would have prevented any action on the part of the U.S. government, even covert action."

"That was your policy," Pearce said. It sounded like an accusation.

"But I'm not the president anymore. He is. It's his administration and it's the law. When you step outside the law, you can't expect the government to support you."

"Do you think I was wrong?" Pearce stood by a large plate-glass window, staring down at the morning rush hour ten floors below. She came up behind him, wrapped her arms around his waist.

"You did what you thought was right, and you did it for the right reasons. But you were on the outside looking in."

"Meaning?"

"Sometimes it's easier to get things done when you're on the inside."

"You mean, go back into government service? The CIA?" His face soured. He'd left the special operations group because he'd lost too many friends in the War on Terror for the sake of political expediency. It was the whole reason why he started Pearce Systems—to pick and choose battles with a certain moral clarity, and to deploy drone technology to protect his people, and all of it without the intervention of self-serving politicians peering over his shoulder. He'd come to love running his own company and valued his independence after more than a decade of taking orders.

"No. Not that. I just think you should reconsider Lane's offer to head up Drone Command." Before Myers and Pearce had been dispatched on a secret diplomatic mission to Asia earlier in the year to try to prevent a war between China and Japan, President Lane had offered Pearce the chance to start a new department within his administration. Pearce hadn't turned him down but he still hadn't accepted it, either.

Pearce turned around and faced her. "So you want me to be a suit? Another pencil-pushing bureaucrat?"

"You'd hardly be that. You're the CEO of the world's best drone security company. That makes you uniquely suited to help the United States shape its drone acquisition program in the coming decade. That means you'd be changing America's war-fighting policy more than anything. And policy is where the game is at."

"I'm used to being in charge now. Kind of hard to put my neck back in someone else's harness."

"As I recall, you'd be relatively independent, reporting directly to the president. And you'd be building an entire agency from scratch. You'd be setting all of the rules, not following them. It's about as independent as you could possibly be in federal service."

"Except for congressional oversight, media scrutiny—"

"It would be all black budget. Minimal congressional oversight, total media blackout."

Pearce scratched his chin. Shrugged. "I'm sure Lane has found somebody else by now."

"As a matter of fact, his chief of staff called me just last night and asked if you were still interested."

"Why'd Jackie call you?"

"Because she tried calling you for the last three days and you weren't picking up." She took him by the hand and led him to the white leather couch. Pearce remembered another white leather couch slathered in blood on a cold winter day in Moscow. They sat together, still holding hands. Pearce was still processing.

"I remember the first time we met," Myers said. "I think we both had trust issues."

"Yeah," he said. He'd come to loathe politics and, by extension, politicians. Only Early could've persuaded him to meet with then–President Myers who had a job for him to do—off the books. But the two of them took a chance on each other. And she'd proved to him beyond a shadow of a doubt that there were at least a few good men and women in elected government service who could be trusted to do the right thing. President Lane was another one.

"So I need you to trust me on this." She kissed the back of his hand. "You're one of the most remarkable men I've ever known, and everything I know about you tells me that your heart's desire is to serve this country. You've sacrificed a lot, and you've lost a lot of dear friends for reasons that don't make a lot of sense."

"My dad, too." Long since dead of a brain tumor probably induced by Agent Orange. Or more accurately, the lousy VA treatment he never actually got for it.

"But you said that Mossa helped you find your way back."

He nodded. It took a long, strange trip through the Sahara with a Tuareg chieftain to remember that he was a warrior and that his ultimate purpose was to fight for his country—even though his country was too often governed by half-wits and hustlers on both sides of the aisle. Fortunately, President Lane was neither.

"And you've been trying to do things your own way for a long time. I get that, I really do. But maybe it's time to stop and reassess. Or at least try something different."

"You mean counseling?"

"For a start. I mean, give it a try. If it doesn't work, walk away. Whatever you need to do."

Pearce's breathing slowed. He was trying to process everything Myers had said.

"Let's just both sell our companies and run away," he finally said. "See the world."

"Sounds like heaven. I think we'd both love it for at least a month or two. But then what?"

"I dunno. Just . . . live. Like normal people. Let the world run itself for a while."

"And the next time a friend calls and asks for your help? Will you tell him you're too busy cutting the lawn?"

"Maybe I'll get rid of my phone."

"Yeah, right."

Pearce scratched his head. Point taken.

Myers curled up against him. "The next time someone calls, you'll be on the inside. The world's too complex and too dangerous to try and fix it on your own."

"Maybe."

"I'm not saying to rush into anything, but at least give Jackie a call. See what Lane is actually offering. If you don't like it, walk away with my blessings. And if that's what happens, we'll try it your way. Maybe we'll even buy a sailboat." She snuggled in closer. He stroked her hair.

"Okay. I'll call. But you better start looking for that sailboat."

6

The early-morning rush hour in the underground Metro was jammed as always, even at Dupont Circle.

He could only afford to own the historic brownstone in the popular D.C. suburb because he was a childless six-figured federal administrator and his wife an administrative assistant with twenty-seven years of tenure at the Department of Labor. They'd lived there for more than twenty years, long before it became the hipster-yuppie enclave it was today. Still, it was a great walking neighborhood, with some of his favorite restaurants, shops, and markets.

He loved the Metro because he was a people watcher. Liked to size up folks and guess what they were all about. He was pretty good at it, too. He even liked the peculiar smell of sparking steel and burnt rubber and the feel of the circulated air beneath the big half-dome ceilings. It reminded him of his youthful adventures running around on the metros in London, Paris, and West Berlin on summer holidays from college.

The commuters pressed in closer as the Red Line train slowed out of the tunnel, pushing a blast of warm air onto the platform that tousled his thinning hair. Secretaries and systems managers, court clerks and tourists. The D.C. Metro was the last great democratizing institution in the gentrifying metropolis. Of course, the Metro wasn't exactly voluntary. Outrageous parking fees, horrific traffic, and subsidized rail passes all conspired against driving a car in the city. Besides, he was just three stops away from his office on 14th and K, and the office reimbursed him for the annual pass.

The federal administrator bumped shoulders with a tall, handsome man in a custom-tailored suit, sporting a hand-tooled leather briefcase and yammering into the Bluetooth jammed in his ear. The douchebag didn't even bother to look up or say "Sorry," which would have been the polite thing to do. A typical lobbyist. Probably a litigator, too.

On the other side of him was a twentysomething white kid in a ball cap and dark glasses with his nose pressed against a smartphone. He wore a cheap sport coat with a narrow tie and chinos. A tattered canvas messenger bag was slung over one shoulder. Probably an intern at one of the agencies, he decided. Reminded him of himself some thirty years earlier. Might have even owned the same brand of messenger bag.

An attractive young thing was just in front of him. Her straw-blond hair was gathered up in a tight bun. He was close enough to smell her perfume, floral and sweet. He studied her fine neck and admired the lacy bra straps flashing beneath a thin silk shirt filling out with her full figure. He began to imagine the possibilities with her in an afternoon romp at one of the downtown hotels. If she worked in his office he'd tell her—carefully—to mind the dress code, but down here he was happy to survey the goods if she was willing to show them. He raised up on his toes and tried to glance over her shoulder for a better look at her cleavage, but she moved forward.

The crowd pressed mindlessly closer as the train approached the platform, air brakes squealing. The door to the last car swooshed open and just a handful of people exited. The rest of the passengers in the crowded car, especially the ones in the seats, didn't budge. Now it was his turn to surge in. The space inside was filling up fast. The twentysomething intern with the smartphone stopped short just in front of the door and turned to the administrator. "Go ahead."

"You sure?" he said back.

"Yeah. I'm sure."

The administrator leaped into the car, snagging the last possible square inch of space. He turned around to thank the kid before the doors shut, but he was already back at his smartphone, thumbs flying on the screen.

Just as the automated voice warned that the doors were about to shut, a black four-rotored quadcopter marked with DHS letters on its fuselage and a Department of Homeland Security logo came roaring down the stairwell from the street. A tubular package was slung underneath the drone, marked with bright green dollar signs on both sides.

The quadcopter dashed into the Metro car just above the administrator's head as the doors slammed shut. The electric-powered blades whirred like angry hornets in the confined space. The railcar lurched as it leaped forward heading for Farragut North station.

People next to the drone reflexively ducked. A heavyset woman screamed as she fell to the ground, knocking people down with her like bowling pins.

The administrator was smashed against the closed doors by the others trying to get away from the spinning blades. His face pressed against the door glass. He caught a glimpse of the intern still working the smartphone, gyrating it in his hands as if trying to run a BB through a maze game.

A black teenager in a hoodie in the back of the compartment shouted, "Hell no!" and took a swing at the quadcopter with his backpack. He missed.

The cylinder exploded with a crack.

The compartment filled with a white gas as the train pulled away from the station. The drone lunged forward, banging into the low ceiling and scraping along it, clouding the rest of the car as it wobbled toward the far end. Screams, panicked shouts, and choking coughs filled the air as the drone finally crashed against the far wall and tumbled to the steel floor, blades spinning, gas still pouring out of the cylinder.

COMMUTERS ON THE FARRAGUT NORTH platform weren't paying much attention when the Metro train screeched to a halt. But when the doors of the last car swished open, dozens of passengers surged out like crazed zombies, gasping for air, eyes bloodshot, screaming, coughing, vomiting. Some fell to the redbrick landing while others surged ahead, scattering the startled commuters on the platform, still waiting to board. Someone screamed, and the waiting crowd suddenly panicked at the terrifying sight. More screams and terrified shouts rose up as the mob broke and ran for the escalators.

The panic swiftly spread to the rest of commuters farther up the platform, uncertain of what was going on. They soon quailed at the sight of the screaming mob. In less than a minute fifteen hundred desperate people were kicking, screaming, and clawing at one another in the manic stampede up the long, crowded escalator toward the light.

As the first of them emerged out of the escalator and into the sunshine, clothes torn, gasping for breath, passersby on the street began to notice. The human flood disgorging out of the escalator exit spilled onto the sidewalk, one after another, including a few of the gassed passengers, clothes slathered in vomit, red faces wet with tears and snot, palming their bloodshot eyes. Some cried out in agonizing pain, others gasped for breath. Others retched on the sidewalk or collapsed to the ground. A few of the passersby moved in to help, but most stood around with their cell phones held high like kids at a rock concert. Even more panicked and ran away as whispers of "poison gas" filtered through the injured crowd. Police and ambulance sirens wailing in the distance grew louder as the subway crowd spilled further onto the sidewalk.

None of them noticed the bearded young black man in a ball cap and dark glasses with a canvas messenger bag slung over one shoulder standing across the street, snapping photos with his smartphone, grinning ear to ear.

7

"The president will see you now."

Pearce was ushered into the Oval Office by the young Secret Service agent. She was as tall as Pearce and broad in the shoulders like a volleyball player, only armed. Cool and professional, she wore her suit more comfortably than he wore his, his new uniform of the day. He preferred his blue jeans and ranch coat and the cold, crisp Wyoming air to the stiff suits and stultified swamp gas of Washington.

"Troy, it's great to see you again." President David Lane stood from behind his desk and crossed over, meeting him in the center of the famous room with his wide boyish grin and a firm handshake. There was genuine affection in his commanding voice. The former air force pilot was the third-youngest president in history and looked it. They hadn't laid eyes on each other since the East China Sea incident the previous May.

Pearce nodded. "You, too, sir."

Lane gestured toward the two others standing next to him.

"I don't know if you've met Vice President Chandler." Pearce and Chandler shook. Pearce squeezed Chandler's soft hand a little more firmly than usual and held it.

"Mr. Pearce and I met several years ago, back in Iraq," Chandler said.

"Good memory," Pearce said. "You were kind of a big deal. I was just a grunt."

"I was just a lowly congressman. But you made quite an impression.

On all of us," Chandler said. He was four inches shorter than Pearce and narrow shouldered, with neatly groomed silvery hair and a tailored Brooks Brothers suit that fit him like a glove. He wore his signature blue silk tie that perfectly matched the color of his eyes. His voice was soft and slightly southern. A casual observer could have easily mistaken him for a genial bank manager or a solicitous funeral director.

But Pearce knew better. Besides his own brief but personal encounter with the man years before, Myers had filled him in on the particulars of his ambitious political career. Chandler was an Atlanta lawyer in private practice before he was elected to Congress in 1998, serving four terms. He was a skilled campaigner, receiving at least 60 percent of the vote each time. Chandler ran for the U.S. Senate after the eight-term senior incumbent announced his retirement. Chandler was reelected to a second term in 2012. Always the opportunist, he resigned from his Senate seat only after he and Lane won the 2016 election.

Despite his personal misgivings about the man, Pearce knew that Chandler was the right person to help shepherd him through the process. Not only had Chandler served on the Senate Appropriations Committee, one of the most powerful positions in the legislative branch, he had been both chair and ranking minority leader on the Appropriations subcommittee on Defense—the largest component of discretionary federal spending. Defense appropriations would be one of the primary oversight committees for Drone Command, and Chandler knew all the players. Pearce would just have to grin and bear it. He doubted this would be the last unpleasant relationship he would have to endure in the next few years.

Chandler gestured toward the woman on his left. She was a stunning redhead with shoulder-length hair. Her slim figure was perfectly complimented by a form-fitting pale yellow designer dress. Pearce guessed she was in her mid-thirties.

"This is my chief of staff, Ms. Vicki Grafton."

Pearce extended his hand. Grafton took it. Her dark green eyes sparkled with an intense curiosity and intelligence.

"A pleasure, Mr. Pearce. I've heard so much about you from the president. He's your biggest fan around here. I look forward to working with you."

"Same."

Lane gestured to the couch and chairs. "Something to drink, Troy?"

"No, thanks."

Lane checked his watch. "Then let's get to it. Troy, first of all, I want to thank you again for accepting my offer. I know it probably sounds like a real step down to head up a new, small federal agency, but Drone Command is going to have a profound impact on the future of all things drone-related."

"I'm still not quite sure why you picked me, Mr. President, but I'll do my best."

"I picked you because you're the perfect person for the job and you have my utmost confidence, which is why you'll run it with complete autonomy."

Chandler shifted in his seat. "Well, sir, that's something we're still negotiating with the Senate."

"It's nonnegotiable," Lane said. "I expect you and Vicki to make that happen."

"Mr. Pearce's hearing tomorrow will go a long way to bolster the committee's confidence in that regard," Grafton said. "After that, we lobby like it's 1999. But I'm sure we can make it happen."

"Good." Lane turned to Pearce. "I know you're a man who knows how to take orders, but I also know you prefer to give them. Your independence is as important to me as it is to you if Drone Command is going to do what we hope it will do."

"No arguments here."

"And as I promised, if at any point in this confirmation process you don't feel comfortable or you think this thing is going the wrong way, you can bail out with my blessing."

"I appreciate that," Pearce said. He glanced at Grafton and Chandler, both smiling. "But I'm not big on quitting something I've started."

"Excellent." Lane stood, ending the meeting. The others rose as well. "If you'll excuse me, I've got a meeting with the DNI in two minutes."

Lane extended his hand to Pearce again. "If there's any problem, you know how to reach me. Otherwise, Clay will be the point man on this."

"Understood," Pearce said.

The vice president ushered Pearce toward the door. "Let's go to my office. You'll meet with Vicki a little later. In the meantime, I'd like to catch you up on a few things."

Pearce nodded and stepped into the hallway. He could already feel the noose tightening around his neck.

8

Chandler steered Pearce out of the Oval Office and into the corridor, past the Roosevelt Room and to the far end of the West Wing and into his own office.

"Take a seat," Chandler offered, pointing at one of the two chairs opposite his own desk. The rectangular room had the same formality and furnishings as the Oval Office, but it wasn't quite as large and the walls had been painted light blue.

Chandler pulled off his coat and hung it on a hanger as Pearce dropped into one of the ornately carved period chairs.

"Can I get you anything?" Chandler asked as he took his seat behind his desk.

"I'm fine, thanks."

Chandler leaned back in his chair. "So, tell me, what do you make of the drone attack this morning?"

Like everyone else, Pearce had heard all about it on the news. Details were still sketchy, but a couple of shaky cell phone videos had gone viral on YouTube, posted by the anarchists who had launched the attack.

"It was a helluva publicity stunt. Surprised no one got killed in the stampede out of there."

Chandler nodded. "Thank God for that. DHS says it was only aerosolized ipecac and tear gas."

"Plan on more of the same from other groups. From what I hear, the attack was pretty low-tech."

"What can we do about these drones? How can we stop this kind of thing from happening again?"

"You can't. Not unless you get rid of them all."

"Why can't we?"

"Why should we? Whoever did this probably used cell phones, too. Maybe even drove cars or rode bikes to the scene. Do you want to get rid of all of those? The drones aren't the problem."

"Then we need to register every one of them."

"We already register cars and guns. At least, law-abiding citizens do. And they aren't your problem."

"People need cars. Some of them might even need guns. They don't need drones."

"Drones are the future. I don't think we should stand in the way of technology. You never know where it will lead."

"That's what I'm afraid of."

"The economic and political superpowers of the future will be the countries that best develop and deploy drone technology. We can't hide from the future, so we might as well embrace it."

An uncomfortable silence fell between them. "I want some coffee. Sure you won't join me?" Chandler finally said.

"No, thanks."

Chandler buzzed his intercom. "Lucy, could you bring me a pot of fresh coffee, please? Thank you." He signed off without waiting for a response. He turned his attention back to Pearce. "The reason why I wanted to meet with you is to put our heads together. This confirmation process is a long, grinding business. We're going to have to pull together as a team."

Pearce nodded.

Chandler leaned forward, putting his elbows on the desk and tenting his fingers. "But as I recall, you weren't much of a team player back in Iraq."

"Maybe you and I just weren't on the same team."

"I see you haven't changed."

Chandler forced a smile. "No, I guess not."

Chandler nodded. "Well, we can set that unpleasantness aside. It's all water under the bridge as far as I'm concerned. Right now we have more pressing problems. We've got to convince some very stubborn senators on both sides of the aisle that you're the man for the job."

"What do you think about my nomination?"

"Me? I serve the president."

"But clearly you don't think I'm the man to do it."

"Doesn't matter what I think. This administration owes you a great deal. My understanding is that if it weren't for you, we might be at war with China right now instead of preparing for the Asia Security Summit." Chandler's eyes narrowed. "I don't know all the details, of course. I was in Europe on a fact-finding mission at the time. But President Lane thinks highly of you, and that's good enough for me."

"So what's the problem?"

"In case you didn't know, most senators don't give a fig for what this president, or any president, thinks about anything. They think they're one hundred little presidents, or presidents-in-waiting. Convincing them to do anything is a Sisyphean task unless they think it directly benefits them."

There was a soft knock at the door, and then it swung open. The vice president's middle-aged secretary wheeled in a small cart with a pot of coffee, cups, and amenities.

"Thank you, Lucy."

"Not at all, Mr. Vice President," she said as she parked it near his desk and left.

As she was leaving, Chandler poured himself some coffee into a piece of fine bone china marked with the vice president's seal.

"You sure you don't want some?" Chandler asked. He poured a generous splash of heavy cream into the cup.

"Positive."

"That just means more for me, then," Chandler said half-aloud, scooping heaping teaspoons of sugar into the cup. The silver spoon tinked on the ceramic as he stirred up the sweet, creamy slurry. "So if you don't mind my asking you a personal question."

"Shoot."

"Do you really want this job?"

Pearce hesitated. "Do I want to be a bureaucrat behind a desk wearing a monkey suit? No. Do I want to have to deal with self-serving political hacks all day long? No. Play all of the stupid games you people play around here? No. Do I want to serve my country and this president?" Pearce paused, still trying to convince himself. "Yes."

"We might want to work on that answer a little bit before we go into the closed-door meeting tomorrow. Maybe just go with the 'I want to serve my country' and leave it at that."

"You asked."

"You're right, I did. We self-serving political hacks tend to ask those kinds of questions in Senate hearings."

Pearce knew he'd crossed a line. Didn't really give a shit.

"Look, Mr. Pearce, I was never in the military, but I'm a good soldier. Whatever the president wants, he gets, as far as I'm concerned."

"Why? What's in it for you?"

"It's my duty and my responsibility to serve the president. That's what I was elected to do."

"But what's the payoff for you?"

"What was the payoff for you when you were in government service?"

"Duty, honor, country. Quaint notions like that."

"And why do you think I'm any different just because I never put on a uniform or picked up a gun?"

"You and I are cut from a different cloth. I have a hard time believing we hold the same views on the subject of service."

"Then you'd be wrong. I love my country as much as any man, including you. But I will grant you this: I loyally serve and obey the president because when it's my turn to sit in that office, I expect those below me to serve and obey me. I expect duty, honor, and loyalty to me in the same measure with which I have given it—and God help the man or woman who doesn't render it."

"So you plan on being president?"

"Why else would I be sitting here? The vice presidency is little more than a game show greenroom. A one-term senator has more authority and respect than I do."

Myers had informed Pearce that Chandler was a last-minute compromise that Lane had to make in order to keep the Democratic party establishment from dumping him at the convention despite his clear win in the primary over the disgraced senator Barbara Fiero.

"You're honest, I'll give you that," Pearce said.

"I'll do my best to get you confirmed. I'm not without a few friends on the Hill, and Vicki is a real go-getter. I'd sooner lose my right arm than her. But I just want you to be aware of what's in store for you. The closed-door hearing is just the first step. You've already had your preliminary FBI background check and you passed, though there are a few glaring holes in your record. I presume that's because of your previously classified status."

"Presumably."

"But you need to understand that anything goes in a closed-door session and you'll be under oath. It's going to be a group anal exam. They have long fingers and big flashlights and they don't miss a thing."

"You really know how to paint a picture."

"Is there anything you want to tell me about now? Anything I might need to fix or massage before you're sitting under the gavel?"

Pearce wondered just how much Chandler really knew about his time in Asia earlier that year. Was he alluding to his role in the sinking of the Chinese aircraft carrier? Or was Chandler referring to his failed mission in northern Iraq a few weeks earlier?

Or was he just fishing?

Pearce shook his head. "There's nothing else. But if there was, anything I'd say right now would implicate you and the president. So I'm not really sure why you're asking."

"Just trying to be helpful. But if you'd rather play it your way, fine. Just know this: We're looking at a hat trick. If you screw up this hearing tomorrow, it will not only cost you the job but it will likely kill the whole program and, worse, you'll hand the president a humiliating defeat."

"I get it."

"I hope you do. Because the other thing at stake is the president's upcoming Asia Security Summit. He's hyper-focused on it, and rightly so—it's the biggest change in American security policy in Asia since the Vietnam War. If we drop the ball on our end, we endanger whatever treaty might come out of it. Are you following me?"

Pearce clenched his jaw, clamping his mouth shut. He earned a master's degree in security studies from Stanford before he joined the CIA as an analyst and, later, worked in the field as a SOG operative. He had a far deeper grasp of what was at stake than Chandler could possibly imagine. Chandler had no idea—or so he hoped—of his role in bringing about the Asia summit. The sinking of the *Liaoning* was what had allowed China's President Sun to overcome his militant opposition in the Party and begin the new march toward peaceful relations with China's Asian neighbors and the United States.

"Yeah, I think I'm following you."

"Fine. Then it's time for you to go see Vicki. She'll prep you." Chandler took another sip of coffee. The Victorian pendulum wall clock ticked heavily.

"Anything else?" Pearce asked.

"No, you can go. She's in the EEOB. Do you need me to have someone show you the way?"

Pearce stood. "I can find it on my own. But thanks."

Pearce turned and headed for the door.

"Pearce, one more thing."

Pearce turned around, his hand still on the doorknob.

"I know we've had our differences in the past, and I'd like to put those behind us."

"Okay."

"But I need to remind you. This isn't Iraq. It's about kid gloves around here, not kicks in the groin."

"Yeah, I get it."

Chandler leaned forward, his face narrowing like a knife's edge. "More important, whatever you do, don't fuck me on this."

9

EISENHOWER EXECUTIVE OFFICE BUILDING
WASHINGTON, D.C.

The specially marked VIP security badge on Pearce's lanyard raised a few eyebrows, but he passed easily through a series of security checkpoints. It was the slow ride up the windowless elevator to the fourth floor that nearly got him in trouble. His claustrophobia was getting worse lately. A flashing memory of a man cut to ribbons in the blood-soaked elevator car didn't help. His breathing shortened and quickened, but the doors slid open to a wide corridor before the panic struck.

The stone floors were a diagonal black-and-white checkerboard with cast-iron baseboards and stately pilaster columns lining the walls. He'd been in the enormous building only a few times but had always been impressed with its French Second Empire architecture. The building was a perfect fit for the broad avenues of Paris and the decadent colonial French empire of the nineteenth century, which is when it was built. Now it served as a vast complex of government offices for many of the senior administrative executives, including the vice president, who enjoyed an extraordinarily large and ornately decorated ceremonial office here. Was he the only one who caught the decadent empire metaphor? Probably not. He pushed the thought aside.

Pearce was ushered into Vicki Grafton's interior office by her secretary. He was surprised how utilitarian it was. He assumed that a woman with Grafton's personal style would want to be surrounded by something equally ornate. But then again, the eye would be naturally drawn to her in the rather spartan office. Only the grand view of the interior courtyard below and the dozens of framed photos of Grafton posing with power elites in politics and business on the walls competed for attention.

Grafton was on the phone. She winked and nodded at Pearce and motioned for him to sit while she finished up.

"Sorry about that. Senators are like babies. When they cry, you've got to whip out the boob or else."

"How many kids do you have?" Pearce asked.

"None, thank God. Can I get you anything?"

"I'm fine, thanks."

"All ready to get started?"

"That's why I'm here."

"Yes, of course. Did you get a chance to read the brief I e-mailed you?"

"Cover to cover."

"Any questions?"

"Nope."

"Really? The brief covered quite a bit of ground. I would think—"

"You did a great job laying everything out. Besides, you're going to be there tomorrow anyway, aren't you?"

"Of course."

"Then if I get stuck, I do that thing"—Pearce mimicked covering a microphone with one hand and leaning sideways to whisper to an aide—"and you can bail me out."

She smiled, amused. "It was a lot of information, wasn't it?"

"President Lane and I already share of lot of the same views. It wasn't like trying to learn Greek grammar."

"Still, it's important that we present a united front. Some of the senators are looking for a weapon to use against the administration. If you get off script, you might hand them the dagger they need."

"Won't be a problem. Worst-case scenario, I'll plead ignorance and offer to get back with them."

"You might not get away with that."

Pearce offered his first smile. "That's what I have you for."

"Did the vice president tell you how I came to be his chief of staff?"

"No. But he has a great deal of confidence in you. That's good enough for me."

"Thanks. But for the record, I used to work for the DoD, and that's how I first met him, when he was chairing the subcommittee. I was giving testimony. He gave me one hell of a grilling. I can still feel the burn marks."

"But you must have passed with flying colors."

"Yeah, I did. It wasn't long after that he offered me a job on his staff, and when he got on Lane's ticket, he brought me along."

"How long did you work for the Seven Rivers Consortium?" Pearce asked.

Grafton smiled defensively, pretending not to be surprised that Pearce had done his homework. "Six years. Five before I went to work for DoD, one after."

"The SRC is the world's largest lobbying firm, isn't it?"

"That's what I hear."

"And you were putting together defense contracts?"

"That's how I started on the Hill. Earned an MBA from George Washington. Interned at Lockheed-Martin. But you already knew that, didn't you?"

"So, Seven Rivers, DoD, Seven Rivers, and then Chandler?"

"And you do math. Very impressive, Mr. Pearce."

"I can scramble eggs, too. And a few other tricks you might never have seen."

Pearce tried to hide his disgust. Not so much with her as with the whole damned system. Washington's famous revolving door between government service and the lobbying agencies made him sick to his stomach. More than a hundred formerly registered lobbyists now served on congressional staffs, many of them chiefs of staff like Grafton. Worse, more than four hundred former congressmen and senators were now highly paid registered lobbyists, leveraging their congressional relationships and influence into multimillion-dollar second careers—as if their gold-plated, full-salaried retirement plans didn't already put them in the top 5 percent of American income earners.

Grafton leaned back in her chair, folding her manicured hands in her lap. "Is my work history going to be a problem for you?"

"You're clearly more than qualified for the babysitting job Chandler handed you. If this is what it takes, well, it's what I signed on for, isn't it?"

She flashed another smile, nodded. "Faint praise, Mr. Pearce, but good enough for me. Let's get to it, shall we?"

Pearce leaned back in his chair. "Fire away."

"Your first hurdle is going to be Senator Floyd. He's practically a hood ornament for the aerospace industry. He'll try to wear you down by playing stupid—which he isn't, I assure you—and he'll start with some innocuous question like, what is Drone Command exactly?"

"Drone Command is a new unified combat command within the Department of Defense. Its purpose is to oversee the acquisition of all new drone and drone-related systems for both military and civilian applications within the DoD and all other federal agencies. Though Drone Command is technically a Defense Department entity, it would be the only unified command headed up by a civilian."

"I.e., you."

"Yes."

"Good answer."

"Of course it is. You wrote it. I just loaded it in here." Pearce tapped his forehead.

"From there Floyd will start drilling down into the minutia of the organizational plan, personnel, et cetera, et cetera. I strongly recommend you just refer him to the appropriate addenda included in the same report I sent you."

"Works for me."

"But that's the easy stuff. It's the 'why' of Drone Command that will be the heart of the battle."

"The 'why' is because those money-sucking vampire squids won't do the right thing on their own. An independent, autonomous agency with the sole authority for development and acquisition is the only way we're going to avoid the massive maldistribution of scarce resources."

"Let's steer away from 'vampire squids' and lean more toward 'efficiency, economy, and efficacy.'"

"What part of 'to tell the truth, the whole, truth, and nothing but the truth' does 'money-sucking vampire squids' not satisfy?"

Grafton sighed, shaking her head. "You're not going to make this easy, are you?"

"Didn't realize that was part of my job description."

She pursed her lips. "No, I suppose not. But it would help me do mine better."

Pearce shifted in his chair, studying Grafton's frozen stare. "What else do you need from me?"

Grafton pulled up a page on her laptop computer. "I did a little digging myself—legally. I've managed to find a few public statements you've made over the years."

"Such as?"

"Foreign policy stuff." She looked away from her computer screen and back toward Pearce. "I'm surprised a fighting man like you would be an isolationist."

"I'm not. But either you're all in to win or you're out. You can't take the middle ground."

"And in regard to the Middle East?"

"Like I said, all in or all out. Since we won't commit to all in, I think it's better to get out."

"But you're a smart guy. A master's degree in security studies from Stanford. You know we can't withdraw from the world."

"I didn't say withdraw from the whole world. But maybe it's time to let that part of the world take care of its own problems and spill its own blood."

"We're the strongest military power on the planet. Who else can stabilize the region?"

"After nearly twenty years of military intervention, do you seriously believe the Middle East is more stable and secure than before we went in? That *we* are more secure?"

Grafton's frozen stare betrayed nothing.

"But we have important allies in the region. The Saudis are vulnerable. They can't possibly defend themselves without our help."

"The Saudis are a royal dynasty teetering on the edge of collapse." Grafton shrugged. "Desperate allies are more reliable."

"They don't share our values. It's practically a dictatorship."

"Sounds like you're channeling Jimmy Carter."

"They're not our friends. They've been the power behind the OPEC cartel, screwing with our economy and politics for decades."

"They pursue their own national interests, just like we do."

"You know that ISIS sells a lot of its sex slaves to Saudis, right?"

"All the more reason to take out ISIS as quickly as possible."

"Why not stop the Saudis from buying them?"

"We've already raised the human trafficking issue with them. It just can't be the top priority right now."

"It would be if you were the sex slave."

She shrugged. "I'm sorry. I guess I'm just a realist."

"So are the women being trafficked, believe me." Pearce sighed, frustrated. "Can I ask you a question?"

"Sure."

Pearce leaned forward. "If fifteen of the nineteen terrorists that took down the World Trade Center had been ethnic Russians, do you think we would have given the Russian government a pass? Called them friends and allies in the War on Terror?"

Grafton's face hardened.

"Me neither."

"The Saudis have powerful friends on the Hill, and especially on the committee. If you say anything like this to them, you're dead in the water."

"I won't lie if I'm asked."

"Then it's my job to make sure they don't ask, isn't it?"

Pearce nodded. "Guess so."

Grafton was feeling cramped in her spacious office. "Speaking of the Saudis, Senator Kelly will want to know your position on Saudi drones," Grafton said.

"It's a bad idea."

Grafton drew a measured breath, clearly trying to calm down. "One of the biggest drone manufacturers in the country is headquartered in his state and they've been approached by Riyadh. A ten-year, billion-dollar contract for MQ-9 Reapers."

"Anything we sell to the Saudis will eventually wind up in the wrong hands. If an internal rebellion doesn't overthrow the princes, the Iranians will overrun them eventually with Iraqi help, and maybe even the Russians."

"Warts and all, the fact remains the Saudis are our most important ally in the region right now."

"Don't you mean Israel?"

"Israel can't help us stabilize the situation. You know the reasons."

"The 'reasons' are why our Mideast foreign policy has been a Hungarian cluster dance for the last forty years."

"If the Saudis are on the edge of falling, doesn't that prove we need to bolster them?"

"Drones won't be enough to save them."

"You do realize that Saudi Arabia is one of our largest defense customers? Their defense purchases put a lot of Americans to work."

"Especially high-dollar lobbyists."

Grafton threw up her hands. "I don't get you."

"Maybe you're not supposed to."

Her features softened but her eyes were searching. "Can I ask you a personal question?"

Pearce shrugged. "Sure."

"You and the vice president have a history. Care to fill me in?"

"He's an asshole."

"Vice President Chandler is the second most powerful man in the world."

"Then that makes him the single most powerful asshole in the world."

"If Chandler heard you say that, he'd run you out of D.C. on a rail."

"Call him. I'm happy to repeat it. Hell, I'll even draw him a picture if that's easier for him."

Grafton laughed. Her eyes raked over him again, sizing him up. "I'm starting to like you."

"Are we done?"

"That was the easy stuff. Let's cut to the chase." Grafton opened up a file on her desk. "You passed your FBI background check with flying colors. Unfortunately, some of your record has been redacted." She held up one of the file pages. Three-fourths of it was blacked out entirely.

"Maybe you don't have the clearance."

Grafton bristled. Security clearance was about the biggest status symbol in Washington there was these days, and hers was pretty damn high.

"You don't have to worry about my clearance. Your government service is strictly 'need to know.' But Senator Floyd is also on the intelligence committee. He'll 'need to know,' and if there are any skeletons you're hiding behind these black lines, he'll find out and use them against you."

Pearce searched her face. What did she know? Pearce had left a trail of corpses across the globe, starting with his CIA service in the Special Operations Group in the War on Terror. Even Pearce Systems had been involved in the sanctioned killing of dozens of people around the world, including the United States. But in his rage and grief and sense of justice, he'd personally killed dozens more—in Africa, Asia, and even Russia. Was she just fishing, like Chandler, or did she really know?

"Shouldn't be a problem."

"We all have skeletons, Troy."

"Show me yours first and I'll show you mine."

Grafton rubbed her forehead. A headache was coming on fast. "It's going to be a long day today, isn't it?"

Pearce checked his watch. "Not really. I've only got another five minutes before I have to leave. Got a plane to catch."

"What? I've cleared my entire calendar today just for you."

Pearce shrugged. "I'm sure you can fill it back up. Or, better yet, take the rest of the day off. The wheels of government will grind on without you."

"I hope it's damn important."

Pearce stood. "It is. I don't have a cushy government job yet. Still gotta pay the bills."

"Then be here bright and early tomorrow so we can go over a few more things. Trust me, you're walking into a minefield."

"Won't be my first." *Literally*, he thought.

"Hearing's at ten. Can you make seven?"

"Eight-thirty works."

Grafton stood. "Why do I get the feeling you really don't want to do this?"

"Maybe because I don't."

"Then why are you doing it?"

"I owe my country a lot. It's the least I can do, even if it makes me want to puke."

10

Pearce gunned the motor again, flipping the paddles on the steering wheel, pushing the tachometer into the red again. The pit of his stomach dropped as the Mini Cooper S convertible went slightly airborne over the sudden dip in the paved two-lane road. The rental bounced on its stiff, sporty shocks when it landed and Pearce downshifted into a sharp hairpin curve. He knew he was driving way too fast on a road with too many blind curves. He didn't care. He was having fun.

He loved this part of the country. He'd been here only once before a few years back, but it was beautiful here near the Smoky Mountains, and the people he met were great.

The road wound through rolling, grass-covered hills dotted with variegated greens of pine, maple, hemlock, and several other species he couldn't identify. It was farm and ranch country with houses and outbuildings to match. But there were long stretches of road blemished by broken-down trailers or ancient barns crumbling into ruin, too. They weren't much for building codes in this neck of the woods, and pride of ownership was optional. Around here he saw mostly cattle dotting the steep pastures, but he knew that farther east there were a knot of apple orchards, and the fishing was pretty good on Douglas Lake—not that he'd have the time to dip a line this trip.

The next curve jumped up on him like a snake out of a hole and he turned hard into it, downshifting fast and letting up on the gas. The centripetal force threw him against the shoulder belts, but the sturdy little car gripped the asphalt like a Formula One racer. The road dived violently down and then took another hard blind curve. He punched the gas anyway and geared up, turning the wheel hard, but he was moving too fast and the car crossed the faded yellow line—

A step-side Chevy pickup blared its horn and swerved hard out of its lane and into the soft gravel shoulder. Pearce barely missed sideswiping it by inches. He caught a quick glimpse of the driver, a thick lump of chaw pouching his cheek, his mouth open in a cursing scream. Pearce downshifted and slowed enough to check his rearview mirror. The truck was throwing dust as it skidded to a stop just inches from a rocky outcrop. Relieved, Pearce punched the gas again and raced ahead.

The GPS map flashed when he arrived at the address twenty minutes later. Good thing. He nearly sped past the weathered hand-painted metal sign that read Goose Gap Farm. He turned in toward the shuttered steel gate and stopped. An incongruous security camera was perched on one of the gateposts. A blinking red light finally turned to a solid green and the steel gate swung open. Pearce nudged his car forward past the security camera and over the thumping cattle grate before his tires began crunching on the gravel road. The narrow track headed straight toward a steep hill, beyond which stood his destination. He punched the gas again and the tires spun. Pearce felt the rocks spanging against the undercarriage and no doubt stripping off some of the paint. He didn't care. The rental was fully insured.

To hell with it.

PEARCE STOOD BY the half-ton Ford flatbed pickup, faded red and rusting. GOOSE GAP FARM was stenciled in white letters on the battered driver's door.

"Good to see you, Virgil," Pearce said.

"Same, for sure." The two men shook hands. *At least his grip is still strong*, Pearce thought.

At nearly six foot six, the sixth-generation Tennessee native seemed even thinner and more gaunt than Pearce remembered him. He assumed it was the chemotherapy. The drooping Hickory shirt and baggy overalls added to the effect. The skin beneath Dr. Virgil Ponder's neck was loose and his bald head was flaking badly beneath the stained orange-and-white UT Vols ball cap. Behind the thick lenses of his Soviet-styled frames, his big brown eyes seemed larger than normal. Other than the crazy glasses, Pearce thought Ponder could have been the stern-faced farmer in Grant Wood's famous *American Gothic* painting. All he needed was a pitchfork to complete the ensemble.

Pearce saw that Ponder was irritated.

"Sorry I'm late. Got held up."

"Time's a scarce commodity these days."

"I know. I blew it." He nodded toward Stella Kang, his Korean American security officer. "I see you've already met Stella." Stella was ten yards away, directly behind the flatbed, fiddling with a radio-controlled transmitter in her hands, its lanyard looped around her neck. A homemade radio-controlled Styrofoam airplane with a six-foot wingspan lay in the grass in front of her. The rear-mounted pusher-styled airframe featured a double tail and a boxy front fuselage that held the engine and electronics. Ponder had built the drone entirely from sheet insulation from Home Depot for about ten bucks. It was meant for function, not beauty.

Ponder grinned. "Stella's a pistol, all right. Where'd you find her?"

"On my island of misfit toys." Pearce had recruited Kang years ago, straight out of the army, where she'd flown Raven surveillance drones, and she'd since become the mainstay of his personal security team. But she was still a helluva drone pilot.

"Well, I supposed we'd best get after it," Ponder said. "Time's a wastin.'"

"Show me what you've got."

Ponder waved Pearce toward the back of the flatbed. Pearce followed.

He'd first met the towering physicist at Operation Black Dart several years before. The Pentagon's annual anti-drone exercise lasted two weeks and only select corporations and government agencies were invited to participate. The event was designed to showcase advances in anti-drone technologies and tactics. The Pentagon understood that both advances and failures at Black Dart could provide useful information to America's enemies in the looming drone wars, so the results were kept secret from the press.

Failure at Black Dart was not only expected but encouraged. The anti-drone technologies still lagged behind the galloping progress of military and civilian drone advances. If participants believed that failure might lead to a loss of a potentially lucrative DoD contract, they might not bring their latest and greatest "bleeding-edge" systems to the anti-drone game. Pentagon simulations at the event provided participants with real-world and real-time scenarios—the perfect venue to test and improve new designs. Black Dart had seen successes from mundane approaches like snipers in helicopters to more extreme ones like suicide drones. But the most exotic solution, and the most promising, was the laser.

After graduating from the University of Tennessee with a BS in physics, Ponder went on to earn a PhD from MIT. He later worked briefly for MIT's prestigious Plasma Science and Fusion Center before striking out on his own and starting his own company, specializing in antimissile laser technology. He invested heavily but lost out on a bid for developing the U.S. Navy's Laser Weapons System (LaWS), which was first deployed in the Persian Gulf in 2014 on board the USS *Ponce*. Laser shots to knock out missiles and aircraft cost less than sixty cents each, and the laser "ammo" supply was infinite so long as the ship's power plant was intact. Standard antiaircraft missiles cost tens of thousands of dollars each, were finite, and, like other kinetic systems, had to be manufactured, transported, resupplied, and reloaded.

Starting from scratch, Ponder set out to construct a viable antidrone laser system. The one Pearce saw demonstrated at Black Dart impressed him, but it was too large and expensive. Two years ago he put up venture capital for Ponder's new company, Goose Gap Photonics, in exchange for first right of refusal for a smaller, portable version of his modular laser system. Ponder wanted to sell his entire operation to Pearce Systems. His health was failing and he wanted to leave a sizable inheritance to his seven grandchildren.

Ponder pointed at the old flatbed. "I call her the War Wagon. You know, after the John Wayne movie."

"That's it?" Pearce asked as he climbed onto the truck bed. There were four separate modules, each self-contained but linked to each other with a single connector. All four modules could be packed up in hard plastic shipping cases for transport, each light enough to be carried by one or two people. Three of the modules were long, rectangular shapes. The third was a mounted tripod with a gimbaled head, its legs fixed to the truck bed.

"The War Wagon ain't much to look at now. I designed everything so that you can shove all of this gear into a Humvee and mount the beam director on the roof like a machine-gun station. Completely self-contained. Only thing is, I don't have an extra Humvee lying around to fix up or I'd have shown it to you."

"I can get you a surplus Humvee if you want one. No charge."

Ponder nodded. "I'd appreciate that."

"System weight?"

"Six hundred and fifty pounds, total." Ponder pointed a large, bony index finger at each module. "That's the power source, a battery—rechargeable, of course. Next to it is the water-cooled chiller. And that one there is the actual fiber laser."

"The fiber is infused with rare-earth elements, right?"

"Right. It's the latest and greatest. A lot of advantages over the solid-state units."

"Is that going to be a problem?" Pearce had boned up on REEs after his adventure in the Sahara. China still controlled nearly 90 percent of all rare-earth element exports, and 100 percent of those used in high-tech military manufacture.

"You mean the Chi-coms? I don't think so. This is a standard industrial single-beam unit. Completely off-the-shelf. Plenty of them around and more where they came from."

"How powerful is the laser?" Pearce read that the laser on board the USS *Ponce* was 30 kilowatt. It was meant for anti-drone, antimissile, antiaircraft, and even small antiship deployment. It would eventually replace the navy's 20mm chain-gun Phalanx cannon system.

"Ten kilowatt."

"What does that mean?" Pearce knew that General Atomics—the company that invented the iconic Predator drone—was trying to mount a 150-kilowatt laser on board the jet-powered Predator C (Avenger). Pearce thought the rigged Avenger looked like something out of a sci-fi flick. It was yet another technological answer to the enduring question: How can America find security in this highly insecure world? Pearce built a company on cutting-edge drone technologies, but he also knew that every war his country had lost had been to technologically inferior opponents.

"Have you ever heard of a cement drone?"

Pearce chuckled. "Not likely."

"Good, because even if you did, I got it covered. They use five-kilowatt lasers to drill through cement, and we're double that." Ponder patted the laser module with his large, spotted hand. "We can punch through sheet aluminum, carbon fiber, you name it, with this little wonder."

"Range?"

"Twenty-two miles. Units like this have been used to knock down mortar rounds and missiles. A drone won't be a problem."

"We'll see, won't we?" Pearce pointed at the tripod. On top of the tripod was a device that looked like a projector with a huge glass eye. "Is that the beam director?"

"My own design. The lightest unit of its kind. You can make all of your money back just selling those to the Pentagon."

"Are we ready to rumble?"

"Been ready. Been waiting for you." Ponder's stern farmer's face almost broke into a smile.

"One sec," Pearce said. He leaped down off the flatbed. He pulled a four-inch magnetic square out of a jeans pocket and slammed it against the driver's-side door with a thud. It was a red bull's-eye target.

Ponder harrumphed. "What's that for?"

"You'll see."

The lanky physicist flicked a switch and the laser unit engaged. The beam director shuttered briefly as it aligned itself. He climbed down uneasily from the flatbed, refusing Pearce's offer of help with a dismissive grunt. The two of them took up position by the back bumper. Ponder flipped open a laptop. The laser's gun-sight reticle was centered in the middle of the monitor.

"Let 'er rip," Pearce said.

"Your gal there will need some help with the launch."

"Right." Pearce jogged over and picked up the Styrofoam airplane. Despite its massive wingspan and overall size, it was surprisingly light.

Ponder raised his fingers to his mouth and let out a shrieking sheep whistle.

Stella frowned, holding up the transmitter. "This is really old-school. We should've linked one of our tablets."

"Next time," Pearce said. "Did you bring our little friends?"

"Of course."

"Did he see you?"

"I used to shoplift, remember?"

"And your army career began the day after you got caught."

She laughed. "No worries."

Pearce grasped the fuselage in one hand and held the aircraft back behind his head, as if he were throwing a javelin. "Ready to launch."

"Aim for the far end of the valley!" Ponder shouted. "Nice and straight!" Low hills on either side of them stood a quarter mile apart, and shouldered for more than half a mile due north. Plenty of room for Ponder to land his ancient Piper Cub on the grassy airstrip.

"Fire in the hole!" Stella flipped the throttle switch. The airplane's powerful electric motor fired up.

Pearce ran a few feet and tossed the gangly plane into the air toward the far end of the valley. The plane wobbled as it came out of his grip but quickly righted itself.

Pearce jogged back over to Ponder's laptop. Saw the reticle tracking perfectly with the airplane.

"Push the F1 button when you're ready," Ponder said.

Pearce pushed it.

The laser fired. It made a *Star Trek*–style phaser beam sound.

The beam locked directly onto the engine in the Styrofoam fuselage. The plastic blades melted instantly as the engine coughed and then died two seconds later. The rest of the plane broke apart and tumbled to the ground.

The old farmer's face finally cracked into a wide grin. "So, whaddya think?"

"Not bad, so long as the bad guys are invested in Styrofoam platforms." Pearce scratched his chin. "What's with the crazy sound that thing makes?"

"The laser is completely silent. I added sound effects so that an operator would know it was firing. You've got ten more sounds to choose from, if that makes a difference."

"You never know," Pearce said. "Some of my clients like that kind of thing." He cast a glance back at Stella. She nodded and pulled the transmitter from off her neck.

"Seriously, Troy. What's the verdict?"

"It's damn impressive. But you had Stella fly in a straight line and it's still a slow-moving target."

"Like I said, this system uses the same components the Pentagon deploys to shoot down mortars. I just made it extremely portable. Targeting drones won't be a problem."

"That's why I'm here." Pearce pointed at the laptop. "That thing still ready to go?"

"Yup."

"You got a 'laser blaster' sound?"

"You mean, like *Star Wars*?"

"Yeah."

"Sure." Ponder ran through a pop-up menu. Made a selection. "All ready, Boba Fett."

Pearce turned to Stella. She had a tablet in her hand. "Go."

Stella stabbed at the tablet. In the distance, small motors whined to life.

"What's this?" Ponder asked.

"I guess they're like Remotes."

"Huh?"

"*Star Wars* reference. Never mind."

The laser gimbals twitched as the onboard radar searched for targets. The monitor image shifted back and forth, almost randomly.

Pearce pointed toward the tree line on the far hill. "Here they come."

Ponder squinted. "I can barely see them. Three of 'em, I think."

"Four. They're cheap, palm-sized quads I bought on Amazon. Dr. Rao rigged them with a simple homing device."

"The target you put on my War Wagon."

"Yup."

Seconds later, the four drones buzzed clearly into view. They rotated in circles around each other in a randomized swarming dance as they plowed toward the truck.

The laser snapped into position, pointing high into the sky.

A laser blaster sound echoed.

A scream.

A large black crow exploded in feathers. Its smoking corpse tumbled into the grass a thousand yards away.

"Darn," Ponder said. He pulled off his ball cap and scratched his flaky scalp. "I figured you'd try something like this. I narrowed the filter to try and pick up smaller targets."

"You succeeded. Sort of."

Four sharp bangs rattled the truck door as the four screaming drones slammed into the magnetic target one after another. They broke apart on impact.

"And just like that, we're a smoking hole," Pearce said.

Ponder sighed as he tugged on his cap. "I guess this means no sale."

Pearce patted the older man's shoulder. "You guess wrong. It's a helluva system, Virgil. Exactly the kind of thing I'm looking for. But it's the really small drones I'm worried about. The hobby-sized stuff. Ten pounds or less."

"Target acquisition is the hardest part. If you set the filters too small, you start targeting everything that moves." Ponder glanced at the dead crow. "Maybe we should call the *Duck Dynasty* fellas."

"How much more time do you need to get it right?"

"I'm not sure how much more time I have," Ponder said. His voice trailed off.

"What can you do for me in thirty days?"

Ponder approached the laptop. Tapped a few keys. His eyes brightened. "I might be able to pull a few tricks out of my bag by then."

"Do what you can. We'll figure something out."

Ponder turned to Pearce. "It's not about me, you know. It's about my grandkids."

Pearce saw the anguish in the old man's eyes. He understood it, but in a different way. In his heart of hearts, Pearce wanted to sell his own company and get the hell out of the game and leave it all behind. Take Margaret on a trip around the world, maybe hole up in Bora Bora or Fiji and just let the rest of humanity slip away into its own madness.

"I know. It's just not quite there yet. Keep pushing."

"I'll do my best."

"You need us to help you pack up or anything?"

"Nah. I just need to rest awhile and think on a few things."

Pearce and Stella shook hands with Ponder and drove off in separate rentals, heading for a plate of pulled smoked pork at a little joint Pearce remembered just up the road. He hoped the old man would figure out the laser problem. But the clock was running out on the cancer.

And maybe the nation, too.

11

CHEBOYGAN, MICHIGAN

Norman Pike was in a foul mood.

The group charter he was supposed to take out for chinook salmon this morning was running an hour late already when they called and canceled on him. Sure, they'd lose their deposit and they were apologetic, but the *Ayasi*, his thirty-six-foot Tiara, was kitted out and ready to go, and so was he. He loved to fish and was disappointed he wouldn't be heading out.

But Pike's mood brightened when a late-model Ford Taurus pulled up to the curb and a man came strolling down the pier and straight for his dock. He was built like an athlete. He flashed a broad smile with gleaming white teeth. Pike thought maybe he was Italian or Greek, or maybe even from the Middle East.

"I'm looking for a day charter. I don't suppose you're available?"

Pike noticed the man's West Coast accent. He had a polished L.A. vibe about him, too. Merrell boots, Oakley sunglasses, Columbia fishing shirt, and a Tag Heuer wristwatch. Typical yuppie tourist, Pike thought. More money than sense. He'd hauled a thousand of them out onto the lake over the years for good money.

"Your timing is impeccable. It just so happens I am."

The man extended his hand. Pike shook it. The man had a strong grip. "Great, man."

Pike glanced around. All of the other charter boats were already out on the water. "I'm usually all booked up this time of year. I had a last-minute cancellation."

"Then it's my lucky day."

"Climb aboard. I'm all ready to go. Even have five box lunches if you get that hungry."

"Awesome. Let's get going."

Pike quoted a full-day rate and the man counted off five Benjamins from a stack of ten in his wallet. Pike asked for ID and the man showed him a California driver's license. His name was Daniel Brody. Twenty-seven years old. Los Angeles, California. Just as Pike had guessed.

"Got a fishing license, Mr. Brody?" Pike asked.

"No. Do I need one?"

"Yes, but I can sell you one, no problem. A twenty-four-hour license is only . . . twenty dollars." *Ten for the license, and ten for my trouble,* Pike told himself.

"Sounds good."

The man pulled out a twenty and Pike pocketed it. "I'll write that up as soon as we get under way."

"Awesome. So we can get going now?"

"Soon as we untie. You're in kind of a hurry, I take it?"

"Just excited, I guess."

More like nervous, Pike thought. *Maybe he's afraid of the water. Probably means he's going to be hurling his guts out, too. Should've charged him more.*

LAKE MICHIGAN
ON BOARD THE *AYASI*

The water was choppy but Captain Pike was trolling with the swell and Brody hadn't complained, even after devouring a roast beef sandwich with horseradish.

Pike had fished these waters for fifteen years, first as a hobby and then as a paying gig. He was a good fisherman. He knew all of the tricks that all of the other charter captains knew as well, and his charter boat carried state-of-the-art fish-finding radar. Pike knew Lake

Michigan like the back of his hand, and he knew chinook, and that this late in the morning the big salmon would be running around 120 feet deep in the cold, dark water. To get the bait rigs down to that strike zone he fitted Brody's rod with copper line and down riggers and trolled at twelve miles per hour, about the speed the fish ran, especially with the current.

Pike was a loner by nature and wasn't the talkative type, but Brody asked the same questions that the beginners always asked about bait and reels and how to hook the big ones, and Pike was happy to answer them because the answers never changed. He also liked the kid's enthusiasm. Brody pulled in his first fish within an hour and seemed genuinely thrilled. Pike reset the hook and showed him how to cast and Brody was back at it while Pike cleaned the five-pound fish.

And then Brody's questions turned personal. How long have you been a charter captain? How long have you lived in Michigan? Any kids? Were you in the service?

It started to feel like an interrogation instead of friendly chatter. There was something about the guy that bothered Pike. He couldn't put his finger on it. When the next fish struck Brody got distracted trying to reel it in. The pole bent nearly in half, as if a bowling ball were hooked to the other end. Pike fetched the net. A twenty-three-pounder—big fish. Not a record, but respectable. At this rate, Brody would hit his legal limit of fish in a few hours, and then they'd be heading back to the marina.

"Can I use the restroom?"

Pike pointed at the cabin door with his filet knife. "Right down there. Hard to miss."

"Thanks." Brody flashed a smile and descended the short stairs, closing the door behind him.

Pike stood at the cleaning station, thinking. He cut the chinook's head off with a single pass of the razor-sharp blade, then took off the tail.

He didn't like personal questions.

CHEBOYGAN, MICHIGAN

It was late. Pike's boat was the last one to tie up for the night. Nobody around.

The high-speed grinder shrieked beneath the stainless-steel tub, mulching the carcass into a fine slurry that ran straight back into the lake. The sound bounced off the blue cinder-block walls. A real racket. But the enclosed fish-cleaning station was always neat and clean whenever he came into it, and Pike intended to leave it that way, too. Always had. He used the sprayer to push the last little bits of flesh and bone into the drain. The city of Cheboygan had built the handy little facility in order to make the fishing experience that much more convenient for the public. They knew how to treat sportsmen right up here, especially in the UP. It's why he loved living in Michigan—for six months out of the year, anyway.

Pike's phone rang. He checked the number. A call he'd been waiting for. He hung up the sprayer and punched the grinder motor's red Stop button. It quieted instantly.

"Pike here."

Pike listened to the urgent voice on the other end but kept spraying the tub, washing away the last drops of blood.

"I understand. The charter is all ready. I'm just waiting for your last deposit."

He nodded, listening. A smile creased his face. "Excellent. I appreciate the vote of confidence. Then we can get started right away. It should be a lot of fun."

Pike rang off. He checked the sink. Spotless, just the way he'd found it.

12

The Kairos Club was traditional, elegant, and private, like Ilene Parcelle herself. Vicki Grafton admired both institutions. Despite its privacy—or maybe because of it—the Kairos Club had been the place to be seen in D.C. for the last forty years.

It was an early dinner, barely five p.m. The last-minute invitation was both propitious and unsettling. It felt more like a summons than a dinner date, but that was to be expected. The former congresswoman had climbed the pinnacle of power after her time in government. Parcelle was used to people clearing calendars and canceling important family events when her assistant called. But when Parcelle was on the other end of the line? One of the senior partners at the Seven Rivers Consortium? Governments fell, countries rioted, markets collapsed. Ilene Parcelle was Vicki's sponsor and, perhaps, even a friend. Grafton admired her immensely but also feared her.

For now.

Grafton arrived early. She always kept a fresh dress in the office for moments like this, with shoes and jewelry to match, of course. Parcelle would be expecting nothing less than her best. Grafton even managed to freshen her light makeup and brush out her thick red hair on the drive over. She took great pride in her beauty and was smart enough to know that her stunning good looks had opened more doors for her than less attractive women could possibly have hoped to pass through. Her vanity allowed for that despite her feminist sensibilities, but no one doubted her keen intellect once she opened her mouth.

Parcelle was decked to the nines as well and, in her late fifties, could still turn heads. She arrived with a small entourage, whom she waved away at the front desk, and she and Vicki were escorted to the table by the maître d', who was himself a formidable establishment figure and social statesman. Politicians, CEOs, and foreign dignitaries of every stripe had dined there over the years, and he had escorted all of them, too. Grafton feigned indifference but secretly reveled in the leering gazes and jealous glances from the tables they passed by as they were seated in the place of honor near the great bay window overlooking the garden. Very private. Grafton smiled. Her Klout Score would jump five points before the evening was through.

They ordered drinks—a gin and tonic for Parcelle, whiskey neat for Grafton—and waited for their dinner to be served.

"You look stunning," Parcelle said. "You must live in a gym."

"I wish I had the time. I'm lucky if I get to run in the morning."

"How do you keep so trim?" Parcelle asked over the rim of her glass.

"I'm eating paleo these days."

"Is that the caveman diet I've been hearing so much about?"

"Something like that. Well, except tonight. Might have to cheat a little bit."

"Cheating is one of life's great pleasures, don't you think?"

"You look ravishing yourself," Grafton said.

"Thank you, love. You're too kind. I can only imagine the hordes of grasping gray-haired old men you have to fight off on the Hill. They were quite the bother even in my day."

Grafton fought the urge to laugh. She knew that Parcelle wasn't one to actually resist those advances back in her day. She'd gone down on more senior political figures than the White House elevator. Rumor had it, she'd once done the big nasty *in* the White House elevator. "Viagra hasn't done us any favors, has it?"

"At least not in that regard," Parcelle said. "But the little blue pill does have its merits." She grinned mischievously as she took another sip of her drink.

"The problem now is that every octogenarian out there thinks he's a twenty-year-old frat boy." Grafton smiled, remembering a recent run-in with the junior senator from Vermont just forty years her senior.

Parcelle's chuckle was gold in Grafton's ears. The elder stateswoman had mentored her through the maze of Washington politics, grooming her for the next big step in her career. Unfortunately, that next step was taking longer than either of them expected. Parcelle must have been reading her mind. Her face soured.

"My colleagues at the consortium are becoming impatient."

"I understand. I'm beyond impatient. Unfortunately, patience is the virtue required here."

"Not for them. They have other projects, other . . . possibilities."

Grafton felt the blood drain out of her face.

Parcelle smiled. "I thought that might get your attention."

"I'm working as hard as I can to make it happen."

"Is Lane any closer?"

"Yes, I'm certain of it."

"Tell me, dear, truthfully. Do you really want to make partner?"

Grafton nearly spilled her drink. "Why would you ask that?"

"It's just that you were so effective on the Senate subcommittee. And now, well." Parcelle finished the rest of her gin and tonic.

Grafton had brilliantly shepherded several multibillion-dollar projects through the congressional budget maze for SRC clients while working as a senior senate staffer. But Grafton's ambition was loftier than that. One project at a time was too cumbersome. She didn't want to be a dealer or a floorman or even a pit boss. She wanted to game the whole casino.

The project she'd proposed to Parcelle a year before seemed like a sure bet at the time. It was only possible because Chandler was VP now, and that gave her direct access to the president. Chandler, unwittingly, was her strongest ally in her plan, along with Ambassador Tarkovsky. But President Lane was still on the fence. His instincts were to avoid another war in the Middle East, despite the neocons in both parties clamoring for it. Grafton's goal was to change his mind. A new war meant every SRC client would benefit, all at the same time, and guarantee her a partnership at the SRC.

Grafton began to fear she might have promised Parcelle more than she could deliver. She knew her plan was good—selling a president wasn't any different from selling a committee chairman—and the odds were in her favor. She was a great lobbyist and staffer because she was a master persuader and media manipulator, the two most important talents in politics. There was no rational discourse in Washington anymore. It was all about creating narratives, and she was the best in the business.

But the dice still hadn't landed right. She steeled herself. It was time to make her own luck.

"You were on the fast track, Vicki. I put you there myself."

"And I'm forever grateful. I won't disappoint you."

"I'm afraid you already have."

Grafton's heart sank. "Please don't say that."

"You see, I put myself at some risk by advocating for your plan despite your lack of specifics. You made promises to me and I made promises to the other partners who, in turn, made promises to our most important clients. And yet, here we are."

"It will happen soon. You'll see."

"When? Exactly?" Parcelle's eyes narrowed.

"I can't say exactly. A week. A month. It's not like baking a cake."

"Frankly, you reminded me of myself at your age. Your proposal was terribly ambitious and I greatly admire ambition."

"Thank you. And I intend to deliver."

"But intentions, no matter how ambitious, are worthless unless they're realized."

Grafton felt a cold panic tingling in the back of her neck. Failure wasn't an option. Neither was sideways. Only up. Only more. If this door shut it would never open again, and there weren't any other doors for her in D.C.

The food arrived. The tuxedoed waiters were swift and silent in their service.

"Another gin and tonic, ma'am?" a waiter asked in a small voice.

"Of course," Parcelle said. She forked a piece of grilled halibut into her mouth.

"And you, ma'am?"

"I shouldn't."

"Vicki! You know I hate to drink alone."

"It is early, isn't it? Yes, I'll have another whiskey, please. Only this time, make it a Yamazaki. The eighteen."

"Excellent choice."

Grafton waited for the waiter to get out of earshot. She leaned in close anyway, lowering her voice. "I've got one last arrow in my quiver and I intend to use it."

"When?"

"Soon."

"What kind of arrow are we talking about?"

Grafton sat back, smiled conspiratorially. "I'd rather not say at the moment."

Parcelle searched Grafton's sparkling eyes, certain Grafton was lying. "I'm intrigued."

"You know you can trust me. I've always delivered before, haven't I?"

Parcelle set her own fork down and sighed. "All right, dear. I'll choose to believe you. But you really must land this awfully big fish you've promised."

"It will be the great white whale."

"You know I only want what's best for you."

Parcelle laid a cold, smooth hand on Vicky's and squeezed it. "I can press for a little more time. But the longer you wait, the greater the risk we both face. Do you understand my meaning?"

Grafton nodded grimly. She was all in now. "Yes, and I'm grateful." Grafton sighed with relief.

Parcelle picked up her fork and knife again as their drinks arrived. "So tell me, how did your meeting with Ambassador Tarkovsky go last week? I want all the dirty details."

"He's an interesting man. Chandler's convinced he'll be the next president of Russia."

"I only met him once. Quite handsome. But quiet. An engineer, as I recall."

"He attended the Moscow Power Engineering Institute with a degree in high-technology management and economics, and then earned a master's degree at the All-Russian Academy of Foreign Trade before entering diplomatic service." Grafton sounded like she was citing a brief, which she was.

"You've obviously done your homework."

"Sorry. A bad habit of mine."

Parcelle's mouth curled into an envious grin. "I don't suppose it's his arrow that's in your quiver?"

"Me? Hardly."

"Tarkovsky's quite a catch."

"Yes, I suppose he is."

"You could do worse."

"God knows I already have. More than once." Grafton winked as she took a sip of whiskey.

"Oh, do tell."

She did, after ordering more drinks. Anything to get the subject off the Russian ambassador.

13

Vice President Chandler dried his hands over the blower, waiting for his bowling ball to return, studying the pin reset.

"A seven-ten split, Mr. Vice President," Tarkovsky said. "How will you negotiate that one?"

"I've seen worse," Chandler replied. His tie was uncharacteristically loose and his French cuff sleeves rolled up. He'd draped his suit coat over one of the two chairs at the scoring station, where Tarkovsky was sitting.

"It's the hardest split in bowling. You don't have a chance."

The sweeper arm cleared and the automatic pinsetter lifted. Chandler analyzed the bowling pins standing on either side of the rear of the pin deck. The dreaded 7-10.

"Actually, the four-six-seven-nine-ten Greek church is the hardest split in bowling. You only have a point-three percent chance of catching all of those. The seven-ten has a point-seven percent chance."

"You take your bowling seriously!" Tarkovsky said.

Chandler's custom ball chunked into view out of the return. "I take everything seriously, Mr. Ambassador. Especially bowling."

"Why bowling, if I may ask?"

"I was raised in the back of a six-lane alley in Devereux, Georgia, by my maternal grandmother. Started setting pins and frying hush puppies when I was nine years old."

Chandler whipped a microfiber cloth out of his pocket and polished the ball lightly before picking it back up. He stepped up to the approach dots in his custom-fitted bowling shoes and raised the ball with both hands to the front of his face like a prayer. Chandler's tailored shirt highlighted his narrow shoulders and back but couldn't hide the spare tire bulging just above his waistband. But when Chandler stepped into his throw, he lifted the ball far behind him and swung it down hard with a vicious curling spin. The ball exploded out of his hand and down the lane, hugging the right gutter until it smashed into the ten pin just right of center. The force of the strike was so strong it threw the ten pin crashing into the back wall at an oblique angle from whence it rocketed back out onto the pin deck and smashed into the seven pin.

"That's a spare, I believe," Chandler said, grinning ear to ear.

Tarkovsky stood to his feet and slow-clapped his admiration. "And that's the game. Congratulations." He added, "Again."

Chandler fell back into his chair and grabbed up the can of Coke in the koozie marked with the vice presidential seal. He held it aloft. Tarkovsky raised a bottle of water and they toasted. "Cheers." Chandler took a long, satisfying pull. He loved the burn.

The two of them were all alone in the little two-lane White House bowling alley Nixon had originally built in 1969. It was one of Chandler's favorite hangouts. It thrilled him to think that every president from Nixon to Greyhill had stood exactly where he was and bowled the same game he loved so dearly. It was a good omen.

Few people outside the White House knew about this place—most were familiar with the Truman bowling alley over in the EEOB—and even fewer had access to it. Thankfully, neither Lane nor his children cared for bowling, so Chandler had it all to himself. White House staff knew to stay clear of it no matter the day or time. It was Chandler's sanctum sanctorum.

Chandler liked to bring down very special guests to his secret sanctuary. It made them feel like insiders. It was also one of the rooms that he could keep his Secret Service detail out of when he was using it without arousing any kind of suspicion, and he was assured by the senior agent that the room was free of surveillance cameras and recording equipment.

"Next time you're in Moscow, I'll have to take you out on the ice for a little hockey. Bowling is too hard."

"You'd wipe the ice with me like a Zamboni. But I appreciate the invitation." Chandler took another sip, wondering if Tarkovsky had finally made his opening bid.

Tarkovsky pointed his water bottle at one of the muted TV monitors. CNN was showing footage of yet another village in the Middle East. Still more crying women and dead children in the midst of fire and ruin. "So tell me, Clay, how would you navigate something like this?"

Chandler rose and crossed over to Tarkovsky. "Are you asking me personally, or the American government?"

"The two aren't the same?" Tarkovsky smiled.

"I'm a loyal servant of this administration, no matter how misguided it can sometimes be."

"Are you referring to the 'no new boots on the ground' policy? The so-called Myers Doctrine?"

"It's a glorified form of isolationism. The world goes to hell without strong American leadership."

Tarkovsky nodded thoughtfully. "Some would argue that 'strong American leadership,' as you have put it, has caused just as many problems."

"Strong American leadership means forming strong alliances with reliable partners to manage the world's problems. We haven't done that. The world is in chaos now because we've failed to bring order."

"And out of that chaos comes the Four Horsemen, flying the black flag of ISIS."

Chandler nodded. "We must first deal with ISIS and then with all of the other Islamic terror groups. The Europeans have proved to be largely worthless in that regard, especially in the Middle East. Only your country has proven it has the strength and determination to tackle the Islamic terrorism issue."

Tarkovsky raised an eyebrow. "I'm surprised. I thought your country viewed mine as an international pariah."

"President Titov has made a few strategic blunders of his own, and the political class in my country has exploited those blunders for their personal political gain."

"Your sanctions have crippled our economy. It would be hard to form a strong relationship without first removing them."

Chandler sighed. "Unfortunately, the president has been advised that removing the sanctions would send the wrong signal to the rest of the world that we're weak on human rights and the rule of law."

"A very strange idea, considering the fact you make alliances with governments that behead, whip, cripple, and imprison their own citizens for minor civil and religious infractions."

"We aren't consistent in our moral umbrage, I'll grant you that."

"You in the West don't play a very smart game. Israel funded Hamas to discredit the PLO when Arafat was preeminent, but now Hamas is built up and they are Israel's implacable enemy. The same with Bin Laden and the CIA. Over and over, you keep supporting religious terrorists as a weapon against your secular enemies, but you create worse enemies in the bargain."

"We supported Bin Laden and the mujahideen in response to your invasion of Afghanistan."

"We invaded to stop an Islamic uprising that was overthrowing the secular government. If we had been allowed to crush the rebellion and restore the government in Kabul, would you or the world be any worse off? Would there have been a Bin Laden or 9/11?"

"Perhaps not. But the way you brutalized the Afghan people—"

Tarkovsky raised a hand. "I was speaking only in geopolitical terms. I make no excuses for the brutality of Brezhnev and the Communists. Good riddance to all of them. But from our perspective—you and me, here, just friends speaking in a friendly way—I think we can both acknowledge that mistakes were made on both sides. The fact we have been and still are competing at the tactical level causes our respective governments to make strategic errors. By not cooperating with each other on the grand strategic issues, we become desperate to find weaker allies to achieve our goals. In my country, the scoundrels invoke historic paranoia to justify their irrationality. In yours, selective humanitarian concerns."

Chandler nodded. "The purpose of national security is to protect the nation from its enemies, period. We need statesmen at the helm, not Sunday-school teachers."

"You are one of America's most articulate leaders. If I may be so bold, I'm not sure why you made common cause with President Lane, who so clearly does not favor Realpolitik."

"I'm just a soldier, Aleksandr. I serve my country any way I can. I hope to serve her even more effectively once I'm president."

Tarkovsky's eyes widened. "You intend on challenging Lane in the next election?"

"Not at all. He's a very popular president, and while I might not agree with many of his policies, he possesses one priceless talent above all others."

"You mean his military background?"

"No. His luck. And like Napoleon said in regard to his generals, it's better to be lucky than clever, and Lane is the luckiest politician I've ever known."

"And you are hoping his luck will rub off on you?"

"I make my own luck. I agreed to run as his VP only because the party assured me that Lane would endorse me after his eight years, but I'm no fool. I need to lay my own firm foundation in the interim. President Lane is about to conduct the Asia security initiative with China as his partner. My intention is to launch a European security initiative with Russia as a partner. A true partner. It's time we bring stability to the European continent, not to mention the Middle East."

Tarkovsky smiled. He knew that it was actually Vicki Grafton that had planted the idea in Chandler's head, part of the plan the two of them had engineered. "What you are proposing is quite brilliant, actually."

"Do you think Titov would be supportive of a mutual alliance between our governments?"

"Yes, wholeheartedly. I have even heard him mention the possibility. But not until the sanctions are lifted."

"That's unfortunate."

"It seems we're at an impasse."

"I'm sure we can figure something out." Chandler crossed over to a replica vintage vending machine. "Another water?"

"I'm still working on this one, thank you."

Chandler swiped a White House debit card and selected another Coke. "If we can't put our boots on the ground, perhaps our Russian allies will do it for us. I have several friends in the Senate who would support a quid pro quo like that."

"Our forces have trained for just such an eventuality. No one has a longer history of fighting these cockroaches than we do, with the possible exception of your own government."

"It won't be easy to pull it off. The moralists and the isolationists don't understand what's at stake."

"A war between civilizations," Tarkovsky said. "A war between modernity and brutality."

"Exactly."

"How shall we proceed?"

"Let's start by having a chat with the president. Feel him out. Maybe we can tie our proposal into his Asia security initiative. Part of a new, comprehensive, global strategy."

"But if the president disagrees with our assessment?"

Chandler sighed. "Then we must do whatever it takes to get both of our governments moving in the right direction."

Tarkovsky nodded. "I couldn't agree more."

14

It was Pearce's turn to cook tonight. He fried a couple of steaks in olive oil and pepper and whipped up a mess of cauliflower mash, trying to keep the carb count down for both of them. He finished out the meal with a spinach salad dressed in a light balsamic vinaigrette and a 19 Crimes cab sauv for her. He was never great in the kitchen, but he was learning to enjoy cooking for the woman he adored. He'd been accused of many things in his life, but domesticity wasn't one of them.

Pearce and Myers were halfway through the meal, the bottle of wine, and their usual chitchat before she turned the conversation in another direction.

"How was your meeting with Chandler?"

"He's a piece of work." Pearce cut into his steak. It bled onto his plate, just the way he liked it.

"He's very smart and a skilled politician."

"So was Stalin."

Myers nearly snorted wine out of her nose. "Please."

"You like that guy?"

"No, but I respect him. Chandler was one of the few Democrats who supported my budget freeze. He's never lost an election and never received less than sixty percent of the vote when he ran four times for Congress and twice for the Senate."

"Chandler's nothing but ambition and self-interest," Pearce said. He'd never told Myers about his experience with Chandler in Iraq.

"Like most politicians. But he was the best-looking horse at the glue factory and Lane was in a tough spot. The DNC threatened to run a third-party candidate unless he agreed to put Chandler on the ticket."

"Sounds familiar." Pearce knew that Myers had gone through a similar meat grinder when she won her presidential primary as a libertarian Republican.

"Sometimes arranged marriages work out. Sometimes they don't. But Chandler isn't stupid, and he knows if he bides his time and plays the game he'll probably be the next POTUS."

"That sailboat is sounding better and better. Have you picked out a color yet?"

"Don't get your hopes up yet, Popeye. You're about to head up the federal government's newest and most exciting agency."

"Maybe." Pearce took a thoughtful sip of ice water.

"What's the hesitation?" Myers tried to hide her concern. Pearce had begun seeing a counselor for his anger issues, which she still believed to be symptoms of PTSD or at least exacerbated by it. Myers knew that his road to full recovery would be long and hard. Pearce was born a warrior and built to serve his country. But that service had involved killing many people, and despite what the genre movies and novels suggested, killing was an unnatural thing for a well-adjusted person to do, and killing the nation's enemies—even for the right reasons—exacted a terrible psychic cost.

She also knew that the loss of his father and the needless deaths of people closest to him in the War on Terror caused Pearce to feel betrayed by the politicians who ran the country he loved so dearly. It was only through the trust he placed in her as president, and later in President Lane, that Pearce felt he could serve again. She feared he would slide back into his black hole of self-recrimination and bitterness if he stepped away from this appointment. She would never abandon him, but she couldn't stop him from withdrawing from the world and from her.

"I know what the job entails," Pearce said. "It means we'll see even less of each other. And I'm not crazy about that idea."

"You like having me around, do you?"

"Yeah. Something like that."

"I might have a solution waiting for me in Germany."

"Was ist das?"

"You speak German?"

"A little. And poorly. What's waiting for you in Deutschland?"

"I got a very interesting call today. Someone in Frankfurt interested in buying my company. If the price is right, well, I'm open."

"Really?" Pearce couldn't believe it. She was as proud of her company as he was of Pearce Systems.

"How else are we going to pay for that sailboat? You're only going to be making government wages."

"When do you leave?"

"Day after tomorrow. The buyer insists on a face-to-face."

"I'll go with you."

"No way, José. Your Senate hearing tomorrow is just the beginning. I'll be back by the end of the week."

"I don't like it."

"You mean traveling by myself? I've done it for decades."

"Security?" Pearce respected the fact that Myers had turned down taxpayer-funded Secret Service protection, which she was entitled to as a former president. But absent formal security, he liked to keep close.

"It's Germany, not Uganda. I'll be fine."

Pearce sighed. He knew that when Myers dug in her heels, there was no way to get her to budge. "Fine. But we're going to stay in touch. Understood?"

Myers was a strong, independent woman. But it thrilled her to know someone in the world cared for her so deeply and wanted to protect her, even at the cost of his own life. She threw a mock salute. "Yessir." She took another sip of wine. "Any other hesitations?"

Pearce stabbed his salad with a fork. "The last time I offered to help Lane, a lot of people died."

"If it wasn't for you, there would have been a lot of dead American sailors."

Pearce held up his hands. "There are a lot of dead Chinese on the ocean floor, thanks to these."

"That wasn't your fault. You didn't launch the missile. They started the war. You ended it. That makes you more than qualified for the job. But there's an even better reason."

"What's that?"

"Lane has surrounded himself with several people who would dearly love to go back to the Middle East and ramp up the war all over again. He needs at least one voice of reason to keep that from happening."

Pearce cut another slice of steak. "I'm not against going to war. It's just that we can't do another half-assed job of it. If Lane isn't willing to ask for a declaration of war and commit every resource to winning it as fast as possible, then he needs to stay the hell out, no matter where he wants to fight. And I know you're against it, but I still think we need a national draft. Every family needs to feel the pain of war, and every son and daughter needs to be at risk. If these chicken-hawk politicians have to send their own kids into the meat grinder, they might think twice before pulling the trigger."

"If you really feel that strongly about it, having virtually unlimited access to the Oval Office might give you the chance to make your case."

Pearce pointed a fork at her. "Why do I get the feeling you're gaming me?"

"I'm not. But I want you to remember that not only can you do good for the country as Lane's advisor, but you can also keep bad policies from happening. I trust you more than anyone else I know to do the right thing. Even Lane. Believe me, that office changes you, and this town is full of people whose only job is to turn his head around."

"You really want me to do this? Or are you just trying to get me out of your apartment?"

"I think your doing this is what's best for the nation, and for you."

"Even though I'm a broken man?"

"Because you're broken. And you have your counselor to help you."

Pearce forked the last piece of steak into his mouth and chewed.

"You are still seeing your counselor, aren't you?"

Pearce chewed some more. Swallowed. "Wasn't helping."

"Maybe we can find you another one."

"I'm dealing with it, in my own way." Pearce's jaw set.

"Okay." Myers knew when to back off, too.

"And I'm not doing the drugs anymore. It messes with my head."

"I understand."

She poured herself another glass of wine. "You all set for tomorrow?"

"Ready as I'll ever be."

"Was Vicki Grafton helpful?"

"She was trying to get my mind right."

"And how did that work out for her?"

"Give her an E for effort."

"Keep your eyes on her."

"That won't take much effort." Pearce winked.

Myers punched him playfully. "Yeah, I get it. She's gorgeous. But Grafton's playing a bigger game than just trying to get a mention on *Page Six*. She was trouble when she was just a Senate staffer. I don't like her being that close to Lane."

"Chandler's got her on a pretty tight leash."

"I'd be willing to bet it was the other way around. Either way, watch your six, buster."

Pearce laughed. "You've read too many Tom Clancy novels."

"Not possible. You feel ready for tomorrow?"

"I think what you're really asking me is if I still plan to attend the Senate hearing tomorrow."

"The former CIA analyst doesn't miss a trick."

"I can read you pretty well, Madam President."

"Seriously, do you feel prepared?"

"That's like asking me if I'm ready to get shot."

"Are you ready to get shot?"

"Depends on where they aim."

"You remember that old saw about flies and vinegar?"

"I won't bullshit them, but I won't go out of my way to piss them off, either. Lane knows that."

"Are you sure you don't want me there with you?"

"No, Mom. I can cross the street by myself. But thanks." He stood with his empty plate and kissed her on the head. He didn't really give a shit what the senators might think of him. He just didn't want to embarrass her or hurt Lane in any way. But then again, they both knew he was damaged goods.

They just didn't realize how damaged he really was.

15

Pearce smelled the tobacco stink on Tanaka's breath. The man's bulging eyes were just inches away, mouth twisted in a rictus of hate, arms trembling with exertion.

The dim blue LED barely lit the black void they fought in. Tanaka's fingers dug deeper into Pearce's throat. He panicked, but not from the fight. The closed space was a coffin with the lid nailed shut. He couldn't breathe.

Pearce gripped Tanaka's fingers and twisted with all of his strength, but they were steel bands, unyielding. Pearce was bigger and stronger but Tanaka's hate was stronger still. He felt the man's murderous rage coursing through his quaking hands, cutting off the last air in Pearce's throat.

Now he really couldn't breathe. The oxygen was gone. His lungs burned. Pearce's strength gave way. He strained every muscle to break Tanaka's iron grip. Useless.

Pearce's heart thundered in his ears. Pain exploded inside his skull. The light snapped out.

Pearce shuddered. Tried to scream.

Nothing.

PEARCE'S EYES SNAPPED OPEN. It was dark but not completely, thanks to the blue glow of the digital clock.

3:17 a.m.

His heart raced. He breathed deeply to push away the panic. He rolled his head to the side. Myers was still asleep. Thank God. Sometimes his nightmares woke her and she could never go back to sleep.

He lay as still as he could, waiting for his heart rate to drop. Reminded himself it was just a dream. The same dream that came to him night after night. There were others, too, but this one was the worst.

He shouldn't have killed Tanaka the way he did. His anger always got the best of him. He fought angry. Always had. Since he was a kid. And all the way through the cage fighting in college. And in the war. Especially the war. Didn't know any other way. He could turn the rage on like a fire hose. Instincts cut in, fear melted away. Early called him the Zen master in battle. Pearce always appeared calm, cool, emotionless. There was machinelike efficiency in his target selection and dispatch. But that was on the outside.

He quit the war, but the fury remained, a smoldering ember deep inside. The slightest breath, and it became a roaring fire.

Tanaka lit the flame when he killed Pearce's old friend Yamada. In his mind's eye he saw Yamada's butchered corpse again, and just like that, the rage welled up like a flash fever.

3:18 a.m.

Pearce tamped the fury back down. Willed his friend's corpse away. He took a deep breath. Told himself again that he shouldn't have killed Tanaka the way he did.

Shouldn't have buried Tanaka alive.

It was the worst death he could imagine, but Tanaka deserved it for the crime he had committed. But then again, who was he to end a life? And who was he that he could end Tanaka's life in such a terrible way?

Pearce sighed. Myers stirred. He froze. Waited for her breathing to slow again. Lying here wouldn't do any good. The dream had dumped adrenaline into his bloodstream like the crack of a large-caliber bullet zipping over his head.

He carefully worked his way out from beneath the sheets and gently lifted himself out of bed. Might as well get prepped for a damned long day. He glanced over at Myers's nightstand. Her bionic pancreas was on the wireless charging pad. The levels looked good.

Pearce went into the walk-in closet to grab his robe. Technically, they still weren't living together, but she'd bought him a few more things since he was there a lot of the time anyway.

Yeah, she was old-fashioned, for sure.

PEARCE STOOD BAREFOOT in the kitchen as he watched the last of the boiling water disappear in the pour-over filter. It took longer to make coffee this way but it tasted better. He was getting tired of everything he put into his mouth first having to run through plastic tubes. Steel and glass were better. The aroma of the rich, dark roast reminded him of cramming for his comps at Stanford, and of nights hovering over a smoking fire in the stone-cold mountains of Afghanistan. He'd been drinking green tea for years for health reasons, but lately his mouth was watering for coffee again, black and strong. He was wide awake but he knew he'd need the caffeine kick before going back over the mountain of pdfs Grafton had loaded into his secured e-mail folder. No point in showing up to the Spanish Inquisition unprepared. If they were going to burn him at the stake, let it be for telling the truth, not for being stupid.

At least the end of the day would be pleasurable. A drive in the Maryland countryside would be a nice diversion. It would be an important meeting with an old friend developing a new anti-drone system that could prove to be very interesting. But he didn't dare get his hopes up. Building drones turned out to be a whole lot easier than knocking them down.

Tanaka's screaming face flashed in his mind again. Not the dream face. The real one, raging with terror in the fish-eye camera Pearce had installed in the cylinder. In his mind's eye he saw the light snap off again and heard Tanaka's feral screams in the dark.

Pearce tossed the filter and grounds into the trash can and pulled down the biggest coffee cup he could find in the cupboard. He filled it up halfway and took a sip. A smooth, dark roast on the edge of burnt. Perfect.

He set the cup down gently and listened for Margaret. She was a light sleeper but she was exhausted when they came to bed and she had taken a Tylenol PM for a splitting headache.

Certain she was still asleep upstairs, Pearce knelt down in front of the sink and opened the cabinet. He reached far behind the rows of cleaners and detergents until his fingers wrapped around a slim half-pint bottle. He carefully removed the whiskey. He stood and cracked the cap on the brand-new bottle. He sniffed the open mouth. Not the best label he'd ever had, but it was the right size and good enough for a brace against the day ahead. He listened once again for Margaret stirring upstairs. Nothing. He poured until the coffee reached the brim of the cup, then sipped hot coffee down halfway. He set the cup down and poured in some more booze, then sealed the bottle carefully and returned it, closing the cabinet door as quietly as possible. He promised himself he wouldn't buy any more after this one ran out. He wouldn't need it after today anyway, one way or another.

16

The thirty-four-foot Carver cruiser was docked at the end of the pier. Boating in the Potomac was usually done in the evenings or weekends. The only people who could afford the big boats generally worked during business hours. Nobody was around at this time of the day. That's why nobody noticed the sudden whir of six electric engines exploding into gear and the triangular foam FireFLY6 aerobot lifting gently off the rear deck like a helicopter. The small drone was painted red, white, and blue and looked like a hobby store toy.

The VTOL airplane inched forward until it cleared the Carver's bridge, retracted its landing gear, and rose thirty feet in the air. Its six engines—four on two-engine mounts on the leading edge of the wings, two on a single mount in the rear—were in the vertical position. The FireFLY6 increased its speed marginally as it made its way across the Washington Channel, where it hovered for a just a moment above the East Potomac Tennis Center, its first waypoint. As soon as the autopilot program coordinated with its inertial and optical navigation systems, three servos rotated the six engines into the horizontal position, converting the helicopter into an airplane. It sped effortlessly northwest toward the Tidal Basin, where it reached its next waypoint, the Thomas Jefferson Memorial, then turned north toward the World War II Memorial, the third coordinate in its program. From the World War II Memorial to the target was less than half a mile to the northeast.

It took just two minutes and thirteen seconds for the VTOL aircraft to reach the airspace over the South Lawn of the White House.

WASHINGTON, D.C., AIRSPACE is the most restricted and protected in the United States. Maybe even the whole planet.

The first line of defense was a layered array of surveillance and detection devices—dedicated satellite, mobile radar, stationary cameras, and acoustic mics around the district and on the White House campus—designed to locate and track conventional aerial assault long before it reached the president's official residence and work office.

The second layer of defense was kinetic. Air defense systems, including mobile antiaircraft missile and machine gun platforms, combined with dedicated combat air patrols circling overhead twenty-four hours a day, were tasked with neutralizing aerial threats like a sea-launched missile or a hijacked passenger jet.

The White House grounds were similarly armed with a variety of antiaircraft systems. As a final defense, hundreds of Secret Service agents and Capitol Hill police guarded the White House grounds, and they had access to a wide variety of weapons—rifles, machine guns, shotguns, semi-auto pistols, and even shoulder-launched antiaircraft missiles—that might conceivably be deployed in a last-ditch effort to take down intruding aircraft.

Unfortunately, none of the layered air defense systems worked if the object itself couldn't be located electronically or visually, typically a problem with smaller, nonconventional airframes like drones. Two solutions to this problem were put in place.

The first solution was the FAA's recent requirement that manufactured consumer off-the-shelf (COTS) drones feature navigation firmware automatically preventing drone vehicles from entering the airspace of airports, military installations, important national monuments and buildings, and other sensitive locations around the country, including Washington, D.C.

The second defense solution was more active. Following a number of accidental drone landings on or near the White House grounds in recent years, a limited electronic shield was installed. It amounted to a dome of signal-jamming radio waves blanketing the likely approach routes of errant vehicles to the White House compound. Once either a radio-controlled or GPS autopiloted drone entered the invisible dome, the signal from the radio controller or GPS satellite signal would be disrupted. In both cases, COTS drone systems were designed to land immediately.

That morning, both solutions failed.

Once the FireFLY6 VTOL crossed the outer White House fence, its servos turned and the engines reoriented to their helicopter position and the landing gear extended. Moments later the aircraft landed dead center in the outdoor basketball court due west of the South Lawn Fountain, scaring the hell out of the groundskeeper emptying a trash bin.

Per security protocols, the groundskeeper immediately radioed the Capitol Police, who, in turn, notified the Secret Service. The basketball court was cleared and cordoned off, and a specially equipped panel van arrived. The drone seemed harmless enough. An accidental flyaway, most likely. The special agent in charge (SAIC) wasn't concerned but she was a stickler for procedure. You just never knew.

Twenty minutes later a remote-controlled ground unit approached the red, white, and blue drone. Infrared and optical cameras, a Geiger counter, and a battery of electronic sniffers found no traces of dangerous explosives, chemicals, or biological or radioactive elements. It appeared to be exactly what it was: a harmless hobby store drone.

It was getting late and the crowd of first responders was growing. Since the drone was most likely harmless, there was no point in drawing attention to it. If the SAIC wasn't careful, a reporter with a camera would show up, and this thing would be all over the nightly news and her ass would be in a sling. She only had six more years until she could draw retirement, and now was no time for a reprimand for wasting scarce Treasury resources. The White House was gearing up for a round of important visits later that day and the Secret Service detail was already stretched to the limit.

The SAIC told the others at the van to stay back as she snapped on a pair of latex gloves. She walked over to the drone, hoping like hell her instincts were correct. She knelt down and gave it one more visual inspection. No unusual wires or canisters. No suspicious or provocative markings or badges. A digital camera was located in the nose, confirming her theory that the drone was just an expensive toy that got away from some knucklehead with a radio transmitter and too much time on his hands. She lifted the lightweight drone as she stood. She turned it over. On the vehicle's underbelly was another downward-facing digital camera. But what caught her attention was the four-inch square hatch door and a latch marked with a directional arrow and OPEN embossed in the plastic.

She took a deep breath as she turned the latch. The door popped open. She should've stuck with procedure.

17

Pearce cleared the security station and made his way to the stairs leading up to the first floor, avoiding the elevator. Another man, tall and well dressed, was heading down in the opposite direction. He stopped.

"Excuse me. You are Troy Pearce?"

"Yeah." Pearce noted the Russian accent.

"Aleksandr Tarkovsky."

"The Russian ambassador. Pleasure to meet you." They shook hands. Pearce noted the firm, calloused grip. Tarkovsky was a lifter.

"I've heard a lot about you. You are the nominee for the Drone Command directorship, yes?"

"Yes."

"Congratulations. I hope sometime we can have lunch. I am very interested in drones." He sensed hesitation in Pearce. His handsome face grinned broadly. "Nothing classified, of course. I am just fascinated by the possibilities of the technology. I am a science fiction geek."

"Happy to oblige. I'll call your office next week." Pearce checked his iWatch even though he knew the time. "I'm afraid you'll have to excuse me, I'm late for a meeting."

"Of course. Please call my office. And best of luck." Tarkovsky nodded curtly and sped down the stairs.

Pearce watched him for a moment. Strange. He wondered how much Tarkovsky really knew about him. There were elements in the Russian SVR who had put a bounty on Pearce's head for killing

Tarkovsky's predecessor in Moscow a few years before. The Russians could never prove anything, but the SVR wasn't organized around the concept of due process. Without divulging the reason for his concern, Pearce recently had made an unofficial inquiry with an old contact in the CIA, who privately assured him he wasn't an official person of interest to the Russian government. That meant Pearce was probably safe while he was stateside.

The man who would take over Pearce Systems if he actually took the Drone Command job was also monitoring Russian sources. Ian McTavish was a cyberwarrior of unparalleled skill.

Pearce shrugged off his concern and headed for the Oval Office.

VICE PRESIDENT CHANDLER, Vicki Grafton, and the secretary of the Department of Homeland Security, Melinda Eaton, were seated on the couches. President Lane sat in a chair. Pearce entered the room.

"Just in time for General Eaton's brief. Seems we had a little incident a few hours ago."

"Incident?" Pearce asked. He was confused. He'd arrived for a final prep meeting with Grafton before the Senate confirmation hearing. He was halfway to her office at the EEOB when he received a text instructing him to come to the Oval Office instead as soon as possible. No reason was given.

"I've got something I want you to look at," Lane said. He held up a sheet of paper in his hand.

"Of course, sir." Pearce took the paper and the chair opposite the president.

All eyes were on him as he read.

President Lane,

All praise is due to Allah, the Glorious, the Majestic! We praise Him, seek His aid, and ask for His forgiveness. We seek refuge with Allah from the evils of our souls and the wickedness of our deeds. Whomsoever Allah guides cannot be misguided, and whomsoever Allah leads astray cannot be guided back.

Allah has said, "Fighting has been enjoined upon you while it is hateful to you."

And the poet has said, "The walls of oppression and humiliation cannot be demolished except in a rain of bullets."

America has waged a cowardly war against the Ummah. It has waged war with cowardly drones against the Lions of the Caliphate around the world. A cowardly war that kills hundreds of innocent Muslims as your own secret documents testify against you.

But the Lions of the Caliphate do not act cowardly. They fight even amongst themselves for the privilege of killing Americans all over the world. Our Young Lions have begged to fight even in the heartland of America.

Today that day has arrived.

We soldiers of the Islamic State will erupt volcanoes of jihad throughout your nation. Allah will deal with America. He will defeat America with the worst of defeats. He will dismember America completely. In humiliation America will lay down in her own dust. In humiliation and failure and degradation she will weep tears of blood. You Americans will sleep with impotent rage in your hearts and fear pounding your beds. How good you are to prove to the world that we Muslims will not be defeated as long as we hold firm to the Book! How good you are to prove to yourselves that we Muslims will not be defeated as long as we hold firm to the sword!

But we are not without mercy, because Allah is merciful. Today we offer a hand of peace. Submit! Submit to the religion of peace. Submit to the Caliphate. To submit is easy. It will be a simple thing. Do not rage. Do not hesitate. It is but a single drop of rain compared to the great storm that awaits you if you do not submit.

You must submit in this way:

Inside this drone you will find the glorious Black Flag of the Islamic State. You must fly this exact flag only at high mast on the White House by 12:00 tomorrow (EST). You must leave it there for 24 hours so all the world can witness your submission and your testimony that Allah alone is God and Muhammad (peace be upon him) His Prophet.

If you do not fly the Black Flag of the Islamic State by 12:00 tomorrow the first blow will crash down upon your head. And each day thereafter the flag is not flown, a worse blow will be struck—another upon another until you submit or until the fifth day, when you will be utterly destroyed in a storm of unquenchable fire.

O Allah, there is no God but You! We fight for Your cause. You are exalted. We ask forgiveness and repent to You. All praise is due to Allah the Humiliator and the Subduer and to Muhammad (peace be upon him) His slave and messenger.

Inshallah.

Caliph Abu Waleed al-Mahdi

18

"What's your opinion, Troy?" Lane asked.

Pearce frowned, still processing. He started out his CIA career as an analyst, not a fighter. Combat required instant decisions. Thoughtful data interpretation took a little more time.

"The language is generally right. Almost reads like a fatwa except there are no suras referenced. No reason to think it's not a genuine ISIS threat."

"We're inclined to agree," Lane said.

Grafton nodded gravely, fighting back a smile. The timing of the drone threat couldn't have been better. *It's almost like I'd planned it myself.*

"There's an identical note in Arabic," Eaton said. "I've sent it over to the ISIS desk at the CIA for exegetical analysis. Maybe there are grammar or syntactical clues as to the authenticity."

"How did the Arabic read to you?" Pearce asked. He knew the retired army general was fluent.

"I'm no linguist but it seemed grammatically correct. Sophisticated syntax. Educated. An adult, I presume. Native speaker would be my guess. But that's all I could glean from a quick read. The two pages were laser-printed so we won't have any clues from handwriting analysis."

"Printed? Did it arrive in the mail?"

Lane chuckled. "Airmail. A drone, actually. Landed on the South Lawn basketball court. The damn thing looks like something you'd buy down at HobbyTown." Lane picked up a tablet from the coffee table and handed it to Pearce. The Secret Service had sent over photos.

"That's a cool toy. It looks like it has VTOL capabilities. Helicopter means you can land or take off from anywhere, forward flying increases speed and drops the energy cost in half. Where is it? I'd like to see it."

"It's over at the FBI lab right now," Eaton said. "They're doing a complete forensic workup on the vehicle, the letter—what you have in your hand there is a photocopy—and the flag. It might be a day or two before we get any hard clues, if there are any to get." The attorney general was out of town at the moment and out of the loop, so Eaton was taking point with the FBI at Lane's request—an unusual but temporary necessity. He wanted to keep the circle small for now. No need to drag the assistant attorney general into this.

"The FBI lab is the best in the world," Chandler said.

"Agreed. But it isn't like those idiot TV shows," Eaton said. "There aren't any magic machines to pull fingerprints off an eyelash. We might come up empty if there's a pro behind this. We're also running through the SIM cards to see what images were recorded by the two onboard cameras."

"I've read that a large number of hobby drones get out of the range of their radio controllers. Maybe it's just that?" Grafton said.

"They're called flyaways," Pearce said. "But the newer systems are designed to land immediately or return home if that happens."

"So you're certain this isn't a flyaway?" Chandler asked.

"Not at all. But if you check the make and model of the drone you can find out how it's programmed. Just call the manufacturer. But by the looks of it I'd say it was one of the newer ones. I doubt it was a flyaway, but we might as well double-check."

"What if this thing wasn't purchased at a store? Just assembled from parts?" Grafton asked.

"You can still check the part numbers on the components. I'd focus on the flight controller. There's a slim chance that sourcing the components could lead you in the right direction—assuming the same person who bought the parts also assembled them and was kind enough to have it all sent to a single physical address."

"Already on the to-do list," Eaton said. "Like you say, it's a long shot, but the FBI has one hell of a sniper rifle."

"Could this drone be connected to yesterday's subway attack?" Chandler asked.

"Anything's possible, but I doubt it. Yesterday was a protest attack. No threats were made, no demands issued," Eaton said.

"I agree. The operator yesterday used a controller and line-of-sight navigation. Not nearly as sophisticated as today's event," Pearce said.

"I've sent over some agents this morning to have a little conversation with our subway attackers," Eaton said. The college-age anarchists had posted their drone gas attack videos on social media anonymously, but the FBI quickly found and arrested them. "Maybe they heard something on the grapevine. Or maybe we can get them to put their ears to the ground in exchange for lighter sentences."

Lane glanced around the room. "Assuming this is a genuine ISIS threat, how credible is it?"

"What would be the point of making a worthless threat? Wouldn't that just make them look weak?" Grafton asked.

"Maybe it's a test to see how we'll react," Chandler said. "Probing our defenses."

"Or lack thereof," Grafton said. "How did that thing even get over the fence?"

"Too small to detect on radar," Pearce said.

"But commercial drones are supposed to be programmed with firmware that won't allow them to navigate near high-value targets," Eaton said. "It's called 'geo-fencing.'"

"Must have been overwritten or deprogrammed," Pearce said.

"And what about the other anti-drone defenses? The signal-disruption stuff?" Chandler asked.

"You said there were cameras onboard?" Pearce asked.

Eaton nodded.

"Have your people download the navigation software. My guess is those cameras were used for a visual navigation system to locate physical waypoints. You should have the FBI check for inertial navigation gear, too."

"Accelerometers? Gyroscopes?" Lane asked. "Is that even possible? The ones on my aircraft were huge."

"Everything's smaller these days. Even your smartphone has them. But the sophisticated kind of inertial guidance system you need to fly an aircraft like this is no bigger than a ring box. Wiring it into a piece of autopiloting software is no problem if you know how to do the programming."

"And ISIS has access to that kind of skill?" Lane asked.

"Without question," Pearce said. "A thirteen-year-old can do it. Go to any online DIY website. The do-it-yourself crowd is very generous with the info, and the hardware is widely available."

"That's terrifying," Grafton said.

Eaton tapped notes into her iPad. "I'll have the software techs check on that right now."

"Landing on the basketball court was smart," Pearce added. "Far enough away that it didn't appear to be a threat. Otherwise one of the Secret Service people might have shot it down with a service weapon."

"But close enough on White House property to get our attention and make sure it got delivered," Lane added.

"Smart thugs," Chandler said.

Pearce nodded. "Smarter than you know." He picked up the tablet again. Stared at the picture of the VTOL aircraft. "Whoever sent that letter was sending an even stronger message by flying this thing."

Chandler frowned. "How so?"

"These things are small, low-tech, programmable, cheap. You can get them anywhere or build them yourself. They're capable of small but significant payloads, especially with extended battery packs. You can't see them, which means you can't stop them. Whoever deployed this is telling us that he can strike anywhere at any time."

"So you believe this really is a credible threat?" Lane asked.

"Yes, sir, I do."

"What should we do about it?"

"Ground every one of them until they're all registered and accounted for," Chandler said. "Better yet, just get rid of the things."

Pearce couldn't believe Chandler wanted to continue the argument from the other day. "There are more than seven hundred thousand assembled commercial drones sold every year in this country alone. You can't possibly locate them all. More important, why ground them?"

"Because they're a damn threat," Chandler snapped.

"There isn't an industry in the world that isn't rushing as fast as it can toward automation. Drones are used in a wide variety of vital economic, research, and rescue activities. We have no idea how far or fast this technology will go, but stopping it now would be like banning the personal computer in the 1980s. Our competitors will lap us economically and militarily if we don't keep spurring this technology."

"Even these civilian models?" Eaton asked.

"You never know where the next big thing is coming from. It was the private sector that developed the Predator drone, not the military."

"Then we need to at least get all of the pilots licensed and the drones registered, just like cars," Chandler said.

Pearce stifled a laugh. "You think an asshole like al-Mahdi is going to run down to the DMV to register his drones so we can keep track of them?"

"So what's your solution?" Chandler asked.

"Right now there isn't one," Pearce said. He didn't even want to think about small drones that could easily incorporate inexpensive stealth design features like wave-bouncing facets or even sophisticated radar-absorbing materials. Both would make them even more difficult to detect.

"Maybe we should send out some kind of alert to local police departments and state agencies. Give them some kind of heads-up for extra precaution, especially around infrastructure—dams, power stations, nuclear facilities," Grafton said.

Pearce shook his head. "I wouldn't waste the manpower. It's not as if law enforcement doesn't already have its hands full these days. This threat is too nonspecific and the points of vulnerability are nearly infinite. If the locals are doing their jobs, they're already on alert for suspicious activity. Tell them to watch out for suspicious drone activity and they might accidentally start arresting innocent real estate agents, farmers, and park rangers. Besides, if you put out a bulletin like that, the press will get wind of it."

"Agreed," Eaton said.

"Should we cancel Pearce's hearing this morning until we get a handle on the situation?" Chandler asked.

The president shook his head. "No. There's nothing to get a handle on and I need Troy more than ever, especially in an official capacity. Canceling at this late hour will send the wrong message about our intentions—might even raise suspicions. Right now I want everything we've discussed to stay between us and off the record. No point in raising alarms or causing a general panic."

"And we still haven't officially ruled out the possibility that this was just some kind of sophisticated hoax or a publicity stunt," Eaton said.

"Fair enough," Lane said. "Though I'm strongly leaning in the other direction."

Grafton nodded in agreement with Lane. So did Chandler. "Feels like a genuine threat to me."

"We've asked local law enforcement to scan their security cameras and try to get a visual on the drone's flight path. They're mostly pointed at the street but we might get lucky. If we can trace its launch point, we might get another clue about who's behind it," Eaton said.

"Even if the threat is real, you can't comply with this demand," Pearce said. "Ever."

"Hell no." Lane picked up the paper again and studied it. "It would send the worst possible signal to our enemies and allies alike. All hell would break loose. And if it turns out to be a hoax, after all, I'd be a laughingstock." He glanced at Chandler. "How long would it take for your friends on the Hill to file an impeachment resolution after a FUBAR like that?"

"Half of a New York minute, and there'd be fistfights in the aisle to see who got to file it first."

There was a soft knock on the door before it swung open. The tall Secret Service agent Pearce had seen before stepped in, carrying a sealed paper evidence bag.

"This just arrived from the lab, Mr. President. The contents have been cleared."

"Thank you." Lane took the bag and she left. Lane opened it. Stood up. Pulled out the familiar black flag with the *Shahada* in white Arabic text above the seal of Muhammed. He shook it out and displayed it for the others.

"ISIS calls it the Black Banner," Eaton said. "It's the most famous symbol of terror in the world now."

Lane shook his head. "It's a big piece of black toilet paper as far as I'm concerned."

"We need to bomb these savages back into the Middle Ages, where they belong," Chandler said.

"They're already halfway there," Pearce said. He thought about Tariq again, and the women ISIS had butchered that night not so long ago. He wished now he'd taken the ISIS fighters out preemptively with the Heron's missiles before they had had the chance to murder. He wouldn't make that mistake again.

Lane wadded up the flag and tossed it onto his chair. "Fuck 'em. We'll just have to wait and see what their next play is. Until then, we'll stay the course. Mel, you're on point for this. Keep us all posted as things develop on your end. And please, everyone, let's keep a tight lid on this. You especially, Troy—the Senate subcommittee will go apeshit if they get wind of this."

"Of course," Pearce said. He saw something familiar in Lane's eyes. He'd seen it before in combat, many times.

The look of a man about to charge in, knowing his number's up.

19

Pearce and Grafton were seated at the long witness table facing the imposing semicircle of elevated chairs where the senators sat behind their nameplates. Chairman Jim Floyd sat in the center, flanked by George Kelly and Claire Earlywine. The other sixteen seats were vacant. No one else was in attendance, not even committee staffers.

Pearce leaned over to Grafton, whispered, "That's it?"

"That's a good sign. That means the others aren't interested or concerned. Trust me, when you're in the stirrups, you don't want nineteen pairs of hands in the exam room. These three are bad enough."

"Mr. Pearce, I see you've brought along expert help today," the chairman began. He spoke in a slow midwestern baritone.

"Yes, sir. I'm pleased to introduce Ms. Vicki Grafton, Vice President Chandler's chief of staff." Even from where he sat, Pearce could see the sparkling blue eyes beneath the huge bushy silver eyebrows.

"Yes, we're quite familiar with our dear friend Ms. Grafton," Floyd said with a grin. "How are you, Vicki?"

"I'm very well, Senator, thank you for asking."

"And how's old Clay treating you?"

"Best boss in the world."

Floyd laughed. "Good thing you're not under oath today." The other senators laughed.

Floyd continued. "Mr. Pearce, as you know, this is a closed-door hearing. We're conducting the people's business but sometimes the people don't need to know how the sausage gets made. No media is present nor will today's meeting be recorded in any fashion or reported, out of national security concerns. I plan to keep our time together as short as possible and the conversation informal. I won't ask you to swear in because I've seen your service record and I know you to be a man of honor and integrity who's sacrificed much on the field of battle and on behalf of your nation."

"Thank you, Senator. I'll answer everything to the best of my ability. And if I don't know the answer, I won't bull—" Pearce caught himself. "Pretend I do."

The senators got a laugh out of that one, too.

"I can't make the same promise on my end, but we'll just see how it goes," Floyd said.

"Mr. Chairman, if you don't mind my jumping in, I'd like to ask Mr. Pearce a question before we get started," Earlywine said.

"Please do."

"Mr. Pearce, what is your opinion of the drone attack?"

Pearce felt his gut sink. How did she know? He cast a quick glance at Grafton, equally puzzled. He needed to buy some time. Lane said to keep his mouth shut but he didn't want to start the meeting with a bald-faced lie or betraying the president's confidence. He decided to stall.

"Is there something specific you had in mind, Senator?"

"Yesterday's subway attack," Earlywine said. "Are we likely to see more of that kind of thing? And if so, what can we do about it?"

Pearce's blood pressure dropped. A bullet dodged. "Unfortunately I'm afraid we're due for more of the same. And for the moment, there's very little we can do in the way of prevention."

"We're damn lucky that attack was only with tear gas and not some WMD," Kelly chimed in. The others nodded in agreement.

"I agree with you, Senator. But luck is a lousy defense strategy. One of my top priorities is drone defense. I know it's a problem the Pentagon has been looking at for years. We're all concerned."

"That's it? Anything else?" Earlywine asked.

"There's nothing else to say. We're behind but we're working on it." Pearce didn't want to tell her it was his worst fear, or the fact that his worst fear might have come to pass just a few hours earlier.

"That concerns me."

Pearce nodded. "It should. But like I said, I won't bullshit you."

Earlywine's face soured. "Decorum, Mr. Pearce."

"Sorry, ma'am."

"Apology accepted." She turned to the chairman. "I stepped in front of you. Please, have at it."

Floyd cleared his throat, then launched into his inquiry. Just as Grafton had predicted, he began by asking Pearce what Drone Command was supposed to be. Pearce gave Floyd the answer he'd rehearsed with her, only adding that Drone Command would be like a more focused, pared-down version of DARPA combined with the U.S. Transportation Command (TRANSCOM). He summed it up neatly. "We find new drone systems, acquire them, and on occasion, deploy them."

Not entirely satisfied, Floyd pressed further, wanting to know more details about organizational structure, personnel administration, and other particulars that Grafton had again warned him about. Being a quick study, Pearce threw him the answer that Grafton had fed him the day before. "I'd refer you to the appropriate addenda included in the report I sent over to your office."

"Not a detail man, eh?" Floyd said.

"I'm a delegator. I leave the details to those best suited to handle them."

Floyd scratched one of his bushy eyebrows with a thumbnail. "Then let me cut to the chase. I'm still trying to wrap my mind around the whole reason for this new federal bureaucracy. President Lane insists on holding the line with the budget freeze that's been in place since the Myers administration. Seems to me we should be cutting departments, not adding them."

"In both the short and long run, Drone Command will save you money."

"How?"

"By trusting the private sector to do what it does best—create and innovate. The Pentagon's weapons procurement system is just a glorified version of Soviet central planning. The technology is galloping ahead too far and too fast for bureaucrats to keep pace with."

"Are you denying the fact we have the most powerful and technologically advanced military on the planet?" Floyd asked.

"No. But the systems we acquire are often over budget, off schedule, buggy, and behind the technology curve the day they're deployed. The Pentagon only knows what it knows, so it keeps acquiring weapons systems for battles it plans on fighting. The problem is, it never does fight those wars—and every war we lose is to technologically inferior opponents. We haven't fought a carrier duel since the Battle of Leyte Gulf in 1944, but we're building three thirteen-billion-dollar *Ford*-class aircraft carriers to add to our fleet of ten *Nimitz*-class carriers. Currently the Russians have one carrier. Same with the Chinese." Pearce's voice trailed off. "At least, until recently." He was suddenly distracted by the memory.

Earlywine nodded gravely. "A terrible tragedy."

"My older brother was killed at the Chosin Reservoir. I'm not losing any sleep over it," Floyd said.

"You're suggesting we have too many carriers, Mr. Pearce?" Kelly asked.

The question snapped Pearce back to reality. "Not my department, sir. But I do know that both the Russians and the Chinese are pursuing hypersonic 'carrier-killer' missile programs, each at a fraction of the cost of a single American aircraft carrier. And such missiles are, technically, drones."

"But wouldn't you agree that our military technology, including carrier technology, is key to our continued military dominance?" Floyd asked. "Just look at the F-35. It's the world's finest air-superiority fighter."

"We're all familiar with the F-35 budget boondoggle and the ongoing technical problems it suffers, including the bugs that kill our pilots. We also know some of that technology has been hacked by Chinese cyberwarfare. The only problem with building an overly expensive and underperforming air-superiority fighter is that we haven't fought an air-superiority engagement in over twenty-five years. No disrespect to anyone in the room or in this building, but we're going to lose the next war because we're spending too much money on the wrong systems for the wrong battles for the wrong reasons."

"And what would those reasons be?" Kelly asked.

"The fact that the F-35 Lightning is manufactured in forty-five states and Puerto Rico tells me a lot about the procurement process."

"Like what, Mr. Pearce?"

"Defense procurement is more about securing votes back home than it is about acquiring the best weapons systems at the least expense."

"That's quite an indictment of the people in this room and in this building, Mr. Pearce."

Pearce glanced over at Grafton. Her frozen smile and desperate eyes told him to stand down. He thought about everything that Chandler and Grafton had warned him about. But he couldn't play the game. "I suppose it is," Pearce said. "Respectfully."

"And your little department is going to right the ship?"

"We're going to give it one helluva try, at least as far as drone technologies go."

Senator Kelly broke in. "No offense, Mr. Pearce, but you're just one man with considerable but still limited experience with drone operations. What makes you think you're more qualified or better at predicting the future than the Pentagon in these matters?"

"I'm not. Not at all. I have no idea what the next war will look like. Maybe it will be a carrier duel in the Pacific or the Battle of Britain 2.0. But nobody knows because nobody can predict the future, including the Pentagon. That's why it's better to let the technology determine the path forward rather than for any of us to try and guess the future."

"The Pentagon has been rushing headlong into drone development. Why do they need you and this new department?"

"The Pentagon has a bad record regarding drones. The basic technology is from the nineteenth century—the first patent for what we would call a drone was issued to Nikola Tesla back in 1898. The

Pentagon—especially the air force and other flying services—fought like hell to ignore it for decades. It was the CIA that finally shoved their noses into the technology when the air force couldn't provide needed surveillance over Bosnia in the early 1990s during our air campaign against the Serbs. It was only after civilians had developed the technology and pumped live video images of enemy combatants to commanders in the field and back in the Pentagon that the Predator's extreme value became understood. In other words, the Pentagon often doesn't know what's possible. My job is to show them what's possible and then let them decide how they might want to use it without the technology getting sidetracked by the lobbyists and log rollers. National security shouldn't be sold to the highest bidder."

Kelly shook his bald head. "I'm the Pentagon's number one fan up here. I think our men and women in uniform do an amazing job defending this country, day in and day out."

Pearce swore Kelly was looking for a camera to bloviate into while he was delivering his campaign speech. He kept his temper in check. "I support the troops as well, Senator. It's the waste, fraud, and abuse of the Pentagon procurement system I question." Pearce wanted to tell the old bastard off. Too many retired congressmen landed on the corporate boards of big defense contractors or as partners in big K Street lobbying firms after spending their congressional careers bloating the defense budget on behalf of their future employers. But President Lane deserved better than him flying off the handle.

"My state is home to some of the nation's finest defense contractors. I'm one of those old-fashioned people who happen to believe that national security wouldn't be possible without them," Earlywine said.

"I agree with you. And if any contractor—big or small—comes up with a viable system, I'd take a look at it. But the days of negotiated weapons designs have to be over. What's the old saying? Camels are horses designed by committees?"

"And so you'd be the person to make the call? What about congressional oversight?"

"Oversight, yes, but not micromanagement. And to tell the truth, I wouldn't trust me, either. So let me run with this thing for two years. See what we can come up with. If I drop the ball, can me. Better yet, I'll quit. But President Lane trusts me to do what's best for the country, not what's best for him or for his party. I'm making that same promise to you today. How well I do it is for you to decide."

Floyd coughed, a wheezing smoker's hack. When the phlegm cleared, he leaned into the microphone, his head resting in his big farmer's hand. "You must think we're a bunch of moneygrubbing dimwits up here on the Hill, pissing away the national treasury while we play with ourselves."

"Senator Floyd, I assure you, Mr. Pearce means nothing but respect—"

Pearce cut her off. "I wouldn't put it quite that way, Senator," Pearce said. "But I'd like you to prove me wrong."

Floyd's blue eyes bored into his. "I appreciate your candor, Mr. Pearce."

Grafton gaped at Pearce in shocked disbelief. He had crossed the line.

The committee spent another hour grilling Pearce on foreign policy and security issues. Pearce repeatedly deferred to administration officials tasked with those policies, and the informal hearing ended on a polite but formal note. Pearce seemed satisfied but it was clear to Grafton that the Drone Command pooch was officially and royally screwed.

20

The eight-bladed octocopter sped toward FedExField, an ominous cargo box fixed beneath its fuselage. It flew at an altitude of 125 feet, high enough to clear the upper tier of seats in the open-air complex. At full capacity, the Washington Redskins FedExField could accommodate nearly eighty thousand cheering fans whose attention would be focused on the game, not on terror in the sky.

The drone roared forward at more than sixty miles per hour. It was only seconds away from breaching the airspace directly above the stadium when it suddenly slowed and wobbled before making a violent 180-degree turn, its speed plummeting as it dived toward the asphalt. It settled on its skids just two yards away from Pearce, standing in the parking lot.

"Impressive," Pearce said as the eight motors cut off. His back was to the olive drab Iveco Light Multirole Vehicle (LMV), the Italian version of a Humvee. An array of radar, sensors, and cameras—optical, infrared, and thermal imaging—were fixed on a rotating turret along with a dish and what appeared to be a firing tube. He heard the rear doors open and the heavy thud of boots hitting the ground.

Wes Klein flashed his used-car-salesman smile. The forty-two-year-old former submariner and Annapolis grad built his own security company based on a license for the Selex ES Falcon Shield combat system. His techs improved on the Falcon Shield with a few proprietary tweaks to the software and hardware. "My rig works as advertised. But you don't have to take my word for it. Run it through whatever tests you've got."

Pearce shrugged. "The specs on paper look good. It's the real-world stuff that usually bites you in the ass." Klein's system was similar to the Israeli Drone Dome. He was hoping it was even better.

"You can swap out a number of components and customize the Falcon Shield according to the threat profile."

"But essentially the strength of your system is you get a visual lock on the target, and then you can take it out?"

"Visual, electro-optical, and signal lock. We have radar, too, but it's hard to pick up the really small ones with it."

"Yeah. Tell me about it." Pearce hoped Dr. Ponder would come up with a fix on that particular bug in his laser system. "How does the electronic defeat system work?"

Klein shook his close-cropped head. "*Segretissimo,* old buddy. Top secret. My Italian investors would bris my sizable foreskin with a pair of rusty pliers if I told you."

Pearce grinned. He liked Klein. Reminded him of his old friend Mike Early, who had a mind as filthy as a coal miner's butt crack. "But you actually managed to seize control of the unit and were able to fly it?" That was an important feature. Merely disrupting the GPS or controller signals might actually result in a drone flying out of control. With the wrong payload, that could prove just as problematic in a crowded venue as a controlled hostile flight.

"It's worked on every hobby and commercial drone system we've tested so far. We've been able to disrupt the signal and seize control of vehicles and land them where we wanted. Of course, we haven't tested every available system out there—there are way too many of them. But we're confident this is the way to go for the vast majority of small, civilian UAV threats."

Pearce thought about the VTOL that had landed at the White House that morning, or even his own test against Ponder's laser system the day before. "So what do you do about autopiloted vehicles?"

"We've been able to seize a few of them, depending on the hardware. But if we can't seize control, we can deploy a focused high-power microwave to fry the circuitry."

"Another add-on?"

Klein rubbed his thumb against his first two fingers. "Cha-*ching*, baby. But it works."

"Every time?"

"Unless it's shielded."

"You mean like a Faraday cage?"

"Or something similar. Again, we're talking high percentages on kill rates. There aren't any absolutes in this business."

Pearce headed for the rear of the LMV. "Any other defeat solutions?"

"You always have the kinetic option."

"Bullets and missiles in an urban environment?" Pearce asked, poking his head in the back of the truck. The compartment was packed with electronic gear and video monitors.

"Security Ethics 101, friendo. Depends on what the payload is on the drone you're trying to knock down. A few killed and wounded by your kinetics, or thousands killed and wounded by your adversary."

"I'm looking for a third option."

"Have you thought about lasers? That's something we're looking into."

"It's crossed my mind." Pearce's phone rang. It was President Lane. "Excuse me, Wes."

"Of course. I've got to check the gear anyway." Klein crawled back into the LMV to give Pearce his privacy.

Pearce answered. "Mr. President."

"Troy, I wanted to give you a heads-up. The FBI came up short on the forensics. No fingerprints, no DNA, no purchase orders to trace, no addresses to raid. Whoever did this knew what they were doing."

"Must've been a pro."

"Yeah, but a 'pro' what? Terrorist? Prankster? Social justice warrior?"

"Doesn't really matter at this point. We just have to wait for the other shoe to drop."

"Come up with any bright ideas for stopping these hobby drones?"

"Not yet, but I'm working on a few things."

"Vicki wants you back in her office tomorrow at eleven a.m. You need to start working the phones, pay a few visits. Time to hustle up some votes."

"I'd rather get tased."

Lane laughed. "I feel for you, brother. Call me if you need anything."

How about a rum and Coke? Pearce wanted to ask. Instead, he thanked the president and rang off.

"We good?" Klein asked.

Another dead end, another ticking clock, Pearce thought. He forced a smile. "I'll be in touch."

WASHINGTON, D.C.

It was two hours before Grafton appeared at the vice president's door. He ushered her in and ordered a late lunch for the two of them. They had a lot to discuss, and even more to accomplish.

Chandler leaned back in his chair and folded his hands. "So how did our boy do today?"

"Frankly, he shit all over the subcommittee. I've just spent the last two hours wearing out my knee pads trying to mend fences with Floyd." Chandler looked concerned. She quickly added, "Figuratively, of course."

"Good for Pearce. Nothing like a good evacuation of the bowels to clear the mind."

"His mind might be cleared, but his chances for getting the nomination are zeroed out. He sinkholed himself, but the administration might be falling in after him."

"How so?"

"Floyd thinks Lane is going to go all Comanche on his gravy train."

"Floyd's half-right. Lane is a reformer at heart. His attention is occupied with the Asia summit at the moment, and now with this crazy drone threat we got today. For now, he's delegating the heavy lifting to others, including Pearce. Even if the Senate passes on him, they've got to know there'll be others just like him next in line."

Grafton frowned, confused. "So you support Pearce? I was under the impression you two weren't on the best of terms."

"Support him? Heavens no. He's a first-rate prick." Chandler's phone alarm rang. He checked it. "Jesus, Mary, and Joseph. I nearly forgot. I've got a meeting with the Saudi ambassador in thirty minutes. You want to come with?" He stood.

"I need to pass. Pearce is coming in. We've got a Rolodex of calls to make. Maybe even knock on a few doors."

"Good luck with that." Chandler pulled on his suit coat. "At least stay and eat your lunch. You look peckish."

"If you don't mind my asking, what exactly is your beef with Pearce?"

"We knew each other, briefly. A long time ago. Our time together wasn't exactly . . . friendly. If you think he's a hardcase now, you should've known him then."

21

The sun burned high overhead and the air shimmered with stifling heat. The twenty-four newly minted Shia recruits from nearby Samarra stood ramrod straight in the courtyard, roasting alive beneath their brand-new Iraqi army uniforms. Their young, stern faces beamed with pride and glistened with sweat as Representative Clay Chandler droned on with the help of an overly enthusiastic translator.

Pearce muttered a curse through his bearded lips as another drop of sweat trickled down his collar. The barrel of his carbine was blistering hot even though it hadn't been fired in days. Bad enough to be out in the middle of this heat. But it was security he was worried about. He and Early stood a nervous watch over the ceremony taking place at the palace—one of maybe a hundred Saddam had built for himself after the first Gulf War. It now served as the headquarters for the regional commander of the Iraqi army, General Ali Majid, a Sunni from a nearby province.

"How much longer with this guy?" Early said. The hulking Ranger whispered in his comms set.

"He's begging for a mortar round," Pearce said. He was linked to Early on a secure channel.

"From us or the bad guys?"

Pearce laughed. "Roger that."

"You should be ashamed." A thickly accented Kurdish voice whispered in their comms. "He is one of your countrymen." Tariq Barzani was the third man on the team. Two more team members, Luckett and Rowley, were back in Baghdad for the day.

"Your problem, Mother, is that you Kurds haven't yet mastered the subtleties of democracy," Early said. "It's our constitutional right to hate our elected idiots."

"And if you ever run short of idiots, we've got extras we can send you," Pearce said. "Plenty more."

Tariq laughed. "Trust me, we have more than enough of our own." His hearty laugh filled their headsets. The Kurdish translator had grown close to Pearce and Early since their arrival. The battle-hardened peshmerga was a decade older than they were. He was out beneath the blistering sun with them, working the perimeter. Tariq watched the Americans like a hawk, constantly worrying for their safety. He knew Early and Pearce had fought with Kurdish forces in the liberation of Kirkuk in 2003. This made him feel even more protective of the men he called his "sons." They returned the favor by calling him Mother, but they were big fans of his, too.

"We're walking point in the hottest, sweatiest sphincter of the known world—no offense, Mother. Hard to believe that Babylonian civilization was born here," Early said.

"Babylon was founded by Nimrod, the grandson of Ham, who was cursed," Tariq said.

"That figures," Early said.

"Stay frosty, Mikey." Pearce kept his head on a swivel, scanning the rooftops and perimeter through his Oakleys. He shared Early's concern. The general's own troops were stationed at regular intervals outside and inside the palace compound, but he didn't trust them. They were as likely to turn their guns on the Americans as they were to drop them and bolt like scalded cats if any real trouble came loping through the gate. Tikrit was in the heart of Indian country, the nutsack of the Sunni Triangle. Worse, it was Saddam's hometown. Every swinging dick seemed to be an angry cousin with a murderous grudge against somebody, especially Americans. All of them were secretly armed or had access to weapons. An AK-47 rattled off a few rounds in the distance. Not unusual.

Pearce didn't put much stock in the six private contractors the general had hired on as personal bodyguards. They were mercs, straight up, all ex-special forces beholden to no one but the general. An Aussie was in charge. One Brit, one American, one South African, and two Russians rounded out the complement. Pearce trusted the Russian mercenaries the least. It wasn't unusual for them to do double duty for the SVR. Today the mercs stood in loose knots in the shaded areas on the periphery, content to the let Pearce, Early, and Tariq do all the heavy sweating.

Pearce checked his watch. Chandler's speech was running twenty minutes late. An American press photographer snapped endless photos of Chandler and the recruits. Publicity photos for his upcoming Senate campaign, Pearce surmised.

"He must not have counted on the time it would take to translate," Pearce said in his comms.

"Especially with a translator like Elmer Fudd over there. Nothin' like a cousin with a stutter."

Despite himself, Pearce burst out laughing.

Six of the dignitaries sitting in the shade were scowling Sunni tribal elders. Seated across from them were their counterparts, a half dozen glowering Shia elders. Seated between them in the place of honor was General Majid in his desert camo BDUs, jaunty black beret, and Saddam Hussein mustache.

"And finally, let me just say," Chandler said, pointing at each of the recruits, "while the future of Iraq belongs in your strong and capable hands, never forget that America will always be here as your faithful ally and reliable friend. We will never abandon the Iraqi people. We have willingly shed our blood in your sand and we will do so again in the future to ensure democracy and freedom for Sunnis and Shias alike." Chandler turned to the general and dignitaries. "Congratulations to all of you on this historic day. Sunni and Shia joining hands in the fight together against the forces of tyranny. It's a fine down payment for the price of freedom. You all should be very, very proud." Chandler began clapping his hands.

General Majid took the cue and stood, clapping. The other dignitaries rose and clapped as well. The photographer dashed over just as Chandler and Majid clasped hands, then followed Chandler as he shook the hands of each tribal elder.

"Is he running for mayor?" Early asked.

"Yeah. The mayor of Bartertown."

"Who . . . run . . . Bartertown?" Early asked in his Master Blaster voice.

"Master Blaster runs Bartertown!"

They both laughed. Pearce and Early had a running gag about the similarities between the post-apocalyptic Mad Max movies and postwar Iraq. They called Majid's palace the Thunderdome.

"Gentlemen, please," Tariq said.

General Majid barked an order and the Shia recruits finally relaxed. Chandler waded into the middle of them, shaking more hands, photographer in tow.

"Criminy," Early said. "How long is this Gomer going to take?"

Pearce shook his head. "Good thing they pay us by the hour." He scanned the roof again. He couldn't shake the feeling his skull was in somebody's crosshairs, but three tours in the Sand Box did that to a guy. He and Early kept moving, walking an irregular circuit on the periphery, cutting in and out between whatever obstructions they could find.

On the last turn, Chandler was standing back beneath the shadowed portico, wiping his dripping forehead with a kerchief, and chatting earnestly with General Majid. Chandler glanced over at Pearce and Early. The general nodded and left, heading past the guarded bas-relief bronze entrance doors. Chandler waved Pearce and Early over with his hand.

"You're Troy Pearce," Chandler said, extended a hand. "CIA, right?"

"Yes, sir."

"And you must be Mike Early. U.S. Army Rangers."

"Yes, sir. At least, that's what the dog tag says."

"Well, I appreciate you guys. I saw you out there in the hot sun. I hope I didn't go on too long."

"Hadn't noticed, sir. Just trying to keep an eye on things," Early said.

"I'd like the two of you to come inside and join me for a cold beverage." Chandler glanced over his shoulder at the two wary Russian mercs standing back in the shadows. "And I'd like to have a private word with you."

Pearce and Early glanced at each other.

"Of course," Pearce said. "Can we bring our translator?"

"No need. It will be just us Americans talking."

"Our translator is as thirsty as we are," Early said. "And the sun is just as freaking hot on him as it is on us."

Chandler shrugged. "The general has informed me that the Kurd isn't welcome inside. I'm sorry. But you know how it is around here. When in Rome."

Pearce started to protest but held his tongue. Chandler might have a legit reason to keep the meeting small. "You're the boss."

22

Chandler led the way across what seemed like acres of polished red marble floors, past towering green marble columns. It reminded Pearce of a temple in the old Hollywood sword-and-sandal movies, only gaudier. The walls were of patterned stone and the ceilings featured brightly colored mosaics illuminated by expansive crystal chandeliers. The cost of building a pleasure palace like this must have been as enormous as the place was gauche. Clearly the architect was attempting to evoke the grandeur and majesty of ancient Babylon. The aesthetic felt more like Tony Montana than Nebuchadnezzar. Considering whom it was built for, the architect made the right choice. Pearce wondered how many starving Iraqi children could have been fed by the cost of this one palace alone.

They passed through two more sets of guarded, bas-relief bronze doors and into the interior section of the palace where Majid's personal residence was located. The first room they entered took the gaudy, overwrought architecture of the earlier rooms and exploded it by a factor of ten. A welter of brightly colored marbles, geometric inlays, gold leaf, gemstones, and crystal bombarded Pearce's eyes, but it was the massive swimming pool and the bikini-clad women who frolicked in it that commanded the room.

Chandler led the way toward a lush banquet table piled high with roasted meats, fresh fruits, and other delights neither Pearce nor Early had seen before. Huge buckets of ice were larded with Cokes and beers. "Gentlemen, help yourselves. There's plenty to choose from."

The Sunni elders were piling plates high with food and pulling out drinks from the bucket. Pearce didn't recognize any of the sullen Shia waiting their turn. The Salah al-Din district was the heart of the infamous Sunni Triangle, and Tikrit, its capital, was strictly Sunni. Samarra, on the other hand, contained some of Iraq's holiest Shia shrines, even though it was also in the district. The fault lines of the Iraqi Sunni-Shia conflict intersected in this part of the country. Pearce had become friendly with several Samarran Shia leaders in the past few weeks that he'd been stationed in the district. He wondered why they weren't here, too.

General Majid huddled in the corner with the Russian mercs, the three of them seated in gilded red velvet chairs, devouring their food.

Early stopped at the edge of the pool, his eye fixed on one particular beauty. He nudged Pearce. "Think she's up for a game of Marco Polo?"

"You can play hide the explorer after we grab some chow."

"Roger that."

EARLY AND PEARCE sat on a marble bench, finishing their steaks, grease dribbling into their beards. Four empty beer bottles littered the tabletop.

Pearce watched as two of the Sunni elders disrobed and leaped into the pool, their pale white flesh covered in thick carpets of curly black hair. They chased around a couple of the squealing girls, who managed to stay just out of paw's reach.

Chandler pulled up a red velvet chair and sat down next to Pearce and Early.

"How are the steaks, fellas?"

"Great," Early said, gnawing away at the last remnants of his T-bone in his thick fingers.

"Wonderful. I flew them in with me, along with everything else. Just my way of saying thanks to all of you out here doing the Lord's work."

"Amen, brother," Early said.

Pearce finished the last of his third beer. "Yeah. Thanks." He burped.

Chandler forced a smile. "What did you think about our little ceremony today?"

"Good to finally see some Shia in army uniforms," Pearce said. "If we can't get these guys all on the same team, this country will collapse into a civil war."

"I couldn't agree more. We need them all on the same team, fighting al-Qaeda together. Too many foreign fighters have come across the Syrian border, not to mention Iranians. A unified Iraq is our only chance of stopping the spread of radical Islam throughout the region."

Then you should've left Hussein in power, you flipping idiot, Pearce thought. Sure, he was a murderous dictator, but he kept even more murderous bastards at bay. Now that Hussein was gone, the demons were unleashed.

Chandler seemed to read Pearce's mind. His smile faded. "My understanding is that the two of you were primarily responsible for training the Shia recruits."

"Just the small-unit tactics and weapons training," Early said.

"They're still pretty green, but they're all good kids. They want to fight for their country, especially now that the Shia have a chance for a voice in the government," Pearce said. "I like them a lot."

"General Majid said you made quite an impression on them. Said that you two were pretty close to them. That's good. We want to give them our best efforts."

"Roger that," Early said.

"But I'm concerned about your attitudes regarding General Majid. He's under the impression you don't approve of his methods, or his governance of the district."

Early and Pearce looked at each other.

"We've been out to the villages. People are scared shitless of him and his men. There are stories—" Early said.

"Think Colonel Kurtz, only without the pajamas," Pearce interrupted. "Batshit crazy."

"I read the last two reports you filed with your boss. Quite a colorful edge you put on them," Chandler said. "Cutting off ears for trophies? Really?"

"I only reported what I saw," Pearce said. "Did Grainger have a problem with them?"

"No, she didn't. In fact, she passed your reports up the chain of command and they eventually landed on my desk." Chandler scratched his beardless chin. "The only problem is that General Majid is on our team."

"You sure about that?" Pearce said.

"What do you mean?"

"Rumor has it he's on the Russians' payroll, too."

"That's ridiculous," Chandler said. "He's one of ours. His assignment was to pacify the district and he's done it. We didn't give him a rule book."

"Maybe you should have," Early said. "Ain't that the whole point of 'ensuring democracy and freedom' for these folks?"

Chandler didn't blink, even though Early was throwing his own speech right back into his face. "You can't have democracy and freedom without security. Security comes first, and the general is bringing that."

"Security I get," Pearce said. "But what he's doing is called terrorism."

Early added, "Not to mention the tens of millions of U.S. taxpayer dollars he's stolen, the public works projects he hasn't completed but claimed he did—or if they were, they're half-assed and built with slave labor. Half these people think Hussein was a Santa Claus compared to him."

Chandler nodded. "I understand your frustration, believe me, I do. But you've got to back off on the general." Chandler looked around the room, lowered his voice. "In case you haven't noticed, this isn't America. These people do things differently over here. We're not here to judge, we're here to win the war against terror, and for good or for ill, that means partnering with people like General Majid."

Pearce leaned in. "If you want to win the war on terror, then arrest that terrorist son of a bitch. The Shia around here will call you a hero—and so will half the Sunnis. He's worse than any of the fucksticks we've been chasing down."

Chandler shook his head. "Not going to happen. He's Teflon as far as Washington's concerned. His brother is one of the most important tribal chieftains in the Sunni Triangle. The Pentagon is pushing a new antiterrorism strategy called the Sunni Awakening. We're going to ally ourselves with all of the Sunnis and use them to help us get rid of AQ and the foreign fighters once and for all."

"The Sunni chieftains are the ones who've been giving us so much hell," Early said. "We should be hunting those guys down, not partnering up."

"This is all bigger than the three of us, believe me. I'm just the messenger."

"And just so that we're clear, what exactly is the message?" Pearce asked.

"Stop filing your reports. Quit rattling the cage. Just keep doing your jobs."

Pearce darkened. "That is our job. We're on a special mission. Grainger's tasked us with keeping tabs on Majid. He's the reason why we were sent here to begin with. That asshole has a history, and Grainger wants us to document it so we can press charges and clean this shit up."

"Not going to happen."

"Take it up with Grainger," Pearce said. "I don't do politics."

Chandler stood. Pearce and Early didn't.

"Grainger won't back you up."

"Why not?" Pearce asked.

Chandler checked his watch. "Grainger's been reassigned. About an hour ago she boarded an air force transport. She'll arrive in Burkina Faso sometime late tomorrow."

"What the fuck?" Early said.

"The world is full of security challenges. Apparently her superiors at Langley felt that her talents would be better deployed over there."

"I don't suppose you had anything to do with it?" Pearce asked.

"Me? Hardly. Like I told you, I'm just the messenger. But don't be surprised if you find yourselves joining her if you don't toe the line."

Chandler pointed at the buffet table again. "Help yourselves to more, gentlemen. Otherwise, I'm sure you have a lot to do around here."

"Yeah, we do," Pearce said, standing up. Early joined him. The two of them towered over Chandler.

The diminutive congressman wasn't intimidated. "There's one more thing."

"What?" Early said. He saw the press photographer approaching out of the corner of his eye.

Chandler flashed an oily smile and extended his hand. "On behalf of the people of the United States and the citizens of the great state of Georgia," he said, in his smarmiest southern accent, "I want to thank you for your service." The whirring high-speed camera flashed like a strobe light, anticipating the moment.

Pearce and Early shook their heads in disgust and stormed away, leaving Chandler's pale, empty hand hanging in the air. An angry glance from Chandler finally stilled the whirring camera.

Pearce and Early hit the refreshment table, snagging a couple of bottles of cold beer, a carton of Marlboros, and a large bag of Skittles for Tariq before pushing their way through the big bronze doors, headed for another beat-down in the relentless Iraqi sun.

23

The Secret Service driver sped through traffic with his emergency lights flashing. Completely illegal, given the circumstances, but when the vice president tells you to do something, you do it.

Arriving a fashionable five minutes late, Chandler was ushered into the ambassador's spacious office and told that His Royal Highness would be down shortly. Coffee was offered. Chandler took it. He was starved. No telling when he'd eat again.

The ambassador arrived with his male secretary and the coffee service. Chandler stood. The two men embraced. "Clay, it's good to see you again."

"And you, Your Excellency."

"Clay, please. We're friends. Come, take a coffee and have a seat." The tall, handsome Saudi steered the vice president toward a luxurious chair. His Royal Highness Ambassador Faisal bin Salman al-Saud dressed and acted like a young Westerner. The forty-year-old prince had attended a Swiss boarding school, graduated from Harvard, and later earned an MBA from Wharton. His Swiss mother's fair complexion along with his short cropped beard softened his Semitic profile. He was the new, youthful face of the royal house of Saud, with the reputation of a reformer.

"Old habits," Chandler said. "Forgive me. My grandmother raised me to believe that good manners are a sign of godliness."

"I defer to your grandmother's wisdom out there in the world. But in here, please, it's Faisal."

"Of course. Thank you again for agreeing to meet with me. I thought our first conversation was extremely enlightening."

"As did I. I hope we may continue in the same spirit of frankness."

"I would expect nothing less."

"Excellent. How shall we proceed?"

"First of all, I want to reiterate that I completely understand the existential threat that ISIS presents to your country as well as mine. President Lane understands it as well."

"And yet, strangely, he still refuses to commit American combat personnel to the war."

"I understand the need for new boots on the ground, even if the president does not."

The Saudi cocked an eyebrow. "Should you be telling me this?"

"It's important that you know there are still plenty of us who reject isolationism. ISIS isn't just going to go away on its own. It's a cancer that needs to be cut out."

"*Daesh* is a great evil that plagues the minds of far too many people. The world isn't ready for what will come should they ever seize control of an entire nation, especially one with resources like ours." Chandler noted that Saud referred to ISIS only by the more derogatory *Daesh*, an acronym for ISIS that sounded like a few other unfavorable Arabic words. ISIS hated the term *Daesh* so much that they threatened to cut out the tongue of anyone who uttered it.

"It was a damn fool mistake to knock off Hussein. Bad as he was, he was at least a devil we knew, and kept his boot on the throats of the other devils we didn't know. Same for Qaddafi."

"If I may be so bold, you Americans have been terribly selective in your foreign policy morality. I'm glad that some of you have seen the difficulty of such selectivity. We have never suffered that particular malady. We hate *Daesh* for what it is. Only recently did it kill my own nephew."

"I'm so sorry to hear that. My condolences." Chandler took a sip of coffee.

"Thank you. The circumstances were difficult. His mother, my sister, is still unconsolable in her grief. The young fool was seduced into the witchcraft of *Daesh*. He perished in a drone strike." Al-Saud paused for effect. "An American drone strike."

"American? On Saudi soil?"

"Northern Iraq. I assumed it was your government behind it. Who else has the capability?"

"I assure you, unless there was some secret mission, it most assuredly wasn't American. President Lane hasn't authorized any such strike in Iraq in the last six months. He's questioning the entire program. In fact, the whole War on Terror. Believe me, if there had been a drone strike against ISIS, I'd know about it, because I've been pounding the table for it since I was sworn in."

"All the more reason to allow my government to purchase and operate our own drone systems."

"I agree wholeheartedly. President Lane isn't yet fully open to that option, but he'll come around to it."

"And this man, Pearce. The nominee? My understanding is that his position is not supportive, either."

Chandler's jaw tightened. Pearce was a stubborn ass. He wouldn't let him ruin this relationship. He'd have to find out later who al-Saud's source was in the administration. "His position will be exactly the same as mine before he's confirmed—or he won't be in the position."

Al-Saud nodded, smiled. "I am truly grateful. Our nations share a profitable history and a long alliance. I look forward to our relationship blossoming even further, especially during a Chandler administration."

"As do I. Saudi Arabia is our best and most natural ally in the region now. I'm sick and tired of the outsize influence Tel Aviv has had on my government for far too long."

"Something else we can agree on," al-Saud said.

They chatted pleasantly for another twenty minutes and agreed to the date and time of their next meeting. The ambassador even escorted him to the front door, where they shook hands, all smiles.

And all of it caught on video by two Israeli Mossad agents.

24

Myers was in bed reading a tablet, with a pair of reading glasses perched on the end of her nose. Even though she was wearing silky lingerie, she looked as if she were studying for an exam.

Pearce quietly entered the room. It was after ten o'clock. He crossed over to the bed and kissed her. "Sorry I'm late. Long freaking day."

"Aren't they all?" she said.

He loosened his tie. "What's that you're reading? Something racey, I hope."

"Fifty Shades of Financials. Thought I'd better go over them before the meeting tomorrow."

"Germany." Pearce wanted to raise the security question again with her but thought better of it. "Mind if I catch a quick shower?"

"A shower sounds great, especially if you plan on getting lucky tonight, mister." Myers pulled off her glasses and set them on the night-stand. "How was the hearing?"

Pearce sat on the bed, untied his shoes. "Like a root canal without the novocaine."

"That bad?"

"Not really. They kept it pretty informal. Mostly they wanted me to commit to keeping the pig trough slopped. I couldn't do it."

"Good. Lane wouldn't want you to. I can make a few calls if you need me to."

"I'll hold you in strategic reserve."

"How did the time with Grafton go? Any success in the calling campaign?"

Pearce placed his dress shoes neatly in the closet rack and tossed his socks in the hamper. "Smiling and dialing. Supposedly I was trying to get votes lined up. It felt more like I was selling vinyl siding."

"Any commitments?"

"No. I guess that's better than flat-out rejections."

"They seldom plunge the knife in while looking you in the eyes," Myers said. "It's a backstabbing, mealymouthed kind of town."

"Thanks for the vote of confidence." Pearce frowned from a throbbing headache. Loosened his belt.

"Just trying to keep it real. But for what it's worth, the worm turns in both directions. Not committing might be a good thing at this point."

"It is what it is." He hung his pants up. Wrestled with telling her about the drone on the White House lawn and the threat from ISIS it contained. If she knew, she might not want to go to Germany. He decided against it.

Myers set her tablet on the nightstand. "How'd the Falcon Shield test go today?"

Pearce unbuttoned his dress shirt. "It's a great system. All we'd have to do is buy a thousand of them and put them everywhere we need them. Not gonna happen."

"At least it's another step in the right direction."

"Yeah, for sure."

"Something on your mind?"

He shook his head. "What will you do with the cash if the deal goes through?"

"If you're still thinking about that sailboat, well, I suppose now is the time I should tell you I get seasick."

"I'll settle for a lake house in the Rockies."

She smiled. "Someday, I promise. There's just so much to do. Now's not the time to run away."

Pearce clenched his jaw. He wasn't a coward. Never ran away from a fight in his life. But he was tired. So damn tired.

And he wanted a drink.

He stepped over to the clothes hamper and began to undress.

"I don't want to argue tonight," Myers said. She softened. "Not that we argue."

Pearce nodded. "Me neither. Sorry. My head's killing me." He peeled off his shirt, his back turned to her.

"What's *that*?" Myers said.

Pearce shut his eyes. Shit. He completely forgot. He heard her feet hit the floor. He turned around. She looked good. Mad, but good.

"I totally forgot to tell you. I'm sorry."

She leaned in close. Stared at the dark river of ink spread across his broad back. "A tattoo? Really?"

"I lost a bet with Ian."

"It's . . . huge."

Pearce spread his arms to his sides like Leonardo da Vinci's *Vitruvian Man*. The black ink tattoo was an abstract interpretation of an eagle in flight. The wings extended down the length of his arms all the way to the wrists. The tip of its beak extended up into the base of his skull.

"And you didn't think to tell me about this?"

"It was kind of a last-minute thing."

Myers sat back on the bed. "When did you get it?"

"This afternoon. Ian flew in with Dr. Rao. They put it on."

"I don't understand. You're supposed to be the head of a federal agency, not a biker gang."

He explained the purpose of the tattoo. She was impressed but not completely satisfied.

"I hope you like to wear long-sleeve shirts. You've got to keep that thing covered up while you're on the job."

"That's the plan. It touches my wrists but shirt cuffs will hide it." Pearce touched the back of his neck. "I keep my hair a little long anyway and any shirt collar will cover the rest."

"I feel like you kept this from me on purpose."

"I just didn't think about it. And it's temporary. It will come off by itself in ten or twelve days. Or I can use a chemical peel. It's just an experiment. If it bothers you that much, I can take it off right now."

She shook her head. "No, it's your call. What bothers me is that you're keeping a lot of things from me lately."

Pearce wondered if she knew about the drone this morning, after all. He gambled she didn't. "Not the important stuff. You've got a lot on your plate, too." Pearce kicked off his underwear and headed for the glass shower.

"Maybe I shouldn't go tomorrow. You're under a lot of stress, whether you want to admit it or not."

"No. I'm going to be up to my neck in it for the next few days anyway." Pearce flipped on the shower. Water poured out of the rain head.

"Okay, but promise me you'll go back to your therapy sessions this week."

"My schedule is slammed. Missing a few more sessions won't matter."

"I think that's a mistake, but you know what's best." She stepped over to the shower. Pearce was testing the water temperature with his hand. The glass was already fogging up from the steam. "I'll get back as soon as I can. I promise."

"Don't sell the company because of me," he said over his shoulder.

"I'm not. I'm doing it for us."

He turned around. "Sorry about the tat. It's no big deal, I promise. I'll take it off tomorrow—"

Myers traced the tattoo with her finger from the edge of his wrist up the back of his muscled arm. "I dunno. It's kind of growing on me." Myers slipped off her nightgown.

Pearce grinned. "Maybe we can get a matching set."

Myers pushed him gently into the shower and followed him in. "Let's talk about it later."

TARKOVSKY TOOK ANOTHER DRAG of his cigarette, then handed it back to Grafton. They were both naked beneath the sheets in her Georgetown loft.

"I met him today."

"Who?" She finished the last pull and stabbed out the butt in the ashtray on his chest.

"Pearce." He set the ashtray on the nightstand.

"Was that smart?"

"It was an accident. We were both at the White House. I introduced myself. He said he was late for a meeting. Seemed like he was in a hurry. Something urgent."

"It was."

Tarkovsky rolled onto his side to look her in the eyes. "How urgent?"

She shook her head. "You don't want to know."

He grinned. Touched the end of her nose with his finger. "Must I torture you for details?"

Her heart raced. He was a beautiful man. The catch of the city. She wanted to show him off to her friends and, better yet, her enemies. Rub it right in Ilene Parcelle's Botoxed face. "Better for you not to know. At least not yet."

"Tell me about Pearce, then."

"Surely you have a file on him?"

"Of course. But it is very thin. CIA Special Activities Division, Special Operations Group. Afghanistan, Iraq. But not much more than that. His record was expunged when my department was finally able to access it. Now he is a private security contractor." He didn't tell her about Ambassador Britnev and Pearce's suspected role in his death. It was a state secret. Worse. He was on a special SVR list President Titov kept.

"You know as much as I do. Except that Chandler hates his guts."

"Why?"

"He's an arrogant prick."

"So am I."

"That's why he intrigues me."

Tarkovsky rose up on an elbow, laughing. "Should I be jealous of this Pearce?"

"There's something about him."

"What?"

Grafton sat up in bed. She weighed her answer carefully. "Rage. You can see it pacing back and forth behind his eyes, like a caged tiger at the zoo. I'd hate to see what would happen if it ever got out."

"You little liar." Tarkovsky sat up, too. "You like dangerous men."

She smiled. "All men are dangerous. Some more than others."

"So Chandler hates him. What does it matter?"

"Pearce has Lane's ear. And worse, Pearce has Chandler's number. Chandler can't move forward with Pearce in the way. Neither can I."

"Do you want me to dig a little deeper on Pearce?"

"Yes. And someone else. Chandler mentioned an Iraqi general named Majid."

"Why? What's the connection?"

"Pearce and Chandler have a history with each other, and with him."

"Do you know what that history is?"

"If I did, I wouldn't need you to dig, would I?"

"I have a contact in the SVR that owes me a favor. I will reach out to him right away."

She flung the bedsheets aside and crawled on top of him, wet and ready. "Tomorrow will be soon enough."

25

Pearce and Grafton were in her office reviewing the list of phone numbers and talking points for the day's round of calls. Pearce was impressed with Grafton's encyclopedic knowledge of the senators in question and even more so with their senior staffs. Nearly a quarter of the Senate was age seventy or older; several were in their eighties. If Hillary Clinton had been flummoxed by fax machine technology in 2009, then how many other septuagenarians were likewise unable to keep up with the startling technological changes today? Whatever thoughts the aging Senate might have on drone tech, they would have to have been informed by their younger, more knowledgable staff, who formulated most of their policy positions anyway.

Pearce and Grafton divided up their workload accordingly. Pearce would call the senators to massage their egos and ease their concerns after Grafton vetted the appropriate staff personnel. It was a decent plan, and Pearce knew Grafton had a long record of success in corralling votes for Chandler.

"You about ready?" Grafton asked. She slipped a sheet of paper across her desk.

"Yeah. I guess so." He had ten calls to make, the first to Senator Floyd, a follow-up.

She saw his reluctance. "It won't be that bad. Just close your eyes and think of England."

Pearce picked up the phone. "Isn't Floyd a waste of time?"

"Floyd's been telling his staff you practically bitch-slapped him in the hearing. But he figures that if you're willing to speak your mind when your nomination is on the line, you won't hold back when it really counts." Grafton's offered a half smile. "Good job, cowboy."

Pearce glanced at his iWatch: 9:55 a.m. Better to wait a few more minutes for Floyd to get settled in before he called. But it wasn't Floyd he was worried about. It was today's twelve o'clock ISIS deadline that was really on his mind.

THE OVAL OFFICE

President Lane, Vice President Chandler, and Ambassador Tarkovsky were seated on the couches and chairs facing one another. Coffee and croissants sat on the table in front of them. Chandler tried to hide his obvious enthusiasm behind a mask of thoughtful reflection. Lane's hands were folded, his face dark with skepticism as Tarkovsky spoke.

"The United States and Russia have many more things in common than not, including our enemies, especially ISIS. We share the same strategic imperative to eradicate them."

"Some of my advisors think you only oppose ISIS because you support Assad, a tyrant and despot." Lane reached for his coffee.

"We only support Assad for the same reason your country supported Mubarak, Qaddafi, Saddam, and even Assad himself, as well as his father, in the not-too-distant past. Not because you are in favor of totalitarianism, but because you knew they were the strongest hands to keep the lid on the revolutionary and radical forces always simmering underneath."

"In the long run, it's never in our best interests to support dictators," Chandler said. "That puts both of our countries on the wrong side of history."

Tarkovsky nodded thoughtfully. He anticipated Chandler's rebuttal. The two of them had already rehearsed today's conversation by phone. Chandler knew that Lane would get his back up if the two of them appeared to be making common cause. Chandler decided a little good cop/bad cop was in order.

"The wrong side of history? Perhaps," Tarkovsky said. "But history has many sides. By abandoning the shah, you got the Iranian revolution. By pushing us out of Afghanistan, you got the Taliban and gave al-Qaeda an operating base. By toppling Saddam, you got ISIS. By toppling your ally Qaddafi, you gave ISIS a foothold in Libya. By promoting the Arab spring in Egypt, Mubarak fell, and the Muslim Brotherhood took power—until a right-wing coup by the army overthrew them. If I may be so bold, you Americans have a strange history of destroying secular regimes in the Middle East, and yet you are surprised when they're replaced by theocratic dictatorships."

Lane sat up. "May I be frank?"

Tarkovsky smiled. "Of course."

"My hunch is that President Titov wants to fight ISIS only to bolster his credibility with the West in order to end the sanctions we've imposed on his government for the invasion of Crimea. This is all about economics, not security."

"Economics and security are inseparable. The purpose of the 9/11 attacks was to collapse the American economy. If ISIS seizes the oil fields of the Middle East, they will have an even greater weapon to use against every Western economy."

Lane sat back, tenting his fingers in front of his face as if in prayer, thinking. A strategic partnership with Russia wasn't the worst idea in the world—certainly out of the box. But his gut was telling him that something wasn't right.

He glanced up at the analogue clock on the wall. It read 11:55 a.m. He hadn't thought about the letter until now.

He caught Chandler studying his face.

"Something on your mind, Clay?"

Chandler shrugged. "Maybe it was just a hoax." He spoke cryptically. Tarkovsky was out of the loop.

Lane glanced back at the sweeping second hand. "We'll know soon enough."

26

The Airbus A380 taxied to a stop on runway 36R, facing due north (000 true), waiting for permission from the tower to take off. The red-and-white kangaroo logo on its eighty-foot-high tail glimmered in the late, high morning sun. Qantas purchased the world's largest commercial airliner in order to create what had been, until recently, the world's longest nonstop commercial flight of 8,578 nautical miles from Dallas/Fort Worth to Sydney, Australia. With a cruising speed of 560 miles per hour, the flight time was just under seventeen hours. Today's particularly efficient ground crew put them on the flight line two minutes ahead of schedule.

Qantas Flight 8 was oversold again and every seat occupied. Five hundred twenty-five passengers were located in three different classes on two flight decks arranged like a London double-decker bus.

To make the long trans-Pacific flight, the A380's four turbofan engines required more than eighty-five thousand gallons of highly flammable aviation fuel stored in tanks located in the wings. The nine-foot-long turbofan blades spun at supersonic speeds, feeding air into the three-thousand-degree inferno of the engine's combustion chamber.

If the spinning blades ever broke off, they'd turn to white-hot titanium shrapnel. The plane, in effect, was a flying gasoline bomb, and the supersonic blades were giant spinning matches. An exploding engine could also damage or disable wing surfaces, landing flaps, and a dozen other critical airframe components, along with the plane's hydraulic, electrical, and braking systems.

Sitting on the tarmac, fuel tanks full and cabin crowded to the gills with anxious passengers, the A380 finally received the tower's signal for departure.

The captain pushed the throttles forward and released the brakes. The turbines whined as the engines accelerated. In order to achieve takeoff, the A380 had to reach a speed of at least 170 miles per hour. When the engines were fully engaged, the plane would reach that speed after covering nearly ten thousand feet of 36R's thirteen-thousand-foot runway. Through the miracle of brilliant human engineering, the fully loaded A380 could cover that distance in just seventy-eight seconds.

Forty seconds down the runway, the copilot pointed at a familiar shape speeding just a few feet off the tarmac directly toward them. He shouted in his headset.

"DRONE!"

No way to avoid it.

The five-pound drone slammed directly into the number-three engine. The captain didn't panic. The spinning forward fan blades were like a giant Cuisinart married to the world's biggest vacuum cleaner. They were safety-engineered to suck in and push out all kinds of objects while in flight, including torrents of ice and water and even frozen birds. With any luck the drone would be shredded, burned, and spat out the other end like a hapless duck.

Unfortunately, the drone was carrying a small payload of brick-orange Semtex, a plastic explosive.

The Semtex erupted.

The blades on the forward fan disc in number-three engine ripped away like loose teeth. In less than a second, the titanium fragments exploded through the compressor and combustor assemblies like a shotgun blast, shredding gearboxes, casings, vanes, discs, and bearings.

The plane shuddered.

People screamed.

27

Lane, Pearce, Chandler, and DHS Secretary Eaton sat around the long table in the Situation Room. The attorney general, Julissa Peguero, was on a secured videoconference display as was Lane's national security advisor, Jim Garza, on board a flight from California. Eaton had briefed Peguero and Garza earlier by phone at Lane's request as soon as the first attack occurred.

"Dallas, Chicago, Atlanta, Los Angeles," Eaton said. "The four busiest airports in the United States."

"Four damaged aircraft at four different locations at nearly the same time can't be a coincidence," Garza said.

"And no fatalities?" Lane asked.

"The closest was Dallas," Eaton said. "Captain's a hero. She was past V-one. Not enough room to hit the brakes so she took it up and around and brought it back down. No serious injuries but a lot of angry customers. I asked Qantas to file it as a mechanical problem for now. They were good enough to comply."

"The Airbus is an amazing airplane," Chandler said. "They're engineered to stay aloft on three engines."

"Even one, in an emergency. But that was good flying for sure." As a former air force pilot, Lane appreciated more than the rest what that kind of emergency situation felt like. He made a mental note to call the captain later and congratulate her personally.

"What about the other aircraft?" Peguero asked.

"Same attack profile but the engines were disabled while the planes were still on the ground. No serious injuries. All of the attacks occurred between twelve oh five and twelve seventeen Eastern Standard Time."

"And still no news reports?" Chandler asked, staring at the video monitors. None of them displayed any of the disabled jet aircraft.

"The networks were compliant, and they promise to sit on the affiliates," Eaton said. "But I'm not sure how long they'll keep quiet on this, even if it is a national security issue."

There was already a media plan in place for just this kind of contingency that the broadcast and cable news network executives had agreed to. It wasn't out of a sense of patriotism. If the media put out the word that the nation's airports were under attack, not only would the public panic but so would stock markets around the world, including media stocks. Air travel and aviation transportation were key components of the global economy.

"Likelihood that another drone attack will occur today?" Lane asked.

"Hard to say," Eaton said. "But at least we've got some breathing room for now."

"Then let's use that to our advantage," Lane said. He turned to Pearce. "Why weren't there any fatalities? They could've killed hundreds, even thousands."

"Either it was a technical failure on their part—which I doubt—or they're exercising restraint."

"Why do you doubt it?" Chandler asked.

"From what little video we've seen from Dallas and Atlanta, those eight-bladed octocopters could've easily carried enough explosive material to take out the entire engine assembly—but they didn't. Me? If I wanted to take the plane down, I would've delivered the package straight to the wing where the fuel tanks are located."

"I agree," Garza said. "So why didn't they?"

"I don't know, unless they're sending a message."

"What message?" Chandler asked.

"They're saying, 'You see what we could've done. Unless you want us to escalate, you better do as we say immediately.'"

"Sort of like holding a knife blade against our throats," Garza said. "Ready to chop our heads off if we don't comply."

"Makes sense," Peguero said.

"Except ISIS doesn't stop with the threat. They always cut the head off," Chandler said. "We need to quit fooling around and start making plans for an escalated bombing campaign. Take out every strategic site in the Caliphate we can find while minimizing civilian casualties."

Pearce shook his head. "The only way to completely exterminate the Caliphate is to wage a total ground war with American boots on the ground. That means killing a lot of people. Some will call it genocide. Are we prepared to do that?"

"If we do, we just prove to the rest of the Muslim world we're the butchers and war criminals they say we are," Peguero said.

"I don't give a shit what the rest of the Muslim world thinks," Garza said. "This is war."

"Then you better give a shit about all of the Americans who already hold that opinion of our government," Peguero said. "There's no political support within our party for an American ground war, let alone a mass extermination event."

"For the record, I'm against American boots on the ground as well," Chandler said, careful to support Lane's campaign position publicly.

Lane frowned. "We don't need to discuss the ground war option yet. I need to know exactly what we're dealing with and what other options are available to us right now."

Chandler hid his surprise. Lane had just said "yet." Apparently a ground war was, indeed, a viable option for him. That was the crack in the armor he'd been waiting for.

Lane turned to Pearce. "Troy, you're the drone expert here. If ISIS wants to escalate these attacks, what can we do to stop them?"

Pearce shook his head. "That's the problem. It's all low-tech, low-cost, off-the-shelf stuff. They're so small that radar isn't much good. They aren't much more advanced than the VTOL drone that delivered the threat in the first place. Depending on battery pack and payload weight, these octocopters could have forty-five minutes or more of flight time. Assuming the same people operating them are the same ones behind the VTOL, it means these new drones have prepro-grammed flights, shielded avionics, and proprietary firmware. Our conventional anti-drone systems won't work against them, as we saw yesterday. Short of getting eyes on them early on, it won't be possible to stop them with any degree of certainty."

Eaton's phone rang. She picked it up. Her face darkened. She cov-ered the receiver. "Denver just got hit."

"Damage?" Lane asked.

"A Delta 737, outbound for San Francisco. On the ground, no injuries."

"That's a twin-engine jet," Pearce said. "Not good." He was thank-ful Myers's flight had long since departed for Frankfurt. She was some-where over the Atlantic now. "What's the chatter like out there?"

Eaton shrugged. "Social media is blank. And the terrorist channels we follow are just as quiet."

"You'd think they'd be shouting from the rooftops about this," Pearce said.

"Unless it's a very small circle of operatives. A single cell, based here," Garza said. "No one's talking about it out there because no one else knows about it. It's all about opsec for them right now."

"But they always talk about it. They're the best propagandists in the world," Chandler said.

"After the fact," Eaton said. "We're still in the middle of an attack."

"If we can't shoot them down, what are our options?" Lane asked.

"Shut down the airports, ground all flights," Eaton said.

"That might be exactly what they want. The whole point of attack-ing New York was to panic Wall Street," Pearce said. "The economic collapse of Western governments is one of ISIS's stated goals."

"But we can't just ignore this and hope it will go away," Chandler insisted. "Maybe the next strike really will take down one of these planes. Then we'll have blood on our hands." Chandler was angling for a way to introduce his Russian security ploy.

"Maybe waiting is a chance worth taking," Peguero said. "Why assume they'll start killing now?"

"Because that's who these animals are." Chandler saw the disapproving look in Peguero's eyes. "Terrorists are the animals, of course. Not Muslims."

Pearce couldn't believe his ears. Chandler must be atoning for his guilty conscience. He didn't remember the visiting congressman having such politically correct sensitivities back in Iraq.

Lane's eyes narrowed. "Don't doubt for a moment my intention to do whatever it takes to defend my country. But I won't be shoved headlong into a war that nobody wants."

"Nobody ever wants war, Mr. President," Garza said. "But war comes knocking anyway. I respectfully suggest it's time for us to answer the door."

Lane drummed his fingers on the table, weighing options.

Pearce could see the stress in his face. Couldn't blame him. He'd hate to be in his position right now. Pearce felt useless as crap. He racked his brain for an alternative. Something rattled loose. "What if we have the FAA issue a warning? Something to the effect that the National Airspace System is experiencing a temporary software glitch. Keep all current landing schedules intact for aircraft still in the air but stop all outbound flights. That puts all of the planes back on the ground in good order and maybe it won't cause a panic."

"That's a good idea," Eaton said. "But it's still going be disruptive as all get-out for the airlines."

"Not as disruptive as their jets crashing all over the country," Garza said.

"For how long?" Chandler asked.

"Twenty-four hours," Pearce said. "We can always extend it."

"Then what?" Chandler asked. "What does that get us?"

"Time," Pearce said.

28

"Time for what? You just said that we can't stop these things."

"I was just out on a demo yesterday. Gave me an idea. There was an old plan that my colleague Dr. Ashley put together a few years ago. It was called Gorgon Sky. It was based on the Pentagon's Gorgon Stare program."

"Gorgon Sky was WAPS, right? Wide-area persistent surveillance?" Eaton asked.

"Exactly. We can put the entire nation under continuous real-time physical surveillance from fifteen thousand feet. See anything that's out of doors, including small commercial drones that might be flying in for an attack."

"How's that even possible? And how long would it take?" Lane asked.

"We can loft our inventory of Predators, Reapers, and other persistent platforms. Some of them are already equipped with ARGUS-IS camera pods. We can retrofit the others. We'd have to roll them all out as units come on line, and it wouldn't be completely comprehensive, but it would be better than nothing."

"You're talking about Total Information Awareness," Peguero said. "I'm not comfortable with that."

Pearce's gut boiled. More PC bullshit from another liberal attorney. Pearce and Myers had deployed variations of ARGUS-IS when they took on the Castillo cartel and the Iranian Quds Force that came over the border, but since then the civil libertarians had shut the programs back down. Even the Domain Awareness Systems that connected citywide surveillance cameras for crime deterrence had been under legal attack all over the country.

"What exactly is your concern?" Pearce asked.

Peguero frowned. "Putting every American under surveillance means we're going to observe many instances of questionable behavior, including criminal behavior."

"And why is that a problem?" Lane asked.

"The Constitution forbids warrantless search and seizure. What Mr. Pearce proposes would be a clear violation of that idea."

Pearce took a deep breath, trying to tamp down his rising anger. "Just so I'm clear, if we happen to catch a rape in progress, you don't want to notify the local PD and stop it because we don't have a warrant?"

"Don't be ridiculous. I was thinking more along the lines of drug transactions and other nonviolent crimes."

"So you wouldn't want to prosecute drug dealers even if you had the visual evidence?"

"Not without first obtaining a warrant."

"Unbelievable," Pearce said. He was thinking something far worse. His face showed it.

Lane leaned forward. "I brought in the attorney general just for this kind of insight, Troy. Whatever actions we take to stop this terror attack, we want to be sure we don't tear up the Constitution while we're doing it."

"So you agree with her?" Pearce asked.

"I'm willing to at least listen."

"The Constitution isn't a mutual suicide pact," Garza said. "This 'security versus privacy' debate is great for dorm room bull sessions, but right now we've got a real problem on our hands and Troy's handing us the tool to fix it."

Thank God for Jim Garza, Pearce thought. The former Green Beret had served the president well in the last crisis. Didn't pull any punches. Myers was right about people like Peguero. Lane had been forced to surround himself with all kinds of political appointees who wouldn't necessarily reflect the president's best interests. But Lane wouldn't be served by his trying to win a civil liberties debate with the AG. He needed to find solutions.

"Look, I don't care what anybody does with the nonrelevant data that comes in. That's for you all to decide. Maybe we can find a way to put the attorney general in the information loop."

Lane turned to the attorney general. "That work for you, Julissa?"

Peguero shrugged. "I'm looking for safeguards. That's all I'm asking."

"I'll have Dr. Ashley contact your office," Pearce said. "You two can figure out some kind of system." He turned to the president. "But I wouldn't let that slow down the Gorgon Sky deployment if you want to get a visual on these drones before they hit, and maybe even their operators. It's not perfect but this is about the best we can come up with right now."

"Agreed," Lane said. "But have this Dr. Ashley loop in Julissa at the earliest possible moment."

"But there's still one problem," Pearce said.

"What's that?" Lane asked. Pearce heard the tension in his voice.

"It's crazy to think that drones are their only option."

"You mean a conventional attack?"

"Yes. And possibly worse. The letter used the phrase 'unquenchable fire.' That might be figurative but I doubt it. No telling what they'll hit us with next, or where. But it sounds like it's leading up to something we don't want to see."

"Best guesses?" Lane asked the room.

"ISIS was talking about using drones as a delivery system for nuclear materials a while back," Garza said.

"That's right," Chandler said. "I remember that now."

Lane leaned forward. "What's the likelihood of that, Jim?"

"All we heard were rumors. I wouldn't put too much stock in it."

"They could just keep hitting the airports," Eaton said. "That would be devastating enough."

Pearce shook his head. "But now we know they've done that, so they'll assume we're prepping defenses against it. They'll try something else. Surprise is their best weapon."

"They hit airports today. We all agree that's an economic attack as much as a political one," Eaton said. "I wouldn't be surprised if other economic targets are next."

"Ports, the power grid. Jiminy Christmas," Chandler said.

"Another reason to put Gorgon Sky up fast," Garza said.

"We have a list of key infrastructure facilities. We'll quietly bump up the threat level. Get more locals out on the beat and deploy ours, too," Eaton said.

"Good." Lane turned to Pearce. "Troy, I'm putting you in charge of reviving Gorgon Sky."

"Me? The Senate hasn't even voted on me yet."

"I don't care. This is a national emergency. I'll have an executive order drafted authorizing you to act on my behalf. Pull any piece of equipment you need from any department and put it up in the air as fast as you can. Anybody gives you grief, call me directly."

"Yes, sir. But the word will get out now. Has to if I'm going to be pulling assets."

"Do what you have to, but keep it strictly need-to-know, and tell them to keep quiet for now."

Chandler shook his head. "Even when we get Gorgon Sky up, we're still just playing defense. We need to go on offense."

"Give me an option other than American boots on the ground," Lane said.

Chandler fought back his desire to gloat. This was exactly the moment he'd been driving toward. "Ambassador Tarkovsky said the Russians are prepared to put their boots on the ground."

"Are you kidding?" Garza said. "Why would we invite the fox into the henhouse?"

Chandler turned toward Garza's image in the monitor. "We can't beat these criminals with just airstrikes. We've been pounding them from the air for years. We need troops on the ground and we aren't sending ours. Do you have a better suggestion?"

"Yeah. Let's go straight to the source. Tell al-Mahdi or whoever the hell is in charge over there that sand turns to glass at seventeen hundred degrees Celsius, and we have the firecracker to make that happen if he doesn't back off this right now."

"And if he denies he's any part of this?" Chandler asked.

"He signed the letter, didn't he?" Garza said.

"Technically, he didn't. It was printed on a laser jet," Peguero said. "We're not even sure if he's alive. Getting some kind of confirmation about the source makes sense, legally."

"He can always blame a lone wolf working on his own. That way he can take credit but not the blame," Pearce said.

"If there's a lone wolf behind this, then we need to shake up every radical mosque in the country. Detain every radical imam as an enemy combatant," Chandler said.

Peguero's dark eyes widened. "I'm surprised at you, Mr. Vice President. You're a trained lawyer. Surely you know that would be a clear violation of the civil rights and religious liberties of Muslims."

Chandler threw up his hands. "Lincoln was a lawyer, too. Didn't prevent him from suspending habeas corpus. Extreme times require extreme measures."

Peguero turned to Lane. "I can't condone that kind of action at all, Mr. President. And neither will the party leadership." As the daughter of illegal Dominican immigrants amnestied under Reagan, the attorney general was particularly sensitive about the rights of the foreign born.

Pearce couldn't believe his ears. He fumed. *We're in a war, not a pillow fight. These people still don't get it all these years after 9/11. These social justice warriors will get us all killed.*

"Let's bring in Ambassador al-Saud for some perspective. I think he'll agree with me," Chandler said.

"Bring a Saudi government official into a national security meeting?" Pearce asked.

"Why not?" Chandler protested. "He's a great friend to our country and a staunch ally in the War on Terror. He'll tell you that the radical mosques are the rat nests behind a lot of these shenanigans."

"For one thing, Saudi Arabia has a horrific human rights record, and as far as I know, the Saudi ambassador is not an American constitutional scholar," Peguero said. "I don't see what value he brings to the table."

Lane held up a hand, frustrated. "All right, everybody, let's put a lid on this. Give me a minute to process." Lane stood and crossed the room, lost in thought.

Pearce pulled out his smartphone and started scrolling through his list of contacts. Pulled up Dr. Ashley's. He couldn't pull off the Gorgon Sky project without her. He sent her a priority text, encrypted.

Lane crossed back over to the table but remained standing. "Jim, I like your idea. Call the director of national intelligence. See if he can get someone in al-Mahdi's face in the next few hours."

"The CIA won't have a direct contact. We'll have to go third party."

"Can we get a direct message to him at least?"

"Probably. But it will have to be all hand-carry. ISIS is scared to death of the NSA, even with encrypted cell phones. That means more people in the loop on our end. I can't guarantee the message will remain secure."

"We'll have to take the chance. Let's do it."

"I'll get right on it," Garza said, signing off.

"Melinda, contact the FAA. Let's get these planes grounded for twenty-four hours. We'll use the software glitch as the excuse. And whatever happens, we've got to keep the media away from this story for as long as we can."

Eaton nodded. "Understood, Mr. President."

Lane turned to Pearce. "Get Gorgon Sky launched as fast as you can. And for heaven's sake, keep pushing on an anti-drone solution."

Pearce nodded. Didn't have the heart to tell the president there just weren't any good ones at the moment. He asked himself if Ian might have any ideas. Pearce sighed. No. Ian didn't.

"Everybody, stay close and expect a call from my office. I've got a bad feeling the day's a long way from over," Lane said. "I'll want all hands on deck if something breaks."

"The only easy day . . ." Pearce muttered to himself, his voice trailing off.

Lane forced a grim smile. "Is yesterday."

29

The Cool Breeze bar was packed with tourists and locals perched on high seats around club tables enjoying Manhattans and daiquiris and good Czech beer. The music from the small stage echoed on the ancient stone floors and arched brick ceiling. The place looked more like a medieval church basement than a jazz joint. The band was Indian. They played bass, sax, drums, and a sitar. Most of the patrons were talking among themselves, ignoring the skilled improvisations.

Mehmet Zorlu had never heard that kind of jazz before. He liked it. He sat at the end of the long mahogany bar with the locals. He was bald and clean-shaven, with a thick braid of gold chain looped beneath his double chins. In his sport coat, slacks, and loafers, he looked more like Alfred Hitchcock than a member of the Turkish mafia. One of his underlings nicknamed him "Tony Soprano" a few years back. He liked the American TV show, so he took no vengeance on the fool, a second cousin. He stabbed out his cigarette butt in a crowded ashtray and lit another one with a Zippo.

Zorlu knew the owners, Fipps and Robson, a couple of British expats. They were both behind the bar tonight, mixing drinks and laughing it up with the regulars. His sources inside the MIT, Turkey's National Intelligence Organization, had vetted the two men three years ago. If they were MI6 or CIA, they hid it well. High-dollar escorts were always in tow and dirty money swam in their cash registers. Some of that dirty money he'd placed there himself over the last year. He liked them, and their whores.

He checked his watch again. The courier was late. He wiped away a bead of sweat from his massive forehead. It was cold outside but hot enough inside to bake *pide* on the butt-strewn floor. He finished off the martini—his third—with a last gulp, then plopped the olive into his mouth. He caught the eye of Fipps, a blond with a brush cut and bulging biceps. Zorlu pointed at his empty martini glass. Fipps nodded and grabbed a clean glass and got to work.

Zorlu checked his watch again. The call he received came from the very top of his organization. A pickup, then a delivery. Very simple. Only not so simple. "Fail to receive the envelope and you die. Fail to deliver it, and you'll be skinned alive. You and your wife, your mistress, and your sons."

Where the hell was that drink?

He knew what lay ahead. He'd made the trip once before. A two-hour ride in the back of car if he was lucky, in the trunk if he wasn't. Bag over his head, hands cuffed behind his back, straining his heavy shoulders. And then another trip by boat. There he would meet the man who would take him the rest of the way to Raqqa. A man he'd only met once face-to-face. A disturbing face. Cruel and certain, like all such fanatics. His contact in the ISIS oil-smuggling ring he ran between Syria and Turkey. They had a sort of trust, thin as a piece of old thread, but still intact. When Zorlu called him, he heard the suspicion in his voice. Suspicion that made him even more dangerous. Still, what choice did he have? He had his orders and his ISIS contact was his only hope.

The fat Turk stole a glance at the German woman seated next to him. Wide hips, big breasts. Very nice. He remembered his years in Düsseldorf fondly. Money, drugs, or force had spread many pairs of such legs in his youth.

Fipps approached with the new martini and set it down in front of him. He leaned in close. Nodded toward the staircase.

Zorlu turned around with difficulty. The courier, he guessed. A Turkish kid in his twenties. Leather jacket, long hair, dark. A British passport in his pocket, no doubt. One of the infamous Tottenham Turks, a violent gang his own organization used to distribute drugs in the U.K. in exchange for guns. His nervous young eyes scanned the room. No doubt he received the same grim threats.

Skinned alive wasn't a metaphor.

For a moment he weighed the option of running. He carried a forged Panamanian passport and had enough cash stashed away in banks in Cyprus and Portugal to live modestly for a long while. He could start over. Even make a life for himself in the States. But he thought of his sons and their flayed corpses. He had seen such things. His stomach soured at the thought and he pushed it away.

Zorlu picked up the martini and drained it in one long gulp. He took one last puff on his cigarette, then crushed it in the overflowing ashtray. This message he was supposed to hand-deliver to the Caliph must be damned important.

Zorlu twisted around in his seat. The kid's eyes finally landed on him. Zorlu acknowledged the courier with a nod, and with a sideways lean of the head, pointed the Tottenham boy toward a door leading to the back room.

Zorlu lifted his heavy girth off of the chair. *Maybe it will all work out,* he hoped as he made his way through the crowded, smoke-filled room. He better take a piss before the car ride, though. Otherwise it could be a long night in the trunk lying in his own cold stink.

30

"Thank you all for getting back here on such short notice," Lane said. Everyone present was seated around the table in the Situation Room.

Garza had come straight from the airport but Peguero was still stuck in California, thanks to the FAA's "software glitch" grounding of her commercial flight. Pearce had commandeered an extra office in the EEOB and spent the previous four hours pulling together the updated Gorgon Sky plan with Dr. Ashley's help. Like Peguero, she was stuck in Texas at the university where she worked, but Pearce was in the room.

Chandler sat between Eaton on his right and, for the first time in the crisis, with Grafton on his left.

Grafton's presence bothered Pearce no end. Why was she in the loop? But it was al-Saud's presence that really chafed his hide.

"His Excellency, the ambassador, has kindly agreed to offer his opinion on the matters before us," Lane said. "DHS has briefed him on the events so far. The ambassador has assured me that everything we discuss in this room will remain in this room."

"He's willing to withhold vital information from his own government?" Pearce asked, his voice thick with skepticism.

"Yes, Mr. Pearce. More than willing. This is a time of crisis, not politics. However, as soon as you are prepared for me to speak with Riyadh, I will do my best to accurately portray the opinions expressed here today. But let me assure you all now that my government stands ready to do whatever is in its power to assist you at this time."

"That's all we can ask for," Chandler said.

"Have you read the letter, Mr. Ambassador?" Grafton asked. Her green eyes locked with his.

Al-Saud nodded, smiling. "In both Arabic and English. It appears to be authentic."

"The good news is that there haven't been any more reports of drone attacks on any aircraft at any airport since Los Angeles. That doesn't mean there won't be any more, but our assumption is that they're waiting to see if we'll raise that flag by noon tomorrow."

"Mr. Ambassador, we have several options on the table right now," Lane said. "But the most extreme option that has been put forth is to launch an all-out ground assault on ISIS and the Caliphate. What is your opinion?"

"I completely agree. You must retaliate. Any sign of weakness will only encourage *Daesh* to escalate their attacks."

"What about negotiations?" Peguero asked from the video monitor.

"Negotiations? Perhaps you can ask for death by beheading instead of crucifixion, but little else. *Daesh* intends to conquer the whole world and usher in the new age under the rule of the Mahdi. Some *Daesh* believe al-Mahdi is the Messiah. How does one compromise on one's holy faith?"

"How should we retaliate, short of American boots on the ground?" Lane asked.

"If I may speak freely, Mr. President."

"Yes, of course."

"You must put boots on the ground, as well as tanks and guns and whatever else you have in your arsenal. You must exterminate *Daesh* totally and completely, as soon as possible."

"Exterminate?" Peguero asked. "I don't like the sound of that."

Al-Saud stabbed the table with his finger. "Every day they survive, they grow, because their very existence proves to the Muslim mind that they have withstood your power. But they have an Achilles' heel. Unlike al-Qaeda and the other borderless gangs, *Daesh* has claimed territory and a capital city. To keep their legitimacy, they must defend the land. With the others, you are chasing the wind. But *Daesh* is a tree fixed in the ground. You must lay the ax to the tree and cut it down, roots and all."

Lane shook his head. "The American people are tired of war."

"As is the rest of the world, especially my part of the world that has borne the brunt of casualties and destruction. Nobody wants war less than we do, but war is here one way or another. Europe was tired of war, too, after the War to End All Wars, but that war gave rise to Hitler and the other fascists. The Western powers hesitated to act because they were tired of war. They could have strangled the fascist infant in its crib if they had acted resolutely. Their reluctance gave time for Hitler and the other fascists to grow in strength. In the end, the Allies came to understand that the only way to stop fascism in Europe and Asia was to wage a total war against it. Defeat it in the field. Occupation, trials, hangings."

"Terrorize the terrorists," Chandler said.

He's right, Pearce thought. *But what does that make us?*

"Exactly," al-Saud said, nodding toward Chandler. "I know the murderous radicals who kill in the name of Allah. Death in combat against the infidels is salvific for them. They won't negotiate and they won't compromise because there is nothing you can offer them that is better than an eternity in Paradise."

"We can get them on the express train to Paradise tomorrow by launching a squadron of B-52s tonight," Garza said.

Chandler nodded in agreement but kept his counsel. *No point in piling on,* he thought. *Let Lane reach his own conclusion in his own time.*

"Right now, I'm taking American troops on the ground off the table. What other suggestions do you have?"

The Saudi spread his long fingers on the table in front of him, weighing his thoughts. "As I'm sure you know, we recently formed ISMAT, an antiterror coalition of over thirty Muslim nations. But it still is not as effective as a single fighting force. NATO would be more powerful but even less committed. The Europeans share your concerns about war fatigue among their populations."

"What about the Russians?" Lane asked.

Bingo, Chandler thought.

Al-Saud raised a sculpted eyebrow. "Russian boots on the ground in the Middle East? I thought American foreign policy since Potsdam was designed to prevent that very outcome."

"It has been," Grafton said. "I know the Senate wouldn't support that idea at all." She felt Chandler's eyes burning holes in the side of her head. She didn't care. She knew her boss was pushing hard for a partnership with the Russians—after all, it had been her idea in the first place—but she sensed in that moment that Lane wouldn't go for it. Her goal was to get the United States into a war, not the Russians.

"What about an American-Russian alliance? Their boots, our air support. A limited action. I'm sure we can draw up some sort of boundaries to keep the Russians contained," Chandler said. "A shared burden with limited objectives."

Lane shook his head. "I'm with Troy. If we do this, it's got to be a maximum effort. Total war, total victory. Annihilate every last one of the bastards. I'm just not convinced yet it's time to go to those extremes. I made a campaign promise. If and when I'm ready to go to those extremes, I won't wage an undeclared war. I'll go to Congress first and get a formal declaration. If we're going to wage a total war, I want the full support of Congress and the American people."

"If we brought some of the congressional leadership into the loop, I think you'd see that they would be in complete support of a war declaration," Grafton said. "A total war to eliminate ISIS is something they could sell to their constituents, especially if we released the threat letter and told them about today's attack."

"If we release this information to the public, there will be a war whether you want one or not, Mr. President," Peguero said. "I strongly advise against inflaming public opinion."

Pearce ignored the AG. "If we're serious about going to war, then we need to talk about bringing back the draft."

"Amen to that," Garza said. "Everybody needs to pay the price for this, including the sons and daughters of Congress and Wall Street."

"What would convince you it's time to go to war, Mr. President?" al-Saud asked.

"Right now we're only dealing with a bloodless event. The kind of

war I'm talking about will be anything but bloodless, and a lot of innocents will get caught in the meat grinder. I still can't shake the fact that
over a million Iraqis might have died in the fighting since Saddam's fall.
I'll make that call for war, but only if the threat has truly escalated."

"For what it's worth, the Open Source Indicators show chatter's up,"
Eaton said. "The word's starting to get out on this mess and they're
expecting more. Apocalypse and all of that."

"I'd say al-Mahdi got our message," Chandler said.

Pearce shook his head. Something wasn't adding up. DARPA's OSI
program was designed as predictive software, vacuuming up every spec
of Big Data it could find on the Internet and in social media to try to
predict future events. A few years back, one Georgetown scientist
proved the concept by using Open Source Indicators to retroactively
predict the location of Bin Laden's hideout in Pakistan. If the OSI was
now predicting future trouble, it was probably right, but it didn't take a
crystal ball to figure that out, either. The ISIS assholes were always
talking about the end-times. The whole point was to provoke a war that
would bring the ultimate apocalypse. Why drop a private message on
the White House lawn instead of broadcasting the threat on global
social media?

Garza's cell phone rang. "Mr. President, I should take this."

"Of course."

Garza picked up. All eyes were on him. He listened, nodding.
Finally, "I appreciate the heads-up." He hung up the phone.

Garza turned to the rest of the room. "That was the DNI. The guy
who delivered our letter to al-Mahdi just arrived at the home of the CIA
chief of station in Sarajevo twenty minutes ago. Sort of."

"Meaning?" Lane asked.

"Technically, only his head arrived. In a box. *Allahu Akbar* was
branded into his forehead and an ISIS gold dinar coin was shoved in his
toothless mouth."

"Well, there's our answer," Chandler said. "Poor fellow."

"He was senior management in the Turkish mafia. Nobody will
miss him, not even his own mother," Garza said.

"Why were we dealing with the Turkish mafia?" Grafton asked.

"Dirty war, dirty friends," Eaton said.

Pearce checked his watch. Margaret should be landing in Frankfurt any minute now—if her plane didn't get blown out of the sky by a drone on approach.

"If the worst is over for today, I'm assuming we have until noon tomorrow before the next shoe drops," Lane said. "Let's make the best use of that time possible." He turned toward the Saudi ambassador. "Thank you for taking the time to come over and answer our questions."

"Of course. I'm happy to remain here as long as you need me."

"Mr. President, a word, if you don't mind," Pearce said. He stepped over to the far side of the room. Lane followed him.

"Is there a problem, Troy?"

"I don't think it's wise to keep the ambassador in the loop."

"Clay assures me he's reliable and discreet."

"The vice president forgets the ambassador is a Saudi national and a royal. He's honor bound to promote the interests of his government over ours. And frankly, I'm not sure why Grafton is here, either."

Lane studied Pearce's eyes. "Is there something you know that I don't? Or is this personal?"

"Let's just say I have some trust issues." Pearce glanced over Lane's shoulder. Saw Chandler glowering at him. "But it's your call, of course."

"I'll take it under advisement. Anything else?"

"No, sir. Just had to get that off my chest." He checked his watch. "The first Gorgon Sky launch was ten minutes ago, over D.C. New York will have one in about an hour. I should get back on the horn and see how the other systems are coming along."

"Thanks, Troy. For everything. We'll get through this."

"Yes, sir."

Pearce left the room. *No doubt we'll get through it*, he thought as he passed through the hallway. He just wasn't sure what they'd all look like on the other side of the wood chipper.

31

After passing through customs, Myers proceeded through the packed terminal, her mind still on the news flash that pulled up on her smartphone when she powered it on after landing. A "software glitch" in the U.S. National Airspace System sounded awfully suspicious to her but it was a plausible reason to ground air traffic around the country if that really was the problem. Pearce had left a terse voice mail telling her he missed her and to call him as soon as she landed but she decided to wait because she was running late. The American air traffic shutdown had international flight ramifications, especially for Germany, one of America's largest trading partners. With so many passenger and cargo flights scheduled for the United States now canceled, airport terminals around the world were jammed. Her Lufthansa flight circled above Frankfurt airport for an extra forty minutes before it could land. German customs was mercifully short.

The terminal Myers was passing through on the way to baggage claim was packed shoulder to shoulder. She loved airports. They always gave her the feeling of an adventure about to take place. It was particularly thrilling to hear so many languages being spoken here in Frankfurt, the third-busiest airport in Europe. In addition to German, she heard Hindi, Swahili, Polish, and Italian spoken around her as she made her way down to Level 1 and the baggage claim area.

Arabic, too.

And yet while she was appreciating the beautiful mosaic of global humanity all around her, she had been with Troy Pearce long enough to pick up some of his security habits. She was never a worrier either before or after becoming president, which was one of the reasons she refused Secret Service protection after she left office. Her first line of defense was keeping a low profile. A big security entourage, press coverage, and official welcomes only drew attention to her value as a target. As for her personal defense, she worked out and was very fit despite her adult-onset diabetes, and had trained in aikido for years, as much for fun as anything else. Back in the States, she had a concealed carry permit and was proficient in the use of a Ruger LCR 9mm snub-nosed revolver.

But Pearce was by nature a worrier, always on the lookout for potential trouble. He'd taught her how to spot suspicious behavior even in large, anonymous crowds. And the bearded man in the dark leather jacket and sunglasses on the far side of the luggage conveyor definitely fit the description of suspicious.

She queued up with the other passengers on her flight, waiting for the luggage to trundle onto the conveyor belt. She was careful not to put eyes on him, but kept his Nike Swoosh ball cap in her peripheral vision. She checked her phone again. A new message from Herr Grauweiler confirmed her new appointment time at seven p.m. local. She was grateful for the respite. That would give her enough time to check into her hotel and freshen up before the meeting. Maybe even catch a quick shower.

She easily caught a glimpse of her first piece of turquoise-colored luggage tumbling onto the far end of the belt, not far from the man in the leather jacket. Her eyes remained fixed on her eBag, but when she saw the man's earpiece, he suddenly commanded her full attention.

She never caught sight of the tall man in the graying beard several feet behind her, pushing his way politely through the impatient crowd, heading straight toward her position.

Myers's bag finally came within reach and she snagged it up. Her other turquoise bag was just a few feet farther back. By the time she looked back up, the man in the leather jacket had melted back into the crowd and she lost sight of him. She shrugged. Maybe he wasn't a problem, after all. As her second bag approached, she began to lean over to grab it, but felt a strong hand on her lower back—

"Let me get that for you, Margaret." The lanky German reached down and lifted her heavy bag effortlessly off the carousel and set it down next to the other to form a matching set.

"August! What are you doing here?"

"A little bird told me you would be arriving today."

"Troy." She tried to sound annoyed, but secretly she was happy he thought so highly of her security.

A broad grin emerged beneath his graying beard. "Well, yes. Of course."

"Come here." Myers threw her arms around the tall German's neck and they hugged. She hadn't seen August Mann since the time when she landed in a plane in the middle of a gunfight in the Sahara, snatching Mann and a wounded Pearce out of harm's way at the last possible second. Pearce had told her all about him later. Mann was head of Pearce Systems' nuclear demolition division and the first employee he ever hired into his organization. Mann was in Japan briefly while she was there earlier in the year but she didn't get the chance to see him then.

"I have a car waiting for you," Mann said. "We should go."

"There was a man earlier"—she caught a glimpse of the Nike Swoosh ball cap out of the corner of her eye; she turned—"there. That's him."

Mann shook his head. "One of mine. He's new to civilian work. I'll have to give him a reprimand for being so clumsy. Did you see the others?"

"There are others?"

Mann smiled. "You can reach out and touch two of them right now—if you're quick."

32

The four-armed quadcopter hovered high above the sprawling 3,400-acre ExxonMobil Baytown complex. The second-largest oil refinery in the United States, the Baytown facility refined 573,000 barrels of oil per day and produced 7.2 billion pounds of petrochemical products annually.

The noise of the drone's whirring rotors was masked by the industrial din of the bustling, 24/7 operation. The drone's familiar mechanical shape was hardly noticeable in the jagged skyline of overhead power lines, coker units, distillation towers, and storage tanks.

Except that Willard Dynes did notice it. Leaning against the company pickup with his hands cupped around his eyes, the rail-thin security guard tracked the drone's cautious movement, threading its way between twin steel towers.

Dynes was an amateur drone pilot and sold units part-time at the local hobby shop. Just last week he made an appointment with the refinery's assistant plant manager. Dynes had observed drones being used for engineering and safety inspections by plant personnel and wanted to know if he could apply for a job like that. But the assistant manager explained to Dynes that his associate's degree in criminal justice didn't qualify him for engineering work in one of the world's most complex chemical-processing facilities.

SOL, Dynes figured. *Shit out of luck.*

Dynes was no engineer, for sure, but he had a good eye for technical gear and an even better memory. The ExxonMobil engineers flew only

DJI Phantom 3s with ExxonMobil decals. The unmarked drone he saw hovering fifty feet off the ground directly over his head wasn't a DJI Phantom 3. Not by a long shot.

He didn't know what the hell it was.

But he knew it wasn't right. And the day-shift supervisor had put out the morning notice to report any suspicious persons or any unusual drone activity.

Well, a strange, unmarked drone was unusual, he figured. Better check it out.

Dynes dashed over to the steel staircase and began the long climb skyward. He flung himself up, pulling on the metal banisters, his steel-toed boots clanging on every other step. The equipment on his belt jangled and his baton clanged against the rails as he made the turns. By the third flight of stairs he was already winded. Damned Marlboros, he told himself. Time to quit. His thighs burned like acid as he finally reached the steel deck five stories up, gasping for air. He inhaled deeply with his hands on his knees, trying to catch his breath. He felt the asthma coming on. He tried not to panic. His hands shook a little and sweat poured over his face, but he kept his eye on the drone. It hadn't budged.

Now that he was close he could see three small red lights flashing on some kind of electronic component attached as a payload. The drone was hovering near some kind of a security box that had an antenna and three green lights, all lit solid. He watched the red flashing lights on the drone turn to flashing green, and the solid green lights on the box start to flash in the same rhythm as the ones on the drone.

They were synching.

Shit!

Better call it in.

His breathing quickened. He felt light-headed. He pulled out his radio from its holster but his trembling hand dropped the unit. It clanged on the deck by his feet and bounced over the side. He leaned over just in time to see the radio hit the concrete slab and explode into a confetti of solid-state components.

Shit!

Just then, the drone began beeping.

Something told him it was about to fly away.

Dynes grabbed for the pistol grip in his belt. The drone turned ninety degrees to face him. Its one unblinking camera eye mocked him like a giant flying fish-eye cyclops. Dynes pulled the trigger on his Taser. He missed.

Shit!

The two Taser darts passed over the top of the fuselage. The drone's blades whirred faster and it bolted vertically in a flash, but the fifteen feet of hair-thin Taser wire caught up in the drone's rotors and instantly tangled around the propeller shafts. When enough of the Taser's steel wire made contact with the rest of the drone's aluminum frame, the Taser's fifty-thousand-volt charge plowed into the onboard circuitry and fried the electronics. The drone's engines froze in midair and the vehicle plunged toward the ground, dead as a doornail. Despite his shaking hands, Dynes held tight to the pistol grip while the drone hung suspended on the end of his Taser wires like a limp carp on the end of his daddy's Popeil Pocket Fisherman.

"Gotcha, you sumbitch," Dynes said to nobody in particular. But then it suddenly occurred to him.

If this was an ExxonMobil drone, after all, he was in serious trouble.

33

"Showered in the gym downstairs," Pearce said.

"You need to sleep in your own bed, not the office sofa," Myers said. "Don't work yourself to death while I'm gone."

"Look who's talking. How'd the meeting go?"

"You mean with Herr Grauweiler? Or August? You should've told me, you know."

"You would've waved him off if I told you up front. But when you saw him there, I knew you'd fall in line."

"You know me that well, do you?"

"Yup." Pearce stifled a yawn. "So how'd it go with the kraut CEO?"

"Herr Grauweiler is an interesting man. Reserved, in the extreme. Asked all the right questions."

"But?"

"I don't know. I think I'll know more after my meeting today with his CFO and we go over all the financials."

"Sounds boring." Pearce took a sip of strong green tea. He had a bottle of booze in his desk drawer but didn't feel right hitting it this early, especially with Margaret on the phone.

"It is. But that's where the deal is. In the details. Speaking of which, how's the nomination coming along? Got your votes lined up?"

Pearce hesitated. He wanted to tell her what was going on but he knew if he did, she'd cut her trip short and come back as soon as she could. Better to hold off. He could fill her in after she got back if it came to that.

"Troy? You there?"

"Yeah, sorry. Still working on the votes. Grafton says we're a fifty-fifty proposition at this point."

"She knows her stuff. Say, what was the deal with the FAA glitch yesterday? Was that for real?"

Again Pearce hesitated. He didn't want to lie to her ever, but Lane instructed the room to keep a lid on things. "Oh, it was for real, all right." He checked his watch. "The planes should be back in the air in a couple of hours." Or so he hoped.

"Good. Otherwise it's a long swim home."

Pearce's desk phone buzzed on the secure line. "Hon, I've got to go. The president is calling."

"Oh, so you're a big wheel now, are you?"

"Only because I know you."

"Tell David I said hello."

"I will. Take care of yourself, and call me when you can."

"Will do." Myers hung up.

Pearce picked up the other line. "Pearce." The president's chief of staff, Jackie Gibson, was on the line. Told him to check his e-mail for some forwarded pictures and to please come over immediately. Pearce hung up and pulled the photos up on his smartphone as he headed out of his office, dreading what he might find when he arrived.

"IT'S DEFINITELY off-the-shelf technology," Pearce said. The photos on his phone were also loaded on one of the video monitors in the Situation Room. He was glad to see that neither al-Saud nor Grafton was present.

"Just like the other attacks," Chandler said.

"It's an Aerial Assault drone. It's used for wireless penetration testing. It's loaded with Kali Linux to test Wi-Fi networks for security weaknesses. Might even have some spoofing software on board, too, to see if they can trick a network into thinking it's a secure router so they can steal data from the user."

"Who in the world would sell something like that?" Chandler asked.

"The good guys. There are a bunch of white-hat hackers out there trying to make networks more secure. They use tools like this the same way an air force base will ask a SEAL team to try and infiltrate to see how well their security protocols are working."

Eaton switched the photo with a remote control. A thirtysomething bleached blonde in an orange jumpsuit pulled up. "The FBI office in Houston had a line on this woman. She's the head of a radical activist group trying to sue ExxonMobil for 'crimes against humanity and Gaia.' They were using this unit to try and find a way to hack into Exxon's mainframe to scout out any evidence from their database they could use in a federal lawsuit they're filing against Exxon next week."

"A private eye in the sky," Peguero said.

"Signs and wonders," Chandler said. "Signs and wonders."

"What does that mean?" Garza asked.

"Something my dear old memaw used to say. We live in interesting times, for sure."

"So the bottom line is that this isn't the other shoe we were waiting for," Lane said. He turned to Eaton. "Still no word of any new hostile actions?"

"No, sir."

"We dodged a bullet this morning, that's for sure," Chandler said.

"Doesn't mean our bad guys won't try to do exactly the same thing here or at another facility," Pearce said. "Or worse."

"That's comforting," Lane said.

"If ISIS managed to hack its way into the Baytown facility, it could wreck all of the control systems and shut down a half million barrels of production a day. That alone would cause a price spike if not outright panic in the oil markets. Imagine if they shut off every valve, pump, cooling system, thermostat, and heat exchanger. At the very least it would shut the entire plant down. It might take months, maybe even years, to find, repair, and replace all of the busted hardware. Worse, it could start a fire that might take weeks to contain."

"Is that the 'unquenchable fire'?" Peguero asked, quoting the letter again.

"Maybe." Pearce frowned with concern. "Hell, a decent hacker could just open up all the valves and dump hundreds of tons of poisonous chemicals into the Gulf. We'd have another BP disaster on our hands."

"Jesus, Mary and Joseph," Chandler said.

"We need to think through how we want to move forward," Garza said. "We're going to see more and more of these kinds of protest attacks that have nothing to do with ISIS. This technology empowers everyone, including our own homegrown idiots."

"We've raised a generation of malcontents fed on the themes of social injustice and disdain for the rule of law," Chandler said. "We shouldn't be surprised."

"Spoken like a country lawyer," Peguero said. "A southern country lawyer."

"Number one in my law school class and editor of the law journal," Chandler said with a practiced smile.

"The *Houston Chronicle* got wind of this story. I've asked them to sit on it for now," Eaton said.

"I think that's a mistake," Pearce said. "Tell them to put it out there."

"Why?" Eaton asked.

"Make the public aware that a drone was used to break the law, and that it could've caused some real damage. Maybe even cost a lot of jobs at one of the area's biggest employers. Get people pissed off," Pearce said.

"So we can get the public to help us spot more drone activity without knowing the real reason why," Eaton said, nodding. "Smart."

"Bottom line is we got lucky today and we can see what's at stake. I say we call in the Russian ambassador to talk about options," Chandler said. "We can't afford to waste any more time. It will take some planning to get everybody on the same page, let alone actually mount the operation."

Chandler's voice was like nails on a chalkboard to Pearce. What was his angle? "I disagree. There's no point in talking about fighting a war halfway around the world when our job is to find and neutralize the drone threat right here on our home turf."

"The war with ISIS has already started," Chandler said. "Better to let the Russians take it to them on *their* home turf with our airpower for cover."

"We always have the option to escalate later," Garza said. "But I agree with the vice president."

Chandler shifted in his chair, clearly frustrated. "What harm is there in talking with Russians? At least see what the options are?'

"Fair enough," Lane said. "Clay, make the call."

Chandler stole a glance at Pearce, smiled. "Will do, Mr. President."

"If an escalated air campaign really is on the table, we need to pull in General Onstot on this," Garza said. "But if we don't change the rules of engagement, it won't matter how many sorties we fly, they'll all come back fully loaded because the pilots are scared shitless of the JAG lawyers breathing down their necks."

"The ROEs are meant to protect civilian lives," Peguero said. "Indiscriminate bombing creates more terrorists than it kills."

"Rules of engagement are for the junior cotillion, not a war," Garza said. The Vietnam combat vet didn't suffer fools.

"Let's table the ROEs until Onstot gets here," Lane said.

"Shouldn't we loop in the SecDef?" Eaton asked.

The president shook his head. "Not yet. This thing will gallop out of control if we get too many horses in the traces. The fewer people in the loop, the better."

"Hate to ask it, but I'd really prefer that the White House press secretary be brought into this discussion," Eaton said. "It's one thing for me to call a media outlet and ask them to sit on a story for a day or two, but we need a media professional to spin this stuff if we want to try and keep control of the narrative."

"You're right. I'll call Alyssa in a few minutes. Anything else?"

Nobody responded. Everybody felt the weight of the moment. No need to add more to it. Lane looked at the clock.

"If our ISIS friends hold true, we've got just under two hours before they pull their next stunt. Let's convene back here at noon just in case they do."

"Is there any doubt, sir?" Pearce asked.

Lane shook his head, resigned. "No, I guess not."

34

Tarkovsky pointed the assault rifle at the masked gunman's head, just over the trembling shoulder of the woman the gunman was using as a human shield. The warehouse was dark and the gunman poorly lit.

"Get back, or I'll kill her!" the gunman shouted.

The woman screamed. "Help me!"

Tarkovsky pulled the trigger once. The weapon leaped in his hand. The gunman's head snapped backward as blood spattered on the wall behind him. The woman screamed again and dashed away into the shadows as the man's corpse thudded to the ground.

"Nice shot," al-Saud said.

"That felt remarkably real." The Russian smiled. He handed the rifle back to his Saudi host.

Al-Saud racked the Blue Fire wireless smart weapon, a laser simulator rifle with recoil, and pressed a remote control, bringing the lights back on and shutting down the 4K digital projector. "That was a judgmental training system program. JTS is an American device, of course, but our Special Security Forces use it in counterterror training. It's quite effective. My security staff trains on a similar unit at the embassy. I train on this one in my home because it's a pleasure."

"I enjoyed it immensely. I wouldn't mind getting one of these for myself."

"Someday you must visit my home in the desert. I have a live ammo shoot house on the property. Same JTS software but an even more lifelike close-combat experience."

"That is very kind of you."

"Coffee? Or something stronger?"

"Coffee will be fine, thank you."

Al-Saud pointed toward the stairwell that led from the expansive training room to the living area upstairs. The white brick Georgian mansion was a bright shining jewel mounted on top of a gently sloping hill surrounded by an acre of closely manicured emerald-green lawn.

Al-Saud ordered coffee from the attendant in his private salon, and the two of them sat down by the large brick fireplace. The room, like the rest of the house, was decorated in traditional American style. Tarkovsky didn't see any references to the Kingdom, Islam, or the desert. If he didn't know any better, he would have sworn an American lived here, not a member of the Saudi royal family.

Al-Saud looked completely relaxed in his turtleneck and slacks, like a man on vacation. Tarkovsky felt overdressed in his sport coat and tie.

"I'm so glad we're taking the time to get to know each other, Aleksandr. I was pleasantly surprised when you called yesterday."

Tarkovsky nodded. "We have only had the chance to speak briefly in public gatherings. I felt that a private conversation was in order. I didn't expect to be invited to your home. I'm honored."

"It's modest, but comfortable."

A lovely young Filipino woman entered the room, efficient and demure. She set the silver tray down and left wordlessly.

"How do you like it?"

"Black," Tarkovsky said. He assumed al-Saud was referring to the coffee.

"Same." The Saudi poured for both of them.

"If I may cut to the chase, Your Excellency—"

"Faisal. Please."

"Thank you. The reason why I wanted to speak with you was to discuss the situation with the Americans and ISIS. The Americans are unwilling to commit ground troops to battle ISIS on their own soil. However, my country stands ready to do so. But President Lane seems reluctant to accept the idea."

"And you've come to me because . . . ?"

"I would appreciate your assistance in helping me convince him."

"Strange you should raise this now. Only yesterday I was with the president and some of his advisors. They asked me what I thought about Russian intervention."

"Would you mind sharing your thoughts?"

"Not at all. I told President Lane it would be better if the United States committed its own forces to the battle."

Tarkovsky's smile faded. He tried to hide his disappointment.

"However, I also said that if he was still reluctant to do so, that an alliance with your country would be the next best option."

"And did he accept your proposal?"

"No, he didn't." Al-Saud sipped his coffee.

"Perhaps he would be open to further overtures?"

"I'm reluctant to press the matter. My government has other requests for him, and I wouldn't want to jeopardize those for a war he doesn't want anyway."

"I have it on good authority that Vice President Chandler is strongly in favor of a Russian-American security alliance. You would have his support and ours in other matters if you made this petition with the president."

"And what is your 'good authority'?"

"The vice president told me so himself."

The Saudi nodded. "Clay did seem keen on the idea. But no matter. It's the president who is reluctant to allow us to purchase and operate our own advanced drone program, not Chandler."

"Chandler would support such a move."

"I know. But he isn't the president."

"Not yet. If you can be patient . . ."

"Talk to *Daesh*. Talk to the Iranians. Will they wait patiently for President Chandler to assume office before trying to overthrow us?"

"Of course not. Your country's strategic situation is quite precarious at the moment, isn't it?"

"We're standing on the knife's edge." Al-Saud paused. "Your country's superlative aviation industry is now deploying the next generation of drones."

"Yes, we are."

Al-Saud set his coffee down. "Might your government be willing to sell us such systems? We would want complete operational autonomy, of course."

Tarkovsky nodded noncommittally. "Well, yes, perhaps. Though, like you, we don't want to alienate the Americans. As you said, Chandler is supportive of drone sales to your country. So is his chief of staff, Vicki Grafton. Have you met her?"

"Only once, briefly, at an embassy function. She was also in the meeting I attended yesterday." Al-Saud reflected for a moment. Smiled. "A beautiful woman."

"She's quite brilliant, actually. And very well connected with senior defense leadership on Capitol Hill. She would also be in favor of selling drones to your country, as would the American corporations that make them. You should try and meet her again."

"An excellent idea."

"But even if you got your drones, that won't be enough to stop ISIS or the Iranians. You still need vast numbers of combat troops to defend your interests. We stand prepared to do so. Our own interests are at stake in the region also, including Iraq. Events could force us to act unilaterally. However, it would be better if we were invited in."

"By us?"

"Of course. But by the Americans, too. The symbolism would be important to the world. And to us."

Al-Saud leaned forward and poured more coffee for Tarkovsky. "You mean, the sanctions. As in, lifting them."

"Those as well."

Al-Saud set the pot back down, thinking. "So where are we, exactly? Where are our mutual interests?"

"I have some influence with Ms. Grafton as well as a few other resources. I will press your case for American drone sales as well as for an American commitment to dismantle and destroy the *Daesh* Caliphate. If the Americans are unwilling to do so, my government will. And if the Americans refuse to sell you their drone systems, I can safely say that my government stands ready to provide them."

"All of this is quite generous. What is it that you want from me in return?"

"Perhaps you can use your influence to convince the Americans to lift their sanctions against us and to invite us into the war against ISIS."

"In effect, you're asking us to change dance partners in the middle of a dance."

"Only because the other partner won't dance to your tune. If the Americans won't exercise leadership in the region, we will partner with you and the other Sunni governments to protect Sunni interests. But we're more than willing to partner with the Americans as well. In fact, we prefer it. Shared responsibility is in all of our best interests."

"Why do you suppose President Lane can't see that?"

Tarkovsky sighed. "It's a legacy from his political mentor, Margaret Myers."

"Is Myers still playing a role in his administration?"

"It's unclear. However, Troy Pearce is one of Lane's closest advisors. I suspect he is the biggest problem you need to deal with."

"Yes, I met him yesterday as well. A quite unpleasant fellow."

"Former CIA special forces. Very dangerous. And smart. The CEO of his own security company, specializing in drone operations."

"Any suggestions about how we might deal with him?"

Tarkovsky set his cup down and leaned forward. "Yes, as a matter of fact."

THE BRIGHTLY COLORED monarch butterfly stood on the lip of the chimney just above the room where the two ambassadors were meeting. Its polycarbonate wings gently flapped, keeping the piezoelectric nanogenerators powering its onboard microphone and the rest of the unit. The Israeli engineers who built the audio surveillance device had done a brilliant job of biomimicry.

Perhaps too brilliant.

A brick-red American robin perched in a nearby elm spied the butterfly drone. It swooped in and snatched up the mechanical monarch in its yellow beak before the Israelis knew what happened and, worse, before the conversation down below had ended.

35

Kan-Tex was one of the largest independent trucking firms in the United States. It owned and operated a vast fleet of tanker trucks that hauled oil, gasoline, aviation fuel, and other liquid petrochemicals across the entire contiguous United States. It had a number of federal and state contracts, but its primary business was civilian commercial long hauls for refineries and distributors.

When Maria Mejias joined the company twenty-four years earlier, she thought she would spend her entire work life in a cramped, single-wide office trailer, trapped behind an IBM Selectric typewriter filling out dispatches for her boss, Jimmy Haygood, a semi-literate trucker turned businessman. But her boss turned out to be a business genius, building a national trucking empire through the ruthless acquisition of less efficient trucking firms. He also managed to increase his own operating efficiencies through the use of automation, which came relatively late to the trucking industry. Jimmy was famously loyal and generous with his employees, offering great benefits and profit-sharing opportunities. Maria took advantage of his generosity and completed her online bachelor's degree in management information systems. An online pop-up ad during one of those courses led her to contact a San Diego company specializing in automated dispatching systems.

Maria introduced the San Diego company to Jimmy and he instantly understood the system's potential. His company had lost a $56 million lawsuit for a fiery school bus wreck caused by a Kan-Tex driver falling asleep at the wheel. Fortunately, Jimmy's insurance covered the jury award, but his new insurance premiums threatened to eat up his profits along with the sky-high fuel costs he was experiencing at the time. He was desperate for answers, and Maria's contact in San Diego delivered them on a digital silver platter.

Just two years later, Maria was on the top floor of a brand-new office building, supervising twenty dispatchers sitting at automated terminals. Each workstation monitored up to thirty tanker trucks at a time. It was a real game changer for Kan-Tex. Not only did the new automated dispatching system track every single vehicle through GPS and provide real-time locations, it coordinated delivery routes, driver schedules, and even maintenance programs. Every aspect of the truck's mechanics was under automated sensor surveillance. Kan-Tex was able to minimize fuel and maintenance costs because the automated system indicated truck speed, fuel efficiency, engine wear, brake usage, and transmission performance.

But driver safety was paramount in Jimmy's mind, partly because the vast majority of all truck wrecks were caused by driver error. Automated braking systems and automated remote throttle control were installed to prevent drivers from driving too fast or recklessly. Not only did this save expensive fuel, it saved lives and greatly reduced the company's insurance costs. Mounted dash and rear cameras also broadcast real-time traffic video, giving dispatchers a live-action view of road conditions. The truck cabs even incorporated a driver fatigue monitoring system through eye tracking and blinking analysis. When the computer algorithms indicated a driver was overly fatigued, the dispatcher would be alerted and, if necessary, could take remote control of the truck and drive it from the workstation to get it off the road. It was similar to the Uninterruptible Autopilot system Boeing patented in 2006 to remotely seize control of hijacked aircraft.

In order for the system to work across the nation, every truck was connected by satellite link to the Kan-Tex dispatch center. But the entire computer system was serviced, maintained, and repaired remotely from the computer company's headquarters in San Diego.

Maria had just finished her cigarette break when she sat down at her desk at noon. Her master monitor was networked into the other dispatching monitors. This allowed her to remotely supervise each dispatcher as well as select any of the 582 vehicles on the road they were all tracking today. She opened up her current favorite romance novel and dived back into the read, but ten minutes later a gentle alarm bell signaled that the entire dispatch system was down.

Maria glanced up at her master monitor and saw the blinking message: SYSTEM DOWN FOR ROUTINE MAINTENANCE. SYSTEM WILL AUTO-MATICALLY REBOOT IN 0:33 MINUTES. The other dispatchers all turned around to face her, confused and annoyed. Maria shared their concerns. The system was supposed to shut down for automated maintenance tasks only at midnight, when the fewest number of trucks were on the road. She thought about calling up the San Diego help desk but calculated that by the time she actually got through to somebody to initiate a maintenance program shutdown and a system reboot, the current maintenance activity would have already completed. She made a mental note to send an e-mail to her San Diego contact and ask him to change the maintenance schedule back to Saturdays at midnight.

"Everybody take thirty," Maria said.

The frowns evaporated as the dispatchers bolted for the break room. Maria glanced at her screen again. Thirty-two minutes to go. She dived back into the novel—it was just getting to the good stuff. She told herself again it was just routine maintenance.

No big deal.

DALLAS, TEXAS

Completed in 1964, the Woodall Rodgers Freeway Spur connected the two busiest traffic arteries in Dallas, U.S. Highway 75 and Interstate 35E. The only significant change the spur underwent in nearly fifty years was to accommodate the burgeoning arts district in downtown Dallas. In 2009 the city planners shut down a portion of the freeway and began turning it into a 5.2-acre urban oasis, the Klyde Warren

Park, a pedestrian-friendly complex of restaurants, jogging trails, a dog park, a botanical garden, and other urban pleasures. By digging a massive eight-lane tunnel underneath the park, the highly traveled Woodall Rodgers freeway was able to stay in operation.

Georgia Romero's forty-foot tanker sped into the Woodall Rodgers tunnel, hauling nine thousand gallons of aviation fuel. The eastbound traffic was mercifully light at 11:05 a.m. CST and she was making good time, cruising at sixty-five miles per hour. She'd been stuck in this exact spot during the five o'clock rush hour in years past. It was a nightmare she wouldn't wish on her worst enemies, not even her two ex-husbands, both OTR drivers like her. Her thirteen years behind the wheel gave her seniority at Kan-Tex, allowing her to pick the easiest routes, and the new dispatch system was doing a heck of job picking the best times. She didn't like the idea she was on camera all the time and that the dispatchers could be watching her at any moment. It was like OnStar from hell. They didn't even like her to wear her sunglasses because it interfered with the driver fatigue system they installed in her cab. She hadn't had a wreck in eleven years, but the dispatchers wouldn't relent.

Hank Williams blared on the radio and she sang lustily along. Her voice pinched off in mid-warble when her throttle pedal plunged into the floorboard and the truck lunged forward, snapping her head back against the seat. Before she could react, the steering wheel yanked hard left and the left brakes seized. Thirty tons of liquid payload shuddered violently behind her as the tractor spun left, whipping the long silver tank behind her in a hard swing out to the right. She caught a glimpse of the tank in her peripheral vision as it slammed into the tunnel wall in a shower of sparks and splintering metal. She saw the explosion before she heard it, but an instant later she was vaporized in the crushing ball of fiery gas that filled the tunnel like a thermobaric weapon.

36

Every eye around the table in the Situation Room was fixed on the video monitor. Eaton held the remote control. Video footage from the TXDOT cameras inside the Woodall Rodgers tunnel played a brief clip of the Kan-Tex tanker truck rocketing through the light traffic. The image froze.

"There. It looks like the left front brake engaged. See the smoke from the burning rubber?" Eaton said. She hit the Play button again. The image advanced in slow motion. "As you can see, physics took over from there. The tanker swerves, hits the wall, and—"

A fiery explosion engulfed the last camera, killing the image in a haze of digital snow.

"How many dead?" Lane asked.

"Including the driver, seven, possibly more. Hard to tell. Not much left, forensically. Dallas PD is still running down VIN and plate numbers from the wreckage. They'll reach out to the addresses of record and try to piece together a more definitive list of victims."

"Thank God it didn't happen at rush hour. Would've been a holocaust," Grafton said.

"Where else?" Pearce asked.

"The 405 in Los Angeles, not far from LAX, along with Atlanta, Chicago, and Denver. No other fatalities. Mostly lane closures, traffic rerouting. Two of those were fuel spills, so HAZMAT teams had to be called in." Eaton noted the time on the wall. "Some of them won't be cleaned up by evening rush hour, so there are still plenty of headaches on the way."

"Do we have any Gorgon Sky on these attacks?" Lane asked.

Pearce shook his head. "Unfortunately, no. The attacks all happened exactly where we didn't have them in place."

"Of course not," Chandler said, unable to hide his disdain.

"How soon until all of the major metro areas are covered?" Lane asked.

"I've got commitments from Boeing, General Atomics, Northrop Grumman, and three other majors. We're getting camera pods and software packages out to each of them so they can link their systems into our network. We should have seventy percent of the country covered within the next seven days."

"No faster?" Lane asked.

"They're balls to the wall now, but I'll see what I can do."

"I've got a question. Weren't all of the tankers from the same company?" Chandler asked.

"Yes. Kan-Tex, out of Texarkana, Texas."

"Is Kan-Tex on any of our watch lists? Or any of its employees?"

"Not on mine," Eaton said.

"Nor mine." Mike Pia, the director of national intelligence, had arrived just minutes earlier. In his wire-rimmed glasses and tailored pinstripe, he looked like a well-heeled college professor or a Wall Street executive. He'd been both at one time or another in his storied career.

"Shouldn't you guys have the same list?" Chandler asked.

"There are a lot of damn lists these days," Pia said. "Too many."

"I don't have a problem with that," Peguero said. "The last thing we need is one single list of enemies of the state. That's begging for abuse."

Pearce bit his tongue. He personally knew of a case where a man was on one terror suspect watch list and yet passed his FBI background check when he applied for—and received—a concealed carry permit. No wonder most Americans felt that the federal government was too big and too inefficient to be of any use other than sucking away billions of tax dollars to accomplish nothing but employ an army of worthless bureaucrats.

"Can we please stay on topic?" Lane asked. A vein throbbed on his temple.

Chandler waived a hand. "Sorry. Just frustrated."

"Join the club."

"The fact that all of these tankers were from the same company is good news. It probably means it was just that one company that was hacked," Pearce said. He turned to Eaton. "And from the description you gave of their automated dispatch system, it sounds like all they needed was access into one terminal, probably the administrator's. From there they took complete control."

"I'm starting to miss the horse and buggy," Chandler said. "Analogue had its advantages."

"I had a call in from the *Washington Post* ten minutes ago, sir. I told them to sit tight but that will only buy us an hour. Maybe two." At twenty-eight, Alyssa Abbott was not only the youngest White House press secretary in history but also Lane's youngest senior advisor. She was another busty blonde who seemed destined for cable sportscasting or anchoring Fox News. But she was whip smart and rough as a cob, growing up with four older brothers who were all active-duty U.S. Marines. Abbott was an award-winning war correspondent and frequent on-air personality before signing on with Lane's presidential campaign.

"What do they know?" Eaton asked.

"It doesn't take a rocket scientist to see the tanker crashes all happened within thirty minutes of each other. The wire services want to call this a terrorist incident—a case of 'suicide truckers.'"

"Holy Moses," Chandler said. "Just what we need."

"We've got to give them something or they'll go out with it," Abbott said.

"What do you suggest?" Lane asked.

"Environment and Public Works has been pushing for a new highway bill. Money for more roads and bridges. We can spin it that way."

"You want to blame all of this on potholes?" Pearce asked.

"Of course not. But I can feed them some inside dope about new funding legislation we're proposing—"

"But we're not," Lane said.

Abbott smiled. "That's where the spinning part comes in. Let me promise them something exclusive on the highway bill we may or may not be working on, and promise to backfill this other story when we've got more facts to give them. If I toss in the national security angle, that should buy us another day."

"That supposes that we actually learn anything by tomorrow. What exactly do we have right now? Let's go around the room, starting with you, Julissa."

The attorney general shook her head, frustrated. "The Dallas FBI field office is flying up to Texarkana right now with a computer forensics team. They're already remotely accessing the site to monitor it and shutting it down to keep anything else from happening. The San Diego computer services firm Kan-Tex contracts with is cooperating as well. It will be at least a day and probably more before we can identify the hackers."

"Or maybe never, if they're good enough," Garza added.

"Maybe not," Eaton said, shrugging. "Good news is that we managed to piece together enough security camera footage to trace the flag drone's flight path backward from the White House lawn to its point of origin. We discovered it took off from the back of a boat moored at the Capital Yacht Club."

"Please God, tell me the boat belonged to a registered Republican," Chandler said, grinning.

"A Green Party lawyer, actually. A lobbyist for one of the environmental organizations. She was and still is out of the country. We're still digging around but my team is confident she's not the one behind this."

Lane turned to the DNI seated next to him. "Mike?"

"Melinda indicated yesterday that chatter is up. Same on our end. The jihadi sites are all abuzz that something's going on, but nothing specific. If ISIS is behind this, they're keeping quiet about it."

"Any reason to think they're not behind it?" Lane asked.

"Nobody's claiming anything at the moment. Doesn't mean they won't later. And this kind of attack—public, disruptive, newsworthy— is right up their alley. The only thing missing is a high body count."

"They gave it one helluva college try today," Chandler said. "We're just damn lucky they couldn't pull it off."

"Seems to me they could've killed dozens, maybe hundreds more. Those tanker trailers are practically rolling ordnance, and they had complete control of the tractors pulling them," Pearce said. "All they had to do was wait for worse traffic or run those tankers into more vulnerable targets."

"Are you suggesting restraint again?" Pia asked. He'd read yesterday's briefing minutes. Thought Pearce's point was interesting.

"Seems like it."

"Restraint for what purpose?"

"Clearly not terror, at least in the classic sense. I think these attacks are pointed at the president. First it was the airports, now it's the highways. These both have profound economic implications."

"We've already established that ISIS is trying to pull down our economy," Chandler said. "What's your point?"

"The attacks are escalating. That means the consequences for not acceding to their demand to fly the flag only get worse. The goal is to get you to fly that flag, Mr. President, not kill Americans."

"Not yet, anyway," Garza said.

"Why is flying the flag so important?" Lane asked. "Wouldn't a terror strike on our soil be victory enough?"

"This is about humiliation, not just publicity," Pearce said. "ISIS pledged to fly the black flag over the White House back in 2014, the same year they declared the Caliphate. If they fail to keep that promise, they're the ones who are humiliated."

"Believe me, I have no intention of ever flying that black diaper over my own home," Lane said. "Alyssa, spin the story any way you need to to keep the newspapers away from this as long as you can."

"Yes, sir."

"Chairman Onstot will be here in an hour to talk about our military options. Let's break for lunch and reconvene when he arrives. If we can't find the bastards here, we'll have to take the war to them over there."

Chandler and Grafton exchanged a glance. Music to their ears.

37

A late-model sedan turned off the two-lane asphalt and onto a tree-lined path. Tires crunched on the gravel as the sedan crept a hundred yards toward the single-story ranch house. Security cameras fixed to light poles tracked their progress.

"There he is," the passenger said.

The garage doors were open. A windowless black-panel van stood far inside, to the right, leaving the rest of the expansive garage open. A bright yellow-and-red Chinook Charter logo decorated the van's swinging back doors.

The sedan pulled up onto the spotless cement driveway and shut off its engine after parking directly behind the van. The two men climbed out. Sport coats, ties, leather shoes. The driver was heavyset with a dirty-blond mustache. The dark-haired passenger was taller and leaner and clean-shaven but with a heavy five o'clock shadow.

The door leading from the house into the garage opened. Norman Pike stepped into the garage in his stocking feet and put on a pair of slippers. He held a heavy ceramic coffee cup in one hand.

The two men entered the garage. The tall passenger scanned the space. Neat as a pin. No oil or dirt or even dust on the garage floor. Everything was perfectly organized and uniform in storage racks and metal cabinets. There was also a tall mechanic's tool chest on wheels and a workbench with a vise.

"Mr. Pike?" the driver asked, reaching into his coat pocket.

"Yes?" Pike took a sip of coffee, his eyes focused on the driver's hand.

"My name is Agent Barr." He held up his wallet so that Pike could read it.

"FBI?"

"And this is Agent Fowler. We're both from the Milwaukee office."

"Nice to meet you fellas. What can I do for you?" Pike reached out and shook hands with both men. Fisherman's hands, Barr noted. Strong and calloused.

Agent Fowler glanced around the garage. "Nice little shop you got here."

"Helps me keep everything shipshape. I run my business out of my house."

"A charter business?" Agent Barr said.

"Yeah. Out of Cheboygan."

"I always wanted to do that," Agent Fowler said. "Nothing beats a day on the lake, fishing."

"I'm a lucky man, for sure."

"Do you mind if we ask you a few questions?" Agent Barr asked.

"Of course not. You want to come in? Just made a pot of coffee."

"Sure, if you don't mind. It was a long drive."

"Follow me." Pike headed for the door. He stopped at the threshold and removed his slippers, placing them neatly on a plastic pad. He turned around. "If you don't mind—"

"Of course not," Agent Barr said.

Pike went in as the two agents unlaced their shoes, leaning against the wall for stability. They exchanged silent, irritated glances. They set their shoes down neatly next to Pike's.

Inside the door, they entered a long hallway, two doors on each side. One was slightly open. Two were shut. The fourth was secured with a heavy security bracket and a black-dialed combination lock. Fowler made a mental note. The engineered wood floors were as spotless as the garage. They eventually landed in a large open-area chef's kitchen that led into a living room.

Pike set two steaming cups of coffee on the bar. "Please, have a seat."

"I'll stand if you don't mind," Fowler said. "Back's killing me after that drive."

"I'm surprised you came from Milwaukee. Isn't there an FBI office in Detroit?"

"Yeah, but they've got their hands full right now, so we got the call." Barr took a sip of coffee. "Man, that's good."

"Roast the beans myself. That's the secret. You guys want anything to eat?" Pike raised a conspiratorial eyebrow. "Something to fortify the coffee?"

"No, thanks, this is great," Barr said.

Pike leaned against the stove. "So, what can I do for you?"

Fowler reached into his coat pocket for a photo. Set it down on the counter. "We're looking for this man. Daniel Brody."

Pike picked up the photo. "Yeah. He was on my boat three days ago. Why?"

"He's missing. We've been asked to check around. We got as far as Cheboygan and your charter but after that, his trail disappears."

"Oh, God. That's terrible. Super-nice guy."

Fowler set his cup down. "You mind if I use your restroom?"

"Sure. It's back down that hall, second door on your left."

"Thanks." Fowler headed that way.

"Did he tell you where he was headed next?" Barr asked.

Pike scratched his beard thoughtfully. "No, not that I recall. He said he was running through his bucket list. I assumed that meant he was sick or something. Was he?"

"Not that I'm aware."

"He said he always wanted to go fishing on the Great Lakes. We had a great time. Caught his limit, too."

"Did he show you any identification?"

"Yeah. His driver's license. California, I think."

"His rental car never got turned in," Barr said.

"Oh, boy. That's not a good sign. Can't you trace it with the GPS onboard?"

"It was disabled."

Pike's eyebrows raised. "Wow. I didn't even know that was possible."

"The last known position of the vehicle was ten miles north of here. The rental car company sent a man out to the location but didn't find anything."

"Huh. Sounds like your guy wanted to disappear."

"Could be. We haven't closed any doors at this juncture."

Pike smiled. "Must be fascinating to do what you do."

"It has its moments." Barr took another sip of coffee. "Did Brody tell you he was an American citizen?"

"He was, wasn't he?"

"Dual citizenship."

"Really? He never said anything about that. Like, Canadian or something?"

"Israeli."

"Oh. Well, he seemed American."

"He grew up in Los Angeles. Did he tell you about his work?"

"No. We just talked about fishing, the basics. He said he didn't really know anything about it. I even had to sell him a fishing license just so he could go out."

"So you didn't know he was a college professor?"

"No."

"He didn't talk to you about robotics? Drones? That sort of thing?" Barr asked.

Pike shook his head. "No. That would've been really interesting. I would've remembered something like that."

"So how long have you been a charter captain?" Barr asked.

"Going on eight years now."

"Business is good?"

"Yeah. It's really good. Great, in fact."

"I'm surprised you're not out right now. Isn't this high season?"

"Had a last-minute cancellation. Decided to use the time to catch up on my paperwork. The IRS is driving me nuts." Pike caught himself. "I mean, don't get me wrong. I don't mind paying taxes. It's the tax forms and Schedule Bs and all of that crap that kills me."

Barr smiled at Pike's discomfort. "I hear ya."

"So you were in the service?" Pike asked.

"First Marines. Iraq."

"You got the look."

"Funny, I was thinking the same thing about you."

"I was in Iraq for about a year, but not in uniform. Bad eyes. But I worked for a contractor. Tech support, for computers. An IED took out a couple of friends of mine, and that was all it took. I was out of there, man, let me tell you. Not worth the money, even though it was damn good money. It's how I was able to buy my boat."

"And tax free, too," Barr said.

"The good ol' days," Pike said. "More coffee?"

"Sure. Thanks." He handed Pike his cup. *Where the hell was Fowler?*

Pike refilled it. "So, this Brody guy. You're looking for him because he's in trouble, or he *is* the trouble?"

"He's a missing person. That's all I'm authorized to tell you."

"Must be an important guy. Otherwise you would've sent the local PD."

"He's definitely a person of interest." Barr checked his watch.

"I'm sorry I couldn't be more help. I hope you find the guy." A toilet flushed down the hallway.

"Me, too." Barr handed Pike a business card. "If you think of anything else, give me a call."

Pike studied it. "I will, for sure."

Fowler reappeared. "It's getting late. We should get going. We've got a couple of stops we still need to hit."

"Yeah, we should." Barr turned to Pike. "Thanks for the coffee."

"Let me walk you out," Pike said.

THE CRUNCH OF GRAVEL gave way to an asphalt hiss as the sedan's tires pulled back onto the two-lane heading west for the I-75 north and Mackinac.

"What'd you see?" Barr asked.

"Not much. I looked around. I stopped at the shut door but there was no time to pick the combo lock. I listened but didn't hear anything on the other side."

"Probably nothing to worry about. Maybe it's just a torture chamber with a dozen women drugged unconscious and chained to the walls."

Fowler laughed. "He's not the type. Trust me."

"Should we grab a warrant, just in case? Check it out?"

"Based on what?"

"Probable cause."

"What probable cause? A locked door?"

"You don't think he's hiding anything?"

"I'm guessing it's just storage. Rods and reels. Those things can get pricey."

Barr sighed through his nose. "You're probably right. He doesn't strike me as anything but what he seems to be, a charter boat captain. I say we hold off on a warrant. Last thing we need is another federal judge up our poop chutes." The car rose and fell with the undulating road. "So where the heck should we look for Brody next?"

Fowler loosened his tie. "I know a good steak house in Mackinac. Maybe he's hiding out there."

"Sounds like a winner."

Barr shifted uncomfortably. "Pull over at the next gas station, will ya? I never did get a chance to bleed the lizard."

38

President Lane took his customary seat at the far end of the Situation Room table, his mind clearly occupied. The next hour in this room would determine the fate of the nation. Pearce was on his right.

The chairman of the Joint Chiefs of Staff, General Gordon Onstot, sat at the other end of the long table opposite President Lane. The four-star air force general's barrel chest was loaded with hard-earned combat medals, ribbons, and badges. Mike Pia, the director of national intelligence, sat to the chairman's right. Chandler, Grafton, Eaton, Peguero, Abbott, and Gibson sat in the middle.

"We need to talk about goals and means," Lane began. "I want to know from each of you what you would do if you were sitting in my chair. Don't try and second-guess me. Just give me your best thoughts in a few sentences. We'll start with goals. Gordon, let's hear you first."

The JCS chairman cleared his throat. "We need a limited and definable goal that can be achieved rapidly and that addresses the threat at hand. We should mount an immediate air and ground assault on the ISIS Caliphate in Syria and Iraq and its capital city, Raqqa. We should kill or capture all enemy forces, and kill or capture Caliph al-Mahdi and his ruling council as quickly as possible to eliminate the current threat."

"Doable?" Lane asked.

"No question. A matter of weeks if sufficient force is deployed quickly enough. Maybe less."

"The CliffsNotes version of the Powell Doctrine," Garza said.

The press secretary nodded. "A definable objective. I can sell that."

"The chairman's right," Chandler said. "Hit them hard and win."

"Objections?" Lane asked. He glanced around the room. Pearce frowned. "Troy?"

"'Hit them hard and win' is great. But the minute we leave, they'll be back and we'll have to occupy the territory indefinitely, just like South Korea, where we still have troops more than fifty years after that conflict ended."

"I take it you have a different goal?" Lane asked.

"Take out al-Mahdi and his troops and you still haven't killed ISIS—they're operating throughout the Middle East, and they have affiliates all over the planet. The only way to truly win a war is to end it, and the only way to end it with ISIS and its affiliates is to hunt every last one of them down and kill them wherever we find them."

The attorney general scowled. "Aren't you exaggerating the problem? Only a small percentage of Muslims are fanatics."

"There are one-point-six billion Muslims in the world," Pia said. "If just ten percent of them are fanatics, that means we're in a war with one hundred sixty million people. If it's just one percent, we're still talking about sixteen million people devoted to destroying us by any means possible."

"That's a long war, Troy," Lane said. "A global war. A *total* war."

"We're already in a long war," Pearce said. "They launched their campaign against the West in the seventh century. But half a war like General Onstot is proposing promises an even longer one—and denies us victory for the effort. By fighting a limited war against ISIS, we telegraph to our enemies that we're not totally committed to winning. That gives them incentive to wait us out. They will, and we'll quit. We always do."

"You're just a bag of sunshine and rainbows, aren't you?" Chandler said.

"Troy's right," Grafton said. Chandler scowled at her. She didn't care. It was time for her to make her move.

"How so, Vicki?" Lane said.

"Even if we could defeat ISIS by only destroying the Caliphate, all we've done is cleared the field for al-Qaeda to reemerge, or for some other jihadi organization to rise up and take its place. Radical Islam is a hydra with a million heads. Like Troy said, either we make a total military commitment to destroy all of our jihadi enemies over a long war, or we don't make that total commitment, and fight an even longer war and lose to them."

"Sounds like genocide," Peguero said. "Like a war against Islam itself. That's not an American idea. That's not who we are." Her eyes narrowed. "That's not who *you* are, Mr. President."

"You're right," Pearce said, looking a Peguero. "Genocide literally means the killing of a type of person. In World War Two we killed fascists. Millions of them. We killed their soldiers in the field and burned their cities to the ground and their civilian populations with them. It was the only way to defeat them. Do you have a problem with us winning World War Two and defeating the fascists?"

"That's a ridiculous question," Peguero said. "There's no comparison."

"I agree," Pearce said. "Germany and Japan were nation-states. ISIS is not, despite the Caliphate. We could invade Germany and Japan and Italy and occupy them and force their leaders to sign treaties that ended the war. There is no one country to invade and occupy, no one person in authority to deal with, no treaty to be signed to end the war with radical Islam. That means we must kill them all, wherever we find them, if we ever want it to end."

"Religion can't be defeated with guns and violence," Peguero said. "We need to win the argument against radical Islam by showing the world we are morally superior. Islam is a religion of peace. The fanatical killers aren't really Muslim at all."

Garza threw up his hands. "Are you nuts? Who are you to say that Muslims who claim to be Muslims aren't really Muslim? ISIS and AQ and Boko Haram and all of the other murdering bastards all swear by the Koran and by Allah and by Muhammad, His Prophet. Only smug, self-righteous Western elites think those people aren't really who they say they are."

"All I know is that if you wage war against the whole religion, you'll only increase the number of zealots who want to kill us," Peguero said. "Bush understood that. So has every other president since him—at least until now."

"I agree with you," Pearce said.

Eyebrows raised around the room, including Peguero's. "I'm confused."

"You can't destroy religion with guns. Religion, like ideology, is software. It's invisible. It's an idea. So you're right, we can't fight radical Islam with guns." Pearce tapped his skull with his finger. "But we can wreck the hardware that runs it. We put bullet to bone. Turn brain pans into pink mist. That's exactly how Islam spread, isn't it? Muhammad and his successors spread their software by killing Christians and Jews in the wars of Muslim expansion that only ended when the West stopped them by force of arms at places like Tours, Malta, and Vienna."

"So we have to become barbarians in order to defeat the barbarians?"

"In theory, yes. But I know that we don't have the guts to wage that kind of war. I'm not even sure it's the morally right thing to do. But half a war and half the effort will only make things twice as bad in the long run. Wage total war or don't wage it at all is my point."

"How can we not wage war against our sworn enemies?" Chandler asked.

"Containment," Pia said.

"What do you mean exactly?" Lane asked.

"Containment is the Cold War strategy that defeated the Soviet empire without firing a shot in a hot war. It forced the Soviets to live with the internal contradictions of their social and economic system and, of course, it collapsed upon itself."

"That took over fifty years to accomplish," Chandler said.

Pia shrugged. "Only because our two-faced European allies propped them up for decades for profit while we spent the money to defend NATO. Otherwise the Soviet Union would have fallen thirty years earlier."

Grafton frowned with confusion. "So what's your point?"

"The principle of Islamic containment is the same: totally wall off

Islam from the West. It's a civilizational war, isn't it? Let the crazies stay stuck in crazy town. Let the whole Middle East turn into one giant ISIS Caliphate. What do you think would happen? The Muslim world hasn't produced a significant medical or scientific or technological breakthrough in seven hundred years. If they were completely walled off from the West and forced to live according to Sharia law, they'd wind up in a complete dystopia of economic collapse, overpopulation, famine, disease, and ultimately revolution. They'd either completely destroy themselves or reform themselves, and we wouldn't have to fire a shot or shed one drop of blood in a war with them."

"But how do we 'wall off' Islam from the West?" Peguero asked.

Pia shrugged. "That's another topic for another day. I'm just suggesting that war isn't the only alternative here."

Eaton nodded. "Technically, Mr. Pia is right. Containment worked against the Soviets. In theory, it may work again. But we don't have ten years or even ten days to see if it will. The ISIS threat is at our throats right now. We need an immediate solution."

"So you favor General Onstot's position?"

"I do," Eaton said. "Even though I also agree that winning this battle against the ISIS Caliphate won't win us the war."

"There's an even simpler solution," Garza said.

"What's that?" Lane asked.

"Fly the stupid flag."

Garza's words sucked the air out of the room.

Pearce watched Lane's jaw clenching in the awkward silence.

"For the record, I was joking," Garza said.

"That flag will never be flown under any circumstances," Lane said. "Am I absolutely clear about this?"

The room nodded in agreement.

"Don't raise the issue again, Jim. Not even as a joke."

Garza nodded, chastised. "Won't happen again."

"Good." Lane lightened up. "I wouldn't quit your day job, either."

Nervous chuckles filtered through the room, breaking the tension.

Garza smiled. "No, sir."

Lane continued. "To summarize, the three alternatives are a limited engagement, a long engagement, or containment, which is no engagement. The problem is, we're out of time. I agree with Gordon and Melinda. We need a swift and powerful strike to decapitate the ISIS leadership and destroy its forces on the ground in Syria and Iraq right now. That's our best shot at stopping these terror attacks on American soil. So that's our goal. Now it's time we talk about the means of achieving it. Suggestions?"

So far, so good, Grafton thought. *Lane is one step closer to war.*

Chandler leaned forward on the table. "Given our 'no new boots on the ground' policy, the only viable option for ground forces would be to accept the Russians' offer and use their troops with our air support. They're already in the region and ready to go."

Pia shook his head. "The Russians have been driving toward the Persian Gulf since Peter the Great. Now's not the time to hand them the keys to the kingdom."

"I agree with the director," Onstot said. "In the long run, the Russians are our strategic competitor. Handing them the world's primary oil reserves on top of their own energy resources gives them economic leverage we don't want them to have."

"It also conveys weakness," Grafton said.

Chandler shot her another withering look. She ignored him. She knew Lane would never agree to Russian boots. The only chance for war was for Lane to commit American forces. Time to kill the Russian option once and for all.

"How so, Vicki?" Lane asked.

"A Russian alliance communicates to our allies and enemies that we're either too weak or too afraid to take on ISIS by ourselves and that we are no longer the world's preeminent superpower."

"So you think we should go it alone?" the president asked.

"Yes, sir. I do." Grafton felt the power in the room shift away from Chandler and toward her. For once she wasn't sitting in the vice president's shadow.

It felt good.

"It's a limited operation with clearly defined objectives. I'm sure our military can handle it."

Lane turned toward the JCS chairman. "Can we?"

Onstot nodded. "No question. "Twenty thousand troops should do the job, not counting air and naval support. First or Second Marines, 82nd Airborne, 10th Mountain. Any combination of those would work. We can have the lead elements on the ground in twenty-four hours. Just give the word."

39

General Onstot's confidence in American arms defeating ISIS swiftly and decisively sealed the deal. Grafton was thrilled.

Lane was obviously about to commit when a storm of counterarguments broke out. Options for arming the Iraqis, the Kurds, or moderate Sunnis (if any could be found) were put forward. All of them were shot down.

Garza offered the most original proposal. "Why not let the Turks play the hegemon? They want to revive the Ottoman Empire and the 'true caliphate.' There hasn't been peace in the region since the sultans and they're not afraid to break a few eggs."

Chandler countered. "The Russians won't stand for it and the Crimea is already a powder keg."

What about ISMAT, the big antiterror, Saudi-led Muslim coalition, or NATO? Both options were weak, and both dismissed.

Chandler was concerned. The Russian option was slipping away. He knew Lane was old-fashioned, a man of honor. Time for Chandler to play his trump card.

"Mr. President, if you don't want to violate your promise to the American people about putting our boots on the ground in the Middle East, the Russian alliance is the only way forward."

The tactic worked. Lane's face tensed, visibly affected by Chandler's appeal.

But Grafton understood Lane better than Chandler. Lane would never accept a Russian alliance. By appealing to Lane's honor, the president was more likely to not go to war at all.

Grafton glanced furtively at Chandler. He was already pissed off. If she spoke up more against his beloved Russian alliance, he'd fire her before the meeting was over. But she had to get Lane back on track.

"We all agree we're out of time. A coalition with the Russians or anybody simply isn't feasible. Coalitions are notoriously difficult to organize, manage, and lead. By doing this on our own we can act swiftly and in our own best interests. If we want to stop these terror attacks at home, we've got to take the war to them over there, right now, just as General Onstot outlined."

Pia and Onstot nodded. So did Eaton, the former army general, and finally Garza. The logic was unassailable. "Agreed."

Grafton turned to Lane. "Mr. President, I guarantee you that the American people want you to defend their lives with decisive action rather than worry about a campaign slogan that no longer applies."

She turned to Chandler. Time to mend a fence or two. "If necessary, we can always expand the war later. Draw in the Russians or other coalition partners if we need to."

Chandler's angry mask began to soften. He saw the logic of Grafton's argument. "True."

Grafton continued. "We can hunt the other global jihadists down and dispatch them anytime we want in the future. But right now we need to destroy the ISIS Caliphate and stop these attacks on our homeland."

"Attacking Raqqa will only fan the flames," Peguero said. "They'll use it to recruit more fighters."

The press secretary shook her head. "We can put the destruction of Raqqa on social media—show how utterly terrible and complete the destruction of ISIS is and futility of resisting our overwhelming force— we might start de-recruiting fighters from ISIS."

"So we're all agreed, at least, that we need to act militarily," Chandler offered.

"And immediately," Grafton added.

Chandler glanced at Pearce. "Everyone except Troy, that is."

All eyes turned to Pearce.

"Troy?" the president asked.

"I'm against anything short of full mobilization, a declaration of war, a draft, and the pledge to hunt each and every one of those bastards down and kill them, no matter what names they use, no matter where we find them—including on our own soil. Anything less than that is a guarantee of failure."

"That's the call you'd make if you were sitting in my chair? Even if you knew Congress wouldn't go that far?"

"More likely I'd stay out altogether."

"How does that solve our problem? If we don't take the war to them, they'll keep attacking us here."

Pearce heard the edge in Lane's voice but he wouldn't back down. "We stay focused on defending our own territory."

Lane darkened. "I don't want to go to war. Our boots, their boots. I don't care. I'm sick of all of it. I hate war. I'm tired of the waste and the death and the insanity of it. But war is upon us and I'm running out of options."

"We wouldn't be discussing any of these military options if we could find the culprits attacking us," Chandler said. It sounded like an accusation hurled at Pearce.

In fact, it was. And that's how Pearce took it. "Still working on it."

"Not good enough," Lane said.

Pearce saw the look on the president's face. He was clearly at the end of his rope. Pearce got it. He would be, too, if he were in Lane's shoes. He thanked the baby Jesus he wasn't. He had to find the terrorists if he wanted to stop the war.

But how?

"Our best shot at stopping a new attack is to predict where the next one will occur. But the DNI reported earlier that our predictive analytics and NSA surveillance sources are all coming up short. But there is a pattern emerging. By attacking the airlines and trucking, it's clear the threat is economic and it's escalating. So the next target will be even more economically important."

"The power grid is vulnerable to a drone attack," Pia said. "Especially the high-voltage transformers. They constitute just three percent of all transformers but they're responsible for upwards of seventy percent of all electrical output. Terrorists could take out the entire U.S. electrical grid by destroying HVTs at just nine locations. They're all custom-built overseas and would take years to replace."

Eaton frowned. "Our port system is vulnerable, too. Underwater drones could take out ships with explosive cargoes and shut our ports down for days, maybe even weeks, and eighty percent of our foreign trade goes through them."

"Nuclear plants," Chandler said. "That scares the living daylights out of me."

"Could be all the above. Or more. Too much ground to cover," Pearce said.

"All the more reason for immediate and decisive action by our armed forces against ISIS," Grafton said.

"All major infrastructure facilities are already on high alert," Eaton said.

"That might work on a conventional attack," Pearce said. "So far this man or woman or team has been thinking way out of the box."

"So you're convinced it's only a small group of people? Maybe even just one person?" Eaton asked.

"Why else the twenty-four-hour delay between attacks?"

"The delay is a brilliant psychological ploy," Eaton said. "They strike, we react, but then we just sit around for another twenty-three hours waiting for the next catastrophe."

"A large organization could use the same tactic," Grafton said.

"The smaller the number, the better the opsec," Garza said. "One would be best. And the tech deployed so far means it could be just one guy, doesn't it?"

"Possibly," Pearce said. "But it would take a lot of planning and pre-positioning."

"One, few, or many, we don't have a single suspect yet. It's time we rattle some cages," Chandler said. "We know where the bad guys hang out. We know the chat rooms, the university campuses, the mosques. We need to get after them."

"We don't want to become like the people we're fighting," Peguero said. "Besides, you'll cause such resentment in the Muslim community that you'll get more terrorists out of the deal than you're trying to round up."

"So we shouldn't do anything to upset the Muslim community for fear they'll turn into terrorists?" Garza asked. "If angry Muslims are all potential terrorists, then why in the hell do we allow them to immigrate here?"

"That's the kind of racist language our enemies exploit," Peguero said.

"It isn't racist to tell the truth," Garza fired back. "And for the record, 'Muslim' isn't a race, it's a religion. And it wasn't a planeload of Buddhist monks that crashed into the Twin Towers, was it?"

"Even if we wanted to, we don't have the resources to track and monitor that many institutions and individuals. There are approximately thirty-two hundred mosques scattered all around the country now, almost three times as many as existed before 9/11. They're servicing the one-point-six million Muslims we've issued green cards to in that same period," Peguero said.

"She's right. We need to be damn careful we don't misallocate scarce resources. Gotta keep a close eye on the Amish terror networks," Garza said.

"What about martial law?" Chandler asked. "If we can't predict what will happen next or we can't target probable suspects, then let's shut the whole thing down until we get a handle on the situation. Just like the French did after the Paris attacks."

"What would you shut down? The entire country? And for how long?" Eaton asked.

"And we're on the eve of the Asia Security Summit. What kind of message would we be sending about international security if we put the country on lockdown because we couldn't secure our own homeland?" Pia asked.

"And even if you did lock down the whole country, the attacks would resume the day after you lifted it if nobody has been caught," Pearce said. "You'd ruin the economy for no good reason, and all because you're assuming that the attacks are originating inside of the United States."

"The terrorists have to be in the country," Onstot said. "The drones that slammed into those passenger jets were all guided."

"Not necessarily. Airport runways are numbered according to their magnetic azimuth. Plenty of public websites provide every possible data point you'd need to set up an automated attack at any civilian airport around the country, including live radar tracking of aircraft and live camera and video feeds of airport runways around the world. Attacks could be preprogrammed and automated without a line-of-sight operator."

Abbott shook her head. "Holy crap. Don't let the media hear that."

"And the tanker trucks?" Grafton asked.

"All linked by satellite that can be accessed from almost anywhere around the globe, depending on the kind of satellite that was being used and the uplinks the attacker had access to."

"So you think the attacks came from overseas?" Pia asked.

"Not necessarily. Only that they could've been."

"Damn it!" Lane slammed his hand on the table. "I don't need another laundry list of possibilities. I need answers. Now."

Pearce knew Lane wasn't angry with him. He was angry at the situation. The president wanted an answer other than war. The problem was there wasn't one. "I'm working on it."

"We don't have much time," Lane said.

Grafton fumed. Lane still wouldn't commit. Pearce still held the reins. She needed to find a way to get rid of him.

40

TORONTO, CANADA

"What about my assignment here?" Tamar Stern's green eyes narrowed as she jogged on the treadmill. The fitness center in the Trump Tower gave her a spectacular view of the city at night, but she was focused on the voice in her Bluetooth. She was glad she had the place all to herself.

The half-Ethiopian, half-Ashkenazi Mossad agent was on the hunt for a Palestinian butcher who killed a young mother and her two toddlers with a knife before slipping into Canada's refugee program. Tamar had every intention of fulfilling her mission to kill him because he was an enemy of the state and she was a good agent. The fact that he'd murdered her cousin and her children only made the task more gratifying.

"You can finish up later. This Brody thing is important. This is straight from the top."

She tapped the Off button on the treadmill and stepped off. "There's nobody else?"

"Not within driving distance. If there were, I wouldn't be sending you."

"What's wrong with flying?"

"Can't be sure the Americans won't ground their planes again."

Tamar knew the voice on the other end of the scrambled phone well. The head of Mossad's North American operations was her former team leader in Iraq. Refusing an order from Moshe Werntz simply wasn't an option. Ever.

"You're the boss," she finally conceded, barely able to hide her frustration.

"I'll keep working on leads for you on my end. By the time you get back, you'll have your target in hand."

"No one else is to touch him."

"He's all yours, I promise."

"I'll contact you when I arrive tomorrow," Tamar said, ending the call. She toweled off her sweaty face as she headed for the door. Back to her suite for a quick shower, then room service and off to bed. It was going to be a long day tomorrow. Seven or eight hours of driving at a minimum. At least she had a new Alex Berenson audiobook she wanted to listen to, and the long drive would give her a chance to call her old friend Troy Pearce. Maybe he could help her find Brody. After all, it was his backyard and he owed her a favor after Berlin.

WASHINGTON, D.C.

Grafton unplugged the blow dryer just as the knock came. She scurried out of the marble-tiled bathroom and into the sumptuous living room in her fluffy white robe and matching slippers with the name of the boutique hotel embroidered on the toes. The slippers were a little much but comfortably plush, and she couldn't bear the thought of walking barefoot on a public carpet, even an elegant one. She opened the door to a smiling, handsome man of Middle Eastern descent standing behind a cart.

"Room service?" he asked.

"Please." Grafton ushered him in with a wave and held the door for him. He parked the cart in the middle of the Colonial-style living room and began to unload it but she stopped him.

"No need. I'll take it from here." She pulled a folded twenty from one of her robe's deep pockets and handed it to the man.

"Yes, ma'am. Of course." He bowed slightly and headed for the door. Grafton locked it and threw the swing bar over the security latch, then pushed the serving cart into the next room.

"How was your shower?" Grafton asked.

Al-Saud pulled the champagne out of the ice bucket, admiring the vintage. "Excellent. Wonderful choice, by the way."

Grafton stood up on her toes and kissed the royal prince on his cheek, just above his stylish beard. "I'm so glad you approve. This is my favorite hotel in D.C."

Al-Saud popped the champagne cork and poured their glasses as Grafton set up the dinner service on the table beneath the gorgeous period crystal chandelier. They took their seats. Al-Saud lifted his glass. "To us."

"To us." They touched glasses and drank.

"I hope you enjoy what I've ordered," she said.

"I'm famished. Show me."

Grafton lifted the first sterling silver plate cover. "For you we have spiced honey-glazed venison loin with pear, a grits cake, burgundy truffles, savory cabbage, and a combination of pistachios and hazelnuts."

Al-Saud leaned over the plate and inhaled deeply. "It smells fantastic."

Grafton lifted a second plate cover. "For myself I've ordered roasted medallions of Atlantic halibut, sweet potato, and apple mille-feuille, applewood-smoked bacon, tarragon coulis, and razor clam broth. We can share if you like."

"Of course. You plan everything so well." Al-Saud held his knife in his left hand and his fork in the right in the German style. He never understood why Americans insisted on cutting with the right, then switching hands to use the fork.

"I aim to please," Grafton said, taking her first bite of halibut.

Al-Saud smiled. "Is there anything in which you don't excel?"

"I used to think I could run a room. But today the meeting ran away from me."

"How so?"

"In my humble opinion, the United States needs to act swiftly and decisively against ISIS. We can't afford to wait for the Russians or anybody else to join in. But Lane still hasn't fully committed."

"It's understandable, given his campaign promise of no new boots on the ground."

"But things have changed since the election. If people knew about the letter, or the attacks—"

"Attacks? There has been more than one?"

Grafton nodded. "You can't say anything. It's classified."

"Of course not." Al-Saud took another bite of venison. "I could be of more help to you if I were in those meetings."

"It was Pearce that got you thrown out."

"Can't Chandler get me back in?"

"He's working on it, but Pearce has got Lane's ear for some reason."

The prince refilled their champagne glasses. "Tell me more about this Pearce fellow. He seemed rather unpleasant."

"Unpleasant? He's a pain in the ass. Believe me, I have to work with him."

"It is difficult to help him prepare for the Senate confirmation hearing?"

"Let's just say he doesn't play nice with others. I don't know what Lane sees in him."

"My security people tell me he's a very gifted man. The founder and CEO of the world's premier drone security company."

"All of the CEOs I know are interested in making money. I assumed that's why he was in Washington—to play the game. But I think he fancies himself some kind of patriot."

"He is a patriot, isn't he? He served in the CIA's paramilitary organization."

"That's the strange thing. He's the strongest voice in the room against a U.S. ground operation. If I didn't know any better, I'd say he was an old-fashioned isolationist." She took another sip of champagne. "Chandler can't break his spell, either. Maybe it's Pearce's connection to Myers that holds so much weight for Lane. Myers was instrumental in Lane's election."

"Wasn't the 'no new boots' policy originally hers?"

"Yes. She was only following public opinion at the time, which has only gotten stronger on the subject."

"Sounds as if she was leading from behind, to borrow a phrase."

"Lane's no better. Chandler's pushing the Russian option if Lane won't commit American troops. Speaking of which, how did your meeting with Tarkovsky go?"

"A very charming man. Do you know him?"

Strange question, Grafton thought. She wondered for a moment if he knew about her relationship with the Russian ambassador but instantly decided against the possibility. "Mostly by reputation. I've been in the room with him a few times. Smart guy. Don't know if I trust him."

"I agree. He's quite intelligent. And persuasive. He's also a big fan of yours. You must have made quite an impression."

She shook her head. "It's the red hair, that's all."

"Tarkovsky made a compelling case to me that the Russians should get more involved in the region."

"Do you agree with him?"

"My government does. Riyadh fears that you Americans have lost your sense of the balance of power. ISIS is an existential threat to the Kingdom, as is Iran. With Baghdad and Tehran getting closer, we fear an overwhelming sense of imbalance that is tilting decidedly against us. At least the Russians have influence with Iran."

"You said your government supports this. It sounds as if you do as well."

"Me? Not at all. The Russians would cause more problems for my country than they would solve in the long run. Titov is a dictator in all but name, with grand designs of reviving the Russian empire. I much prefer the Americans as alliance partners. There is much to admire about your way of life and worldview. If your government ever decided to live up to its role as the leader of the Western world, my government would follow suit. Tell me, why do you suppose the vice president is so keen on Russian involvement?"

Grafton took a sip of champagne, trying not to laugh. "He has dreams of winning the Nobel Peace Prize."

Al-Saud grinned. "Seriously? How?"

"By forging a grand new security alliance with Russia and NATO."

"For what purpose?"

"He'd tell you it was to bring a lasting peace to the European continent and to solve the trouble in the Middle East, beginning with ISIS."

"But what do you say?"

"He thinks a Nobel Peace Prize will guarantee him the White House."

"And does Pearce support Chandler's position vis-à-vis the Russians?"

"Hardly."

"So it seems that there are three of us that would like to get Mr. Pearce out of the White House."

"Yes, but how?" Grafton forked another bite of halibut into her mouth. She was open to suggestions.

"If he can't be pushed out, maybe he can be pulled out."

"You have any ideas?"

"I'm not that clever." Al-Saud lifted the last sterling silver cover. "What's this?"

"Dessert, my sweet. Caramelized pineapple, bourbon vanilla coconut meringue and passion fruit–mango sorbet." The plate rested in a bed of crushed ice.

"I can't wait to try it. Where's yours?"

Al-Saud felt Grafton's skilled fingers wrap around his manhood.

"Mine's right here. But you better eat yours. You're going to need the energy."

41

Max Garcia slipped the cherry-red Mustang into reverse as the automatic garage door lifted. He turned around out of habit, throwing his right arm across the top of the passenger seat and steered with his left hand, watching for traffic and kids in the quiet but hilly street in the Silver Lake community. He rode the brake pedal as the car edged down the steep driveway until his phone sounded a familiar tone. A text from his girlfriend. He hit the brakes, threw the transmission into park, and checked the message.

    NEED U WANT U NOW!!!

An X-rated emoticon Garcia had never seen before accompanied the text. He grinned beneath his salt-and-pepper mustache. She was ten years his junior and really hot in the sack. He hit the microphone on his keyboard and spoke back the text, "Can't. Big meeting in thirty minutes. Maybe a nooner?"

Another text appeared.

    Won't take long. I have a big surprise for you. Hurry!

Another sexy emoticon.

Garcia sighed. She was a real nympho. Always ready to go, which he liked. Didn't need a lot of talking to beforehand, and glad to grab a quick bite to eat or a drink later, which meant she was easy on his wallet, too.

He checked his watch. He had to leave now if he didn't want to walk in late to yet another meeting. His boss at the water district would write him up for sure after the last warning. He spoke another text. "Sorry, babe. I want you, too. Gotta wait. I'll make it worth your while. I promise."

He watched the three blinking dots on his iPhone as she typed yet another text. He couldn't wait any longer. Traffic on Sunset would start backing up any minute. He threw the car back into reverse when a popping soap bubble sound signaled the arrival of her next text. He backed all the way into the street, turned, then threw the car into drive and sped forward. He picked up his phone and glanced at the text.

> Come now or I'll call your wife. Maybe she'd like to come over and we can have a long talk about all those dirty things you like to do to me.

Garcia swore violently. He thought this bitch was cool. They'd had a thing for months now and she'd been a real sport. What was going on with her? Maybe that time of the month, he grumbled. You never knew with women.

"I'll lose my job if I'm late," he spoke into the phone.

He hit the gas, speeding a little too fast in the narrow residential street, but he had to make the next light if he hoped to beat the first rush of traffic. He heard the popping text bubble again. It was an address in Los Feliz but she lived in Burbank. Had she moved without telling him? She probably wanted to christen the place. Crazy bitch.

> 15 minutes or I call your wife.

Garcia shook his head. His first divorce cost him a three-bedroom rancher in South Pasadena and half his retirement pension. He couldn't afford to lose the new house to his second wife and he was already under-water on the mortgage. He texted back, "Okay, but it's gotta be quick."

> I'm already wet.

The filthiest emoticon he'd ever seen popped up. He felt a rush of blood to his crotch. He'd figure out a way to explain his tardiness to his boss.

Garcia tapped the address and it pulled up on a Google map. Seven minutes away. Good. He was already getting hard just thinking about what she would do to him, but he popped a little blue pill anyway and washed it down with sip of stale coffee.

Timing was everything.

THE WHITE HOUSE, WASHINGTON, D.C.

Pearce was working over a plate of hash browns and hard fried eggs in the wood-paneled White House cafeteria when his phone vibrated. He picked it up. An unknown caller. Not many people had the number for his phone. Against his better judgment he answered.

"Yeah?"

"Troy, it's me, Moshe Werntz."

Pearce recognized the thickly accented English of his old friend. He glanced around the room. Nobody was within earshot but he lowered his voice anyway. "It's been a long time, Moshe." Pearce had heard through the grapevine that his old friend from the Mossad was head of North American operations and chief of station in D.C.

"Too long, my friend. How are you enjoying Washington these days?"

"It's like a slow-motion car wreck. If I manage to walk away in one piece I'll be happy."

Werntz laughed. "I understand completely. I think a firefight is more pleasurable than the games these politicians play, mine included."

"What can I do for you?"

"I just wanted to touch base. I'm sorry I haven't stopped by to see you yet. How are things going with your Senate hearing?"

"Fine. Thanks for asking." Pearce could tell by the tone of his voice that wasn't the purpose of his call. "So what's really up?"

"I'm sure you have a lot on your plate these days," Werntz said.

Pearce wondered how much the cagey old Israeli spy knew about the current state of affairs.

"No rest for the wicked," Pearce said.

"And the righteous don't need any," Werntz said. "But since I have been a negligent friend, I feel as if I owe you a favor."

"Happy to collect them. What have you got?"

The Israeli spymaster paused for effect. "It's a delicate matter. I'm sure I can trust your discretion."

Pearce's eyes kept scanning the room. No one was listening to his conversation, near as he could tell. His phone was encrypted, so even if the Secret Service was scanning calls in the room, they wouldn't be able to hear them. "Of course."

"I thought you'd like to know that Ambassadors al-Saud and Tarkovsky of the Saudi and Russian delegations, respectively, met just yesterday at al-Saud's private residence."

Pearce frowned, concerned. That wasn't good news. Interesting that they were both being invited back into the Situation Room in just a few minutes. "Maybe they're in love and wanted a moment alone."

"Perhaps. But it seems that the Saudi and the Russian governments are suddenly becoming fast friends."

"Why is that a problem?" Pearce asked, fully knowing why.

"Perhaps it's nothing. Perhaps we're just jealous that we haven't been invited to the party with the cool kids. But I thought you should know."

"What did they talk about?"

The Israeli faked outrage. "Troy, I'm shocked. Are you accusing me of spying?"

"Isn't that what you do?"

Werntz laughed. "I wouldn't be very good at my job if I were to answer such a question, would I? And yet you and I are old friends, so I will tell you that we trust neither the Saudis nor the Russians."

"Me neither."

"And yet your vice president seems quite taken with both of them lately."

"Which is why you called me and not him," Pearce said.

"We live in such interesting times, don't we? It's important to remember who our true friends are."

"I do, believe me."

"Yes, of course you do. But does your government?"

Good question, Pearce thought.

"Please give my regards to President Myers," Werntz said. "And President Lane as well, though I've yet had the good fortune to meet him."

Pearce was frustrated that Lane's advisors had kept the Israelis at arm's length since his election. Powerful factions in Lane's party were doing everything they could to ostracize the Israeli government for political and politically correct reasons. He knew Lane was sympathetic to the Israeli situation but he had a lot on his agenda these days and Israeli-American relations were a low priority at the moment. "I'll see if I can't fix that soon."

"I'd be grateful, as would my ambassador. Have a wonderful day, Troy."

"You, too, Moshe. Thanks for the heads-up. My best to your wife."

Pearce slipped the phone into his pocket. He dug back into his breakfast, processing this new piece of information. *Games within games*, he said to himself.

Games they might already have lost.

LOS FELIZ, LOS ANGELES, CALIFORNIA

Garcia parked his Mustang in front of the white stucco rental. He double-checked the address. It was correct. He was going to be late to work for sure but there was no way around it. She was crazy enough to rat him out but she was also the best lay he'd ever had. Lucky for him his current wife never checked his text messages.

Here, he texted.

Great! Come on in! I'm in the back bedroom. Get ready.

Garcia scrambled out of his car and jogged up the short brick path to the porch. He could hear faint salsa music on the other side of the heavy wooden front door. He glanced around the neighborhood but no one was there to see him. He was grateful. He saw a security camera attached to the eaves that pointed in his direction. He'd told his woman she needed to get serious about her personal security. Violent crime wasn't just south of the I-10 these days. It pleased him that she was finally listening to him, but when he found out the front door was unlocked he was irritated again. She didn't have any common sense. Of course, if she did, she wouldn't be fooling around with him.

He stepped inside and called out to her but there wasn't any response. His voice reverberated on the red terra-cotta floors. So did the music, which was much louder now that he was inside. He shut the door behind him.

The house was completely void of any furniture except for a TV dinner tray with the blaring radio. This was getting weirder by the minute. But the little blue pill had kicked in and he was in serious need of relief now. She was easily satisfied and so was he, so this wouldn't take long. The rougher and faster he was, the more she liked it anyway.

Garcia worked his way down the hallway, where another noise caught his attention. A low hum, almost industrial. He called out her name again. No answer. At the end of the hall he saw a closed door and another security camera perched above it.

He approached the door and turned the doorknob and opened it.

His woman wasn't there. The noise was louder.

He paled.

Oh, damn.

42

All eyes in the Situation Room were focused on a crudely shot cell phone video flashing on the screen. The sound was off.

"And this Garcia guy is credible?" Chandler asked.

"He's the operations manager for the Metropolitan Water District of Southern California. He's in charge of delivering water to nearly twenty million people in the L.A. basin, so, yes, I'd say he's credible," Peguero said. She fast-forwarded to a large portable pump, steel pipes, and a fifty-five-gallon plastic drum. They were all connected to the larger water pipes in the bathroom wall, torn away, along with the sink. The toilet had been removed to make room for the equipment. Yellow-suited HAZMAT workers crowded in the frame. Pearce saw one of them wanding the plastic drum with a handheld Geiger counter.

"And Garcia just happened to find this rig?"

"The details of how he managed to find it are still a little sketchy. The FBI ran a quick background check. He's not on any watch list and he doesn't have any felony convictions. I'd say he's above suspicion. Otherwise, why call it in?"

Peguero described how Garcia had called his number two at the MWDSC, who then alerted the head of the security team. The water district had a plan in place for just such an emergency. The FBI was immediately contacted, along with an L.A. County HAZMAT team.

"And we're sure the water district is safe?" Chandler said.

"Not at all," Peguero said. "What Garcia and the water people tell us is that the device found in that home hadn't been activated. That fifty-five-gallon drum contains plutonium-239, at least according to the letter they left behind." She froze the image and pointed to a small metal box with an antenna located on top of the pump. "We believe this is a remote-control unit designed to activate the pump on a cell phone signal."

"How could one drum of contaminated water affect the entire water system? Aren't there controls in place for something like this? Wouldn't water treatment have caught it?" Grafton asked.

"This is our worst-case scenario come to life," Eaton said, her face darkening. The former army general looked like she hadn't slept in days. "It's a system designed to induce a backflow contamination event into the main water supply—the water that has already passed through the treatment process and is made available for public consumption. It's extremely simple and effective. The pump you see in the video is used to overcome the water-pressure gradient coming into the house, effectively stopping the water flow long enough to dump the contaminant in. Then the pump is shut off and the main water system itself siphons and circulates the contaminant throughout the network. In some computer simulations we've run, the right induction point can contaminate whole neighborhoods and even the main trunk lines before the contaminant is even detected. If this device had been activated, we think as many as ten thousand homes could have been affected."

The room was stunned into incredulous silence. Pearce could see the gears behind everyone's eyes as they processed the magnitude of Eaton's words.

Pia cleared his throat. "Aren't there backflow prevention devices looped into these networks to avoid this exact scenario? Water system attacks have occurred all over the world. I thought our people were on top of this."

"Yes. Prevention devices are in place," Eaton said. "But they weren't designed for terrorist attacks. Backflow incidents are usually accidents. So the backflow devices aren't considered strategically important. They're often out in public and not guarded. In fact, the nearest backflow device to this house was just a half mile away. No fencing or protection of any kind. That might even be why this particular location was selected. Apparently that backflow prevention device was disabled with a low-yield remote-controlled explosion just thirty minutes before the house was discovered."

Pearce saw the frustration in the president's face.

"I thought the EPA's Water Security Initiative was supposed to prevent this kind of thing."

"The WSI has been very effective, but no system is perfect and it hasn't been fully implemented across the board. And just like with the electric grid, it's really up to the local authorities to bear the brunt of security. The overall problem we face is that there are nearly one hundred seventy thousand public water systems, many of them serving fewer than a hundred people. The biggest vulnerability is that only fifteen percent of all public water systems provide seventy-five percent of all potable water. Attack those fifteen percent and you've got a national problem on your hands. The other challenge is this: If this attack had been initiated, the Water Sector Initiative alarms would've likely sounded—after the distribution of the plutonium—and the MWDSC would've alerted the general population, according to protocols. That would've led to mass panic on top of the contamination even if we could've stopped or neutralized the contaminant."

"And we're confident the device as constructed would've led to widespread contamination?" Chandler asked.

"No question," Eaton said. "But it isn't only a matter of this single device and location. You can see on your tablets that the terrorists left behind a schematic of the entire MWDSC. We've already discovered two more disabled backflow devices, and the water district is checking all of the others. Worse, the terrorists claim there are five more introduction points in the MWDSC ready to be activated. Where they are is anybody's guess. These people knew exactly what they were doing and how to do it."

The room exchanged nervous glances.

"By the look on your face I take it there's more bad news," Lane said.

Eaton nodded grimly. "They also listed threats to ten other metropolitan water districts, including Nashville, Dallas, Salt Lake City, and New Orleans. We've issued a private security bulletin to every water district in the country, alerting them to potential contamination threats. This could be a mass attack on an unprecedented scale. We're talking millions of casualties. Utterly catastrophic. And I don't use that word lightly."

Pearce felt the rising anxiety in the room, rushing in like a morning tide.

"Please God, tell me that this is all being kept out of the press," Abbott said. The White House press secretary had been fighting tooth and nail to squash the terrorism rumors flying around D.C. for the last twenty-four hours.

Peguero frowned. "While I agree that we wouldn't want to cause a mass panic over the mere *threat* of a water-contamination event, at some point we owe the public an explanation and the opportunity to prepare accordingly."

Garza shook his head in disgust. "And when would that be? You let this story out, the only 'preparation' anyone will take is rioting."

Peguero shrugged. "I'm just saying."

"Any chance of finding the other automated introduction points in L.A. or around the country?" Lane asked.

Peguero shook her head. "You'd have to kick down every door inside of every building all over the county, and then you'd still have to contend with at least six million fire hydrants and thousands of water towers, both of which are also points of access. And that would be the easy stuff to find."

Pearce felt the iWatch tap his wrist—a phone call. If it was important, the caller would leave a voice mail. He hoped it wasn't Margaret. But the call reminded him of his earlier conversation with Moshe.

"The letter said the water was loaded with plutonium-239," Garza said. "If I recall, it has a half-life of twenty-four thousand years."

Chandler paled. "Oh, Lord."

Garza turned to the vice president. "It's really, really nasty shit. What I want to know is, where'd they get it from?"

"No telling," Eaton said. "Most likely stolen from one of our own stockpiles. It's fissile material used in either nuclear bombs or nuclear reactors. There are hundreds of tons of it in storage, a lot of it being converted to MOX to burn in civilian nuclear power plants."

"That stuff is under lock and key. Hard to steal," Pearce said. "It's more likely a country with plutonium-239 stockpiles provided it directly."

"You have someone particular in mind?" Lane asked.

"Who would benefit from the transaction? Wouldn't be the French or the Japanese," Chandler said.

"How about North Korea?" Pia asked.

"They don't produce very much of it, and whatever they produce they keep for their own nuclear weapons program," Pia said.

"India, Pakistan, China—" Onstot threw in.

"Don't see the advantage, especially China with the upcoming security summit. And China fears ISIS influence as much as we do among their ethnic Uighurs."

"Unless there's a rogue element in the PLA behind this," Pia said.

Pearce leaned forward on the desk, folding his hands and shaking his head.

"Come on, Troy," Chandler said, rolling his eyes. "You obviously have your own answer."

Pearce turned to Chandler. "What about the Russians?"

43

"The Russians have more of this in stockpile than anybody," Pearce said.

"The Russians? Are you insane?" Chandler asked. "They're trying to get back in our good graces. If they were behind this attack, we'd be back in another cold war in a heartbeat. Possibly even a shooting war."

Pearce sat back, trying to decide if he should divulge Moshe's intel. Better not, he decided. No point in compromising his Israeli source at this juncture. "I don't completely disagree, but I think we need to explore every option. We're still not one hundred percent sure this is actually an ISIS attack and we still haven't found any culprits."

"What about the rental house in L.A.?" Garza asked. "Whoever rented or owned it might be who we're looking for."

"Checking on it now," Peguero said. "Not likely the bad guys used their real names or left a forwarding address. Neighbors claimed they haven't seen anybody for weeks."

"That explains why Gorgon Sky wasn't any help," Pearce said. Ashley had managed to get three pervasive stare units in the air over the Los Angeles basin last night but nothing pulled up in the digital review except for Garcia's car pulling up to the house earlier that morning.

"As far as I'm concerned, there are only two options on the table, Mr. President," Chandler said. "Either we raise the black flag or we launch the war. This attack proves these animals are willing to kill millions of us."

Pearce threw up his hands. "Whoa, let's back this truck up. What do you mean they're willing to kill millions of us? If ISIS really has dozens of these induction points loaded with nuclear material, why didn't they just use them? Why isn't the entire U.S. water supply irreparably contaminated right now? Or even just Los Angeles? We know they're murderous fucks. ISIS wouldn't hold back."

Peguero read from the letter left behind in Los Feliz. "'An act of restraint, an act of mercy before the final blow if you don't bow the knee and raise the flag by noon tomorrow.'"

"Bullshit," Pearce said. "These guys cut people's heads off, gang-rape children, set prisoners on fire. There's no mercy in their black hearts."

"What's your point?" Onstot asked.

"If this restraint was an act of mercy, then it couldn't have been ISIS. Maybe it's an American or some other Western group with a conscience. Hell, I don't know. But if it really wasn't an act of mercy, it could've been the work of a lone wolf—a radical, a merc, an earth worshipper— somebody who doesn't have the capacity to poison our entire water supply. Maybe he or she or they just want us to think they can."

"That really narrows things down," Chandler said.

"Then why no ransom note? Why the demand to raise the black flag? Why claim to be ISIS?" Garza asked. "And how or why would the Russians be connected to it?"

Pearce ran his hand through his hair, a nervous habit. "I don't know. I'm not convinced I believe anything I'm even saying. I'm verbally processing as much as anything. What I do know is that going to war is a nightmare. Many will die on both sides, and they'll die for no good reason if we get this wrong."

"There's always the flag option," Peguero said.

"I'm not raising that godforsaken flag, Julissa. I thought I made that perfectly clear," Lane said.

"Am I free to speak my mind? Or is this just an exercise in machismo groupthink?"

Lane motioned with his hand. "Go ahead, please."

"It's just a flag. A piece of silk with ink on it. It's all these flags and chest-beating rants that cause all the problems in the world. I say put your ego aside and raise the flag and see if that solves the problem. If it does, you've saved thousands of lives—maybe millions—and avoided a cataclysmic assault on our country."

"He'll be impeached the second he raises that flag," Chandler said. "And we know ISIS doesn't keep its word."

"Just a flag?" Garza said. His eyes were daggers. "Flags mean something, lady." He pointed at the American flag standing on a pole in the corner of the room. "I had good friends who died for that flag. Hundreds of thousands of Americans have been killed and wounded for that flag. I'll be damned if I'll stand by and watch that flag get lowered from the top of this building and replaced with that filthy do-rag."

Peguero remained unflustered. "Mr. President, there will be blood on your hands if you decide to launch a war—American blood as well as the blood of innocent civilians. History will judge you harshly if it turns out you could have prevented all of that bloodshed if you would've set aside your ego and raised that meaningless piece of silk."

Eaton shook her head. "You raise that flag and a billion Muslims will be dancing in the streets before sunset, including Muslims in this country. ISIS's reputation will soar. They'll double their recruitment in twenty-four hours. They'll have ten times as many fighters within the week. They'll all be smelling blood and mocking us in every mosque and madrassa from Mecca to Detroit."

Lane nodded. He stood and stepped over to the box containing the black-and-white ISIS flag. He picked it up and examined it closely, thinking.

Pearce felt his stomach sicken. Was Lane wavering?

Lane held it up for the rest of the room to see.

"I greatly appreciate your comments, Julissa, and I respect your opinion. Thank you for sharing it. This is a flag that stands for death and the destruction of everything I hold dear."

Lane's hands flew apart, ripping the flag in two.

"Now you're talking," Garza said.

Lane tore the flag again and again, then tossed it on the floor. "Is my position on this matter clear?"

Heads nodded all around the table.

"Good." Lane turned to Chandler. "Contact your friend Ambassador Tarkovsky. I imagine he's already been in contact with Moscow. I want to run him through the paces with the rest of our team and see where they stand. Today, if at all possible."

Chandler fought back a grin. "Yes, Mr. President."

Grafton seethed. She needed to get the Tarkovsky option off the table. But how? "Excuse me, Mr. President, but if we're considering a joint international effort, we should bring Ambassador al-Saud in on the meeting with Ambassador Tarkovsky."

"Good point." Lane saw the objection in Pearce's eyes. Ignored it. "Can you arrange that, Vicki?"

"I'm on it." Grafton picked up her smartphone and began texting, telling him to come quickly and to argue against Russian intervention.

Lane turned to Pearce. "I want you there at that meeting. And I want you to ask Tarkovsky directly."

"No problem."

"Him?" Chandler said, pointing at Pearce. "He's a bull in a China shop."

"You'll be there, too, Clay. You can pick up the pieces when he's done."

"To do what? Try and glue them back together?" Chandler forced a smile. "I'll do my best."

The rest stood up to leave while Pearce checked his phone. It wasn't Myers who had called.

It was Tamar Stern.

44

The night air was cool, even though it was summer.

One of Frankfurt's most popular destinations, the Römerberg plaza was brilliantly lit and still crowded with tourists. The tables outside the restaurants and bars were packed with customers downing sizzling sausages and tankards of frothy beer.

"If you had come in the winter you could have seen the Christmas Market, one of the oldest in all of Europe," Mann said in faultless English. His eyes kept scanning the bustling crowds. Quite a few hijabs and Middle Eastern men among them, he noticed. He felt guilty for resenting them.

"I love the architecture," Myers said, standing in front of the famous eastern facade of the Römer and its "stair-step" rooflines. The small plaza off the main boulevard was a circular enclave of tall medieval-styled buildings of various designs in hues of green, red, beige, and yellow. It looked like every postcard she had ever seen of Germany.

"They still register weddings in there," Mann said, nodding at the Römer. "On the weekends there is a traffic jam of wedding parties out here in the plaza."

"Must be delightful to see. I envy you having a country with such a long history. I read on the plane that the Romans first settled this city nearly two thousand years ago." Myers thought Mann looked like a dashing U-boat captain in his scruffy beard, dark woolen coat, and fisherman's cap.

"Don't be fooled by what you see. This city was leveled by Allied bombers during the war. This plaza was rebuilt to appear like a medieval square back in the eighties to celebrate our heritage, but also to bring in the tourists."

"Tourists like me."

"*Ganz genau.* Exactly."

"Still, it must mean something to you that Charlemagne once ruled from here. Maybe even stood exactly where we're standing right now."

"History is a double-edged sword. How it cuts depends on where you stand." He steered her gently by the elbow toward a large commemorative bronze plaque in the midst of the cobblestones. They stood over it. In the center of the plaque were bronze book pages and licking flames with an inscription in German in the center.

"What does it say?"

Mann translated. "In this place on 10 May 1933, National Socialist students burned books by writers, political commentators, scientists, and philosophers."

"That's terrible. What does the rest of it mean?" She pointed at the words circling the plaque.

"It's a famous quote from a nineteenth-century German Romantic poet by the name of Heinrich Heine. It says, in effect, 'Where they first burn books, they will later burn people.'"

"Did the Nazis burn his books?"

"Of course. He was born a Jew, though later he converted to Christianity. In the context of this quote, he was actually writing about the danger of burning the Koran. History is a circle, yes?"

Myers glanced over at the statue in the center of the plaza, surrounded by a fountain. A great bronzed woman with a sword and scales.

"That is Lady Justice, a Roman goddess," Mann said. "This is her plaza and her fountain."

"I like her. She's fierce. Her sword is already drawn and she isn't blindfolded," Myers said. "Justice can never be blind."

"She is fickle, this one, I think. Or perhaps her back was turned when the books were burning behind her." Mann nodded at the head of his security team standing near the Old St. Nicholas Church on the edge of the plaza. He whispered German in his comms as he scanned the crowd for the rest of his team. Once he made eye contact with the others, he turned his attention back to her. "Perhaps we can leave now?"

"We just got here. I'd like to look around."

"There are too many people here. I can't guarantee your safety."

"First let's have a beer and a schnitzel or something. I'm starving."

"As you wish, Madam President."

"Margaret, please."

Mann led the way through the milling crowd toward one of the beer gardens. Myers watched him whisper in a waiter's ear and the surprised expression that lit the old man's pale blue eyes. A smile creased his wrinkled face and he bowed discreetly toward Myers, an old reflex. She smiled warmly in response and the waiter grabbed two younger men, and a small portable table was set up with such efficiency and speed that the other tourists hardly paid attention.

Myers took her seat. She noticed Mann remained standing. "What are you doing?"

Mann looked embarrassed. "I'm standing watch."

"You'll sit down and eat with me. I insist. It's been a long day for you, too."

"But my team—"

"We'll feed them next. Please, this is all such a fuss over nothing."

Mann shrugged, resigned. She had a commanding voice and he was truly famished. He took the seat opposite her. He ordered for the two of them and ten minutes later, two towering mugs of a carefully poured local pilsner were set before them along with plates of steaming potatoes, beef brisket, and two small bowls of green sauce.

"What's this?" Myers said, dipping her finger into the sauce and tasting it.

"*Grüne Sosse.* It means—"

"Let me guess. Green sauce?"

"Your German is excellent."

"Don't kid a kidder, August," Myers laughed. "It's delicious. I'm tasting dill, sour cream, and chives. What do I do with it?" The crowd of tourists around them chatted and laughed, enjoying the festive evening.

"If you were Goethe, you'd pour it all over your potatoes and meat. It was his favorite dish. Or you can just use it like, how do you say, a dip." Mann dumped his bowl all over his food. Myers followed suit.

"Why don't we hear about German poets anymore?"

"Nihilists can't rhyme."

They drank and ate like old friends, which they really weren't, but the shared experience of near death in the Sahara with Pearce had brought them closer than most. Mann was telling a funny story about Pearce when his earpiece crackled with a panicked shout from one of his team, but before Mann could react, the pilsner mug in front of Myers shattered in a cloud of glass and beer foam and she tumbled backward to the stony ground.

45

Lane's Oval Office phone rang.

"Mr. President, Ambassadors Tarkovsky and al-Saud have arrived."

"Show them in, please."

"The cavalry's finally here," Chandler said. Lane glanced at Pearce, who shook his head disapprovingly.

The two ambassadors entered. Chandler greeted them first with enthusiastic handshakes.

Lane, likewise, stood and shook their hands. "Thank you both for coming on such short notice."

"Of course, Mr. President," al-Saud said.

"I'm at your service," Tarvkosky said.

Lane pointed them to the couches. Pearce remained seated in his chair opposite the president, scowling. The two ambassadors noted this but said nothing. Chandler sat back, affecting calm, fighting hard to suppress a gloating smile.

"Gentlemen," Lane said, "there's no time for diplomatic protocols. Events over the last three days have spun out of control. I've called you here to lay my cards out on the table, and I'm asking you both to do the same."

Both ambassadors nodded.

"As you both know, three days ago I received a message delivered by a drone threatening to unleash hell on my country if I didn't raise the black flag of ISIS over the White House. Unfortunately, my security services have been unable either to find or stop the culprits from carrying out these attacks."

"My embassy has been carefully tracking your news services. There hasn't been any reporting on any catastrophic event that we know of," Tarkovsky said.

"How bad have the casualties been?" al-Saud asked.

"Because the casualties have been relatively light, and because of cooperation from our major media outlets, we've been able to keep a lid on these events, but it won't be long before these stories break. As you can both well imagine, if the public gets wind of this before I can assure them we have the situation under control, there will be mass panic. Markets will crash here and around the globe. I'm also concerned about the potential for mob violence against Muslim people here."

"How bad can the attacks have been if there haven't been any casualties?" al-Saud asked.

"Some members of my security council believe that the attacks have been intentionally limited in their lethality, but the potential for mass casualties appears to be very real. The last attack especially so."

"And what is the nature of that attack?" Tarkovsky asked.

"You don't need to know," Pearce said.

Tarkovsky darkened. "Perhaps we would like to prepare our defenses against such an attack ourselves."

Lane waved Pearce off. "You're right, Aleksandr. In the spirit of full disclosure, I can tell you that there was a credible threat against our public water system. The entire national system."

Shock washed over al-Saud's face.

Tarkovsky shifted in his seat, skeptical. "How is such a feat possible?"

"My security people will contact yours shortly with details so you can take the necessary precautions. Yours too, Faisal."

"Thank you," al-Saud said. "My desert country is even more vulnerable to such a water threat than your two great nations."

Pearce nodded, intrigued. "Yes, it is, isn't it?"

"I trust you have decided against flying the *Daesh* flag?" al-Saud asked.

"Of course," Lane said. "Over the protest of some of my cabinet."

"Flying that flag would be as symbolic to the killers as the downing of the Twin Towers. Perhaps greater," al-Saud said. "It would raise up a new army of recruits overnight."

"We agree," Chandler said.

"Many recruits from Saudi Arabia, no doubt," Pearce said.

Al-Saud shook his head, grieved. "Unfortunately."

"Which is why His Majesty's government is as committed to the destruction of ISIS as we are," Chandler said.

Al-Saud nodded toward Chandler. "Thank you for understanding our predicament, Mr. Vice President."

"You must forgive Mr. Pearce. He has a hard time seeing the big picture," Chandler said.

"If you won't fly the flag and you can't find the terrorists, what option do you have other than war?" Tarkovsky asked.

"None," Lane said. "That's why you're both here. I need to make a decision and I need to make it quickly. Maybe I'm naive but I think candor is the best form of diplomacy. And in all candor, I'm trying to assess whether or not I want the cooperation of either or both of your countries in a ground war against ISIS."

"It's obviously not a matter of fighting capacities," Chandler added. "But the president wants to determine if we are all of similar minds on the issue. Whether or not our interests are mutually aligned."

"I am a scientist by training first, and then a diplomat," Tarkovsky said. "I believe in facts and the facts are clear. ISIS is a threat to everyone in this room. We have a large and restive Muslim population within our borders and an even more aggressive population beyond them. My government is completely prepared to join your country in any way feasible to destroy ISIS, including the use of our own troops on the ground."

"Unconditionally?" Lane asked.

"Of course not. The West imposed heavy economic sanctions on my country for the war in Ukraine. Those must be lifted immediately as a sign of good faith. We must also be treated as equal partners in this conflict. A grand alliance, much the same way our two countries allied against the fascists in the Great Patriotic War."

So you'll do the right thing as long as we bribe you to do it, Pearce wanted to say. He held his tongue instead.

"Mr. President, this is a historic opportunity to restore balance and peace in the world," Chandler said. "Thanks to your initiative in Asia, we will be partnering with China to bring stability to that region. Now we can partner with Russia to bring the same kind of stability to Europe and the Middle East."

"Would your government feel comfortable with an American-Russian hegemony over your part of the world?" Lane asked al-Saud.

Pearce felt his iWatch tap the inside of his wrist. He discreetly checked the face. An incoming call from Myers. He hesitated. Pressed Ignore.

"Nature abhors a vacuum," al-Saud said. "Shia and Sunni radicals are rushing to fill it. Nothing but war and bloodshed are before us unless it can be stopped. Frankly, I don't believe you need the assistance of the Russians to accomplish the goal of peace and stability in the Middle East if you're willing to partner with us." Al-Saud turned to Tarkovsky. "But to answer your question directly, Mr. President, my government would feel perfectly comfortable with a joint American-Russian alliance so long as the destruction of *Daesh* and its heretical Caliphate were the objective and so long as we are permitted a role in the campaign."

Tarkovsky smiled appreciatively. "Excellent."

"Outstanding," Chandler said, beaming.

"I have two concerns," Pearce said.

Chandler rolled his eyes.

"Speak your mind, Troy. It's why you're here," Lane said.

Pearce glared at al-Saud. "First of all, a lot of ISIS funding and support have come from members of your own royal family. You just said that ISIS is a Sunni group. Some have suggested that your own government is behind the rise of ISIS as a way to blunt Shia aspirations in the region."

"That's a lie concocted by radical Israelis and Iranian fanatics."

"But if it is true, then what steps will your government take to ensure that ISIS is, indeed, wiped off the map and not supported or protected in some other form in the future?"

Al-Saud felt the heat rise in his face. "I assure you that supporting ISIS by anyone in my country is illegal, whether directly or indirectly. But additional, harsher steps are being taken even as I speak to enforce those laws." Al-Saud calmed himself down. "And it's well known that I and other members of my family are moving as quickly as possible to tamp down the more radical elements of the Salafist intellectuals in our country. My personal goal is to see an end to exporting their zealous interpretation of the Koran through the madrassas they sponsor around the world."

"Can we get that in writing?" Pearce asked. "'Personal goals' are hard to quantify."

Al-Saud turned to Lane. "You asked for complete candor and I'm giving it. If we rush our political reforms too quickly, we will radicalize our own population. But I assure you that those of us in power fully realize that the genie has been let out of the bottle. We're determined to slay the genie and smash the bottle. But it all begins with the destruction of *Daesh*."

Lane nodded. "I understand, and I accept your word on the subject."

"Thank you."

Lane nodded to Pearce. "What was your other concern?"

Pearce learned forward. Time to play the card Moshe had dealt him. "I'd like to know why the two of you met secretly recently and what that meeting was about."

Chandler's eyes narrowed.

"It's not uncommon for diplomats to talk, Mr. Pearce. I make no apology for doing my duty," al-Saud said.

Tarkovsky turned to Lane. "Normally I don't discuss my government's private affairs with other heads of state, Mr. President, but since this is an unusual time, I'm happy to disclose the content of our meeting. Both of our governments are concerned that your country does not have the will to lead at this time. We were exploring the possibilities available to us in the event you decided to adhere to your 'no new boots on the ground' policy."

Pearce's iWatch tapped again. This time it was a text. Once again he discreetly rotated his wrist. He read the text.

"Oh, God."

46

Pearce stood, heart racing.

"What's wrong?" Lane asked as Pearce pulled out his iPhone and hit the speed-dial for Myers.

"For heaven's sake, Pearce, we're in the middle of a very important meeting," Chandler said.

Pearce ignored him. The phone rang. Finally it picked up. "Margaret? Where are you?" Pearce asked.

"It's not Margaret. It's me, August," Mann said. "I'm sorry but I had to use her phone. Margaret was shot. She's still in hospital but she's fine."

"How badly was she wounded?"

"Wounded? Margaret?" Lane asked, obviously concerned.

Tarkovsky and al-Saud exchanged a glance.

"She was shot in her left bicep with a twenty-two-caliber rifle. It passed through the muscle. No significant damage."

Pearce frowned. "A twenty-two? That doesn't make any sense."

"The Israelis use twenty-two-caliber in urban countersniper operations to limit collateral damage. It's quite an effective round at close range. But there's more."

"What?"

"She also hit her head on the cobblestones when she fell to the ground. The doctors ran preliminary tests. No concussion, no internal bleeding. But they want to keep her for a few days for observation. I just wanted you to know in case you wanted to come."

"Let me speak with her, please."

"I can't. She's having an MRI scan. That's how I managed to get her phone and call you. She threatened my life if I told you any of this."

"Troy, you should go and see her. Bring her back safe," Lane said.

Pearce spoke to Lane. "Thanks, but no. My job is here. August will take good care of her."

"*Natürlich!*" Mann said. "She didn't want you to know because she doesn't want you to leave what you are doing. She said it was important for you to stay."

"Any idea who was behind the shooting?" Pearce asked.

"The two culprits are dead. No identification papers, but by looks alone I would guess Levantine."

"Syrian?"

"Most likely. But they could be Lebanese or Jordanian as well. The BND is looking into it now."

From experience Pearce knew the German foreign intelligence service was first rate and their contacts throughout the Middle East impressive. They were as likely as anyone to find out who the attackers were. "You think ISIS?"

"Perhaps, but the attack was professional. Definitely not a lone-wolf assault. And almost nobody knew the president was in Germany, let alone where she was at that moment."

"You think another intelligence service was behind this?"

"We should know more in a few hours. I'll have her call you as soon as she can."

"Thanks, August. I owe you."

Pearce hung up his phone. He felt the familiar, mind-numbing fury burning again in his chest. He wanted to smash something.

"Excuse me," Tarkovsky said. He pulled out his cell phone. Checked the text message. He turned to Lane, "Unfortunately, I must leave on urgent business. But I'm available for further discussion by phone or perhaps later today in person after this matter is resolved."

Lane nodded at Tarkovsky's phone. "Anything I can do to help?"

Tarkovsky smiled as he stood. "No, sir. That is very kind of you. This is an internal Russian matter."

Lane stood, as did the others. Tarkovsky shook hands with him. "I hope I don't need to remind you to keep everything we've just discussed between us. A press leak at this time would be a disaster."

"Of course," Tarkovsky said. "Discretion benefits us all. If you don't mind my asking, have you made your decision?"

"Not yet. But I'll be in touch." Lane turned to al-Saud. "With you as well, Faisal. Again, I urge your discretion."

Tarkovsky left as al-Saud gripped Pearce's hand. "I'm sorry to hear about President Myers. Please convey to her my country's best wishes and my personal concern for her health. If there is anything I can do for her, please don't hesitate to ask."

Pearce peered into the ambassador's dark eyes. "I will on both counts. Thanks."

After al-Saud shut the door behind him, Lane turned to Chandler.

"Can we trust either of them, Clay?"

"No, but you can trust their ambitions. We stand to gain a lot more than we'll lose if we invite them into the fight. It's better than going it alone."

Lane turned to Pearce. "Troy? Of the two, whom do you trust more?"

Pearce's mind was on Myers. He was scared to death for her. Everything in him told him to bolt out of there and head for the nearest plane and go to her. But duty called and she was in good hands.

"Neither, sir. But if it were up to me, I wouldn't go back in, with or without them."

"I think you've made your position clear enough," Chandler snapped as he sat back down on the couch.

Pearce ignored the vice president. "But if you do decide to go in, I know you'll do it because you think it's right for the country. Whatever you do, trust your gut."

"If the American people knew what you knew, David, they'd demand you launch an attack," Chandler insisted.

"Your instincts have gotten you this far," Pearce said, casting a withering glance at Chandler. "Ignore the noise."

47

Meghan Osweiler's phone rang. Hardly unusual for the assistant managing editor for foreign and national news at the *Los Angeles Times*. What surprised her was the message from the unidentified voice on the other end. A woman. It was familiar but she couldn't place it.

"How do you know about this?"

"It doesn't matter," the voice said.

"It's not possible." Osweiler's head ached. She'd missed breakfast and her late lunch was still an hour away. "I have sources in the water department. I would've heard about this already."

"Not if it was labeled a national security issue."

"How did you get my direct number? It's unlisted."

"All that matters is that you confirm what I've told you and get the word out. For God's sake, it's a public safety issue."

"I'll confirm it first. What we do with it after that is up to the managing editor."

"I know you'll do the right thing." The voice went on to provide an address as well as the name of an FBI special agent from the L.A. bureau office, someone Osweiler happened to know.

Osweiler's phone disconnected. She wasn't sure if she should shout with triumph over the story of the year—she was already thinking Pulitzer—or race home, gather up her two shelter cats and Yorkshire terrier, and jump on the next plane to Alaska.

Her throat suddenly parched. She glanced at the half-empty glass of water on her desk. She picked it up gingerly with her thumb and forefinger and poured the contents into the wastebasket, then tossed the glass in after it. She called her assistant and told her to bring a can of cold Diet Dr Pepper and a couple of Tylenol from the break room.

It was going to be a long afternoon.

WASHINGTON, D.C.

Grafton slipped her cell phone back into her purse, flushed the toilet, and stepped over to the sink, still stinging over the snub of getting cut out of today's meeting with Lane, Tarkovsky, and al-Saud.

Damn them. Damn them to hell.

She washed her hands. This was the best way for her to keep control of the narrative. Osweiler was a bulldog. She wouldn't let this story die even if her boss tried to spike it. Osweiler would go over his head or, more likely, step on it—and get his job in the bargain.

Grafton stared at herself in the mirror. Checked her lipstick and her long red hair. Didn't like what she saw. She frowned. Her hair looked tired. Maybe it was too long.

Time for a change, she decided.

BLACK LAKE, MICHIGAN

Tamar had been studying Pike's lake house from a distance all morning. She couldn't hear the crunch of his tires on the gravel driveway but she watched the black windowless Chinook Charter panel van pull out of his driveway and onto the two-lane asphalt road. She checked her watch. It would take him approximately twenty-five minutes to reach his charter boat in Cheboygan and probably another thirty minutes to load everyone on board for the afternoon excursion, which was scheduled to end at five o'clock. She'd wait fifteen minutes before she moved toward the house just in case Pike forgot something and decided to turn around.

She checked her phone again, hoping Pearce had called her back. She would've liked an extra pair of hands on this job, especially his, but he was a big shot in the American government now and probably up to his blue eyes in paperwork and committee meetings. She chuckled.

Poor bastard.

TAMAR MADE HER WAY on foot through the trees, careful to avoid the watchful eyes of the security cameras on the house she'd observed through her binoculars. The cameras didn't surprise her. If Pike was the threat Mossad thought he was, he'd have a security system in place. If not, it was reasonable for a person in a remote location like this to secure his property from thieves. Either way, she'd anticipated the presence of them and had prepared accordingly.

Fortunately the camera over the entrance facing the lake had been disconnected. Probably needed to be replaced, she assumed. She worked her way around to the side of the house, hugging her shoulder bag close. She was reasonably confident that she couldn't be identified. She wore a ball cap to cover her angular face, dark hair, and clear green eyes. Her skin was hidden beneath long sleeves and slacks, and she wore blue surgical gloves to avoid leaving fingerprints. The goal was to keep Pike from knowing that anyone had entered his house at all. She easily picked the keyed lock on the electrical panel and opened it up. She flicked off the main power switch, disabling the cameras and likely alarm systems on the property.

Confident that she could move freely about, she dashed to the front entrance, quickly picked the sliding door lock open, and pushed through the heavy curtains. Without lights and the curtains drawn the house was dark. She pulled out her tactical flashlight and smartphone and shot video as she passed through each room as quickly and efficiently as possible, careful not to disturb anything. At this point she was only trying to locate a hidden safe, military-grade weapons, or, best of all, his personal computer—anything to confirm Mossad's suspicions and, ideally, help locate their missing agent.

Twenty minutes into her search Tamar found the bedroom door with the heavy security bracket and a simple combination lock. Not a problem. Tamar removed an automated lock picker from her shoulder bag and placed it on the lock's black dial. Two seconds later it popped.

She pushed the door open and stepped in.

Inside she found two long workstation tables loaded with video monitors, keyboards, joysticks, and a virtual-reality headset. At first she thought it was a film-editing suite, but the joysticks didn't make any sense. Maybe he was a crazy online gamer. That would explain the VR, too. His brief said he had a background in computer science and did some contracting work for the U.S. government in Iraq.

What bothered her was the electronic hum of the CPUs on the floor below. How was that possible? The power was off. Her heart skipped a beat. Had she missed something? She double-checked the security camera in the far corner. It was clearly powered off. What was going on?

Battery backup power for the computers. Of course. She stepped over to a closet door and saw the power cable snaking through the green shag carpet. She opened the door and found three large battery backup systems. Thank God Pike hadn't thought to do the same with the security system.

She shut the door and turned around. Something caught her eye hanging on the far wall.

It was a small reproduction print in a cheap frame. She recognized it instantly because she had written a paper on French Romanticism for an art course at university. It was Géricault's *The Raft of the Medusa*. A brilliant piece of work, tragic in subject but beautiful in both its realism and construction. *Strange it should be here*, she thought, but then again perhaps not. Pike was a boat captain and its subject was the sea. It was the image of survivors on a raft on the verge of rescue having suffered the fate of people lost a long while on the ocean and the hard moral choices the starving often face. Géricault's meaning was clear, her professor had insisted: Civilizations must sometimes be reduced to savage barbarism in order to survive.

Did Pike know that? Not likely, she decided. He had probably bought the print at a garage sale.

She stepped over to one of the keyboards and pressed the power button. The screen flashed on. It required a password to proceed. That was a lock that Tamar knew she couldn't pick, but Lev could. He was the best in the business. He was the IT officer assigned to her case and he was on standby waiting for her call. If anyone could break into a secured system it was him. She dialed and he picked up instantly. She pulled out the necessary cable and connectors from her pouch to link her phone to the CPU so that Lev could begin remotely hacking into Pike's computer. Once connected, she pulled up the rolling executive chair and plopped down into it, leaning in close to the screen to watch Lev move the arrow and operate the keystrokes remotely from his office in Tel Aviv. He was on speakerphone.

"It's going to take a little while. Not your typical password protection."

"I've got plenty of time. No worries," she said. "Pike is far away and won't be back for hours."

PIKE SAT IN his van on the side of the road, admiring Tamar's lovely face in his laptop monitor. Her green eyes and sharp nose were slightly distorted because she was sitting so close to the computer monitor back at his house, and the glow of the light from the screen muddied the color of her beautiful bronze skin.

He fired up the engine and put the van into gear. He was very much looking forward to seeing much more of that beautiful bronze flesh in a better light very soon.

48

"Assholes! Move!" Mathis shouted, his voice muted by the blaring squad car siren.

Sergeant Vasquez wove skillfully past the slowing cars. She was surprised they'd made it as far as they had on Wilshire, always busy this time of the morning. But the news broadcasts had really thrown a wrench into it. People were losing their damned minds. Helluva training day for Mathis, she thought. Just a week out of the academy. Couldn't be worse than her first week, though, she thought. It was the end of the world, or so it seemed to her that day, thanks to Rodney King.

She wondered for the thousandth time if it was time to retire.

"Should I unlock the shotgun?" Mathis asked. Sweat beaded on his black skin.

"It's a two-eleven in progress, not a riot," Vasquez said. "No point in escalating the situation."

"Yes, Sergeant! I mean, no," Mathis said.

"Take a deep breath. You'll do fine," she said.

She hoped he would. You never knew with probes.

TWO MINUTES LATER Vasquez slammed the brakes and screeched to a halt at the edge of the intersection. A half-dozen cars and pickup trucks surrounded a red-and-white Coca-Cola delivery truck in the middle of the street. Its rolling doors were flung open and nearly empty.

Civilians were stealing the last cases off the racks and tossing them into their vehicles.

"Let's go!" Vasquez shouted. She leaped out of the driver's side, drew her pistol, and charged toward the pickup nearest her. A young Hispanic male was throwing a case of orange Fanta into the back of his Chevy.

"Stop! Put it down! Now!" she shouted in Spanish.

"FUCK YOU, PIG!" the man shouted back in English, laughing, flipping two birds before leaping into the truck bed.

Adrenaline begged her to pull the trigger but her training kicked in. No telling who was driving the truck. A kid could be riding in the passenger seat. If she missed, the rounds could kill innocent bystanders. Besides, it was just a case of soda. Not worth it. The news this morning had caused this panic. Scared people did stupid things.

The other civilians were already scattering, slamming doors and squealing away in blue clouds of burning rubber.

Vasquez charged around to the other side of the Coca-Cola truck, Mathis hot on her heels. She stopped dead in her tracks. The uniformed delivery driver lay facedown in a pool of blood on the asphalt, his head broken open like a pomegranate.

Mathis puked.

"No time for that shit!" Vasquez shouted.

Mathis wiped his mouth with the back of his hand. "Yes, Sergeant."

Gunshots rang out from the corner. A 7-Eleven convenience store.

Vasquez turned and ducked into a low crouch, running toward the 7-Eleven. People bolted out of the front door, hauling armfuls of juice boxes, bottled water, energy drinks, and anything else remotely potable.

A Korean clerk emerged a second later, his face streaming with blood, waving a large-caliber revolver, shouting profanities in his native tongue.

"Drop your weapon! Now!" Vasquez shouted, her pistol pointed in his direction.

The Korean turned toward Vasquez, his bleeding face a mask of mindless rage.

Gunfire exploded in her right ear as Mathis ripped off a half dozen .40-caliber rounds. She winced in pain but through her squinting eyes saw three rounds flowering blood in the Korean's white shirt as the plate glass window behind him shattered. He tumbled backward, screaming, arms wide like the Christ. He was dead before he hit the pavement.

"Got you, motherfucker!" Mathis shouted, a half-crazed smile smearing his face.

"You stupid shit! What did you do?" Vasquez shouted. She laid a hand on Mathis's Glock. The barrel was hot. "Holster your weapon, officer."

Mathis frowned at her, confused. "What?"

"Holster your damn weapon! Now!"

Mathis blinked away his confusion. "Yes, Sergeant." He holstered the Glock.

A blue helicopter thundered overhead. Vasquez glanced up. White call letters plastered the side. A video camera pointed directly at them.

FoxSky 40 News.

Vasquez swore.

Should've retired yesterday.

49

All eyes were on Alyssa Abbott, the White House press secretary. She shrugged and shook her head. "I'm sorry. I did everything I could. I played the national security card. Even threatened to pull their press credentials. But the *Times* wouldn't hold off on the story. Frankly, I would've run with it, too, if I were in their shoes."

Chandler blew out a long breath. "That's terribly unfortunate, Alyssa. It puts us in quite a bind." He glanced over at the video monitors on the Situation Room wall. They silently displayed several local L.A. news broadcasts showing live images of massive freeway traffic jams, looted stores, panicked mothers with babies in their arms. Los Angeles had gone mad.

Lane shook his head. "It's not her fault, Clay. She's right. There are ten million people in the L.A. basin. It's a huge story for them." Lane glanced back down into his lap. The *Times* story was on his iPad. "It looks like they only got the water story. That's a break, at least."

"But the wire services have picked up the scent on the others." Abbott held up her cell phone. "AP has called me three times already this morning, asking for confirmation about Kan-Tex."

"Shit," Garza said. "Pardon my French."

"There's the mayor," Peguero said, nodding at the monitor.

Lane tapped a remote. The sound came up. Ronald Hillman, the mayor of Los Angeles, had just begun his speech. His tailored sky-blue suit perfectly complimented his mane of thick silver hair and permanent suntan. A news ticker identified the other public officials flanking the mayor at his podium, including the general manager of the Metropolitan Water District of Southern California.

"I've been assured by federal, state, and local public health and security officials as well as by the head of the MWDSC that our water system is perfectly safe, that it has not been compromised in any way, and that every effort is being taken to ensure that our water remains safe, clean, and available to everyone in Southern California. I urge everyone to return to work or to their homes. There is no need to leave the area or to panic. Your water is safe." The mayor was handed a glass of water. "This was drawn just thirty seconds ago from the break room here in the building. It came from the tap in the kitchen. This is public water." The mayor took a long drink, draining the glass. He set it down empty and smiled a mouthful of blazing white teeth.

"I condemn in the strongest terms possible the irresponsible and sensationalist reporting by the *Los Angeles Times*. Hiding behind the First Amendment and in the name of public safety, they have created an artificial crisis that has led to the injury and death of an untold number of persons and the destruction of millions of dollars in property, all for the sake of selling a few newspapers. I'll take your questions now."

Lane shut the audio back off. "Has the mayor been fully apprised of the situation?"

Eaton nodded. "Yes. I thought it best to level with him. I didn't want him to be caught by surprise by your speech tonight and made to look the fool. I explained the national security dimension. He's promised to play dumb until we give him the green light."

"God bless Ronnie," Chandler said. "He always was a team player."

Lane turned to his director of national intelligence. "How did the brief with Gaby and Bren go?" The secretaries of state and defense were both in Beijing, making final preparations for the summit. Lane asked Pia to update them and solicit their advice.

"They're both up to speed. SecDef will contact Chairman Onstot later today for further details. Secretary Wheeler has already been in touch with her EU counterparts."

"And President Sun?"

"Secretary Wheeler assured me he's in your corner."

"Good news, finally," Lane said.

Abbott nodded at the business channel on the monitor. "The New York Stock Exchange is down four hundred fifty points," Abbott said. "It's not clear if that's a reaction to the L.A. situation or the rumor that the Fed is going to raise interest rates again."

"Wonder what it will be after my speech," Lane said.

"I think the market will rally," Chandler said.

"Nothing like a war to drive up profits," Garza said under his breath.

"The drive-time talk shows are all abuzz this morning, too, as well as the TV news. People are on edge."

"Maybe you should hold off on the speech," Peguero said. "No point in dropping a match into a gas can."

"The networks are expecting a live broadcast from the Oval Office at nine p.m. Eastern Standard Time. If we back off now, we'll only feed the rumor mill," Abbott said.

"My dad always said the best way to tackle a problem is head-on," Lane said. "I'm giving the speech. But I'm not waiting until tonight."

"Sir?" Abbott asked.

"This thing is spinning out of control. I need to get ahead of it. I want to be live and on air at noon."

Abbott's face blanched. "I don't know if I can pull that off."

"You'll figure it out. Better get to it."

Abbott opened her mouth to protest, then checked herself. "Yes, sir. I'll make the arrangements right away." She sped out of the room.

Lane turned toward the others. "You've all read the speech. Any last-minute suggestions?"

Heads shook around the table. No suggestions. Chandler and Grafton smiled enthusiastically. Peguero appeared resigned. Pearce was grim.

"This will be the most important speech of your administration," Garza finally said. He grinned. "Don't fuck it up."

Lane burst out laughing. He could always count on his salty security advisor to say the most inappropriate thing at exactly the right time. The tension in the room dropped. The room laughed with him.

Except for Pearce.

"Something wrong, Troy?" the president asked, still smiling.

"Just did the math."

"What math?" Chandler said, still chuckling.

"Tomorrow is the fifth day. The day the letter promised we'd be destroyed in unquenchable fire."

The room quieted like a tomb.

Nobody was laughing anymore.

50

President Lane's boyish good looks played well on national television, especially in hi-def. Abbott made sure all of the production details were right, especially the lighting. Unfortunately, the average American was focused more on optics than substance these days. The wrong tie, too much makeup, or a speck of lint on his lapel would garner more attention in the Twittersphere than the speech itself and detract from his message. She sometimes wondered if her feckless fellow Americans deserved the right to a self-governing republic at all.

All the broadcast and cable networks agreed to the last-minute changes, especially after Abbott stressed the significance of the speech and the accelerated schedule. She insisted on Lane delivering an "Oval" because the office of the president, especially the weighty desk—carved from the timbers of the HMS *Resolute* and first used by JFK—conveyed the gravitas of both the man and the moment. The utilitarian James S. Brady Press Briefing Room just wouldn't cut it.

Abbott stood on one side of the camera and the floor manager on the other. Abbott whispered a prayer as the manager counted down with her fingers.

Three, two, one . . .

"MY FELLOW AMERICANS," Lane began, "I come to you today with both hard news and a clear path. Three days ago, my office received a letter threatening a series of escalating terror attacks unless I agreed to fly the black flag of ISIS over the White House. Since then, a series of attacks were made against the American aviation industry, the American trucking industry, and just yesterday, a threat was made to the Los Angeles public water system. In regard to the Los Angeles water attack, I want to assure all of you, and in particular, the residents of Southern California, that your drinking water is perfectly safe. There's no evidence whatsoever that the water has been contaminated in any way and we continue to monitor water quality by the minute in California and throughout the nation. The airline and trucking attacks resulted in minimal property damage, but unfortunately, there are several deaths directly or indirectly associated with the trucking attack. We grieve with their families today.

"Though we continue to pursue the perpetrators of these attacks with all of our resources, we now face a hard but clear choice in the days ahead."

Lane paused for effect. "The first option is to raise the ISIS flag over the White House. Some in my cabinet have argued that it's just a piece of material, nothing more, and that raising that flag might satisfy the terrorist demands. I respectfully disagree with this position. The ISIS flag represents the face of evil in the modern world. It holds a great deal of meaning and significance for those who follow it—and for those who have suffered under it. For that reason alone I could never fly it. More important, the American flag is a flag worth fighting and dying for because of what it represents. I refuse to lower a great flag to honor a lesser one. Too many have sacrificed too much to protect our flag. I won't dishonor their sacrifice in the vain hope of preventing further attacks. Our long history with terrorists shows us that appeasing them only leads to more violence.

"The second option is to do nothing and hope the danger goes away. As some of my other advisors have suggested, while the nature of the terror attacks points to potential catastrophe, in reality almost nothing has been done. The terrorists claim they are restraining themselves out of some misguided sense of mercy. But some of my advisors speculate that the limited scope of the attacks is proof the attackers can't follow through because of their limited resources. In other words, these attacks have been designed to make us believe they are more powerful than they actually are. In my judgment, the attacks have proved to be sophisticated, well designed, and strategic, and the threat of potential catastrophe is all too real. I take them at their word that they are murderous thugs intent on doing us great harm and I refuse to cede the initiative to those who would destroy us.

"The final option is the clear path I believe we must take. It will be a difficult and perilous road, but it's the right one. ISIS has declared war on the United States and the West. Without question this is a war between civilizations. This war didn't begin three days ago or even on September eleventh, 2001. It began in the seventh century, when an army of Islamic zealots began spreading the doctrines of the Koran by the power of the sword. ISIS claims to be a direct descendant of those same zealots, and now they have brought their swords to this country. I do not intend merely to stop the attacks against our homeland. I intend to destroy ISIS in Iraq and Syria, root and branch.

"I have also made the decision that the United States will fight this war without a coalition. We have strong alliance partners in Europe and the region, but we don't have the time to assemble a coalition or manage it. Our goal is simple and measurable. Destroy the ISIS Caliphate. Nothing more, nothing less. And the time to do it is now.

"I have consulted with the House and Senate leadership and have formally requested they pass an unlimited Authorization to Use Military Force against ISIS and their so-called Caliphate with its capital in Raqqa, Syria. I am under no illusion that destroying ISIS will end our struggle with Islamic terror. ISIS is merely one of a thousand hydra heads now biting at our throats, but that is the head I intend to cut off. My prayer is that the destruction of ISIS will be so total and definitive that it will deter other radical Islamic groups from waging jihad against the West.

"Ten minutes ago four U.S. aircraft began dropping emergency leaflets in Raqqa, warning the civilians to evacuate within twenty-four hours, after which a bombing campaign will begin and the city will be leveled. Any civilian still within the city limits after twenty-four hours will be considered an enemy combatant, even if ISIS thugs prevent them from evacuating. Any civilian deaths will be on the heads of ISIS, not the United States government.

"There will be no negotiations with ISIS. There will be no compromises with ISIS. There will be no mercy for ISIS. We will cut off the head of the snake, then kill the snake. Abu Waleed al-Mahdi, the leader of ISIS and the caliph of the ISIS Caliphate, will either be captured or killed, as will each member of his ruling council. The region now identified as the ISIS Caliphate will be occupied and pacified until the territory can be turned over to the legitimate governments from which it was stolen.

"I want you all to be assured that the departments of Justice, Homeland Security, and all other national security and law enforcement agencies have been working around the clock to find and stop the perpetrators. I'm confident that they will do so in the near future. Until then, you can help. 'See something, say something' means you can actively assist us in the search. This is not an excuse to persecute or discriminate, but don't let political correctness keep you from picking up the phone if you suspect anyone who poses a legitimate threat. If you see suspicious activity, do not take matters into your own hands but contact your local law enforcement agency or the FBI immediately.

"Finally, I want to remind each of you that our country has faced many crises in our past, some far worse than this one. We have always prevailed, and we will do so again with courage, determination, and faith. God bless every one of you, God bless all peace-loving people everywhere, and especially, God bless the United States of America."

51

Pearce sat in his office at the EEOB, channel-surfing the television and scanning the news feeds, a dull depression gnawing in the back of his mind. What he saw on the screen didn't surprise him.

The usual flock of neocons, chicken hawks, and posturing politicians all favored Lane's "Kill the Snake" doctrine.

On the other side, the talking heads for the American Islamic Association, pacifist groups, and isolationist and libertarian think tanks all came out swinging against it. Street protests broke out for and against Lane's call to arms in Washington, D.C., and in state capitals around the country. Code Pink, Black Lives Matter, Occupy Wall Street, and pro-Sharia groups made the most noise, but the pro-war protestors fielded the largest numbers. Law enforcement kept them as far apart as possible.

The Russian government filed an official protest with the United Nations, claiming President Lane's unilateral action violated the UN Charter, especially Article 33. They also pressured the rump government of Syria, or what was left of it in and around Damascus, along with Cuba, Venezuela, and North Korea to join them. Anti-American, antiwar, and anarchist protests erupted in the capitals of Western Europe, the largest in London. Only Poland, Hungary, and the Czech Republic formally endorsed Lane's announcement and offered their support.

Al-Mahdi issued a slick new video message on Al Jazeera and on social media sites, urging the apostate Saudis, pagan Russians, degenerate

Americans, and all other "Romans" to "hurry to their doom." He pointed gleefully at a map of Syria, showing them the location of the city of Dabiq in the northwest. "Here is your final destination, in case you don't know where it is," he said, laughing. "Here is where you will die, and where the Apocalypse begins." The video garnered more than seven million views worldwide in less than an hour.

There were also news reports that web traffic on militia group websites was spiking, especially those recruiting new members. Law enforcement officials issued warnings against vigilantism. Local news agencies showed footage of civilian national guardsmen in their uniforms leaving home for active duty, hugging proud spouses and weeping children as they departed. The governor of Massachusetts, a staunch opponent of President Lane during his primary run, announced she would ignore the federalization of her national guard units. Constitutional scholars debated the standoff on C-SPAN.

No doubt the protests on the streets and the shouting matches on the TV shows would only escalate in the days to come—democracy's version of a relief valve. But Pearce knew none of them mattered. Cataclysmic decisions like war didn't take place in front of television cameras or radio microphones. They happened in well-appointed government and corporate offices with period furniture and air-conditioning, by people with manicured fingernails and hair plugs and bleached teeth.

Pearce checked his latest e-mail from Dr. Ashley. Over 60 percent of the country was now under Gorgon Sky surveillance. It would be nearly 100 percent before the week was out, Alaska and Hawaii included. He wasn't sure how she had pulled that miracle off. Lane should give her a presidential citation for her herculean efforts. Pearce wasn't sure how he felt about living in a surveillance state, but he felt even less comfortable living in a war zone without it. The chickens had, indeed, come home to roost.

Pearce shut off the television. The news was only feeding the animal growing inside of him. He turned to his computer. He had a mountain to climb now and few ropes to work with. Lane instructed him to draw up Drone Command plans to conduct long-term operations in the

Middle East. Despite Pearce's strenuous objections, these included supplying the Saudis with all of the MQ-9 Reaper drones they could afford to purchase. In a perfect world he'd coordinate with the DoD and the armed services, but there was no way in hell he could overcome the bureaucratic resistance he'd meet as they each pursued their own drone acquisition and operational plans, especially now that they were on a war footing. That battle would have to wait until after his confirmation. For now, all he could hope to accomplish was to draw up the Drone Command operational plan and lay out his vision for the future of drones without regard to the rest of the federal government.

His fingers tapped haltingly on the keyboard as he tried to formulate the first sentence of the first paragraph of his executive summary, but his monkey mind was in full swing, a thousand ideas crashing around in his brain all at once. He pushed away the keyboard. What was the point? Besides, something was wrong with this whole setup, but what? He couldn't put his finger on it. Too many moving parts, too many players, too many deals getting cut behind closed doors far beyond his reach.

Lane knew the score. He even said it in his speech. Al-Mahdi would never let the civilian population of Raqqa evacuate. Air Force Global Strike Command would unleash holy hell on the city and kill more than two hundred thousand residents in hopes of killing the half hundred lunatics trying to start Armageddon. Of course, al-Mahdi and his closest advisors wouldn't wait around. Hell, they were probably already long gone and hunkered down in the basement of some other third world shithole.

Morality aside, the destruction of Raqqa would be a public relations disaster of the highest order for the United States. Maybe that was the ISIS plan all along. No matter that they were the ones pulling the temple down on their own heads. *They'll still blame us for it*, Pearce knew. *They'll never forget it. They'll use it to recruit more terrorists who will cause more destruction in the West, and the West will retaliate again, and again and again.*

How do you fight the fanatical Muslim mind-set? Pearce had been asking that question for years while trading potshots with them. And the answer was always the same: bullet to bone.

Unfortunately, the murderous cowards liked to take their shots while hiding behind the skirts of women and children.

If they don't care about their own, why should we? He'd asked that question a thousand times, too.

And the answer was always the same: Because we're not them.

And that's why he feared they may win in the end.

Total war was the only answer, he was sure of it. Lane chose half a war, which meant a forever war. Just as many would die in the long run, but there would be no victory for the United States, and the drone attacks at home might continue anyway.

Pearce failed to convince Lane to steer away from starting the war if he wasn't going to finish it. The whole point of getting back into the political arena was to try to change things from the inside. Isn't that what Margaret had said?

Well, he was as inside as he could get. Thousands would die soon and all of that blood would be on his hands, too. "Sins of omission." Where had he heard that before? All because he couldn't stop the drone attacks.

Guilt like snow fell on him, heavy and cold.

He'd failed his country. He'd failed Margaret.

He was useless. More than useless.

Pearce shut his computer down. He needed to get out of this place. Head home.

And get seriously fucking hammered.

52

Pearce called Myers's cell phone from his car, but it was Mann who picked up again. She was sedated and resting under doctor's orders. He promised to have her call Pearce when she awoke. Mann also assured Pearce that the German government was helping with her security—discreetly. The German press hadn't been alerted to the incident or even to the former president's presence on German soil. The last thing Berlin needed was more publicity about immigrants and violence after the incidents of mass rape and beatings that had been taking place since the tidal wave of migration began in 2015.

He thanked Mann again for all his help and rang off. He wished he could have talked to Margaret, though. He wanted to tell her that he was spiraling out of control. But then again, he probably wouldn't have said anything. He couldn't bear the thought of disappointing her.

One more bender was all he needed to clear his system. Then he'd walk the straight and narrow for good.

A SOFT KNOCK on the door of her Georgetown loft sent Grafton scurrying to open it. Tarkovsky stood in the doorway. His two hulking bodyguards remained in the hall, their backs discreetly turned away.

She pulled him inside her loft and threw her arms around his neck and kissed him. He returned the favor.

"I've missed you," Grafton whispered breathily.

The handsome Russian pulled off his sport coat. "Something smells marvelous."

"I've ordered in." She led him by the hand to the dining room. Candles, wine. A feast.

"Before I forget." Tarkovsky reached into his pocket.

She bit her lower lip with anticipation. "Something for me? Something terribly expensive?"

"Not expensive, but something I think you will find extremely valuable." He pulled out a thumb drive. Handed it to her. She examined it.

"It's not Tiffany but it's interesting. What's in it?"

"Your friend Pearce. My contact in the SVR came through. Turns out there was a secret, unauthorized file on him. Not many details. But I think you're going to be quite surprised at what you'll find in there." He loosened his tie.

"Surprised in a good way?"

Tarkovsky poured two glasses of wine. "Only if you want to get rid of him."

Grafton pocketed the thumb drive. "You said a secret file? Sounds like someone had a special interest in him."

"Pearce killed two SVR operatives in Mozambique just a few years ago. They want their revenge. Of course, the SVR would never attempt an operation on American soil without my government's permission. But if Pearce can be removed from service some other way? There's an old Russian saying, 'Never let the perfect be the enemy of the good.'" He laid his hands on her shoulders.

She gazed into his hungering eyes. "I didn't realize Voltaire was Russian."

Tarkovsky began unbuttoning her blouse. "That's what made him such an effective Russian spy."

Grafton's flesh tingled. "What about dinner?" She reached for his belt buckle. He answered with a lingering kiss.

They ate later.

Much later.

———

PEARCE DECIDED TO SPEND the night at his corporate hotel suite. He couldn't bring himself to get drunk at Myers's place for the same reason he would never bring another woman into her home and violate the sanctity of their shared bed. What he was about to do felt like an even worse betrayal than that.

He put up a good fight, at least for a while. When he arrived at the lobby he checked in with the concierge for mail and messages, then picked up the house phone and ordered a steak dinner from the room service menu.

On the long ride up the elevator with the wide glass wall and spectacular view of the city, Pearce suddenly realized the anniversary of his dad's death had passed him by again. The weeds around the old man's lonely grave on the side of the hill in Wyoming would be three feet tall by now. He should've been there to trim them back down and clean the stone.

By the time he unlocked the front door and kicked off his shoes in the foyer he gave in to his lesser, fallen angel. He called the rooftop bar and ordered a bottle of his dad's favorite, Jack Daniel's Old No. 7. It arrived on the room service cart with a sizzling porterhouse and fries. He cracked open the bottle first and poured himself a tall one. He drank it standing up. It went down fast with a familiar burn. It knocked him sideways, just like he hoped it would. He filled his glass again and shoved a few salty fries in his mouth before draining it and then poured another and headed for the sofa.

He never got around to that steak.

THREE-QUARTERS OF THE WAY through the bottle, his iWatch alarmed. It was a text. Bleary-eyed and flushed, he picked up his phone and read it. "Package in the lobby. Marked urgent. Thx. Management."

What could it be? Pearce ran through the possibilities in his fogged mind but couldn't settle on anything definite. Why bother trying? *Just go down and get the damn thing*, he told himself.

He pulled on a pair of Vans and grabbed his pass key and headed uneasily for the door. He tried to be quiet. It was late and the guests in the neighboring suites were probably asleep, and the management was fussy about noise.

It was hard for him to hold a straight line down the long hallway and he brushed against the walls a few times. He finally arrived at the elevator and pushed the button. He stood there, wobbly, waiting for the stainless steel doors to open. It took forever. He leaned against the wall. His eyes were heavy. He closed them. The world spun on a nauseating axis but he was too tired to get off.

The elevator ding startled him.

The doors slid open but all Pearce saw was the massive fist slamming into his face. The force of the blow whipped him around. The pain in his jaw woke him up as he crashed down onto the carpeted floor. Before he could lift himself up to throw a punch, a heavy knee jammed into his spine and a pair of thick hands pinned his shoulders and head to the ground, pressing his face against the carpet. A needle stabbed his neck and a moment later he was gone.

53

The air buzzed with flies. Hundreds of them, thick as thumbs.

Pearce stared at the corpses, their faces covered by swarms of blue-bottle flies already eating away at the soft tissues, laying eggs in the moist cavities of mouths, noses, and gaping wounds where the skulls had been broken open by the bullets.

The twenty-four Shia recruits lay in a rough line along the low, blood-spattered wall, their fresh uniforms smeared in gore and dust.

Pearce, Early, Luckett, Rowley, and Tariq had pulled up their *shem-aghs*, covering their own mouths and noses against the stench. Their weapons were unslung.

Pearce knelt down next to the young Shia lieutenant and brushed the flies off his face with a gloved hand. The Iraqi soldier was just a few years younger than Pearce. They'd grown close over the last few months. He told Pearce he wanted to be an architect but decided to serve his country instead. "All because of you brave Americans. You gave us hope."

Pearce pulled off one glove and laid it across the lieutenant's half-eaten eyes, his lifeless face turned toward heaven.

"Damn flies always show up out of nowhere," Early said.

Pearce rose, wanting to say something smart-ass, but couldn't. He stood, frozen and numb. He glanced over at Tariq. The hardened Kurd's glaring eyes were wet.

"They were lined up and shot, execution style," Rowley said.

"It's a low wall. Made them kneel down first," Pearce said.

Early shook his head. "Poor bastards. I liked 'em."

Pearce said. "Good men, bad war."

"Who did it?" Luckett said, scanning the low roofs.

"Who do you think?" Tariq's wet eyes blazed.

Pearce thought he should pray or something but he didn't have the words. "Let's pull tags and cover them up, then haul ass. We're nothing but targets out here."

THE EMPTY 6x6 CARGO TRUCK pulled out of the wide warehouse door and sped away. Two of Majid's foreign mercenaries, the Brit and the South African, stood outside, guarding the entrance.

A Humvee raced past the 6x6 in the opposite direction, heading straight for the warehouse. Luckett was driving and Pearce was riding shotgun. Luckett stomped the brakes and skidded to a stop just feet from one of the scowling mercs.

Pearce turned toward the others in the Humvee. "Wait here—and stay frosty." He looked at the open machine-gun cockpit, then at Tariq. "Stay off that fifty unless I whistle it up. Understood?"

"Let me go with you. I translate."

Pearce grinned, shaking his head. "You're a hothead. I need you to stay put."

"You need me in there. I fight with you."

"Trust me, I know when I need you. Not now. Later. Got it?"

Tariq nodded reluctantly. "Got it."

Pearce and Early exited the Humvee, leaving their rifles behind but not their holstered pistols. They nodded at the merc standing closest to them. The South African looked them up and down, ignoring the gesture as he lit a cigarette.

Early grinned wide and pointed a thick finger in the merc's direction. "Fuck you too, buddy!"

The South African shrugged dismissively as he took a long drag.

Pearce marched into the cool, dark air of the massive concrete warehouse recently built by the U.S. Army Corps of Engineers. General

Majid stood in the center of the floor, watching a forklift carry a loaded pallet toward him. The forklift driver was one of the two Russian mercs in Majid's employ. The leader of the mercenaries, a short and wiry Aussie, stood next to Majid. When he heard boots clomping behind him, he turned around. He lowered his rifle down to his side in a non-threatening gesture but stepped toward Pearce and Early.

"State your business, gents."

Early turned to Pearce. "You want me to toss this shrimp onto his barbie?"

"Ha, ha. Like I haven't heard that one a million times," the Aussie said. His unshaved face wasn't smiling.

The Russian lowered the pallet down right in front of Majid, then killed the forklift engine and jumped off.

"Need a word with the general," Pearce said.

The Aussie shrugged. "As you can see, he's a little busy at the moment."

Pearce stepped into the man's face. "Won't take long."

"Mr. Pearce! Come!" General Majid smiled and waved them over.

"Sorry, Barbie," Early said, bumping into the shorter man as he pushed by, following Pearce.

Pearce and Early approached the pallet. It was a four-foot cube of newly printed American money. Majid cut open the plastic with a knife. The smell of fresh ink and currency paper filled the air.

The Russian glared at them through his mirrored sunglasses. Pearce could hear the Aussie behind them whispering into his comms.

"What can I do for you gentlemen?" Majid asked.

Early nodded at the pallet. "Nice stack of Washingtons you got there."

"Development funds, courtesy of the American government. Very generous."

"Developing who, I wonder?" Early shot back.

Majid picked up one of the cash bundles and riffled through it. "The people of my district, of course. Schools, roads, farming—my country has been destroyed by the war. This is how we rebuild." He was quick to add, "We are grateful, of course."

Pearce knew this wasn't the first delivery of cash to the general in this quantity. He also knew that very little of it would actually make it to the people it was intended for. He didn't really care. It was all Monopoly money anyway, given the way the U.S. government just printed it out of thin air.

"Yeah. Of course," Early said.

Pearce pulled his *shemagh* out of a large cargo pocket, bundled up and tied off.

Majid tossed the cash back onto the pallet, curious.

Pearce handed the *shemagh* to the general.

Majid glanced at the bundle in his hand. He weighed it and shook it. Metal jostled inside, like coins. "What's this?" Majid asked, intrigued.

"The dog tags of the twenty-four Shia soldiers in your command. They were butchered not fifteen klicks from here, at a village just north of Al-Awja."

"I know it well," Majid said. "I'm sorry to hear this."

"You look like you could cry," Early said.

The general ignored him. "Their families will be notified, of course. Are they buried?"

"No. We just covered them up." Pearce knew the Muslim requirements for burial of the faithful. It would have been inappropriate for the five non-Muslims to do so.

The general handed the bundle to the Russian mercenary. "Take that to Major Raghif and tell him to organize a burial detail immediately." The Russian nodded and turned on his heel, heading for the doorway.

"Those Shia recruits that we were all so proud of a few days ago are now all martyrs for the cause," Pearce said.

"A terrible tragedy. It must have been AQ again."

Pearce shook his head. "AQ hasn't been active in this area for weeks, General."

"Then Baathists. Or even Syrians."

"Not likely," Early said.

"Then who?"

Early's eyes narrowed. "Good question."

"I don't like the tone of your voice, soldier," Majid said. Another Humvee driven by the other Russian merc pulled up behind Tariq's vehicle. Barnes, Majid's American mercenary, stood in the machine-gun cockpit, hands on the weapon.

Early started to say something but a gesture from Pearce silenced him.

"Who sent them to that village? Whose command were they under? And why wasn't their disappearance reported earlier?" Pearce asked.

"Excellent questions. I shall look into them myself."

"Good. Because when I report this back to my people, they'll want answers."

"What are you implying?"

"They were good men. *Your* men. And now they're dead. They deserved better."

"There are a lot of dead Iraqis around here, Pearce," the Aussie said. "Hundreds of thousands. A lot of them killed by your people. What's a few dozen more?"

Majid's eyes narrowed. "So many things you arrogant Americans don't understand. Long after you leave, we will still be here, and there will still be war, and the Shia will butcher us if they come to power. You want answers? You don't even know the right questions to ask."

Pearce felt the heat rise in the back of his neck. Maybe he didn't know all of the right questions. But a bullet in Majid's merciless face had to be the right answer, didn't it? Pearce's training pushed the thought away.

"You and your men have been reassigned to Baghdad. Why are you still here?" Majid asked.

The day after Chandler left, Pearce and the others were ordered back to Baghdad, but Pearce managed to put it off for two more weeks, promising to deliver a major intel score. "Another week and we'll be out of your hair, General."

"I want you gone now. For your own good. Now get out of my sight!" Majid turned and waved a dismissive hand.

The Aussie merc behind them racked a round in his rifle. "You heard the man."

Pearce and Early turned around. The other two mercs from outside were approaching, rifles up. The smiling American in the Humvee kept his hands on the machine gun but didn't move.

Early glanced at Pearce. "You thinking what I'm thinking?"

"Yeah, I am. But this isn't the time. Let's roll. This place stinks."

IT WAS LATE. Pearce sat alone in the mess tent, working on a hamburger and Coke, thinking about Majid and the dead Shia while Early and the others grabbed some shut-eye.

Barnes, the American merc, dropped down opposite him at the table with a tray piled full of food. His eyes were bloodshot and he stank of weed. His unshaved faced was specked with silver stubble.

"Mind?" Barnes asked.

"Would it matter if I did?"

Barnes chuckled. "No." He picked up one of his two cheeseburgers and took a huge bite.

Pearce glanced around the mess tent. A lot of empty tables. "So I take it this is a social call."

Barnes chewed with his mouth open. It took a minute before he could swallow. "Yeah. A social call." He popped his soda can and took a swig.

"So start socializing," Pearce said.

Barnes slammed the can down on the table. Saw the disdainful look in Pearce's eyes. "What the fuck's your problem?"

"You, and asshole mercs like you."

"You judging me? You don't know shit. I been wasting hajjis since before you were learning how to jerk off."

"This isn't just about killing jihadis. We're trying to build a democracy in this godforsaken country, remember?"

Barnes laughed, a barking smoker's rasp. "You think you're all that 'cuz you're in the Cock In Ass club? CIA don't mean shit out here." The merc stabbed a crooked finger on the table. "You've been here six weeks. I've been here six months. You don't know the score. But I can fill you in." Barnes took another bite of his cheeseburger.

Pearce studied the scars on the side of his face. Barnes was an apex predator in a Mad Max world. Cunning and lethal.

"Fine. Fill me in."

Barnes finished chewing and swallowed again. He leaned in close. The dope smell was intense. "You won't stop nothing. You won't change nothing. You won't do nothing but maybe get yourselves killed. So take my advice. You and your buddies—clear out. Now. Like the general said." He grabbed a half dozen french fries and shoved them into his blistered mouth.

"We'll leave when we're good and ready."

Barnes took a long pull of soda. Pearce watched his Adam's apple bob up and down as he guzzled it.

"What were you, Barnes? Army? Marines?"

Barnes wiped his mouth with the back of his hand. Burped. "Delta, not that it matters."

"You swore an oath."

The merc rolled his eyes. "You don't have time for this Boy Scout bullshit. Grab your gear right now and get rolling."

"You swore the oath. That's still gotta mean something."

Barnes leaned forward, glaring at him. "I ain't in service no more. The oath don't mean shit. I quit it." He flashed a card dealer's smile. "I make three times as much as you, maybe four." He winked. "And then some, if you catch my drift."

"Yeah, I think I do."

"I kill the same ragheads you do, get the same rush you do when I do it. But I don't got no 'rules of engagement' and I don't do no ass lickin' like you chumps gotta do." He leaned back, smiling. "And, brother, it's all tax free. If you had any brains, you'd quit, too, and get with the program."

"You gave your word."

Barnes's worn face darkened. "I gave blood, too. Who gives a shit?"

"You're a hired gun."

"And you aren't? Shit. You just don't know who you're working for. You're just a two-bit grocery clerk." Barnes shoved the tray of food away and stood. "See you around, Boy Scout."

"Just tell me one thing, Barnes. Why the warning?"

Barnes shook his head. He looked almost hurt. "I'm an American, aren't I?"

PEARCE AWOKE.

The cold steel of a Beretta 9mm barrel pressed against his forehead.

He focused his eyes. Saw the Aussie's twisted grin on the other end of the pistol.

"Rise and shine, sweetheart."

Pearce tensed for a moment, ready to slap away the pistol and lunge at him. But he caught sight of the two Russians on the other side of the room, pointing their weapons at him, too.

"Don't even think about it," the Aussie said, stepping back. He kept his pistol pointed at Pearce. "Get dressed. We're going for a little ride."

"What about the others?"

"They're already downstairs. Except for the Kurd. Where is the little bald Turkish?"

"I sent him home yesterday. He's done."

"Lucky him."

THREE VEHICLES BOUNCED ALONG the dusty track heading for God knows where. A sliver of pale moon hung low in the dark predawn sky.

At least they didn't blindfold us, Pearce thought. He was cuffed and seated on a bench in the back of a covered 6x6 along with Early, Luckett, and Rowley. Barnes was driving. The Aussie sat in back with them, holding his pistol on them, clearly enjoying being in charge. They were in the middle of a three-vehicle convoy. The Humvee leading the way was manned by the Brit and the South African. The Humvee trailing Pearce's vehicle carried the two Russian mercs along with two of Majid's Iraqi soldiers.

Pearce sat in the rear near the open flap. His ass was sore from all the bouncing on the unpaved road and the heavy springs in the truck. Seemed like the wild broncs he rode in Wyoming didn't buck half as bad as this, he told himself, trying to keep up his humor in the face of his impending execution. He watched the headlights of the tailing Humvee a hundred yards back jerk up and down as it hit the same holes in the road they did. He imagined the Humvee in front was just as far forward as the one in the rear and bouncing just as hard. Pearce glanced up into the early-morning sky. The stars were muted by a veil of haze. It wouldn't be light for another two hours. There was just enough moonlight on the gently rolling hills and scrub to let him know they were out in the middle of nowhere.

"How much longer?" Pearce shouted over the din.

The Aussie checked his watch, grinned. "Time enough to pray or piss, if you do it quick."

Pearce glanced back at the trailing Humvee, calculating. If he jumped out and could hit the ground on his feet, then roll to the side, he just might be able to get out of the way fast enough before the Humvee would slam into him—

WHOOSH! Pearce saw the rocket's flaming tail slam into the trailing Humvee. It ripped apart in an explosion of fire and shrapnel. The shock wave hit Pearce in the face just as the 6x6 slammed on its brakes, tossing everyone forward, including the Aussie, who hit the deck and dropped his pistol. Early saw his chance and fell hard on the smaller merc, who grunted in pain as air blasted out of his lungs from Early's massive bulk. Pearce leaped to his feet and swung his boot hard into the Aussie's gut and he cried out again while Luckett kicked the merc's pistol out of arm's reach.

"What the hell happened?" Early asked, still lying on the Aussie. "And why are we still alive?"

Pearce wondered the same thing. The Humvee in front obviously was hit, too. Why weren't they?

Three Toyota Hilux pickups swerved into view, machine guns firing. A few shouts up front were quickly cut off. One of the pickups skidded to a halt just behind the 6x6. Its headlights blasted into the back of the truck. Pearce lowered his gaze against the intense light. He made out the figure of a man leaping out of the Toyota and heading for the truck. A moment later he climbed into the 6x6, brandishing a knife.

"About time," Pearce said. He and Tariq had worked out a plan for the Kurd to gather his own men and keep an eye on the compound. His second father and CIA mentor, Will Elliott, had taught him a long time ago to always have someone watch the back door. Pearce was glad he'd listened to the old-school CIA fighter—and his gut.

Tariq smiled. "Better late than never, yes?" He cut Pearce's Plasti-Cuffs. Pearce rubbed his sore wrists as Tariq proceeded to free the others. Kurdish voices crackled on Tariq's shoulder mic.

"All secured. No survivors." Tariq nodded at the Aussie still on the floor and pulled his .45-caliber pistol. "Except this one."

Pearce put a hand on Tariq's weapon. "No."

"We can't leave any witnesses."

"Majid will hunt you down, Pearce. You and your mates. Let me go and I'll talk him out of it. I swear."

Pearce leaned over and picked the Aussie up by his lapels, standing him on his feet. "You can do that?"

"Sure thing."

"But you wouldn't."

"I would, mate! I would! I don't owe that man a thing. It's my skin I'm worried about."

"Waste him. We can take our chances," Early said.

"It wasn't personal, mate! It was just business. Following orders, that's all. I can follow orders. You tell me what you want me to do, I'll do it. It's a contract between you and me, and I keep my contracts. You'll see."

"How do I know I can trust you?"

"Trust me? You *own* me."

"Prove it," Pearce said.

"How?"

"Call Majid. Tell him you did the job. That will give us time to get out of here."

"Sure thing."

The four Americans, Tariq, and the Aussie climbed out of the back of the truck. Pearce surveyed the damage. The wreck of the Humvee up front was still burning by the side of the road. The Humvee behind them was closer. The heat from its flames tingled on his skin in the cool air. Bodies were strewn about in the dust, tossed from their vehicles after the explosions or shot by the Kurds. Barnes's corpse was just ten feet away, cut down while trying to run away into the dark.

The Aussie looked at Tariq and pointed at his inside pocket. "I'm reaching for my phone."

"I prefer you reach for a gun." Tariq grinned. "Then I kill you, fair and square."

"A phone, mate. It's just a phone."

The Aussie pulled out his phone and dialed Majid. Tariq pressed his pistol against the Australian's head, flashing a smile, daring the merc to screw up the call.

The Aussie spoke to Majid, calm and collected. "Yeah. It's done. All of them. We're burning the bodies now. Thank you, sir. See you soon." He hung up. Turned to Pearce. "Satisfied?"

"You think he believed you?" Pearce asked.

"I know he did."

"Good."

Tariq's pistol cracked.

A fist-sized glob of brains and bone erupted out of the back of the Aussie's head as more than four hundred pounds of foot energy pushed the .45-caliber slug through his skull. His wiry corpse tumbled into the dust, twitching as it bled out.

"Damn it!" Early said. "How about a little warning next time?" He wiped away the gore splashed onto his camo shirt.

Everybody's ears rang from the stinging pistol retort.

Tariq spat on the corpse as he holstered his pistol. "We cross the border into Kurdistan, be in my village before sunrise if we leave now."

"The Aussie was right," Rowley said. "Majid will hunt us down when he finds out we're still alive."

"He won't," Pearce said.

"How do you know?"

"I'll take care of it."

"How?"

Early loaded a wad of chaw in his lip. "Don't wet yourself, Rowley. He'll take care of it."

Tariq grinned ear to ear. "And if Majid does find out? Let the bastard come to my village. We will welcome him. Ha!" He spat in the dust.

"He won't," Pearce said. "Let's saddle up and roll."

WASHINGTON, D.C.

Congressman Chandler opened his secured server. His contact in Baghdad confirmed that Pearce and the others had finally reported back in, a week late. The debrief indicated that the four Americans had followed a lead that took them to Kirkuk. The contact further indicated that Pearce and Early were being reassigned to JSOC for special security work in Baghdad's Green Zone. Chandler was grateful that Pearce and his friends were finally out of the way.

Chandler took a sip of heavily creamed and sugared coffee and scrolled through his classified news feeds. He came across a CIA report. He set his cup down. Chandler couldn't believe his eyes. The CIA report indicated that at least forty members of General Majid's command had been butchered in fierce fighting in the district over the last few weeks, including, apparently, the twenty-four Shia recruits he'd helped swear in. "Too bad," he whispered to himself, clucking his tongue. He took another sip of coffee and read further. He nearly spit it out of his nose.

Majid was dead. Killed by a bomb in his palace. His private office incinerated. No evidence left behind.

Chandler swore under his breath as he pulled open a desk drawer and lifted out his private secured laptop. His door knocked. "Just a moment, please."

The door pushed open. His secretary poked her head in. "Sir? The Sisters of Perpetual Help are here for your nine o'clock."

"Not now!"

The secretary saw the crazed look in her boss's eyes. She blanched. "Yes, sir." She closed the door in a hurry.

Chandler typed in the password. Majid's Cayman Island bank account screen pulled up.

Zero.

Jesus, Mary, and Joseph, Chandler thought. *All that money, gone.* Only he and Majid had the password for the account. Whoever took it must have tortured the general for it.

Just what a terrorist would do.

54

Pearce heard voices in the distance.

The ache in his shoulders was finally pulling his mind out of the dark abyss of the tranquilizer and into the dim fog of semiconsciousness. He was suddenly self-aware. Aware enough to know that his eyes felt taped shut, but they weren't. He struggled to pry them open, finally managing to lift the half-ton weights holding down his eyelids. A hazy film blurred his vision. He blinked a few more times. Clearer now.

Pearce focused on his lap. He was sitting. Bound to a chair. He was wearing an orange jumpsuit. He was screwed.

Pain shot through his neck and shoulders and his skull throbbed with a pounding headache. The room was nearly dark except for a bright flickering light outside his peripheral vision, coming from the same direction as the voices.

He squirmed and stretched as best he could, trying to work out the kinks in his aching back, but he couldn't move much. His arms were cuffed behind him. The thick plastic strips cut deeply into his wrists. He tried to twist them but they wouldn't budge. He began opening and closing his tingling hands, partly to keep the blood flowing. His ankles were cuffed tightly to the legs of the chair as well.

Christ, Pearce thought, *where am I?*

The voices came from the wide-screen television on the wall in front of him. Arabic. He caught most of it, but the images told the story: ISIS fighters, flags, guns, Raqqa. Then more reporting about impending American airstrikes and stock video images of infrared targets, reticles, smart bombs, exploding buildings. "B-52 bombers are already in the air from bases in the United States," a reporter said, then cut away to a Saudi official. "Yes, thousands of civilians will die, but that is the fault of *Daesh*, and *Daesh* will finally be destroyed."

Pearce's heart sank. How long had he been out?

He wiggled his fingers and thumbs as much as he could. In his mind he wondered if Ian knew where he was.

He glanced over at the plate-glass window. Outside he saw lush green grass in gently rolling mounds lit by buzzing sodium lamps. Long, arcing plumes of water swept back and forth over the turf bounded by palm trees. "A damn golf course," he muttered to himself. "Ian, you're a Scot, and you don't even play golf."

What was going on? Where was he? If he didn't know any better, he would have guessed by the expensive furnishings he was in a five-star hotel or condo on a golf course in Vegas or West Palm. If they were going to torture him, why would they do it here? If they weren't going to work him over, what did they want with him?

His nose twitched. An acrid smell. Urine. His own. He looked down. He could feel his cold crotch. He rocked in the chair. Heard the adult diaper crinkle beneath his jumpsuit. He tried to swallow but his throat ached. He was parched. Probably dehydrated from the booze. Stupid.

The door pushed open.

A barrel-chested monster in desert camo and a bushy beard burst into the room. His dark eyes first scowled at Pearce, then scanned the room swiftly. He left as quickly as he arrived, slamming the door shut behind him.

Was that the goon who would torture him? Cut off his head? Pearce's mind was still clouded. Nothing was making sense.

The door swung open again. The fanatical goon stormed over to Pearce. Ran his thick hands over the PlastiCuffs to make sure they were secure. He turned around and nodded toward the door.

Al-Saud stepped in. He wasn't dressed like a Westerner now. He wore flowing robes and a white keffiyeh, the traditional headdress of

Saudi men. He dismissed the uniformed killer with a wave of his hand. The man sneered at Pearce one last time and left the room, gently shutting the door behind him.

Al-Saud stepped closer to Pearce, leaned down. A smile creased his face. "How are you feeling, Mr. Pearce?"

"Sitting in my dirty diaper, strapped to a chair?" Pearce's voice croaked. "How do you think I feel?"

"I apologize for the inconveniences. My security team insisted upon it. You have a formidable reputation."

"I'm a harmless little fuzzball. You can release me. No worries, I promise."

Al-Saud stood erect. His smile widened. "I think not." Al-Saud stepped over to an ornately carved dining table and pulled out a chair identical to the one Pearce was strapped to. He placed the chair next to Pearce, then sat in it.

"Why am I here?" Pearce asked.

"That's an excellent question. Why do you think you're here?"

"First of all, where is 'here'?"

"One of my properties adjacent to the country club my family owns."

"In the States?"

"Just outside of Riyadh, actually. Do you play golf?"

"I have a Mizuno five-iron I'd like to rack across your skull."

Al-Saud darkened. "I can see the murder in your *kafir* eyes. Tell me, how many men have you killed? I mean, personally. In combat. Not from one of your remote drone strikes."

"Why do pussies like you always want to know how many people men like me have killed?"

"Don't you know it's rude to answer a question with a question?"

"Do you think I care?"

Al-Saud laughed. "You think you're in some kind of a movie, don't you? Like you're playing the tough-talking action hero who finds a way to free himself and take out the villain."

"Something like that."

Al-Saud's fist slammed into Pearce's face with a sickening thud.

Pearce tumbled over sideways, his head crashing to the thickly carpeted floor. His cheek was on fire.

"Damn," Pearce said with a groan.

Al-Saud stood, rubbing his sore fist. "You must pardon my temper." He pulled off his long headdress and set it on the table. "In my country, manners are expected from guests, even ones that stink of their own filth."

Pearce opened a swelling eye. Saw the pistol in al-Saud's shoulder holster.

Al-Saud touched his weapon and shook his head. "Not yet, my friend. We have a few things to discuss. Then I should like to sit here and observe you as you watch the destruction of Raqqa and the beginning of the war that will finally cleanse my land of the filthy *Daesh*." He checked his Rolex. "My sources tell me that the bombing will begin in just three minutes. We haven't much time."

Al-Saud lifted up Pearce in his chair and set him upright again.

Pearce shook his head to clear it. "So what are we discussing?"

"You were an analyst with the CIA before you became a SOG operative. Tell me, why do you think you are here?"

"I guess I pissed somebody off. And I'm guessing it's you."

"Excellent. You are quite correct."

"What I can't figure out is how I've managed to do that. My friend Ian might know."

"Ian? Who's that?"

"The head of my IT department. Smart guy. Knows a lot."

"This Ian fellow might know, but I doubt it. But you do."

Pearce shook his head and shrugged slightly. "Sorry, drawing a blank."

"Why do people become angry with other people?"

"Listen, buddy—"

Another fist cracked into Pearce's jaw. The chair started to tip but al-Saud caught Pearce by the scruff of his neck and stabilized it.

"There's my temper again. I apologize. I come from a proud family. I should advise you, I'm not your 'buddy.' I am His Royal Highness

Faisal bin Salman al-Saud, fifth in line in the succession. However, that's quite the long title. Your Highness or Mr. Ambassador will suffice. Understood?"

Pearce nodded through clenched eyes, his face wincing with pain. "Yeah. Understood."

"I've just given you the answer to my own question."

Pearce tried to clear his mind. *I wish you were here, Ian*, he thought. *I really do.* Pearce opened his eyes, glared at al-Saud. "I guess I did something to offend you."

"Offend? Outrage is more like it."

"How?"

"How do you think?"

Pearce's mind raced. What had al-Saud just been saying? Something about a proud family. "I must have done something against your family or your country."

"My family is this country. But, yes, my family is the issue. Blood is, indeed, thicker than water, especially in the desert."

"Are you saying I killed someone in your family?"

"Very good."

"Who? I don't know of any Saudis I've killed. At least not knowingly."

"Not knowingly? Interesting phrase."

Pearce suddenly understood. "A drone strike."

Al-Saud nodded. "You must have been quite the analyst. I'm sure the CIA regrets having lost you."

"When?"

"Earlier this year. You struck a group of *Daesh* fighters in the Kurdistan region. Fifteen were killed outright. Several others who were horribly burned and wounded died later."

"*Daesh*? What does your family have to do with them?"

"Unfortunately, my nephew had been seduced by the devil's own doctrine. He was a *Daesh* unit commander in the region. He died that day."

"Those sons of bitches were using captured women as sex slaves, then selling them on the open market after they were through with them. They butchered an entire village of Christians. You expect me to weep over that kind of garbage?"

Al-Saud pulled out his pistol and raised it high to slam it into Pearce's skull, but halted in midair. He lowered the chromed weapon. He grinned. "You see? My temper. You shouldn't provoke me. Yes, the *Daesh* behave like barbarians. But my nephew was still my blood, however misguided he may have been. When you killed my nephew, my family demanded retribution. One of my sources in the Turkish army informed me you were the mastermind of the operation. Honor demanded I seek vengeance. Surely you understand the concept of vengeance."

All too well, Pearce thought. "So why am I still alive?"

Al-Saud pointed at the HD television with his pistol. "We're going to watch a little television together first, then I'm going to blow your brains out."

"You don't think kidnapping and murdering an American government official is a problem for you? Your government won't be happy with that."

"No one in my government knows anything."

"You want me to believe your government isn't behind the entire operation?"

"The leadership of my government is as feeble and weak-willed as yours. I was forced to act on my own initiative."

"You don't know President Lane. He won't stand by when an American citizen is captured and killed."

Al-Saud sat back down in his chair, holstering his weapon. "Ansar al-Sharia butchered Ambassador Stevens and the whole world saw it. Your government didn't seem to care at all. But you? No one even knows I've kidnapped you, and no one will know I'm the one who killed you. By this time tomorrow your corpse will be scattered in the desert in small piles of jackal dung."

"When my team finds out where I am, they'll track you down." Pearce kept flexing his hands.

Al-Saud shook his head. "My men stripped you naked when you

were unconscious and destroyed your watch. They even neutralized the transponder unit you and your employees have implanted inside your bodies."

Pearce couldn't hide his surprise. He'd used those trackers for years to protect his people. Dr. Rao warned him the technology was becoming vulnerable.

Al-Saud laughed. "Nobody knows you're here, Pearce. Nobody will rescue you."

"Something still doesn't add up. Why bring me here? Why wait to kill me until after the war begins?"

"Because I know how much you hate the idea of this war. I wanted you to see it begin. And I want to watch your face when you realize your worst fears will come to pass. Your country will be committed to occupying the Middle East for decades. Thousands of your people will be killed or wounded, and you will spend trillions defending my kingdom from *Daesh* and the Persian heretics. And it's all your fault."

"You want this war."

Al-Saud laughed again. "Want it? You still don't get it, do you? I *made* this war, thanks to you."

55

Pearce frowned. "What do you mean, you 'made this war'?"

"Who do you think sent that drone to the White House with the flag and the threat?"

"You?"

Al-Saud shrugged. "Well, not me, personally. But I helped arrange it. You know, Pearce, you're not the only drone expert in the world."

A news report flashed on the television screen. Live images of the bombing of Raqqa suddenly appeared. The Saudi reporters shouted, "It has begun!"

Al-Saud pumped his fists in the air, shouting *"Allahu akbar!"* over and over, laughing and pointing at the TV.

Pearce stared at the gruesome images, a city under bombardment. It made him sick to his stomach. Alyssa Abbott obviously had won the argument that the live video feeds of Raqqa's destruction would be the perfect piece of propaganda to terrorize would-be terrorists. Pearce wasn't so sure.

"How many civilians made it out?" Pearce asked.

"Just a few thousand, according to your satellite imagery."

"Hundreds of Muslims are dying right now, maybe thousands. Don't you care?"

Al-Saud shook his head. "If they die, it is Allah's will that they die. Besides, they're mostly Syrians."

"You're a callous f—" Pearce caught himself. "So tell me, why didn't you kill more Americans while you were at it? Why not drop the planes in midair or poison all the water?"

"Despite what you may think of me, I'm not an uncivilized man. I like Americans. The only purpose of the drone attacks was to finally rouse President Lane to war against *Daesh*. Your country was never really in danger. I only wanted to make it appear that way. There are no other attacks planned for your water system, or any other drone attacks of any kind."

"What if Lane had refused to go to war? And refused to raise the flag?"

"Then the plan would have failed. But obviously it didn't. It was Allah's will that it succeed."

"You wouldn't have escalated?"

"No. I must stand before Allah and give an account of my life someday. I will not have the blood of innocents weighing against me in the balance."

Pearce nodded at the television. "What about *their* innocent blood?"

"Their blood is on America's hands, not mine. But their sacrifice also serves Allah's purpose. Those videos will be used as jihadi recruiting tools around the world for years to come, guaranteeing your country's continued interest in the War on Terror, which means continued interest in protecting the Kingdom, which is Allah's will."

"I don't know what god you think you're serving, but the Koran says that Allah loves the just."

"And you are a Crusader-blasphemer." Al-Saud stood up, pulled his pistol back out. He racked the slide. "Would you care to pray before you die?"

Pearce doubted it would help. He shook his head. "No, but I have a question."

"What?"

"Why did you try and assassinate President Myers?"

"The goal was only to wound her, not kill her. It was an expert shot that guaranteed her life."

"Why?"

"To get you out of Washington, of course." Al-Saud smiled. "She is an admirable woman. You were a lucky man, Pearce."

A loud crack threw the room in to total darkness, killing the lights outside, too. Pearce twisted in his chair. There was enough moonlight that he could see shadowy figures racing across the grass.

Al-Saud's men shouted outside the room. Gunfire erupted. Bullets shattered the door just as the window glass exploded.

Al-Saud lifted his pistol and pointed it at Pearce's head. Squeezed the trigger.

An explosion blinded Pearce and smashed his eardrums. The stabbing pain in his skull was the last thing his brain registered.

"TROY! TROY! Are you with us?" Ian shouted in Pearce's skull.

Pearce's eyes blinked open to a sweating, scowling Saudi face. A wide, toothy grin began spreading beneath the thick mustache. The man wore the uniform of the Saudi Special Security Forces.

"Are you injured, Mr. Pearce?" the major asked. He whipped out a combat knife.

"I'm here, Ian. Quit yelling," Pearce said.

"Excuse me, sir?" The Saudi said as he cut away the PlastiCuffs still pinning Pearce to his chair.

"Who are you?" Pearce asked, his brain still ringing from the flash-bang.

"Major Muhammad ibn Saleh al-Bunayan." He helped Pearce uneasily to his feet. "I see no wounds, sir. How do you feel?"

"I'm fine, Major. Who sent you?" Pearce stretched the kinks out of his back and the strain in his wrists.

"I did," Ian said.

"Hold that thought, Ian," Pearce said. "It's confusing as hell trying to talk to both of you."

Pearce and Ian were communicating through the elaborate "smart tattoo" inked across his back and snaking up his neck. The smart tattoo comprised a multilayered organic transmitter and receiver module. It was powered by a bio-templated piezoelectric nanogenerator activated by Pearce's opening and closing his hands. The tattoo's subvocal speech-recognition technology meant Pearce could simply "think" his words to his Scottish computer genius. Pearce could hear Ian silently inside his head through bone conduction, much the same way Google Glass head-phones operated. Because the smart tattoo was printed with electronically conducive organic hydro-gel, it couldn't be discovered through tradi-tional metal detection. When Dr. Rao inked him with the smart tattoo five days before, he had no idea it would be field-tested so quickly, nor that it would be used to save his life.

The Saudi major frowned with confusion. "Sir? Who is this Ian you are speaking to?"

"Doesn't matter. Who sent you?"

"My commanding officer received the request thirty minutes ago directly from the White House." The major began checking Pearce over. His face was partially swollen where al-Saud had struck him. Pearce knew he looked as beat to hell as he felt.

"Who in the White House sent you?"

"I need to have you examined by my medical officer."

"Don't sweat it."

"I have my orders." The major barked a command in Arabic. A moment later another Special Security Forces officer rushed through the door, a combat medical kit slung over one shoulder. Pearce relented and let the medic take a few minutes and do his duty. Pearce was steered to a more comfortable couch, and the medic gave him a quick exam while Pearce continued questioning the major.

"I don't know who in the White House sent the request."

"It must have been President Lane," Pearce said.

"Permission to speak," Ian said in his buttery-smooth brogue.

"Not yet," Pearce said out loud.

"You must be speaking to that Ian fellow again." The major frowned, scanning Pearce up and down. "Tell me, where are your comms?" the major said.

Pearce shrugged. "It's classified."

"It was Vice President Chandler," Ian said inside Pearce's skull.

"Chandler?" Pearce said. "Why the hell did you call Chandler?"

"I contacted the White House directly, but President Lane is incommunicado, heading for Beijing and the Asia Security Summit. The vice president is in charge of day-to-day operations for the time being. He authorized the mission to rescue you."

Pearce was surprised. He assumed Chandler would have welcomed his disappearance.

"Please tell me you recorded the conversation with al-Saud."

"Of course, but it's rough. I'll have to run it through an audio filter first."

"Forward a copy of it to Chandler as soon as you can. We've got a war to stop." Pearce turned to the major. "Where's al-Saud now?"

The major stiffened. "He's in our custody. He shall be dealt with."

"I need to see him, right now."

"That won't be possible."

"Why not?"

"Orders."

"From whom?"

The major shrugged. "Does it matter? You know how it is."

Pearce swore. He had a feeling he'd seen this movie before.

"Troy, I've arranged for a Pearce Systems plane to land in Riyadh in the next twenty minutes," Ian said. But the transmission was starting to break up. "As soon as it refuels, it's scheduled to bring you back home. There's a doctor on board as well."

Pearce thanked Ian and told him they'd talk later with better comms. He turned to the major, tugging on his orange jumpsuit. "Any chance I can grab a shower, a set of clothes, and a ride to the airport?"

The major sniffed. Pearce's diaper was full. "Follow me."

56

Good as his word, the Saudi major provided Pearce with a hot shower, clothes confiscated from the pro shop, and a ride to the airport in his command vehicle. Pearce's presence in the Kingdom was kept secret from the American embassy as per Chandler's request.

Pearce boarded his company plane and headed straight for the cockpit. He ordered the pilot to radio the tower and get the plane off the runway. "We're not leaving here without al-Saud in custody," he told the crew. "Understood?"

"Yes, sir."

The onboard doctor—a physician's assistant, Sarah Swift—approached him in the cabin. "I need to check you out."

"Not yet," Pearce said. "I've got a couple of calls to make. We'll do it once we're in the air."

"But, sir—"

Pearce's withering glare cut off the former combat medic in midsentence.

"Yes, sir."

"Thank you."

Pearce dashed for his secured comms station and contacted Ian. The smart tattoo was already starting to fail, and it wasn't an encrypted system anyway.

"Ian, have you reached Chandler yet? I need to speak with him now."

"I've tried to connect with him directly. His assistant says he's unavailable at the moment."

"Tell his assistant Chandler either calls me back right now or I call the *New York Times*."

"Will do. Give me a minute."

CHANDLER WAS ON the phone ten minutes later.

"Troy? It's me, Clay. How are you feeling?"

"Fucking fantastic. Did you listen to the digital recording Ian sent you?"

"Thank God you're alive. I couldn't believe my ears when Ian said you'd been kidnapped."

"The recording? Did you hear it?"

"Of course. Al-Saud is a real son of a bitch—pardon my French. I'm glad we're rid of him."

"That's one of the reasons why I needed to talk to you. I need to get my hands on him right now, find out who's running his terror operation."

"I'm afraid that's not going to happen. He's in Saudi custody now."

"Are you shitting me? The Saudis owe us everything. I just need him for thirty minutes. I'll even keep him alive."

"You see, Troy, here's the rub. In order to save you, I had to cut a deal with the Royal House of Saud. The ambassador is one of theirs. They agreed to send in their best and rescue you, but they insisted on keeping the prince in their custody."

"The bastard attacked our country and got us into a war."

"And I've been assured he'll be dealt with harshly."

"I don't give a shit how he's dealt with. I need to find out who he was working with. We need to stop the source of the terror attacks."

"Did we hear the same recording? Al-Saud said the attacks were staged and over with. No more attacks have occurred since the last one, which confirms his statement. As far as I'm concerned, the terror threat is neutralized."

"Are you out of your mind?" Pearce could practically hear Chandler's jaw clenching over the satellite connection.

The vice president hesitated a long while before speaking, obviously trying to calm himself down. "The Saudi government has publicly supported our actions against Raqqa and they're providing important logistical resources for our operations. I won't do anything to jeopardize that relationship. This war against ISIS is too important. Besides, we still have our best people on the case. We'll find whoever was responsible for this in due time."

"Why take the chance? Al-Saud knows exactly who this is."

"We need the Saudis to fight this war. The Saudis won't hand him over. Period. You said there was another reason you needed to talk to me?"

"Yeah. It's time to stop the bombing."

"Excuse me?"

"The war is a sham. Al-Saud said as much. Civilian casualties are mounting even as we speak. Lane would stop it immediately if he knew about al-Saud."

"I'm not so sure about that."

"Call him. Tell him exactly what's happened."

"The president is behind closed doors right now with President Sun and the other Asia leaders. I'm in charge now, and we're not calling the war off."

Rage fell on Pearce like a bad fever. "You callous son of a bitch. This isn't a game. People are dying."

"Everybody dies, Pearce, including you and me. It's just their time, that's all."

"You're killing innocent women and children."

"Innocent? I had no idea you were such a romantic. There's no innocence over there, especially in Raqqa. It's a jihadi Woodstock. Every baby on the tit is just another suckling terrorist waiting for his turn to kill an American."

Pearce's grip tightened around the handset. "So help me God, I'll go to the press with this. Pull the blanket back and expose the Saudis for what they've done."

"The Saudis? No. You mean, al-Saud. He's just one Saudi. Emotionally unstable, certainly. But the House of Saud is our staunch ally in the War on Terror and has been since 9/11. They have powerful friends on the Hill. Besides, we're now in the middle of a war against the most brutal and evil regime we've seen since Hitler. Are you sure you want to muddy the waters now?"

"I don't give a shit. It's the truth."

"Truth is a funny thing, Pearce. Go ahead and tell the 'truth.' But do so knowing that if you stop the war, you'll be saving ISIS from destruction. That means you'll be responsible for every person they rape, torture, and kill from now on. Is that a truth you can handle?"

"Don't try to play head games with me."

"And don't forget. If you go to the press with your story, Lane will be impeached because he's the one that gave the order. Believe me, he's got plenty of enemies in Washington, and the long knives will come out lickety-split. And here's one more truth for you to chew on: If Lane's impeached, I'm the next POTUS." Chandler couldn't help but laugh. "I bet you'd just love that, wouldn't you?"

Pearce wanted to puke. His head swam. This is why he hated politics, and Chandler was everything he hated about politicians. But in his own sick, twisted logic, Chandler was right. The damage he'd cause by blowing the whistle on al-Saud still wouldn't stop a war that everybody in Washington now wanted. He saw Lane's poll numbers after his speech. They were through the roof. Proof yet again that the "rally 'round the flag" phenomenon was the most dependable fact in American political life. Ever since Lane's speech, Americans wanted the war and they craved leadership, and Lane was giving them both. With that kind of credibility, the president could craft a lasting peace at the Asia Security Summit, too. It all made perfect sense—at least politically.

"Are we still connected? I don't hear you running your mouth," Chandler said.

"I'm here."

"The truth is a fickle lover, isn't it?"

Pearce remembered something al-Saud said. "Do you believe in God, Chandler?"

"It comes with the job description."

"Good. Because when you meet Him, you'll have to give an account for what you've done. And so will I."

"I'm prepared to give an account when that day comes."

"That day will come sooner than you think if I have anything to say about it."

"Are you threatening me, Troy? The sitting vice president?"

Pearce heard the mocking tone in Chandler's voice.

"No threat, Mr. Vice President. Just conveying my fervent hope and prayer." Pearce hung up to the sound of Chandler's laughter.

Fuck Chandler, Pearce thought. *Let him play his stupid games.* There were more important things to do.

He knew he could still try and persuade the president to call off the bombing and maybe even the war after Lane's meeting with President Sun. Equally important, there was still a lone wolf on the prowl whom he had to find. Whoever he was, he was dangerous as hell and was roaming free. It didn't matter to Pearce if he had stopped operations for al-Saud. The man was guilty of committing crimes on American soil and he needed to be brought to justice. Pearce had to find him.

But how?

57

WASHINGTON, D.C.

Chandler turned to Grafton. "You heard all of that, Vicki?"

"Yes."

"What's your read on Pearce?"

Grafton had been listening in on Chandler's phone call with Pearce but her mind was elsewhere. She was on cloud nine. A woman totally in the flow of her own giftedness and power. She was sitting next to the second most powerful politician on the planet and he was seeking her counsel, but she hardly cared—like a tenured postal worker who just won the Powerball. Ilene Parcelle had called earlier that morning, congratulating her first for landing her "big fish" and, subsequently, her reward. Grafton was now a junior partner at the Seven Rivers Consortium. Another long and costly Mideast war would replenish the coffers of SRC's international clientele. But there were formalities to satisfy, Parcelle said, and Grafton's official duties wouldn't begin for a few weeks. Ilene advised her to stay put and keep her hand on the tiller and her ear to the ground for as long as possible.

"Vicki?"

Grafton snapped out of her trance. "Pearce sounds like he's out of control. Do you think he'll change his mind about going to the press with all of this?"

Chandler chewed on his lower lip, a childhood habit. "I really don't know. He's a very smart man, but he's prone to rashness. If he falls into some kind of funk or rage, who knows what he'll do?"

Grafton shifted uncomfortably in her chair, trying to decide what to tell her boss. "If he does go to the press, what damage do you think could actually be done?"

"Can't you imagine the headline?"

"You mean, 'One crazed Saudi conspires to launch a series of frightening but essentially nonlethal attacks to get us into a war we should've been fighting anyway'?"

"You never wrote newspaper copy, did you? That headline wouldn't fit if you folded the paper sideways," Chandler said, smiling at his own joke. "The headline I fear is, 'Saudis manipulate U.S. into another pointless Mideast war.' That's the one that will turn this administration upside down, and not a few careers will get poured out into the gutter, yours and mine included."

Grafton's green eyes narrowed, studying Chandler's face. He was scared. That surprised her. She'd always known him to be a decisive and ruthless decision maker. She'd never seen him clutching his pearls before. "You knew Pearce was dangerous. Al-Saud was about to do you a favor. Why did you intervene?"

"Pearce's man Ian alerted me to the situation. That means he was a witness. If al-Saud had killed Pearce, then we'd be in a world of hurt, possibly even planning the invasion of Riyadh right now. Believe me, if I could've let al-Saud dispatch Pearce without getting caught, I would have been in the front row, cheering him on."

"Pearce is a man with a violent history," Grafton offered. "I wouldn't be surprised if someone from his past finally caught up with him." She had a few resources at her disposal now, including Tarkovsky's connection to the SVR hit teams. Pearce was already on their list. Once she was fully on board at SRC she would have access to their private mercenary army to draw upon as well. Pearce was a bleeding wound that needed to be cauterized. That would put Chandler in her debt forever.

"What are you suggesting, Vicki?"

Grafton saw the hope rise in his round, piggish eyes. She'd seen that look before. She was used to being the object of desire, especially for men, and she enjoyed it. The male desire for sexual satisfaction was a powerful weapon in her arsenal, particularly when that satisfaction was first withheld, then granted. But the look in Chandler's eyes was even more desperate. The expectancy of a drowning man the moment before his rescue.

She was about to jump in and pull him out but she stopped. A small voice in the back of her mind warned her that drowning men usually pull down the people trying to save them. Arranging for Pearce to be killed would solve a lot of problems for everybody, but the risk of being discovered for having done so was even higher. What did she care if Chandler went down? She was standing on the high, rocky shores of the SRC. She was invulnerable now.

Or was she? If the war suddenly stopped and the Saudi conspiracy was revealed, she might get swept up in the undertow of the sinking Lane administration. After all, she was in the room when the decision for war was made. She was sitting right next to Chandler. If he became radioactive, so would she by virtue of her proximity. Would the SRC terminate her partnership to avoid the scandal? More important, her value to the SRC was tied directly to her access and influence with a successful Lane-Chandler administration. Her fate was now inextricably bound to theirs.

Dealing with Pearce suddenly seemed a lot less risky. There was one other option.

Grafton reached down into her turquoise Brahmin handbag. "I have something that can help you with your problem."

Chandler brightened, curious. "I like surprises."

Grafton held out her hand. Chandler opened his. She placed Tarkovsky's thumb drive into his soft palm.

"What's this?" Chandler asked.

"A gift from a friend. Now it's my gift to you."

"I should still be mad at you for abandoning the Russian option."

"I didn't abandon it. Just changed the batting order." She nodded at the thumb drive. "You should open that."

"I was taught that regifting was bad manners."

Grafton suddenly wondered if she'd been played by her Russian lover. If so, it didn't matter now. "Maybe it was always meant for you."

"How delightful." Chandler grinned, intrigued. He fingered the drive. "What's in it?"

"Pearce's head. On a great big silver platter."

58

Pearce had given the order to his crew to take off. No point in hanging around. Al-Saud was in protective custody.

At least for now.

Once they'd reached cruising altitude, Sarah Swift unbuckled from her seat and reappeared. "Time for that checkup."

Pearce started to protest but stopped. His headache throbbed so badly he thought there might be a slug lodged in there. Despite the pain, his mind didn't stop racing as he tried to come up with a solution to the problem at hand—how to find al-Saud's operative.

He told her about the headache and she checked his eyes again for dilation and concussion symptoms. Swift was fast but thorough. While she kept checking and recording his vitals, they swapped stories about Afghanistan. The Canadian former combat medic was a thirty-six-year-old blonde from Vancouver with a spray of freckles across her California surfer-girl face. She reminded him a little of dark-eyed Cella, the Italian doctor he had met and fallen in love with during his time in Afghanistan. According to Ian, Swift was just as brave and every bit as talented as Cella in the field. In fact, Swift had been wounded in battle and received both the Sacrifice Medal and the Star of Courage for her service. She was a great asset to the team. Pearce Systems was a civilian contractor specializing in drone applications across a wide spectrum of economic activity, but the company had been born out of security operations. Even with drone ops, human lives were at risk in the field. Swift was part of that team but in between assignments. He was glad to have her on board tonight.

Swift told him he needed to get into a clinic for a more thorough exam and a brain scan when they landed, but for the moment she was reasonably satisfied that he suffered only a headache. She handed him a couple of industrial-strength Advil and fetched a bag of frozen peas for him to press against his bruised face while she headed for the galley to whip up something for him to eat. She explained that their flight was last-minute and they were shorthanded. Pearce complied.

The cold bag of peas felt good against his throbbing face and the Advil already seemed to be kicking in. He had twelve hours of flight time before he reached Washington, D.C., and he was pretty much out of action until he landed. But his brain, busted as it was, could still be put to use. His training as a CIA analyst would have to fill in the gaps.

All of the analytical resources of the federal government hadn't been able to turn up anything regarding al-Saud's lone wolf. Not one single clue. He'd been as brilliant in hiding himself as he had in the design and execution of his attacks. But there had to be a vulnerability in his invisibility shield. What was it? Forensics had crawled all over the original drone that landed on the White House lawn and didn't find anything. The other physical devices left behind, including the water-disruption equipment at the house in Los Angeles, proved equally clean. There was absolutely nothing—not one piece of physical or digital evidence—left behind.

Except al-Saud. He was the only link. Chandler had severed that link. He needed to reconnect it.

Pearce rang up Ian again. "We need to start digging into al-Saud. He's the chink in our lone wolf's armor."

"I initiated a search query as soon as I determined you were in his custody. So far, no luck. His digital shadow has been thoroughly scrubbed."

"Stay on it. And, by the way, thanks for saving my bacon."

"Hated to go to Chandler but I had no choice."

"I would've done the same."

"Cheers." Ian rang off.

Swift came back ten minutes later with a microwaved entree of salmon and scalloped potatoes, along with a cup of fresh fruit. She saw the faraway look on his face. He wasn't in the mood for company. "I'm fixing something for the boys up front. I'll check back on you in a while or you can hit the call button."

"Thanks. This looks great."

"You've got a terrific galley back there. Beats MREs any day of the week." She laid a hand on his broad shoulder. "Soon as you eat, you need to get some shut-eye. Doctor's orders."

"I'm trying to stop a war."

"You're stuck on a plane for twelve hours. Maybe God's trying to tell you to take a breather. At least for a few hours."

"Tell you the truth, I'm exhausted. But I haven't been sleeping well lately."

"For how long?"

"A couple of months."

"I'll get you something for that. At least for tonight."

"Thanks."

Swift left and Pearce cut into his salmon filet, his mouth watering. A little food would help clear his mind.

JUST AS HE FINISHED his last bite Swift reappeared with a couple of sleeping pills and bottled water. "Take these. They'll knock you out, but not too badly. Just enough to get you some rest. You need it." She set the pills in his hand.

He stared at them. "Addictive?"

"Very, if you're not careful. That a problem?"

"Maybe."

"Once won't be an issue. Take them. You need it."

"You're the doctor."

She gathered up his plate and silverware and left him alone. He cracked open the bottle of water and stared at the pills in his hand one last time. His headache had cleared up quite a bit, but his mind was fogged like a Swedish sauna. He needed to sleep. He popped the pills into his mouth and washed them down with a long pull of water. It was entirely psychosomatic, but he already felt a little sleepy.

He leaned his business-class chair back into a reclining position, shut off the light, and closed his eyes. The thrumming turbines and cool cabin air blowing on his face calmed him down. He forced himself to clear his mind by focusing on his breathing. It worked. For a minute. Until the images flooded back. Tanaka flashed in and out of his mind, along with al-Saud's twisted smile. Shame gripped Pearce. If he hadn't been drunk, then al-Saud's security team wouldn't have gotten the drop on him. If he'd been at the top of his game to begin with, maybe all of this wouldn't have happened. Tariq Barzani's bald head and wild Kurdish mustache flashed in his brain. So did the infrared image of the ISIS fighters Pearce had killed in a ball of white fire on a computer monitor. It was an act of mindless vengeance. Al-Saud's nephew died in that explosion. And now many thousands more were dying—all because of him. Who was he kidding? Chandler would be judged in the end, but so would he. Maybe he would be judged even more harshly because he knew what he was doing.

No, it wasn't me, it was al-Saud, Pearce reminded himself. He only used Pearce's attack to justify his actions, and to light the fuse that was setting the world on fire. Al-Saud blamed him for his nephew's death. He used Pearce to get his vengeance on ISIS, then tried to get his personal revenge on Pearce. Why the personal revenge? Because al-Saud obviously wanted the satisfaction of executing Pearce up close and intimate instead of having his lone wolf do it for him.

Wait a minute, he thought. *Al-Saud. Who else knows about him?* The sleeping pills must have been kicking in. He was having a hard time holding on to a memory. It swam like a silvery fish though the fingers of his mind. Something about al-Saud. A phone call. Yeah, but from whom? Pearce rolled through a hazy Rolodex in his mind's eye. It finally stopped. Moshe Werntz, from Mossad. That was it. He'd called Pearce and told him about the secret meeting between al-Saud and Tarkovsky.

Tarkovsky? What did he remember about him? An engineer by

training. Formerly head of some department. International science and technical cooperation? Security affairs? Something like that. Drones would fit in his wheelhouse. The Russians were years behind on drone technology but coming on fast. What they couldn't design they reverse-engineered or flat-out stole—following the Chinese model perfectly. But the stuff that was used over the last week wasn't high-end. It was all easily within grasp of Russian technical abilities.

Could Tarkovsky be the lone wolf? Seemed unlikely. But if not him, a Russian operative connected to him? Sure. Why not?

Pearce turned and twisted the idea in his mind over and over like a Rubik's Cube, trying to solve the puzzle. But the colors faded and the cube got smaller and smaller until the world went black and Pearce disappeared with it.

59

Pearce woke, groggy and dehydrated. He wiped his face with his hands to wake up. He winced. Remembered the beating he'd taken at the hands of al-Saud. But he noticed his headache was gone. The meds worked. He felt the side of his face. It wasn't as sore and the swelling had subsided.

The space around him was dark, save for the eerie glow of blue LED cabin lights. He raised his wrist to read his watch out of habit, but it was gone. Al-Saud's operatives had destroyed it as a security precaution. A wall clock indicated it was around eight p.m. in D.C. How long had he slept? He did the math on his fingers. Six hours straight. Some kind of record for him, at least lately.

He glanced across the cabin and saw Swift fully reclined and sound asleep beneath a blanket. He needed some caffeine but didn't want to wake her. He raised his seat back up and stood to head for the galley but had to catch himself from falling. He was a little dizzy on top of the grogginess. He used the leather headrests to work his way back.

In the well-stocked galley he found bottled water in the refrigerator and drained one in one long pull. The cold water soothed his parched throat and slaked his thirst but his brain craved caffeine. He found the hot water spigot, and a few minutes later he was back in his seat with a steaming hot cup of green tea. He tapped the display on the headrest and saw the plane's location, altitude, and speed, along with the route they were taking. They were over the Atlantic, about one thousand miles due south of Greenland. The ETA to Dulles was still six hours away.

Pearce noticed another benefit to the meds. He didn't dream. For the first time in a long time he wasn't haunted in his sleep by the ghosts of men he'd killed or friends he couldn't save.

He'd slept like the dead.

The caffeine kicked in after a few minutes and the Rubik's Cube he'd been twisting and turning earlier came back into focus. He wanted to call Myers first and check up on her, but it was only around four in the morning where she was in Germany, so he put that off. It wasn't yet midnight in Washington, so he called Moshe Werntz instead.

"Moshe? It's me, Troy."

"Where are you, my friend?"

"Somewhere over the Atlantic."

"On a much-needed vacation, I hope."

"Not exactly. Look, I know you're busy. I just wanted to follow up on that phone call you made to me two days ago. About al-Saud and Tarkovsky."

"How can I help?"

Pearce collected his thoughts. "What can you tell me about Ambassador Tarkovsky?"

"Interesting man. Very smart. An ardent nationalist. Part of Titov's inner circle of advisors—but only recently. A rising star. Surely you know all of this?"

"I read his brief. What else do you have?"

Werntz paused. "The first time I met him in person was at an IAI trade show in Moscow he had arranged several years ago. Have you met him?"

"Yes, briefly."

"Then you know he is charming but unassuming. But he's a big thinker. Not just another bureaucrat. Even back then he was pushing for drone development against the protests of the Russian Defense Ministry. He was seeking our latest export designs."

"Is he a drone operator himself?"

"He struck me as technically well versed in drone systems, but I have no indication he's an operator himself. He's a strategist, not a tactician. Why do you ask?"

"I'm trying to find out who's behind the current troubles. He seemed a good candidate."

"Interesting," Werntz said, his voice trailing off. "Yes, I can see the connection you're making."

"You mentioned that he and al-Saud had met privately. What was that meeting about?"

"You put me in a difficult situation, Troy."

"I'm pulling you into mine."

"Yes, I understand. So, perhaps I can put it this way. If we had eavesdropping equipment at the ambassador's personal residence—I'm not saying we did—and if we recorded the conversation—and I'm not saying we did—I would suppose one could guess that Tarkovsky and al-Saud are forming a strong personal bond wedded to mutual national interests."

"Any talk of a terror attack on American soil? Or the use of drone technology?"

"Of course not. I would have contacted you immediately. I'm a friend as much as I am an ally."

"So what did they talk about?" Pearce wasn't going to allow Werntz to dodge the question again.

"Theoretically?"

Pearce rolled his eyes. A legal fiction but necessary, he knew. "Yes. Theoretically."

"In theory, al-Saud wanted Russian drones and Russian military intervention against ISIS if your government refused either or both. According to Tarkovsky—theoretically—Russia wants the same thing but prefers to be invited into a partnership with the United States. It would be necessary to lift the economic sanctions levied against them for the Crimea invasion, and it would also restore their status and credibility as a great power nation. But all of that is moot now, isn't it?"

Pearce sighed. "So Tarkovsky isn't our guy."

"Why do you say that?"

"Because he failed his mission. Lane didn't lift the sanctions and didn't invite the Russians in."

"Not yet. It's bound to be a long war."

"You're right. It will be. Better not check him off the list." Pearce sensed the Israeli spy had more to offer. "Anything else?"

"Yes. They discussed you."

Pearce suddenly felt as if his head were centered in a sniper scope. "What did they say?"

"We lost contact at that point."

He couldn't tell if Werntz was telling the truth. The Israeli would be a lousy spy if he couldn't lie effortlessly, he reminded himself. But he trusted their friendship. "Anything else?"

"As we discussed previously, both men have a strong relationship with Vice President Chandler."

"How strong?"

"I believe Ambassador Tarkovsky has a lunch meeting scheduled next week with Inger-Marie Ragland. She's on the Nobel Peace Prize committee. Tarkovsky intends to float Chandler's name as a possible nominee for the European security initiative the two of them are trying to launch."

"That's quite the hand job Tarkovsky's arranging for Chandler. Clay always was an ambitious bastard."

"I have a file I can send you—unofficially."

"That would be great. I'll forward it to my team."

"I can send it directly to Mr. McTavish if you prefer," Werntz said.

Pearce was surprised Werntz knew about Ian. He shouldn't have been. Mossad was the best. "I'll handle it from my end, thanks."

"Of course. And I'd appreciate it if you kept the source hidden."

"Not a problem. It's very generous of you. I owe you."

"Yes, you do. So I'd like to cash in the favor now."

"Name it."

"Two of our agents have gone missing. Daniel Brody and Tamar Stern."

Hearing Tamar's name was like a cold slap in the face. "Hold on one second." Pearce put Werntz on mute and quickly scrolled through his phone log. *Shit.* Tamar's call from two days ago. He totally forgot. No voice mail. He took Werntz off mute.

"You and Tamar were friends, yes?"

Werntz would know everything about his relationship with Tamar and her husband, Rudy, killed on the operation in Mexico a few years before. "Close friends." So close, Pearce thought, she ran a risky op in Germany just a few months before that probably saved his life.

"I need your help finding them. I'm shorthanded at the moment."

"What about the FBI?"

"Brody was the first to go missing. We asked the FBI to send their people out but they couldn't pick up his trail. We didn't inform them that Daniel was one of our agents because he was on assignment. When they came up short, we sent Tamar to find him. Now she's gone missing as well. Any chance you can spare some of your people to take a look around?"

"I'll go myself."

"That's more than I could hope for."

"She's done the same for me."

"I know. But your country just went to war and they're going to need you."

"I won't be playing much of a role if Chandler has anything to say about it."

"That would be a foolish mistake on his part, in my opinion."

Pearce's phone dinged.

"I've just sent you all of the information we have regarding Tamar and Daniel's disappearance," Werntz said, "along with what little we have on Norman Pike, the man they were investigating. I'll send Tarkovsky's file along in a few minutes as well. Good luck—and good hunting."

60

CHEBOYGAN, MICHIGAN

Pearce returned to his hotel apartment in D.C., still exhausted and sore from the kidnapping ordeal. He reminded himself again that he was getting too old for this shit.

He called Stella Kang, his senior security operative, and gave her a heads-up about the Tamar situation. The two women were close. Stella was glad to be part of the search. He took a long, hot shower and scrubbed off as much of the tattoo gel as he could, then grabbed some grub before heading out. He met Stella two hours later at the Pearce Systems hangar in Manassas, Virginia, with tactical gear and weapons for the op.

He piloted the two of them in the company HondaJet directly to Cheboygan County Airport. It didn't have a tower but it did have one four-thousand-foot runway, which was just enough to accommodate Pearce's aircraft. They landed and rented the only available car, a white four-door Chevy Impala, and drove into town.

On the flight over, Pearce finally managed to speak with Myers and found out that she was not only okay but boarding a nonstop Lufthansa flight from Frankfurt to D.C. that evening and would arrive at Dulles the following morning. He filled her in on the big picture but left out the minor detail of the savage beating and near-death experience with al-Saud. It was easy for him to say yes to her proposal that they get away for a few days. Pearce was grateful to the Man Upstairs for sending Margaret into his life.

Stella didn't plug the Cheboygan addresses they were checking out into the Chevy's onboard GPS. Ian warned them repeatedly against the hackability of modern cars, especially systems that utilized Blue-tooth, Wi-Fi, and satellite connections. Their own secure phones used Google Maps anyway, so the Chevy's navigation system was easy to avoid. In fact, Ian remotely hacked the Chevy's onboard computer and took the car offline so that even the rental agency couldn't trace their movements while they were in the area.

The thin file that Werntz sent over on Norman Pike didn't contain much information, but the fact that he had been an IT contractor in Iraq for one of the big multinational security firms suggested he had the skills to break into something as simple as a rental car if he was so inclined. More disturbing, Ian was unable to hack Pike's late-model panel van, which likely meant that Pike had taken similar precautions. Even if Pike wasn't guilty of criminal activity, he was behaving as if he had something to hide.

"It bothers me that some of Pike's file has been redacted," Kang said, scrolling through her tablet once again. "Why doesn't Werntz want us to know why they were chasing him?"

"Why do you think?"

"We won't like the answer."

"Bingo."

Pearce agreed with Kang's assessment—it bothered him, too. The Israelis were running ops on American soil—not an unusual practice. The United States spied on its allies, too. The NSA first hacked into Angela Merkel's phone in 2002, partly because of her membership in the East German Communist Party in her youth. It was part of the great game they all played. Pearce wondered if the damage done to relations between the allies was worth the scant information they actually man-aged to glean from tapping into the personal and professional lives of Western leaders. Not only were such activities illegal but they violated the trust that was the foundation for all economic and political transac-tions in liberal democracies. It didn't really matter what he thought. They were going to do it anyway, even if it didn't make any sense.

Pearce and Kang pulled into the marina parking lot and drove past the fish-cleaning house and parked, then walked over to the slip where

Pike's charter boat was permanently docked. They were surprised to discover the ship had been sold to a woman who owned a small fleet of charter boats. She hadn't seen Pike since the sale and wasn't sure how to find him. They showed her pictures of Daniel Brody and Tamar Stern, but she didn't recognize either of them.

Pearce and Kang then visited a local pub where Pike was known to hang out, but he wasn't there. A suspicious bartender with biker tats and a bad attitude loosened up when Pearce slipped him a fifty-dollar bill. He knew Captain Pike, sure, but hadn't seen him for a few days and, no, he didn't recognize the people in the two photos Kang showed him. A lewd comment regarding Tamar's sexual desirability almost got the bartender's teeth knocked out, but Pearce had better things to do than spend the rest of the day in the county jail, so they pushed on. Two more stops were equally frustrating.

The last stop was Pike's house on Black Lake.

BLACK LAKE, MICHIGAN

Pearce and Kang assumed that their inquiries into Pike's whereabouts could have been passed along to Pike himself, since he was a local. That was fine by them. They were shaking the bushes as much as they were searching for him. It would be that much easier if Pike decided to come and find them. They were ready.

It was possible that Pike had disappeared entirely, but it was just as likely that the people they'd spoken to had simply lied to the two strangers searching for one of their own. If Pike were still around, he might be holed up at his home, as obvious as that was. After all, the FBI and Tamar had already come calling there. Pike would know that another inquiry would lead to his place. What better location to set a trap?

Or he was long gone and the house was empty.

It was their last shot for the day, either way. They drove to Pike's place from Cheboygan and arrived less than half an hour later.

The house was situated on Black Lake on two heavily wooded acres that butted up to the two-lane county road. They parked their rental car off the road and made their way by foot to the edge of the property. It didn't take much effort to locate the security cameras directed at the long gravel driveway leading to his house or on the house itself. Ian was tracking their progress via their cell phones remotely from his office in San Diego. Ian was also busy hacking as much of the house as he could.

"Troy, hold on a minute. Can you shoot a pic of one of the security cameras?"

"Sure," Pearce whispered in his comms. He zoomed in as best he could on the closest security camera with his smartphone, then forwarded it to Ian. "That work?"

"Wireless. Interesting."

Pearce heard Ian's keyboard clattering.

"Do you see any kind of antenna or satellite dish on the house?"

Pearce took another look. Pike's house was still some distance away but there was definitely a satellite dish on top. "Yeah." He shot a photo of that, too, and forwarded it to Ian.

"Thanks. Carry on."

Pearce wondered what to do about the security cameras. He brought along a silenced .22-caliber pistol for the express purpose of knocking out impediments, such as cameras and lights. But Pike was still only a suspect and a law-abiding citizen as far as the local authorities were concerned. If Pike were in fact innocent, there was no point in destroying his property. He hoped there might be another way to avoid detection.

Pearce glanced at Stella but she had already read his mind. She pulled out a small surveillance drone and launched it. She guided the vehicle above the tree line and took the time to study the house and property, carefully picking her way around to get a three-sixty view of the place. The extra effort paid off. The drone showed that the camera over the front entrance facing the lake appeared to be disconnected. Strange that Pike, who seemed to be a thorough and cautious man, wouldn't have fixed that issue immediately, Pearce thought. *Sometimes Murphy's Law works for you*, he reminded himself. *Not often, but sometimes.*

Pearce and Kang worked their way through the trees, careful to avoid the sight lines of the cameras. With any luck they were triggered by motion detection and were not on continuous surveillance mode. Once they reached the edge of the trees, Pearce signaled for Kang to stay put and remain hidden while he moved forward toward the front of the house.

61

Pearce searched the house. It was orderly but clearly occupied, and it looked like Pike was coming back soon, judging by the beer and food stocked in the fridge. His clothes closet was full, as were his dresser drawers. If Pike had fled, he didn't take much with him and he had left in a hurry.

There were no electronics to be found in the house—at least, no computers, cell phones, or tablets. Nor did he find a secret safe, ammo caches, or weapons-grade anything except for a collection of flint arrowheads locked in a small glass case and stashed in a sock drawer.

Neither were there any clues that Tamar had been in the house at all. But Pearce didn't find any smashed furniture, bloodstains, or bullet holes, either. If Tamar had been there and had been subdued, it was done quickly and with little violence. Pearce doubted it. Tamar was a skilled operator and a good fighter. Pike looked like a harmless schlub with a talent for computers. But then again, he was a commercial fisherman who navigated the dangerous waters of the Great Lakes for a living. That was a real workingman's job, and it took guts and strength to survive out there.

The garage was filled with neatly stacked and organized fishing and boating gear. A quick perusal didn't uncover any weapons or contraband there, either. He thought about checking the attic but he was getting the feeling this entire trip was a waste of time. He half expected Pike to walk in at any moment with a bucket of fish in one hand and a slew of questions. Pearce wouldn't have any answers.

Pearce began to despair. This was the last stop on the search for his missing friend, at least for today. He wondered if he could call up the attorney general and beg a favor from her despite their recent clashes. The FBI was still one of the world's premier investigative organizations. Perhaps with a little more focus and incentive from Peguero, the local field office might put out a more sustained effort.

Pearce headed for the hallway and stopped at the last unexplored room. There was a heavy security bracket and hasp attached to the door frame and door but no lock. Where was it? Strange.

He pushed the door open.

The room was empty except for two long workstation tables. Pearce stepped inside. A thin layer of dust on the tables outlined the shapes of keyboards, monitors, and other peripherals. Exactly as Werntz's report stated. The IT officer assisting Tamar said that he tried to hack the system but couldn't break in after several attempts. Thirty-eight minutes into the hacking attempt, Tamar's phone went dead and he lost the connection to both her and the computer.

Pearce ran a finger through the dust. No reason. Just habit. Something he'd seen in the movies a hundred times. Like the dust itself contained some sort of clue.

It didn't.

The only other object in the room was a painting on the far wall. It looked familiar, like a museum piece. People on a raft. Pearce shrugged. He wasn't much into paintings.

If he'd have looked closer, he might have seen the micro-camera embedded in the picture frame.

PIKE HAD WARNED al-Saud against going after Pearce personally. "He's a trained operator. Fuck. A trained SOG operator. Those guys recruit from the SEAL teams, not the other way around."

But al-Saud wouldn't listen. Even argued Pearce was one of the few CIA spec ops fighters recruited out of the civilian community, as if that mattered. Pike was a gun for hire and he knew how to obey orders. He also knew how to do an end run. The imperious prince never suspected that his computer contractor might use those skills on him as well. Pike watched the entire Pearce fiasco unfold at the prince's golf course residence. He even tried to warn al-Saud at the last minute that an attack by Saudi forces was imminent, but the prince wouldn't pick up his phone. Too busy putting a gun to Pearce's skull. Couldn't be bothered. *Arrogant prick*, Pike reminded himself. But al-Saud paid well. Very well.

Once al-Saud kicked the hornet's nest, it was up to Pike to keep track of the hornets, and Pearce was the nastiest of the bunch. He had no idea that Pearce was connected to Werntz but shouldn't have been surprised. The espionage community was small and clubby, like an East Coast prep school—but with guns. He was lucky Werntz didn't spill the beans entirely on him to Pearce. But it wasn't luck that kept him one step ahead of Werntz and the assassins he'd sent his way. His mole in Werntz's organization had seen to that. Keeping tabs on Werntz now meant he could keep tabs on Pearce, at least from a distance.

Until now.

Pike watched Pearce through the fish-eye camera lens embedded in the picture frame. It was a guessing game now. Pike hoped Pearce would call his female friend into the house to help search, but instead Pearce wisely left her outside on overwatch. Pearce had checked the place pretty thoroughly. Pike watched him do it swiftly and expertly on the two dozen other micro-cameras he had hidden throughout the house. It was clear that Pearce hadn't found anything because there was nothing for him to find. The only thing that really mattered to Pike was the computer setup at his house that allowed him to remotely control the drone and hacking operations from Black Lake, and he'd already spirited those components away and dumped them in the middle of Lake Michigan before selling his beloved *Ayasi*.

Pike checked his watch, his finger hovering over the switch. Pearce was nearly done. If he wasn't going to call the woman into the house, that meant he'd be leaving soon. It was now or never.

Good thing Pearce didn't bother checking the attic.

———

IAN NEVER DOUBTED his ability as a hacker, especially after breaking into Jasmine Bath's seemingly impregnable system last year. But Pike had proved himself no slouch, either.

The Scot finally found a back door into the wireless camera system and, once there, was able to ride the unprotected video signal all the way back to Pike's remote station, somewhere on the other end of the satellite connection. Suddenly he was watching Pearce through the same fish-eye camera lens that Pike was using, and a moment later Ian discovered the remote triggering software connected to the camera system.

Ian shouted at Pearce through his comms as he tried to disable the trigger, but he was too late.

TROY HEARD IAN SHOUT in his earpiece, "Pearce! The window! Now!"

Pearce instantly lunged for the window directly in front of him. Felt his clenched fists break the glass just as the world exploded.

STELLA KANG SCREAMED as Pearce's huge frame broke through the window, the house erupting all around him. The roof flipped up on one sturdy wall, like a hinged lid, propelled by a ball of fire and shattered lumber, but the other three walls blew out. Pearce's body tumbled through the air like a rag doll. He landed clear of the house as the flaming roof smashed back down onto the remains of the structure and collapsed it.

Stella sprinted through the trees and fell down at the side of Pearce's body, twisted and limp in the pine needles. She called Ian for help, but Pearce wasn't responsive and she couldn't find a pulse.

62

Pearce's eyes blinked open. *Where the hell am I?*

He glanced at his feet tenting beneath the blanket on his elevated bed. Saw the bed rails and the TV attached to the far wall. It was hard to focus. A hospital room. His back and shoulders were sore. He felt the feeding tube snaking through his nose and down his throat. Instinctively he reached up to yank it out.

"Hold your horses, fella."

The voice was familiar. Pearce turned to look.

Myers smiled at him. "Welcome back, sleepyhead. Better leave that tube alone until someone can take it out for you."

Pearce nodded. He couldn't speak with the feeding tube, and his throat was sore and parched. Myers looked tired. She reached for the call button. A pretty Ghanaian nurse soon appeared. She gently extricated the feeding tube and took his vitals. "Everything looks good, Mr. Pearce. I'll call the doctor. She should be back to see you shortly." She poured him a glass of water, which Pearce drank greedily. She left, shutting the door behind her to give them some privacy.

"So what's the story?" Pearce asked in a croaking voice. "The last thing I remember was Ian yelling something in my comms."

"You were in an explosion. Knocked out cold. Good thing Stella knows CPR."

"Stella? Is she okay?"

"She's fine. She stayed here with me the first few days but I sent her home to get some rest."

"How long have I been in here?"

"You've been in a medically induced coma for seven days. She and Ian got you to an emergency room and then arranged to have you transferred here to the neurology department at the University of Michigan. It's one of the best in the nation."

"Neurology? You mean brain damage. I mean, more than usual."

Myers couldn't help but grin. Pearce always made her laugh. "You had some serious brain swelling going on. The coma gave your brain a chance to heal itself. The prognosis is good."

"Speaking of which, how is your noggin?"

"All checked out."

Pearce nodded at her left arm, covered up in a sleeved jacket. "What about that?"

"Passed clean through."

"That's lucky."

"A few stitches, oral antibiotics. Should heal completely within eight weeks. But we were talking about you."

"Oh, yeah." He took another sip of water and coughed a little. Then he took another. "Brain damage, you said."

Myers's grin slipped away. "I'll let the doctor fill in the details."

"I'm a big boy. Tell me what you know."

"You definitely suffered some traumatic brain injury. But the MRI scans they ran showed you had previous brain injuries. Some quite serious. Probably from combat."

"Comes with the job."

"Helps explain the anger issues."

"Some of them." Pearce wanted to fill her in on what he'd been going through the last few days during the crisis but decided against it. She seemed stressed enough.

There was a soft knock on the door before it swung open.

"Mr. Pearce? I'm Dr. Guth." She extended her small, fine-boned hand. Pearce was afraid he'd crush it in his large paw. The diminutive physician looked as if she were in her early twenties. Without the white coat and name tag, he might have mistaken her for a college student.

"Thanks for the help, doc."

Dr. Guth nodded at Myers. "Good to see you again, Madam President. I mean, Margaret. Sorry."

"I'm glad you two finally got to meet," Myers said. "It was a rather one-sided conversation the two of you were having until today."

"She hasn't left your side since the day you arrived," Guth said. "As bad as the food is here, that's saying something. You're a lucky man."

"Don't I know it."

"Have you both had a chance to talk?" Dr. Guth asked.

"Briefly."

"I know you'll both want to catch up, but I wanted to stop by and give you a quick overview of where things stand right now and the path forward. But the good news is that while you've suffered some severe TBI recently and in the past, there's no reason not to expect a full recovery of cognitive and vocational function over time with appropriate therapies. But then there's the other issue."

Pearce raised an unruly eyebrow. "What issue?"

Guth shared a look with Myers. "Since you were unconscious, Margaret was the only person I could consult with regarding your medical history. Everything she described to me sounds like a classic case of PTSD, though technically I'm not able to offer you a formal diagnosis."

Guth pulled up her tablet and swiped it for her notes. "You have extensive combat experience. Combat can cause traumatic brain injury or PTSD or both. The symptoms for both overlap and the treatments for TBI can be different than for PTSD. You need a skilled clinician to fully assess your situation and design a customized treatment plan. The VA has established the PolyTrauma System of Care for people exactly like you, and I'm recommending you to the PolyTrauma Network Site at the D.C. VA center as soon as you are discharged."

"When's that?" Pearce asked.

Guth smiled. "I want to keep you under observation for a little while. You're bound to feel some physical symptoms—blurred vision, headaches, that sort of thing. And don't be surprised if there's some memory loss. But those should all clear up quickly. I'll discharge you tomorrow morning if you feel up to it."

"I'm ready now," Pearce said.

Guth smiled kindly, as if addressing the village idiot. "But I'm afraid I'm not." She tapped her tablet. "I'll have someone come up from the kitchen and take your order. Try to eat and drink as much as you can." She turned back to Pearce. "You can except a full recovery if you decide to do whatever it takes to get better."

Pearce nodded. "That's the plan."

"Good. TBI is nothing to fool around with. And, Mr. Pearce, that means taking it easy for the next few weeks. Your brain needs time to heal. I understand you were up for some serious government post but I highly recommend you put that on hold for a while. You don't need to do anything but rest and maybe watch a ballgame or two for the next few weeks. Okay?"

Myers resisted the temptation to shout amen.

"One more thing," Guth said. Her brow furrowed. "I don't want to cause you any alarm but I need you to be aware of the possibility of CTE."

"Chronic traumatic encephalopathy," Myers said. She had plenty of time to Google it while Pearce was unconscious.

Pearce saw the look on Myers's face. Apparently this was the "not great" part of the news she couldn't share before. He'd heard of it before. "Like the football players get. Comes with repeated blows to the head. That isn't exactly me."

"I agree. But at least one study indicates that a single incidence of blast exposure can cause the condition. CTE is a degenerative disease that eventuates in death." Guth laid a hand on Pearce's shoulder. "I'm only telling you all of this because I want you to take your situation seriously. I have no idea at all if you are suffering from the condition because the only way to confirm a diagnosis of CTE is an autopsy."

"I'd just as soon skip that," Pearce said, grinning.

Guth smiled back. "Me too. But you need to get to the VA as quickly as possible for evaluation and treatment—and follow their directions to the letter. Am I being clear?"

Pearce nodded. "Yeah."

"Good. I'm confident you'll be just fine. I'll check back later this afternoon, but don't hesitate to call me if you have any questions before then."

Pearce and Myers thanked her and she left to finish her rounds.

Pearce asked Myers. "So what's going on with the war?"

"Didn't you hear the doctor? You need to let your brain rest."

"I can turn on the TV if you prefer."

"Just for the record, being a wisenheimer isn't one of your symptoms."

"Seriously. What's going on?"

Myers sighed. Pearce was relentless. "The bombing campaign against Raqqa has ceased. Civilian casualties are estimated to be in the tens of thousands. ISIS has declared victory even though American and Saudi troops are on their way to the city. There have been terror attacks all across Europe. Baghdad, Doha, and even Saint Petersburg have been hit as well. Lone wolf, mostly. Light casualties but lots of press attention."

"Lane needs to stop this war."

"Too late, I'm afraid."

"If I can talk to him, tell him what's really going on, he'll stop it."

Myers glanced away. "He's asked about you. He's worried about your health."

"But he won't talk to me."

"He's unavailable until after the Asia summit."

Pearce saw something else in her eyes but decided to let it go. "So fill me in. What did you find out while I was napping?"

"Ian's been busy putting the pieces together. After he hacked into Pike's computer he found some interesting connections."

"Like what?"

"It turns out the outfit he was contracting for in Iraq was owned by a shell company. Can you guess who owned it?"

Pearce frowned, connecting the dots. "Al-Saud?"

Myers smiled. "You know, even with your brain bruised, you're pretty good at this analytical stuff."

"Was Pike still connected to al-Saud?"

"Ian believes Pike was al-Saud's drone operative." Myers laid a hand on one of Pearce's. "He also confirmed that Pike killed Tamar. I'm so sorry."

Myers saw the sadness fill his eyes. She wished she could take it away. "He also killed Daniel Brody, and at least two other Israelis over the last few years."

"That explains the Mossad connection." He wished Werntz had clued him in. Pearce's eyes narrowed. "What's Pike's status?"

"Disappeared. But Ian's still on the hunt."

"What about al-Saud?"

"Still under 'house arrest.'"

"We've got to get that sonofabitch and put him on trial."

Myers shook her weary head. "Not going to happen. If the American people suspected the Saudis were behind the recent attacks, they'd demand we invade them first."

"That's bullshit. He's guilty. He needs to be brought to justice."

Myers's face darkened. "I'm afraid al-Saud skates on this one—at least for now. I hate what he did to you. I'm tempted to go over there and put him down myself."

"Where's Pike?"

"Missing."

"Tarkovsky?"

"Recalled to Moscow."

"Which makes him out of reach. Convenient."

"Your friend Vicki Grafton has made a move, too."

"Where?"

"She's made partner at Seven Rivers Consortium. They only bring on serious rainmakers at that level. My guess is that they gave her the brass ring for helping launch the war. Their biggest clients stand to make a handsome profit."

"What's wrong with this country?"

"There's more. Your friend Werntz told Ian that Grafton was 'friendly' with both Tarkovsky and al-Saud."

"Are you shitting me?"

"I'm afraid not. A lot of business in Washington is done on the horizontal."

Pearce winced, shutting his eyes. He wanted to scream. He pressed his palms to his throbbing forehead. "Can you get me a couple of Tylenol?"

Myers stood and snatched the call button, pressing it. "I'm getting the nurse." She dropped the call button and sat on the bed next to Pearce, rubbing his head. "I'm so sorry. What else can I do?"

"Get me in touch with Lane right now. Please."

She didn't have the heart to tell him that Lane didn't want to speak with him. "His mind's already made up on the war. There's nothing you can do about it."

"I've got to try."

"Let it go."

"I can't."

The anguish in his eyes broke her heart. She put her hand on his. "Trust me, you don't have a choice." She stroked his head. His eyes closed but his brow still furrowed with pain.

Where was that nurse?

63

Pearce was frustrated that he hadn't been able to reach Lane in the last two days. He'd left messages with Lane's chief of staff but his calls were never returned. The meds that Dr. Guth had prescribed allowed him to sleep a lot more than he was used to. Once Myers got him settled back in at her place she went to her lawyer's office to finish up the last of the paperwork needed to complete the German deal. She made Pearce promise to not turn on the television or Google anything about the war—at least not until she got back later that afternoon. She also gave strict orders to Ian that no Pearce Systems employee was to answer any of his calls, texts, or e-mails for forty-eight hours. Pearce was too groggy to fight back.

When his head cleared up enough, he made his way back down to Myers's kitchen. He opened the cabinet beneath the sink and knelt down, fishing around until his fingers secured the half-pint bottle of whiskey in the back. It was time to clean house.

He pulled it out, only to find a Starbucks card taped to the front of it, along with a note from Myers: "Green tea is better. Refills are on me."

Pearce grinned. She was always one step ahead of him. He pocketed the Starbucks card and opened the bottle over the sink, pouring out the last few ounces into the drain, then tossed it into the trash can.

His phone rang.

Pearce checked the number. "Unknown." He thought about Margaret's admonition to avoid outside contact. He stared at the screen. He couldn't help himself.

"Pearce."

"Troy, it's Clay Chandler. It's wonderful to hear your voice. You gave us quite the scare."

Yeah, right, Pearce thought. Chandler's honey-sweet Georgia accent soured his stomach. "What do you want?"

"Blunt as always. I admire that. So I'll cut to the chase. President Lane asked me to call you directly. Under the circumstances he feels it's best for him to accept your resignation."

"My resignation? Why? Because I got a knock on the head?"

"Hardly. But I think you know that."

"What are you talking about?"

"That business with Werntz you were caught up in."

"What's that got to do with anything?"

"Moshe Werntz is Israel's top spy in North America. He used you on a mission to find two missing Mossad agents. Technically, that makes *you* an Israeli spy."

Pearce couldn't believe his ears. How did Lane and Chandler find out? Did Werntz rat him out? No, not Moshe. Not without reason. He was an Israeli patriot but he was also a friend. Werntz must have a bad apple in his barrel.

"Bullshit. I was doing a favor for a friend. And unless I'm mistaken, Israel is still an allied government in the War on Terror."

Chandler clucked his tongue. "That doesn't give you permission to do spy work for them."

Pearce felt the old demon grabbing him by the throat. "Are you accusing me of treason?"

"Not at all. But it's optics we're worried about. We're trying to fight a war. The president can't have one of his closest advisors appear to be a puppet of the Israeli government. The public wouldn't stand for it."

"That's idiotic."

"Perception is reality. Besides, you never really wanted the job. Why pretend you want to keep it?"

"Because it keeps me close to the president, and gives me a chance to stop the killing before more damage is done."

"You've read history, Pearce. Good wars often start for the wrong reasons. You said yourself we need to exterminate ISIS."

"I said you either exterminate them or leave them alone. We knocked AQ out of Afghanistan and they metastasized. They're in over one hundred countries now. Same thing will happen if we knock ISIS out of Syria and Iraq. You're better off letting them all congregate in one place. Like Pia said, containment might be a better option. But half a war is the worst possible action."

"You're being naive. Containment? Political correctness will never allow us to contain the Islamic threat. Extermination is the only option. Half a war, as you put it, sets us on that road. Eventually the people of this country will accept that reality."

"Now you're the one being naive. The American people will never accept the kind of war you're talking about. Lane won't, either. It's not in his nature."

"With your help we can get him there."

"No. I'll do everything I can to get him to change his mind and stop the bloodshed now."

Chandler's honey-smooth accent turned ice cold. "The president has already made his decision. We're at war, Pearce. Congress is voting on the most comprehensive and far-reaching AUMF in history. There's nothing you can do to change that."

"The president doesn't have all of the facts."

Chandler chuckled. "Facts are analogue, Pearce. Completely out of fashion. I thought you knew that."

"I guess I'm old-school that way."

"The world's too complicated for a reality-based paradigm. Superpowers like us have to create our own reality now."

Pearce gripped the phone tighter. "My job is to tell the president the truth."

"That's not going to happen."

"Then I'll go to the press. They still like facts."

"Not from discredited sources."

"How am I discredited?"

"It would be better if you walked away, quietly and with honor. You still have your company. I'm sure the government will still want to buy your drones."

"You still don't get it, do you? This isn't about money or power. This is about my country. And about shitbirds like you who are going to kill it."

Chandler sighed. "I was afraid this would be your response. Lord knows I tried." He rang off.

Pearce stared at his phone, wondering what Chandler was up to and plotting his own next move. Maybe Ian could find a way to break into Lane's secured communication network and get a message directly to him.

The doorbell rang.

Strange. He wasn't expecting any visitors and Myers had a key. He snagged a Shun carving knife out of the block and crossed over to the door, holding the blade behind his back. He opened it. Two FBI agents stood in the hallway. They flashed IDs.

"Troy Pearce?" one of the agents asked.

"Yes."

The other agent held up a sheet of paper. "A warrant. You're under arrest."

"On what charge?"

"The murder of Iraqi general Ali Majid."

64

CUMBERLAND, MARYLAND

Tanaka's iron grip tightened around Pearce's throat but Pearce wasn't fighting back. The Japanese minister's bulging eyes were just inches away from his face, his tobacco breath stale and foul as always. Suddenly Tanaka's grip slackened, and then his ropey arms dropped. He stared contemptuously at Pearce, grunted, and turned away, shuffling through the thick, watery muck around his ankles, back over to the steel cylinder lying on its side. Tanaka opened it and crawled back in, shutting the door tightly behind him.

Pearce's eyes opened. He wasn't sweating or gasping for breath. He was lying on his cot, staring at the ceiling. Guilt sat on his chest like a familiar dog, heavy and still. But at least he could breathe.

The heavy steel cell door thudded twice. The portal slid open. He saw the prison guard's face.

"Pearce, you have a visitor."

PEARCE SHUFFLED into the sparse but spacious visitors' room. In the center of it was a steel table bolted to the floor and two metal chairs. His wrists were manacled in front of him to a chain wrapped twice around his jumpsuit at the waist. The muscled guard, the shift supervisor, guided him by the elbow to an open chair.

"How much time do we have?" Myers asked. She sat opposite Pearce across the steel table. A digital clock was high up on the wall, shielded by a metal cage.

"You're scheduled for fifteen minutes."

"Can we get more time?"

The grim-faced officer tilted his head. "How much time do you need, ma'am?"

"I'd like a month but I'll settle for thirty minutes."

He nodded thoughtfully. His features softened. "I can make that happen, Madam President."

Myers smiled. "I'm grateful."

The guard left, shutting the door behind him. He took up a position square in the center of the observation window as per standard operating procedure.

Myers glanced over Pearce's shoulder. "Does he have to watch us like that?"

Pearce nodded at the camera hanging from the ceiling. "He's not the only one."

"Good thing this wasn't a conjugal visit."

"That's disappointing to hear." He held up his manacled hands. "I even wore jewelry for the occasion."

"Are they listening, too?"

"I don't think so. The video is just for security purposes."

She tried to hide her concern. It was the first time she'd been allowed to visit. They hadn't even let her call. "So . . . how bad is it in there?"

Pearce smiled, trying to ease her anxiety. "It's just a medium-security facility. Pretty low-key, actually. I'm in my own private cell, which is great."

"You hear stories about prison." Her voice trailed off.

He shook his head. "Only in the movies. The COs do a good job. Mostly white-collar criminals in here, at least where I am."

"You look like you've lost weight. How's the food?"

"Good. Somewhere between an army commissary and a Golden Corral. I just do a lot of push-ups."

Myers fought back tears. She promised herself she'd stay strong for him. "I've been so worried."

"I know. I'm sorry." He reached up to take her hands in his to comfort her but forgot about his handcuffs. The rattling chains stopped him short. That made her even more upset. He needed to change the subject. "Did I tell you I started my new job?"

"No. What is it?"

"I'm making license plates."

Myers shook her head. "You're pulling my leg."

"No, seriously. Cumberland makes all of the license plates for federal vehicles. Do you have any idea how many cars the feds own?"

"I still think you're pulling my leg."

"You always said I should be in government service. At least no one is shooting at me in here."

"How is therapy coming along?"

"Great. The meds are working, too. I haven't felt this good in a long time."

"Glad to hear it. Still dreaming?"

Pearce shrugged. "Sure. Not bad, though."

"One step at a time."

"One step at a time."

They sat for a moment in an awkward silence.

Myers gathered up her courage, brightening. "I met with President Lane this morning."

Pearce couldn't hide his surprise. "I'm all ears."

She smiled hopefully. "The president is prepared to give you a pass on everything you've ever done since the day you swore in at Langley all the way until this very moment."

Pearce frowned, calculating. "On what condition?"

"None, really. Except that he wants you to step away from the limelight. Make no public comments about the war. Stay away from the press."

"In other words, shut up and go away."

"Far away. His advisors feel it will be easier for you to meet the conditions if you left the country."

"By advisors you mean Chandler."

"No. Chandler's praying you won't take the deal. But Lane respects you tremendously and wants to do everything he can to make things right."

"That's easy. All he has to do is open the door and let me out so I can exercise my right to free speech."

"It's not that easy. You know that." Myers leaned in close, whispering. "Besides, you're guilty of the crime they're charging you with, aren't you?"

Pearce thought she was fishing. But he saw the certainty in her eyes. "When did you find out?"

"Lane showed me the files the Russians had on you. It was easy for the FBI to connect the dots after that."

"And he actually trusts the Russians to not hand him a pack of lies?"

Her eyes bored into his. "Did they?"

Pearce darkened. One or both of Majid's Russian mercenaries must have been working with the SVR. "That Majid guy was a dirtbag. I've killed better men for less."

"Probably not your best line of defense," Myers said, trying to make a joke.

Pearce sat back. "No, probably not."

He wondered if she knew the rest of the story. How he stole Majid's money and gave half of it to a charity he trusted and used the other half to start Pearce Systems. Whenever he was asked where he got his original investment money, Pearce always said he had a silent partner. Well, Majid was silent, all right, silent as the grave. He never felt guilty about it. Majid's stolen cash was Pearce's ticket out of the war and a way to do some good in the world on his own terms. If he had left the money alone, Chandler would have just given it to some other thieving warlord to fund the next circle jerk. Luckily for Pearce, the statute of limitations had run out on that particular felony or they might have charged him with that, too. Or maybe Chandler was just covering his own ass.

"What are you thinking?" Myers asked.

"Lane. I thought he was different."

"He's a good man but he has a hard job. He's fighting a war he believes in, and he's fighting it the way he thinks he needs to. Unfortunately, that means he's relying heavily on people like Chandler now."

"So this is really as much about Chandler as it is about me."

"Chandler's determined to ruin you. Lane is offering you a way out."

"The pardon."

"Probation, actually."

Pearce was shocked to hear that. But then he processed it. "To keep me on the leash in case I decide to get out of line in the future."

"Chandler's idea, not Lane's."

"I'd rather take my chances in front of a jury of my peers."

Myers shook her head. "It's more complicated than that."

"How?"

"You're considered a national security risk and the evidence at hand has been classified as Special Access Program. It will take years to bring your case to trial and the restrictions imposed by SAP guidelines means it might also take years to adjudicate. And, no matter what, you won't be able to get your side of the story out to the public."

"I don't get my Clarence Darrow moment?"

"Not even Atticus Finch."

"I'd make a great Atticus Finch."

"I know."

Pearce frowned. "What do you think I should do?"

"The attorney general's office is assembling an airtight case with irrefutable evidence. Frankly, the feds can't lose no matter how hard you fight them. Chandler wants you to know he'll do everything in his power to get you thrown into the supermax prison in Colorado with a life sentence." Myers's eyes teared up. "So what do you think I'd tell you to do?"

"I don't know if I can walk away."

Myers fought back her own rage at the system. Maybe Pearce had been right all along not to trust the government. He once told her that democracy was too important to be left to the politicians. She was beginning to believe it. The people who ran D.C. always did this to warriors like him. Honest soldiers had short careers in the U.S. military these days. She knew Pearce struggled for years with a dilemma. How does a man serve his country when he no longer trusts his government? She thought she knew the answer. But now that it was clear the government no longer wanted his service, she saw another path for him.

"You can't win, Troy. You can't stop the war. And you'll lose your life behind iron bars. Or there's this."

Myers pulled a photo out of her purse and handed it to Pearce. He examined it.

"A sailboat?"

"Our sailboat. A Beneteau First 38. It's waiting for us down in the British Virgin Islands."

"Why did you buy it?"

"Because it's blue, like your eyes."

"Expensive?"

"Terribly. But you're worth it."

Pearce studied the photo more closely. He felt his heart lighten. "You want me to be a pirate?"

"I think you already are one."

"We don't know how to sail."

"We'll have all the time in the world to learn. Or we can just park the boat and fish off the back deck. You haven't been fishing in a long while."

"I miss it."

"I know."

"What happened to the idea that we need to be useful?"

"I can't think of anything more important than you getting healthy and well, however long that takes."

Pearce thought about what was happening in Syria. He knew what kind of carnage was taking place over there. He could smell the cordite and burnt flesh. He wanted to stop it. Felt guilty for not already stopping it. And then his mind flashed back to the ghost-white images of the women being butchered by the ISIS killers in Iraq. He couldn't stop that, either.

He was worse than useless.

He handed the picture back to her. "Let me think about it."

She pushed it back into his hands. "Keep it. It will look great on your windowless cell wall."

He couldn't help but grin a little. "I'll use it to hide my escape tunnel from the guards." He turned serious. "Any word from Ian?"

Her eyes narrowed. "He said everything's being taken care of, as per your orders. He wasn't specific."

"He wasn't supposed to be."

"You've got to let it go. For you. For us."

"I am." He pocketed the photo.

"Really?"

He nodded. "I will."

Myers leaned forward, peering into his face. "Promise?"

He lowered his eyes. "I'll try. I swear to God, I'll try."

"What about Lane's offer?"

Pearce shrugged. "I'll think about it."

"The offer won't last."

Pearce looked up. "Betray my country or betray myself. Hell of a choice."

"I don't see it as a betrayal of your country."

"But I do."

Another awkward silence. Myers heard the second hand ticking on the wall clock. "We're almost out of time."

"I know."

"What shall I tell David?"

Pearce saw the pain in her eyes. He knew his answer.

He just couldn't say the words.

65

It was only the third flight of the recently delivered Saudi Air Force MQ-9 Reaper drone and it was already routine. It could fly continuously for fourteen hours fully armed but it had been in the air for only eight on today's mission, keeping watch over the Kingdom's eastern shoreline on the Persian Gulf. The Reaper ran a continuous circuit from the border of Kuwait in the north all the way down the coastline to Bahrain in the far south and back again.

The nearsighted Saudi captain piloting today's mission sat in an air-conditioned ground-control station parked at King Abdulaziz Air Base, just north of the bustling port city of Al Khobar. He was as newly minted as the Reaper he was monitoring, having just graduated from drone pilot training with the 9th Attack Squadron at Holloman Air Force Base in New Mexico.

The mission had been routine so far. In fact, it was mind-numbingly dull thanks to the vehicle's autopiloting capabilities, just one function of the most advanced navigational software and avionics package available, designed and built by an American company.

The captain stifled a yawn. His sensor operator had stepped outside for a smoke, leaving him alone in the GCS. He thumbed through a well-worn Victoria's Secret catalogue he'd found in the officers' lounge. He succumbed to a second yawn as he flipped to a dog-eared page, struggling to see in the dimly lit room.

The Reaper's direction suddenly turned away from the coast and headed inland. No alarms sounded. The captain was too preoccupied to notice the change until it was too late.

But it wouldn't have mattered if he had.

A DOE-EYED QATARI GIRL from the royal house of Al-Thani swam naked in the vast blue pool inside the expansive stone courtyard.

Al-Saud leered at his newest and youngest wife from the shade beneath the portico and sipped on a minty mojito, his favorite cocktail. She was already pregnant, another sign of favor from Allah, whose blessings were as heavy and real as the thick rope of golden chain around his neck. His villa near the coast was a pleasure palace he had purchased just for the two of them with the dowry he had received from the girl's father.

Life was good, and al-Saud was filled with the gloating satisfaction of all patriots on the winning side of a war. A war he had helped orchestrate. Thanks to him, the Americans were providing the drones his country required for fighting *Daesh* and keeping the filthy Persians at bay. Victory was certain.

But al-Saud's thoughts turned inward. He sighed. House arrest was, literally, a gilded cage. But it was still a burden. His desperate desire was to be back in the good graces of the king. He would be now if it weren't for Pearce. Pike's new contract to assassinate the American was paid in full, a wedding gift to himself. He prayed it would be completed soon.

His mood began to sour until he remembered the comforting admonition of his uncle. "The Americans have long arms but short memories." The old sheikh was right, of course. He would be back in service to his family and his nation eventually. He only needed patience, and a good word from Chandler at just the right time. Until then, he would be forced to endure the sensate life of a pampered Saudi royal. He laughed.

C'est la vie.

Al-Saud drained the last of his glass and slipped off his swimsuit. It was time to pleasure himself again with his young wife in the pool's cool salt water. He padded over to the gold-tiled edge in his bare feet and called out to the girl. She laughed and waved him in. He felt his manhood swelling as he gazed upon her bright and eager face.

A glint of sunlight caught his eye. He glanced up into the pale blue vault. He sensed more than saw the blinding fury of two erupting Hellfire missiles, cutting off his scream in the scalding fire that burned away his world and everything he loved.

SITTING IN HIS OWN GCS in San Diego, Ian turned the Saudi Reaper toward Iranian airspace. With any luck the Saudis would think it was Tehran that had managed to pull off the hijacking instead of him. Thanks to the Reaper's navigational software and avionics package—designed and built by a subsidiary of Pearce Systems—Ian had taken effortless control of the drone and piloted it toward al-Saud's private residence just five miles off its preprogrammed route.

The Reaper's onboard facial-recognition software confirmed al-Saud's identity before Ian launched the Hellfires and the high-powered optical camera captured the astonished look on the prince's face just moments before he and his compound were vaporized.

Too bad about the girl, he thought to himself. But as his nana told him years ago, *You sleep with the Devil in a bed of your own ashes.*

Monitoring the communications channels of the Royal Saudi Air Force, Ian knew that two fourth-generation Boeing F-15SA strike fighters had been dispatched, just as he assumed they would be once the Reaper was discovered off course. Equipped with the AN/AAS-42 infrared search-and-track system wedded to the Joint Helmet Mounted Cueing System, the Saudi pilots would easily find and destroy the slow-moving turboprop Reaper with or without help from Saudi ground-control radar. No doubt they would completely destroy the aircraft along with its black box. But Ian was a cautious man and put a worm in the drone's CPU that already destroyed any evidence of his activity just in case the black box was recovered.

Ian tapped an encrypted message on his console.

"14Gipper."

66

Pike stared at the barrel of a pistol. His hands were raised. She stood well outside of his arm's reach. The weapon was rock steady in her two-handed grip. The Korean was a pro, for sure.

"Irony is a bitch," Stella said.

"I'm not following you."

"Tamar was my friend. We ran an op together with Pearce, right here, in these waters."

Pike wanted to bargain but the cold rage in her pitiless eyes told him it was pointless.

Stella motioned with her pistol. "Turn around."

Pike hesitated. Her fingertip slid gently from the trigger guard to the trigger. Not good.

He turned around.

So this was it, he told himself. He faced the wide blue Pacific and its vast pale horizon. Tiny whitecaps shimmered in the morning light. He could imagine worse ways to go than a bullet to the back of the head, staring at the sea.

"She was an honorable woman and you're a piece of shit," Stella said. "I want those to be the last words you ever hear."

"Technically, my dear, the last words—"

Stella clocked him on the back of his skull with the butt of her pistol. Hard. He moaned as he fell, hitting the deck with a sickening thud. He wasn't dead. She was sure of that.

Couldn't be dead.

That would ruin it.

PIKE WOKE, eyes fluttering, surprised he was still alive.

His head throbbed, an excruciating headache. His shoulders were killing him, too, and pain shot down the length of his back. His wrists were cuffed to the broad wheel of his brand-new yacht, hands purpling. The weight of his body was suspended from his wrists as if he were crucified in reverse on a silver, circular cross.

He stood up on wobbly legs, the locked wheel supporting him. He shook his head to clear it.

He remembered.

That crazy Korean bitch. Something about irony.

He looked around. Miles offshore. Nobody around.

He called out. She was gone.

Thank God for that.

The cuffs dug into his wrists. He twisted them. The plastic bands dug in deeper. He cursed. Tugged again, hard. Tendons popped. He screamed at the top of his lungs, panicked, raging.

A muffled explosion forward shook the deck beneath his feet.

That caught his attention. He listened.

Utter silence.

Except for the gurgling noise.

What the hell?

He twisted all the way around, his stiff neck barely able to rotate enough to look directly behind him.

A boat. About a half mile away.

He squinted. He saw the Korean standing on the bow of another boat with a pair of binoculars.

The deck began tilting forward beneath his feet.

He whipped back around and the deck angled further.

It was going down.

Fast.

———————

STELLA WATCHED PIKE scream and flail, his wrists still pinned to the big silver wheel. She could hear his anguished cries even from here. Probably from the pain in his two wrists, now broken, but maybe from sheer terror.

She hoped it was both.

The bow submerged, filling with tons of dead ocean weight. The stern stood high out of the water like a shark fin.

She zoomed in on Pike's manic, jerking dance as the helm filled with surging sea. A moment later the rest of the ship followed the bow, plunging beneath the surface of the cold Pacific, Pike at the wheel, his screams cut off, steering a course for a deep blue hell.

She lowered her binoculars. Tossed the remote-control detonator over the side.

Her phone vibrated. She checked the message. It was Ian.

"14Gipper."

She smiled. Good timing.

Ian was a good man and a great boss. He owned the company now.

She was glad he decided to tie off the loose ends. They owed Pearce that much, even if he didn't ask for it.

She texted Ian back. "24Gipper."

She wished she could tell Pearce it was over now, but he was gone. So was Myers.

Off the grid. Nobody knew where, not even Ian.

They were on a boat, she heard.

She smiled.

Ironic.

She prayed they were happy.

ACKNOWLEDGMENTS

My deepest thanks again to Ivan Held and G. P. Putnam's Sons for believing in the series. I'm grateful for the guidance provided to me by my editor, Sara Minnich, and I congratulate her on the newest addition to her family, William. Tireless Lauren LoPinto kindly threw in with us and I owe not a little to my copyeditor, David Koral, and production editor, Claire Sullivan.

As always, a tip of the hat to my literary agent, David Hale Smith, and his assistant, Liz Parker, along with the entire team at Inkwell Management.

Angela, my wife, is always my first reader. She never fails to inspire me both on and off the page.